M

Life

Books by Gwyneth Jones

Divine Endurance
London, George Allen & Unwin, 1984; London, Headline, 1993

Escape Plans
London, George Allen & Unwin, 1986

Kairos
London, Unwin, 1988; London, Gollancz (revised) 1995

Flowerdust
London, Headline, 1993

White Queen
London, Gollancz, 1991 (James Tiptree Award 1991)

North Wind
London, Gollancz, 1994

Phoenix Cafe
London, Gollancz 1997; New York, Tor (revised) 1998

Bold As Love
London, Gollancz, 2001

Castles Made Of Sand
London, Gollancz, 2002

Midnight Lamp
London, Gollancz, 2003

Seven Tales and a Fable
Cambridge MA, Edgewood Press, 1995

Life

a novel

by Gwyneth Jones

Aqueduct Press
PO Box 95787
Seattle, WA 98145-2787
www.aqueductpress.com

Library of Congress Control Number: 2004108745
Library of Congress Cataloging in Publication Data
Jones, Gwyneth, 1952
Life / Gwyneth Jones, 1st ed.
1. Gender politics, fiction. 2. Genetic engineering, fiction. 3. Science fiction. 4. Scientific revolutions, fiction. 5. Sociology of science, fiction. I. Title
p.   cm.
ISBN 0-9746559-2-9
First Edition, First Printing, October 2004

Cover Photograph by Lea Lichty (lichtay@mchsi.com)
Cover Legong Keraton dance courtesy the family of I.K. Asnawa.
Dancers: Ni Made Nias Yunirika & Ni Nyoman Nias Yonitika.
Cover Design by Lynne Jensen Lampe
Inside Cover Photo: Courtesy U.S. Department of Energy Human Genome Program, http://www.ornl.gov/hgmis
Lotus Motif by Edgar Hernandez
Book Design by Kathryn Wilham

Printed in the USA
10 9 8 7 6 5 4 3 2 1
This book was set in a digital version of Monotype Walbaum, available through AGFA Monotype. The original typeface was designed by Justus Erich Walbaum.

Acknowledgments

The two books that most influenced *Life* were *The Differences Between the Sexes*, eds Roger Short and Evan Balaban; Cambridge University Press (you can find my overview of this collection of sex-science papers and how it affected my fiction at http://trace.ntu. ac.uk/frame/freebase/free2/gjones.htm, and in the essay collection called *Deconstructing the Starships*, Gwyneth Jones, Liverpool University Press); and *A Feeling for the Organism*, Evelyn Fox Keller; WH Freeman; the biography of Barbara McClintock. My deepest gratitude to Dr Jane Davies, Reader in Developmental Biology and Molecular Genetics at the University of Sussex, who talked to me when I was first writing this book: let me tour her lab, let me sit in on lectures and on a team meeting; who advised me that I must read *A Feeling for the Organism* and altogether was incredibly generous and helpful. The stumbling fiction I made from everything I learned is of course entirely my responsibility. Thanks also to her team and to Richard Crane, who helped to matchmake.

Quotations and References: Ramone's dryad howl (p 11) is from George MacDonald's *Phantastes*, as is her "Alas" reflection (p 72). The "obscure" paper Anna is reading in the library (p 34), "Studies on the chemical nature of the substance inducing transformation of pneumococcal types," Avery, OT et al. 1944..., is the historic description of how Oswald Avery and Macyln McCarty discovered that DNA is the material of which genes and chromosomes are made. Anna's couplet, on lasting affection for a first lover (p 54 and p 116) is from *Love and Age* by Thomas Love Peacock. Lavinia's triumph over her suitors (p 69) is from *The Libertine*, Aphra Benn. KM Nirmal's reflection on the holy of holies (p 92) is from Emily Dickinson, *The Single Hound; 74*. Spence's epiphany on a dead child (p 149-150) is triggered by *John Keats*, Walter Jackson Bate. Anna's rush of springtime in Borneo (p 189) is from Algernon Charles Swinburne's Chorus from "Atalanta in Calydon"; her reflection on mind's emergence in Bournemouth (p 208) is from William Wordsworth, "Intimations of Immortality." Geoffery Hazelwood's lament for the great dying (p 301, Diffugere Nives) is from Horace, Odes iv, 7.

for Kim Stanley Robinson

Roads and the Meaning of Roads, I

On an orphaned stretch of open trunk road, between the urban freeway system and the M6, they stopped at a garage to recharge. The night was warm. The trees in the hedge by the layby raised nets of blurred, dusty dark branches against a neon-tinted grey sky. Spence went into the shop to pay. He could be seen brightly lit behind plate glass, prowling the stacks, peering into the chill cabinet, and moving slowly along the racked magazines, surreptitiously peeking at half-naked ladies. Anna decided that she wanted to drive. She got out of the car and stood on the blackened concrete, feeling the weight of the dull heat and the light-polluted clouds. As Spence returned a girl in a pink jacket and torn jeans arrived on a petrol-engined motorcycle, her boyfriend riding pillion in a complete suit of black leathers. They drew up beside a German van and began to refuel with the reckless, expensive old stuff. A nostalgic reek flooded the air, invoking hot road-movie nights in happier times. Spence and Anna had been travelers together for so long.

"He must be sweaty in there," remarked Spence tentatively.

"I want to drive."

"Are you okay to drive?"

"Of course I am."

"Sorry. Didn't mean anything." He held out his keys, with a wary smile. "Is it peace?"

She could see through the droop of his shoulders to the hostility he denied.

"Sure," she said miserably. "Peace, why not." She ignored his offering, used her own keys, and slid into the driver's seat.

"Shit," muttered Spence. "**Christ**—" He slammed the passenger door and hunched beside her, fists balled against his forehead.

"Daddy said the s-word," Jake murmured, pleased. "Did you get me anything?"

"Not this time babes," said Anna. "But we're going to stop at a Services."

"In the middle of the night?" The child's sleepy voice woke up, fired with enthusiasm. Jake loved midnight pit-stops.

"In the middle of the night," she agreed.

"And have ice cream?"

"We'll have whatever we like."

Anna had lost her job. She had lost plenty of jobs without feeling much pain. Short-term contracts end and are not renewed: there is no stigma. It's the business. But this was different. It was her own fault; it was because she had started to work on "Transferred Y" again. Spence had been making money at last. Anna had thought she was free to stretch her wings, to do something a prudent breadwinner couldn't contemplate. She'd known there would be flak when she published her results, maybe a weird science paragraph or two in the papers. She'd been totally unprepared for the catastrophe that had descended upon her. There was no one to understand. Not her parents, who had taken out an option against bad news. Not her sister (you must be joking). Not Spence; least of all Spence. He said he could not see what her problem was. If she never worked again, which was her overwrought prediction, they weren't going to starve. Why was she so upset? We're talking Anna Senoz here, not Marie Curie. She'd been one of the worker bees, footslogger in a lab coat. Now she was one of the unemployed. Why not? In case you hadn't noticed, it happens to a lot of people.

For fuck's sake, it isn't the end of the world. What makes you so special?

The fact that it was my life.

The fact that you love me.

Anna had said the first of these things. Not the second, because if you have to say that, it is already useless; since then they had not been friends.

It was strange to visit them and see her parents settling into a late bloom of prosperity. Treats, indulgences, new possessions. She felt glad for them but uneasy, as if they had given up her childhood's religion. No car, though. They were true to the old code in that: still acting the way everybody should, but didn't. Still doing the right thing.

The Motorway. They bowled across the wide confusing pan of the interchange: no lanes, headlights coming from all directions, the monstrous freight rigs blazing, bearing down on you like playground bullies, like street gangs—the only thing to do is not be in the way. Anna set her teeth and kept her line, up to one of the automatic gates. They were through, into hyperspace, into the video screen. Suddenly it was fully dark, all solid outlines had disappeared. The road world was made of lights, a rushing void between the unreeling double strands of scarlet and silver, amber and viridian, brake lights in front, headlights streaming towards her in the northbound lanes. Could be anywhere. It should be anywhere, a nameless country outside time and space, but somehow the road was not anonymous. She could sense that tired, familiar sky still overhead: skinny ragged hank of an island, hardly wider than the traffic lanes that braided it up and down.

Oh, but she truly loved this effortless glide through hyperspace. She loved the disembodied concentration that floated up in her: overtake, recover your lane, gear change up, gear change down. Never wanted an automatic or an autopilot, what a sissy idea, get a machine to eat your dinner and fuck for you next. This was a state of grace, hurtling at 140 kilometers an hour (habitual law breaker, like practically every British driver); and then every so often you'd do something wrong, a lapse of concentration or slight misjudgment, a jolt: speed up, dodge, drop back, whew, safe again. Lovely, lovely.

Until, inevitably, they hit a slow patch.

For years now they'd been making this trip, up to Manchester for Anna's mother's birthday. Always ended up doing it on a holiday weekend. Always ended up caught in traffic. When they visited Spence's mother in Illinois, LouLou would insist they didn't have to leave the night before their flight home: cue panic on the freeway, stacked like doughnuts in a box; and Spence's mother's rapture about the gashog-heaven dawn run to O'Hare descanting into an aggrieved wail—it's never like this! For the Goddess's sake, it is barely five am! Anna glanced at the routemaster prompt, faintly hoping for an alternative. But if there was any escape, it wouldn't know. It was dying; they ought to replace the chip, but they wouldn't because they were planning to give up private vehicle ownership. Thus, clinging to the destructive habit, we resort to stupid tricks, essentially punishing the car itself: like an unhappy woman who punishes her own body, poor innocent animal, by failing to groom, by dressing drably, by feeding or starving it into physical distress.

Stop that. Don't think bad thoughts.

She kept her distance; three cars instantly elbowed into her sensible gap. She accepted fate: settled into the nose-to-tail routine, along with the people on either side, and in front and behind for however many miles. It was as if they were all sitting, each of them staring reservedly straight ahead, on the banks of seats in some giant aircraft, doing odd calisthenics to stave off muscle atrophy on a long, long flight through the dark.

Those economy-class long haul flights, in the days when Anna and Spence used to travel the world: chasing short-term science jobs for Anna, in exotic locations. Those airports, the battered transfer lounges where the aircon gave up long ago, the ragged carpets soaked in an icy sweat of condensation, the tumbledown vinyl furniture. The rumor that passes as if through a herd of animals, so that first one or two and then a few people hover by the desk: then there's a surge, an unstoppable rush of bodies that everybody has to join, but which is completely pointless. Someone in uniform peeps around the glass doors and hurriedly retreats, clutching a mobile phone. The people in uniforms are terrified of the crowd. Therefore they put off as long as possible the awful moment when they'll have to admit that they don't have enough seats. Actually the plane was full when it left Lagos/Abu

Dhabi/Karachi/Singapore, because though all of you here have tickets and you confirmed and reconfirmed your onward bookings, the passengers at the point of origin have the advantage: and there are always more passengers. Always. So they wait and they keep us waiting, in the fear that lies behind unthinking cruelty—as if hoping that some of us will decide, having come out to the dead no-man's-land of the airport and suffered here for sixteen hours on a whim, just to while away the time, that we don't want to go home to London or Paris or New York after all.

We make small alliances, we look for people who look like ourselves, or failing that, for people with whom we share a language. Then there's an announcement: our flight will be leaving from a different gate. We all leap up and run, abandoning any semblance of solidarity. Maybe some of us will fall by the wayside, or accidentally rush through a door to the outside and have to start again with Immigration and Passport Control Hell. Maybe some of us will be trampled to death. Maybe that's what everybody's hoping for: that the numbers will be winnowed down, until we, the survivors, are secure. But at every window of the plane that sits out there in the night on the hot, wet, tarmac (these scenes always happen in the dark) there gleams a pair of listless, patient eyes. It's worse than we thought. It's not that there is not enough room for the whole crowd. There is no room at all. There is no drinking water, and the toilets don't work any more. Oh no, it won't do. There's no excuse, not even the thin illusion that you are doing good. If you don't have the moral bottle to take a two-week package tour to The Gambia for fun and sun in a razor-wired and guarded compound, which you'll only leave to visit the crocodiles by armored personnel carrier. (Sorry, crocodile. Sorry, we know there was one alive last year. We'll change the information in the brochure very shortly, honest.) Then you should stay at home. Don't worry. The experience you seek will soon come to find you.

Soon come.

Soon come.

When she was a little girl, Anna had been frightened when she found out that her grandfather Senoz (who was dead) had been born a Jew. He'd eloped with a Catholic girl, something his family took so hard the couple had decided to leave Spain and start again in England. It was supposed to be a romantic story. In Anna's childish mind the word *Jew* triggered an image of a great crowd of people shuffling along, dressed in black and white and shades of grey, towards a destination that obviously terrified them, but they couldn't turn back. **Where are they taking us, mummy? I don't know. Sssh.**

Here we are again, shuffling along, heads down, packed like frightened sheep. . .

The road folds in on itself. Sssh, don't ask where it leads.

The bad thoughts kept coming back, taking any shape they could find. She glanced at her husband. He seemed to be asleep, or if not asleep he was avoiding her as best he could inside a moving car. Spence wake up, talk to me, I'm drowning.

She was no stranger to the harsh realities of her profession. Getting fired was nothing really. The problem was Transferred Y, this outrage about Transferred Y: as if Anna had invented the phenomenon, and was being whipped and driven from the herd as a scapegoat. She wasn't to blame, she'd done nothing wrong; so why did she feel so broken, so desperate? She needed to understand. If she understood her own feelings, maybe she could deal with them. Her menfolk slept. Reluctantly, ruefully, her thoughts turned to the person who used to have the all answers: Anna in the long ago. Staring ahead of her, the silence of memory brimming behind her closed lips, she began to tell herself a story.

For a long time, I used to share a bedroom with my sister. . .

The Spirit of the Beech Tree

— i —

For a long time Anna used to share a bedroom with her sister. They were close in age, incompatible in temperament. Anna was fifteen months older: stoical, reserved, well-behaved, and single-minded. Margaret was a creature of enthusiasms, with a flaring temper and quick resentment of any authority-figure. When they were small, they were often happy together: by the time Anna was ten Margaret's very presence could fill her with despair. She marked her half of their space with string and tape, and begged her sister to respect the law. Margaret took up the challenge energetically, so that whenever Anna opened a drawer, looked for a dress in their shared wardrobe, took a book from her bookshelf, she found defiant spoor: torn and scribbled pages; missing toys; clothes tried out, dropped, stepped on, and left in a grubby, fingered heap among the shoes.

Anna's bed was the one by the window, by right of primogeniture. When she came upstairs, an hour later than Margaret (their parents, pining for child-free time, had tried sending the sisters off together: they'd had to give up the idea), she would pull the curtain round her and sit with a torch and her library book as if crouched in a cave—a mountain between herself and the hateful sound of her sister's breathing; the entrance of her refuge facing through chill glass into the night. Out in the dark there lived another girl. She was Anna's reflection, but there must have been a time when Anna genuinely didn't know this, because some of the mystery of the impossible had survived. The other girl floated in space: cold, wind washed, barefoot, marvelously free. She was both an ideal sister and an ideal Anna. She was closure. Between the shell of the reflection and the shell of her own body, Anna was poised, safe in her own territory, her privacy ensured. It did not occur to her to make up adventures for the wild girl or to invent imaginary conversations. She would simply look up from time to time from her reading, to meet the bright eyes of the other. They would smile at each other. The wild girl vanished at last when Anna was fourteen, which was when her parents had the loft converted and the two girls were able to have a bedroom each. She was not entirely forgotten. It was because of her that Anna, usually so levelheaded, had the curious impression—which she confessed to nobody—that she had *invented* Ramone Holyrod the night when they first met: called up this mischievous, erratic guardian spirit from nothing and darkness, with a past and circumstances all complete.

It happened like this. Anna was wandering the campus alone in the middle of the night. This was supposed to be dangerous for a female undergraduate. Anna, accustomed to street life on an inner-Manchester estate where the Rottweilers went around in pairs, saw no reason for alarm. Her sister had been staying for the weekend, sleeping on Anna's floor; it had been a strain. Her mind was buzzed and bruised from lack of sleep, but either her room or her head was still full of Maggie (still Margaret in Anna's interior monologue, for old time's sake), so she had been forced to come out for a midnight stroll. She was trespassing at the Arts end of the campus. Owing to savage prejudice on the part of the planners, the grass was literally greener up here, because there was more of it. The library was here (do they think we can't read?); and the great beech trees that Anna loved. Light from uncurtained windows and security lights along the paths and roads filled the dark valley, but when she looked away from them the sky above her was cobalt clear and bitten by more stars than you ever saw in inner Manchester.

She had been stupid enough to confide that she was in love.

"Do you sleep with him?" demanded Margaret.

"It's not like that. We're friends, we're in the same. . .social group, I suppose. He...he isn't interested."

She *must learn* that you didn't have to answer those kinds of questions. You could ignore them, or change the subject, or lie. Everybody did it.

Margaret laughed. "You don't have to wait for him to be 'interested.' Make him an offer. Men will fuck anything, the pigs. Didn't you see that thing on the news last week, a ninety-three-year-old great grandmother gang-raped by a bunch of thirteen-year-olds? Or something like that. It's always happening. I don't mean to be crude, but if *she* can get some, what is your problem? Offer sex, you don't have to worry about anything else. He'll fuck you once, he'll fuck you twice, he'll get used to the idea, you become a habit, and bingo!" Margaret waved her white hand in the gloom of Anna's sleeping cell, spreading the fingers daintily. "The engagement ring!"

"You're nuts," muttered Anna from her bed, wishing to God being drunk made Margaret fall asleep like a normal person.

"What d'you say?"

"I'm going to sleep."

If Margaret was right about the way things had to be between men and women, then Anna wanted no part of the business. The idea that you could carry on in such bad faith to the point of *marrying someone* was disgusting. Margaret said they expected nothing else, wouldn't understand if you were honest. Anna couldn't believe that the boys, the men, she knew were really like that. Straightforwardness and fair-dealing must be better. It only needed somebody to make the first move. If it was true that human beings were the helpless puppets of their sex hormones, then why didn't Anna herself have six children by this time? Surely men must be human as well as sexual, same as women? Surely they must be. Suppose Margaret was right? Anna shuddered. Then too bad; she would stay celibate her life long. Can't play; won't play!

Getting married young was crap anyway. When she married—if she married, it wasn't essential—it would be at the end of an extended and intense single life, and with somebody she had met long after this callow apprenticeship as an undergraduate. The cold kiss of dew on her bare ankles, she lifted her face to gaze at the stars: distracted by reasoned argument and comforted by exquisite dreams. The house in the country where she and Rob would live together. Their cats, their dogs, their two children, Richard and Delphine. But as she approached one of the beeches, a solitary tree that she regarded as her particular refuge, a dart of anguish pierced her: *he doesn't love me and he never will.*

It was the truth. She could read the game-board; she knew her hopes were doomed. She could see other couples moving together, possible or probable configurations: *not* Anna with Rob. Either he had a girlfriend elsewhere, though he'd never mentioned one, or he was gay and shy about letting people know, or (the most likely) he simply did not want to do it with Anna. These things happen at first sight, or at least soon: chemicals are involved. Sexual attraction is not something people ponder over for weeks. He must know that Anna wanted him. She hadn't offered herself on a plate, the way Margaret would advise, but she'd made her moves. She had gone as far as self-esteem allowed, done and said all the things people do and say that code for *would you like to do it with me?* The answer was no.

She huddled down between two of the tree's massive roots, feeling very glum. It was not to be. She'd been wanting him for too long, anyway: weeks, *months*. If he turned to her now it would be no use. She'd transformed him into the object of desire; she couldn't make him human again. How could a happy relationship be built on such an unequal foundation? Perhaps she should try a modified version of Margaret's way, smuggle herself naked into his bed one night. That way at least she'd get to fuck him once. And then walk away. That would be noble. But if he turned her down? If he said, *um thanks but I have an essay to write*, or *um thanks, er, meet my girlfriend/boyfriend.* Awful, awful: and not untypical for the results of taking Margaret's advice.

Her worldly wise little sister! If Margaret was so smart, why wasn't some merchant banker loading her with jewels right now? No, Anna would be Rob's friend, not even a close friend; that was best. Free to look, free to stay near that gorgeous body, to catch a smile from those wonderful lips. . . Oh, but the night was beautiful. If you managed not to hear the dance music from someone's late night party. It was the end of April, dry and fair. The beech tree was in fresh and trembling leaf; the breeze that touched her face carried scents of sap and blossom. It was bliss on a night like this to be alive. And free, and at the beginning of things. . .

Suddenly she heard a strange voice, a woman's voice chanting softly.

I may love him, I may love him
For he is a man and I am only a beech tree. . .
And then, a low musical wailing.
Oooooooooooooh, Ooooooh. . .
Oooooooooooh, Ooooooh. . .

Anna said sharply, "Who's there??"

There was a rustling pause. She wished she hadn't spoken, she'd probably interrupted a pair of lovers—damn it, how embarrassing. But there had been something truly scary about that long moan. Maybe it was murder not sex that was going on. Then what would she do? Her skin crept, her heart thumped. A figure emerged from around the bole of the tree. It was a girl, a girl with long draggled hair, a round and pallid face, a nose ring, and wire-rimmed glasses. They stared at each other. Involuntarily, Anna brushed a hand across her cropped, dark curls and touched the bridge of her own nose. Her skin felt warm.

"Hi," said the girl. "I'm sorry, did I frighten you?"

She was small, shorter than Anna. She was wearing a long skirt, and her feet were bare. A large, fringed shawl was wrapped around her shoulders. Her eyes were round behind the round-rimmed glasses, her mouth curiously wide and thin lipped. It was almost comical, a cartoon sketch of a face; and yet somehow arresting. The question, *did I frighten you?*, was definitely aggressive. Anna admired this: you had to admire a person caught moaning behind a tree who was instantly ready to snatch the initiative.

"No." Anna knew she was now expected to get up and go away, but she sat her ground. The girl sat down too, tenting herself in the shawl like a savage in a blanket or a cloak of animal hide. Her bare feet were dirty. The colors of her shawl and skirt were lost in deep twilight, but the skirt seemed to be covered with unraveling machine embroidery, and the tasseled fringe of the shawl was a mess. Someone who did not iron or mend. A hippie, possibly a tree-hugger.

"Do you often wander around the campus late at night?"

"Sometimes," Anna answered coolly. "Do you?"

"Aren't you afraid of rapists?"

"No. Aren't you?"

"I'm all right. I can scare people." She raised her shawl in dark wings and shook out her unkempt locks. "Oooooh! Oooooooh! I was practicing when you came along."

Anna nodded politely.

The strange girl laughed aloud. "Actually, I was masturbating. You yelled out at *just* the wrong moment."

"Well, don't let me put you off. Go ahead."

Silenced, for a moment, the girl started to pick at the skin around her toenails.

"Are you a first-year?" asked Anna.

"Nah. I'm a drug dealer. I hate students. I prey on them. I take all their money and ruin their little lives. Are you? You look clean enough."

Anna folded her hands around her ankles beneath the neat hems of her jeans. Her deck shoes, blue and white gingham canvas, were very clean. She had cleaned them herself. She wished she had not. "I think you're a first-year. I think I've seen you around."

The girl wrinkled her long lip, looking like a very intelligent chimpanzee. She shrugged. "Okay, you're right. I'm Ramone Holyrod. I'm doing Modern Cultural History. I bet I've seen you around too, it's a small world. But I don't remember."

One of those do-nothing made-up Arts courses, thought Anna the Unmemorable. Just what I would have guessed. "My name's Anna Senoz. I'm doing Biology." She noticed that the other girl had said *I'm Ramone*, not "my name's Ramone." As if being Ramone Holyrod was important.

"Oh, a *scientist*!" Ramone Holyrod had the conventional reaction: Anna was disappointed in her. Suddenly she laughed. "Hey, I *do* know you. You're a friend of Daz's, I've seen you with her and her boyfriend, and that rich guy, Tim Oliver, and the American Exchange student, whatsisname. He's in my tutor group."

"It's Oliver Tim. Everyone makes that mistake. His Dad's family's Korean, I mean that's where they're from originally. I didn't know Daz had a boyfriend."

Ramone rolled her eyes. "You know what our sexual behavior is like. It's all so fucking hierarchical, teenage sex: alliances and humiliations conferred by who pokes whom, and here we are with no proper hierarchy set up. Therefore nobody wants to go public on who they fuck *in case it turns out to be the wrong move.* She's been doing Rob Fowler for weeks. I reckon they've both just about decided they're the right, nice, middle-class, clever-but-not-too-clever rank, because I saw them holding hands today, coming out of his hall of residence. The sly bastard, I hate him."

Anna's blood started running cold and slow.

"Girl scientists always go for Biology," remarked Ramone. "It's a fucking crime. They get better A level results than the boys for everything, but they 'ant got the bottle to go for Physics or Chemistry. I read about it. You have to go for the big idea if you're into hard science and girls can't face that. They don't like the loneliness. And they don't want to look unfeminine. You'll never find a pretty girl taking Physics. They stick to the soft teamwork, modest efforts, and second class degrees of their own free will. It's a fact."

"Shows how much you know about science," retorted Anna. "Do you call Biology second class? That's ridiculous. You're living in the past. Do you really think people are going to be worried, a hundred years from now, about missing Z particles and up and down quarks? It'll be like phlogiston or something, people will laugh. Just look at the board, look at the evidence. They have big money, but that alphabet soup is dead in more ways than one. The boys go for Physics because they're conformists. I mean, really, doesn't it remind you of Alfonso of Castile?"

"Who?"

"You know. King of Castile in the fifteenth century. When they showed him the latest cat's cradle of celestial spheres that was supposed to reconcile astronomers' observations with the stationary earth. He said, *If God had consulted me, I would have suggested something simpler.* Haven't you read *The Sleepwalkers?*"

"I couldn't give a shit about Alfonso of Castile——"

"I thought all Arts Students had to read *The Sleepwalkers.* Even if they had to tie you down and drug you. That and a few other old sacred popular-science texts. It's about the Copernican revolution, the birth of the modern world-view."

"Fuck, no. Not until they force-feed the nerds with Deleuze and Guattari." Ramone's long lip curled in a secret, speculative smile. "Did you get good A levels?"

"The best," replied Anna firmly. She's started to enjoy this game.

"So did I. I'm going to do something great, you know? That's my single-minded purpose in life. I'm going to be famous. What do you think about animal experiments?"

"I think they'll continue to be important," answered Anna. "For the foreseeable future. But I'm more interested in plants."

Ramone didn't persist with the animal rights line.

"Are you ambitious? Will you get a first? Do you think you'll make it?"

Anna would have liked to explain that the world rank of upper-second is the best there is. You do what you do, you do it *well*. Being famous, high-flying, is a different category, reflecting happenstance, personal need, hunger for attention. . . But she guessed that actual argument with Ramone would not be much fun. Better stick to verbal tennis.

"I don't see why not."

Ramone cackled. "Modesty will get you nowhere!" Then she sighed. "Really, I was moaning and crying because I am unhappy in love."

The Spring night, which had been somewhere else during their volleys, returned, with the scents of new growth and the mournful sighing of the breeze.

"With Rob Fowler?"

Ramone bristled indignantly. "With *Daz*. I worship her. It was love at first sight, and now she's in an out-and-proud heterosexual romance I know it's a hopeless passion."

"She *is* very pretty,"

"I don't mind for myself so much as for Daz. When you love someone you want the best for them. Maybe I'm no good, I come on too strong, I'm not her type. But I don't see how any intelligent woman can be interested in men, in *male undergraduates*. They detest us. You can see it in the back of their eyes. They hate and fear us, we're the alien hordes. Any guy on campus who pretends to think you are a human being is faking it in the hopes of getting laid."

"I only asked because you were saying 'I may love *him*,' just now. When you were pretending to be a dryad."

"It was a quotation. From a writer called George MacDonald. You wouldn't know anything about him." Ramone gave Anna a suspicious look and raised her voice. "A weird reactionary Victorian nutcase, but interesting in a bizarre way."

Anna didn't know George MacDonald from a Beat Generation poet, so she merely shrugged. Touché for Alfonso.

"All the women at this place have the mentality of freed slaves," growled Ramone. "We ought to be the Goths and Vandals, sweeping in to rapine and pillage, but no way, not a chance. It's like the fall of the Roman Empire, but the *wrong part*, you know what I mean? Freed slaves, getting rich but absolutely no fucking idea of taking power, no self-esteem, no political perspective. You can't bring people up for millennia to have zero rights and suddenly expect them to understand what freedom is, what it means to control, to rule, to have authority. They're out for what they can get. All these pretty shiny rich girls, they don't know they're privileged, they take it all like, like *cat food*. They're aspiring to nothing more than some smug fucking dishwasher-proof two-car garage career-housewife lifestyle. Or if they succeed in a man's world, it's going to be by using their stinking rotten femininity, by whoring in other words. It's a sin to give them an education, they're *cattle*. Are you rich?" she demanded abruptly.

"No. I'm poor. About as poor as you can be and still be an undergraduate."

She spoke without thinking, instinctively placatory. Ramone cast a skeptical glance over Anna's neat and tidy attire. "Yeah? I bet your parents support you. . . Mine don't. I've got a scholarship from some rich shit foundation for the needy, and when that runs out, I starve. What do they do?"

"My father's a fashion designer."

"Hmm. That doesn't sound poor."

"If you're unemployed, it doesn't make any difference what your profession is."

"Who employs fashion designers? I can't imagine."

Anna was ashamed to admit that she didn't know. Another thing she'd discovered over the months, besides the depth of her poverty, was her ignorance about the grown-up world. Her parents' lives had been a blank, beyond the veil, until the moment she left home. She felt that this was old-fashioned and embarrassing.

"He had his own business. It failed, and his partner ran out on him. I don't know the details, but we were left with huge, horrible debts."

Ramone sucked her teeth, affecting shock. "We? You mean they made you *sign* things?"

"Well, no but. . ."

"I suppose *Mummy* couldn't be expected to go out to work."

Anna's mother was a doctor. She'd started out as a pediatrician, shifted into educational counseling for job security and regular hours. Her salary had poured away for years into the debt pit, leaving very little for the household bills. Anna's parents had never dreamed of trying to escape from the trap: they had to do the right thing. She decided not to explain. She noted that Ramone's tirades were to be treated with respect. They could knock you off balance and spoil your next shot.

The thumping beat of party music reached them relentlessly, filling up their pauses. "Fucking MDMA," muttered Ramone. "Sometimes I wish no one had ever heard of that stuff, don't you. What happened to *tender is the night, and haply the queen moon is on her throne?*" A gang of male students passed noisily along the path at the foot of the slope and disappeared in the floodlit, shadowy maze of buildings. Ramone lay back and started shifting about. She rolled over: Anna jumped, startled.

"Don't worry, I'm not making a pass. I was lying on a rock."

"Are you going to sleep out here?"

"Maybe. Why not?"

It was time to admit defeat. "You'll get very cold." Anna stood up and walked away, leaving the victor in possession. "See you around," called Ramone, happily.

"Yes, sure. See you around."

Her room was free of Margaret. As soon as she walked in, it began to be full of Ramone. Ramone's round eyes surveyed the neat interior: basic, shabby, battered, anonymous. Ramone's cartoon grin mocked Anna's humble decorations. Her chimpanzee lip curled at the stack of text books, she shook her head over the well-nigh complete absence of Fiction or Social Comment or Style Statement in any form. The Narnia and Tolkien paperbacks on the beside shelf made things worse. One might as well keep soft toys. Anna felt judged, but the judgment was invigorating. She wondered if Ramone was really a lesbian, or was that part of the act? She was full of admiration, which she would do her best to conceal when she met the wild girl again. She felt that she had met *somebody*.

On her desk lay the draft of an essay, which should be handed in tomorrow. She was short of an elusive reference. Charles Craft, the best of the boys and the only person on the first year Biology course to offer Anna any competition, laughed at her for acting the baby academic. First year work, he said, is make-work, it's crazy to treat it seriously. But Anna was physically uncomfortable if she didn't get things right…to her own satisfaction at the time. She would sleep, get up early, go to the library and check through back issues of *Plant Genetics*. Simple, no problem.

But Rob was with Daz!

Daz and Anna had met at the Freshers' Fair. Daz was a scientist too—in computing, which made her less of a nerd. They were both serious people, interested in doing real work, yet they'd both made friends across the Great Divide. But Daz had black shiny hair half way to her knees, a beautiful walk, and a rangy coat-hanger figure on which clothes fit like a dream. Of course, Daz! Anna, who had been standing in the middle of her small space, tingling with Ramone-induced energy, dropped onto the bed. Thank God she'd heard the news before she tried Margaret's evil recipe. So that's it, she thought. I'd better start getting over him.

➤ ➤

Ramone returned to her grubby cell in The Woods, by far the scruffiest hall in the valley, about an hour after Anna had left her, chilled to the bone and bruised by the rocks in that friendly looking hillside. She flung herself at her keyboard and into full flow.

Some people never leave the childhood home. They grow up, move house, marry, divorce, remarry, have children, but do all of this without separating themselves from a certain psychological landscape. The setting may change out of all recognition, buildings destroyed, trees uprooted, the old furniture sold. The human icons remain: Uncle Sam and Auntie Betty, the cousins, old family friends. People who live like this may say: I will do that thing; I will hold that opinion. . ., but not until my mother dies. They spend decades as adults of the second rank, dancing on the spot, waiting for their moment. Those of us who leave, who extract ourselves from the matrix, will always feel lost in the world, unsure of our place in any hierarchy. But, our emotional lives can be tranquil. The child who stays attached has axes to grind, stakes to protect, territory to mark. Her relationship with society is cluttered with rusty weapons, bad wiring, amended treaties. The child who abandons family lives in equality, having nothing to gain from subservience. We have given up the sweet recursions of the first world for the beauty of beginning. We are not free, but we see our bonds for what they are. We have no obligations.

Save it. In the folder called *Commentaries*, or *COMMENT*. Don't call it *Anna*!

She unearthed a small tin of processed peas from her clothes cupboard, pondered briefly (it was the only treat left this week), opened it, and drained it into the washbasin; added a dollop of mayonnaise from a rather festering jar and buttered two slices of bread, while licking fingerfuls of the green and primrose mixture. She applied salt and vinegar. Wonderful! Crumbs and butter gobbets fell among the clean socks and knickers she'd brought up from the Laundromat but forgotten to stow away. Lying on the bed with her sandwich in one paw and her life's companion, Pele (a blue and once furry toy rabbit, scoured by age), tucked under one arm, she leafed through a crumpled notepad of lined paper to find the latest record of her grief:

"Dido and Aeneas in the Underworld"
I remember
The pyre, and how I climbed it
The sword, and the little mastheads sinking below the sea
I remember too the blow I got

Deep in my side and how I ran confused
Lost, and my hooves snicked on the herby stones
You should have been behind me. . .

━ ━

Deeply affected by her own words, she sobbed aloud around masticated primrose-green and whole-meal mouthfuls. "Oh God. OH GOD. God, God, please don't do this to me, I can't bear it. AWOoooooh! AWOoooooh!"

The people in the cells on either side woke and groaned. An Iranian Media Studies student pulled her pillow over her head and stuck her fingers in her ears. The American Exchange smacked the on switch of his ghettoblaster and slammed it against the wall, full blast drastic thrash right in the monster's ear hole. Made no difference. He switched it off and lay grimly enduring. Amplified music in the small hours was a chucking-out offence, whereas there was no obvious sanction against Howling Wolf's behavior. He was a timid soul.

Ramone did not have a bedtime. She fell asleep at about four, dropping like a stone into oblivion in the middle of a sentence in *Anti-Oedipus*. It was the only way she knew.

➤ *ii* ➤

Anna Senoz preferred male company, because guys tended not to interrupt her when she was explaining things. Patrick Spencer Meade, the American Exchange student, had noticed this. When she talked to fellow females they would speedily glaze over and soon it would be *yes, yes, yes, but what about my new hairdo?* Okay, to be fair, *yes, yes, yes, but what about <something intellectual>?* Result: Anna bewildered. She didn't know how to leave a thought unfinished. She had no idea why the average male undergraduate let her gab in peace. She had no idea she was sexy. Picture it: Marilyn Monroe is sitting beside you—a *brunette* Marilyn, which is so much classier, and *brainy*, which to the male is subconsciously incredibly attractive, resist the dreadful idea as he will. Holy baloney! Those lovely, clear, taffy-colored brown eyes are gazing into yours, that body is staying nice and close, as she explains to you the role of small particles of molybdenum in the process of photo-synthesis. No sir, you are not going to interrupt, not for your life.

The guys didn't know what was going on either, not consciously. Anna's signifiers were neat and sober clothing, hardly-there make-up, an air of cool comradeship. There was nothing about her dress or manner that said THIS WAY TO THE HONEYPOT. The guys, who jumped up slavering whenever anything marked GIRL walked by, if the body under the labels belonged to Dumbo or to a stick insect, never mentioned Anna in their parodic, hard-on discussions of female first-year talent. But they kept quiet for her, and in a puzzled way they *gravitated.* He guessed they had to be aware, at some level, of her wide shoulders, hand-span waist, and curvaceous little bottom; of the pert, round-as-apples breasts under her clean and modest tee-shirts.

Or maybe Spence was partial.

She had been pointed out to him at an early stage in his Exchange Year, by Charles Craft whom he'd met at the Computer Club. She was the girl in Biols who had read everything on the reading list and then some, the one who spent hours in the library reading science journals that had nothing to do with any first-year course. Charles had laughed unpleasantly and called her Mr Spock. Spence, who'd already discovered to his personal cost that Craft was full of shit, had detected envy and insecurity, and looked on the cause of these emotions with approval. Then, one weekend, they all went up to London for a critically vital music gig. *They all*, meaning those members of the loose group of friends who had the funds for a daunting ticket price, plus Spence and Anna Senoz, poor but scraping by. They'd hardly spoken to each other at this point. *They all* had stayed at Rosemary McCarthy's parents' house. Rosey and Wol (otherwise Oliver Tim) had cooked a large Sunday meal. Spence and Anna, both of them maybe feeling socially marginal, had independently decided to clean the kitchen, which was in a heap big mess. Stacked the dishwasher, cleaned pans. She washed, he dried. They didn't talk. He felt that she was shy and wondered idly why she didn't know she was gorgeous. Mean older sisters putting her down? Father who considered girls second-rate? Was she a previously unappetizing teen, who had just blossomed into glory? She handed him a large cast-iron frying pan, which still had a gob of burnt Bolognese sauce adhering to its butt. Spence returned the article, silently pointing out the failure in her technique. Anna nodded and flashed him a beautiful smile before bending to the task of scrubbing it over again.

Hey!

It isn't often you get to be in at the birth of one of your own legends.

She made him think of his mother. Louise Davinia Spencer Meade, the poor widow-woman he'd left behind him in Annandale, Illinois, lending her large spirit and presence to whatever attempt at counter-culture you could find in a small town on the Manankee river. Spence's Mom—who liked him to call her Louise, or LouLou, but he preferred Mom—was a vintage feminist. She'd have been proud of him. The menfolk of Annandale were an unregenerate lot, stubbornly resistant to the siren allure of female intelligence, which was one reason why Louise had remained more or less single since her husband died. The other was Spence, of course. She adored him, as he well knew.

Spence remembered his father only as a querulous and smelly sick person of whom his mother was inexplicably fond. He had come to feel grateful, as he grew older, that the man was dead, not merely divorced and hanging around wanting to take his son to the ball game alternate weekends. He didn't like to think of the life he'd have had, between Mom and a male rival. Sometimes, in the darkest dreams of kid fantasy, he'd entertained the idea that she had actually *killed* his Dad. This surely wasn't true, but it gave a fellow pause, nonetheless. She had brooded over his childhood like a sweet, capricious thunderhead. He dreaded her rages (which were hardly ever turned against him, but against abstract principles, things the government did, programs on the tv) and lived for her smiles, her gallant *joie de vivre*. When he flew over the Atlantic for the first time, the dazzling soft masses of cloud below his plane had looked poignantly familiar. She had weaned him late, hippie earth-mother style. He did not remember, or barely, his possession of her large breasts. But there was Mom: snow crème and eiderdown.

He was sure she wanted him to have a healthy sex life, but he felt strange about feeling anything serious, so far from home. He needed good clean casual sex, not a love affair. So he had decided not to do anything about Anna; or rather he'd procrastinated, through the dull British winter and the chill but pretty springtime: missing his Mom, thinking about Anna, enjoying his friends, paying little attention to his studies, and hating his cell in Woods. Everything in Britain seemed to Spence unclean, especially the food. The university residence hall was *disgusting*. Noisy, too.

◆ ◆

"At its inception, a telephone network was perceived as a tool of commerce, without application outside the exclusively male sphere of business or the schematically male emergency services. Telephone communication as a social phenomenon in its own right was unforeseen, until the telephone was discovered or imagined into cultural being by women or women-analogic social males. In 1881, when the first public telephone service was initiated in Paris, Marcel Proust was ten years old. Some ten years later, according to the chronology of *In Search of Lost Time*, Proust—as a homosexual and a Jew, a doubly marginalized male—became one of the first of those to re-present and real-ize this novel technology, by fervently mythologizing the

Young Ladies of the Telephone—the obscurely necessary, menial yet all-powerful, female agency interposed between the telephone and the world: midwives of an applied technology balanced on the brink of meaning. Proust's paen of praise for the telephone operators of Paris is not, of course, a serious expression of respect. Yet it is literally true that women, the secret arbiters of cultural significance, by annexing for their own use this male instrument, transformed the concept of telecommunication. It was another socially marginalized male, a science fiction writer, who invented the term 'cyberspace.' Here on the threshold of the third millennium, can we doubt that a similar female agency, erased but necessary, will emerge in the new industry of telematics? Note how often, in popular mythology texts, the *voice* of the computer is female: the voice of the dominatrix, teacher, mother. . ."

The other students gazed out of the window; or doodled or frowned in feigned concentration. The tutor, semi-recumbent behind his four-square, sixties desk of blonde and grainy pine, occasionally lifted his lizard lids a trifle and thought, it's never the pretty ones. Ramone Holyrod had lost some puppy-fat over the course of the year, but the improvement was slight. It's always the childish ones, he added. The adult-looking undergraduates are the monkey-do accomplished (we won't say intelligent, that would be a premature judgment indeed); but the most childish, the most unfinished are the only ones with any kind of originality. He wondered if there were any scientific rationale to back this idle observation. One would have to include young Spence of course, whose face was as formless as an egg—an egg with a mop of Dylanesque ringlets on top of a stringy male child's body—but whose sense of humor was surprisingly sharp. But that could be the accent. Quite possibly Spencerisms would not be in the least entertaining if expressed in graceless UKC1ese.

Ramone had finished.

"Very nice," said their tutor. *Very nice* meant I wasn't listening. *Interesting!*, which never came Ramone Holyrod's or Andrea David's way, meant Good. Lucy Freeman heard it often. She was the pretty one. "Comments, anybody?"

Ramone gritted her teeth and glanced fearfully at Spence, who was a computer nut and probably knew what a modem did. But the

American Exchange was preoccupied. Martin Judge, the other male member of the group, took issue, as usual. "I don't understand why you have to bring sex into everything, Ramone."

Relieved, she turned on him, "What do you think I *should* bring to a discussion about Technology in Society? Jars of marmalade? Sex is in everything. I didn't put it there. The most significant thing in your entire social and cultural life is your assigned gender. Everything else comes after that fact, including your relationship with technology. Don't you accept that?"

"Jars of marmalade would make more sense. Whoever invented the screw-top lid made more positive difference to women's lives than political feminism, if you ask me——"

"Okay, if sex doesn't come into it, why did you say *women's* lives——?"

"Children, children. . .Telephones. The subject was telephones. Ramone's essay. Could we return to our *moutons*?"

At the end of the session Ramone, bright color in her pasty cheeks, bundled up her belongings into her shoulder bag. She tried to take the essay with them; she was now ashamed of it and miserable. The tutor made her leave it on his desk. His resigned glance at the butter-stained first page cut her to the heart. She stomped out. Lucy and Andrea had departed to some girly lunch-date, but the appalling Martin was lying in wait pretending to talk to Spence. She had to walk down the corridor between the two of them, feeling hatefully small and untidy, a heaving maggoty mess.

"Look, Ramone," began Martin. "I'm sorry I upset you. It's just that I don't think our Technology and Society tutorials are the place for sexual politics. It's not the subject of the course, and it's not fair on the rest of us. I'd honestly love to sit down with you some other time and have a proper discussion about the whole sex and gender thing."

The term *shit-eating grin*, she thought, was coined for occasions like this. She stared, fascinated, analyzing the precise content of that exposure, male teeth with a fat juicy turd locked behind them. It means, *I'm stealing something from you.* I'm being obnoxious and we both know it, but you can't prove it and you can't stop me. I'm getting something for nothing from a female. I'm copping a feel here.

"I know what's wrong with you, Martin. You're afraid for your life. You don't want me to mention sex because by mentioning sex I insist that I'm here at the university as a woman, whereas you still think women ought to accept that they're here as second-rate men. Your privileges aren't protected any longer. I'm not going to keep the rules of the little boys' club, I'm not going to pretend to be inadequate. I'm going to claim to be a complete human being. And if that's what I am, where does that leave you, you titless freak!"

Spence wondered what 'a God's name would happen next. Martin opened his mouth and closed it. Knots of muscle on either side of his jaws worked visibly.

"Well, see you around, Spence." He strode away.

Spence cleared his throat. "I don't think you can claim William Gibson for a marginal male, Ramone. In the US it's okay for a guy to be a writer, was in the eighties anyway, as long as he makes good money. And science fiction is some kind of heartland. Maybe it's different over here, but to me bracketing Gibson with Proust sounds weird. I mean, not in a good way——"

She shook her head. She could not talk about her work. Her essays were creations; they stood or fell. It was over: another stillborn, another fortress leveled. They dawdled, to avoid the awkwardness of bumping into Martin again. Ramone seemed surprised that Spence was still by her side as they passed out into the May sunshine.

"Are you two going to go on like this for the whole degree course?" he asked.

"Maybe not. He didn't say 'until our next encounter, dear lady' this time. Arsehole. I got to him. Maybe someday he'll learn to *leave me the fuck alone.*"

This reading of the situation was enough to make a basilisk blink, but Spence let it stand. "I thought he was going to do a Dr Johnson on you that time."

"Say what?"

Spence took a violent swing at the air. "I refute you *thus!*"

Ramone glowered, her hands bunching into two ready little fists. She bared her teeth: plain fury behind them, no shit. "If he did, he would get a surprise."

He'd been trying to think where he'd seen a likeness of Ramone Holyrod. Now he knew. It was an Aubery Beardsley drawing of Messalina. *Messalina, Going To The Bath:* snakelocks, glowering cheeks—a dumpy Queen Victoria bundle of garments full of pugnacious forward movement. . . He'd have to tell someone this: it was too good to waste. Not Ramone. Much as she'd bite your head off if you dared to suggest it, he knew she longed to be better-looking. She was a pig to live with, but his heart went out to the kid. Her absurd, bantam hen bravado: *he'd* get a surprise! Martin Lodge was six two and built like a linebacker. You could only hope that crazy Ramone would never meet the man callous enough to hit her. Because *she was asking for it.*

He had caught himself wondering if she knew about that in herself.

"I'm moving out," he announced.

"Huh?"

"I'm moving out of the Woods. I met some guys—"

"But it's the end of term next month. I mean, why bother?"

"Yeah, well."

"You won't get your rent back."

"That's okay. I'm moving into a squat. The fact is—" Spence was wondering why the HELL he had told Ramone, the LAST PERSON IN THE WORLD he wanted informed of his escape plans—"I'm thinking of staying in town for the summer. I have an open ticket. I can temp with a software house, make some easy dosh, and head home in September."

She beamed, round eyes glowing. "Cool! When are you moving? Can I help?"

He didn't have the balls to refuse. "Sure. Sure, why not?"

◆ ◆

The day that Spence moved into his squat *they all* went along to help, in Rob Fowler's battered but capacious old Volvo and Daz Avritivendam's glossy Renault: a version of *they all* that meant Rob and Daz and Ramone, Anna and Spence and a computing friend of Spence's called Simon Gough. Everybody stared, lost for words, at the three tiny old cottages, their picturesque flint walls gruesomely painted-over in coarse bright colors. A junk metal man with a frilled yellow head, possibly representing the sun, stood where roses should have clustered over the middle one of the three front doors. The other two doors were roughly boarded-up.

Spence was moved to apologize. "That's the way it goes for us tourists these days. There's no romance left in the Old World. You schlep into the interior to rubberneck the savages in their traditional murdered-bird hairdos and find them sporting war-bonnets made of flattened Coke cans and Radio Shack parts—" He blushed. Daz, the lissome, elegant black girl with the confusing English accent, was an ethnic-origin Tamil from Borneo. "Er, meaning no offence—"

The World's Most Gorgeous Malaysian patted him kindly on the shoulder. "We do our best to stay ahead of your games, Americano. We do our best."

In the kitchen the head of the household, a skinny smoke-dried individual going by the name of Mr Frank N Furter, was transacting business with three oldish men in work clothes. It was a surprisingly clean kitchen, although doing double service as a menagerie. A black and white rat sat in a cage by the cooker, next to an iguana the size of a rabbit in a glass vivarium. A grey parrot peered down from an old-fashioned drying rack slung from the ceiling; there was a cat with kittens in a basket under the table. Frank seemed distant. Spence was nervous and hustled them away before Ramone—who had shed ten angry years the moment she saw the animals—could ask to play with the rat or get her busy paws into the vivarium.

Everyone cheerfully hauled everything up to his room: cardboard boxes, a secondhand mattress, a murderously heavy suitcase full of books, an old dining table from the Salvation Army, orange crates for chairs. When Spence became absorbed in wiring his computer rig, *they all* faded away. The squat was too interesting; it produced strange noises: bongo drumming, wild laughter, rapid furtive footsteps. Spence's neighbor, a friendly brown-skinned Aussie blonde in a bikini, who introduced herself as Alice Flynn, popped in and explained that there was sunbathing on the roof. . . Before long, the only removal assistant left was Anna Senoz.

"Sorry about this," said Spence, blushing. Someone had recently rewired the cottages, which were linked by casual breaches in the interior walls. Socket plates dangled everywhere, over heaps of fresh dust: but the only power point in this room was not conveniently sited for Spence's plans. "I need to get back online, my Mom worries. If she sends me one email that bounces, she'll be on the next plane——"

Anna nodded, more impressed than she liked to admit by an emailing mother.

She didn't mind being left alone with the American Exchange. She didn't know what to say to him, but it was restful to sit quietly. So many hours she'd spent like this when she was a little child, watching while Daddy did things. . .

"Do you know what his real name is, downstairs?"

"You mean Frank? No, I don't. What business is it of mine?"

Where Anna came from, horny-handed sons of toil who spent their afternoons cutting up lines of white powder were not good news. She was concerned. He was a tourist, as he had admitted: seeking thrills, taking risks he didn't recognize because they didn't look the same as at home.

"It might be your business if the police come calling——"

Spence finished connecting his printer, set it on its base, and stepped back. "They won't. The Bournemouth police are cool, Frank told me. They don't bother recreational users. What's wrong with the guy providing a service? You use drugs, I've seen you do it."

"I think my parents have smoked dope most of their lives, and they know I do it. If taking alcohol is okay, there's nothing much wrong with cannabis. But there are limits."

"And different people have different ideas about where the limits are." He gave her a look, assessing new information: and added, not really changing the subject, "Where d'you think Ramone comes from? She's a phenomenon, that kid. Having the room next door to her on campus, I got to know her habits. She never sleeps. Likes to scream, too. It was a wild party for one, all night and every night."

Anna frowned.

She was right, it was a shame to tell tales. "I *suspect* she may be the smartest person I've ever met. I couldn't prove it; most of her work is a disaster. I just have a weird feeling she may be brilliant. And doesn't have an idea how to deal with it, because no one ever told her or showed her how—"

"I think her parents are sort of hippies."

"That would figure. Brought up in a cave, by dog-food-eating drop outs—"

He'd heard that Anna and Daz were planning to stay on and work through the summer. He wanted to ask her about that. But what could he say? Secret lust made it impossible to form the most innocent remark—

"I'm gonna have to use the light socket as an interim auxiliary power source. Damned wiring in here is totally inadequate—"

"Who did it, anyway?"

"Ah, hm. Me, actually." He dragged one of his orange crates into the center of the room, tucking a connecting block and an electrical screwdriver in his pocket. "Make sure it's switched off at the wall, will you?"

"Er, don't you think you should disconnect at the mains?"

It was Spence's mother, the original Ms Fixit, who had taught him to be a handyman, infecting him at the same time with her own cavalier impatience. He knew it but he couldn't help it. "Not yet, I'll just see if this is going to work—" He unscrewed the lightbulb, handed it to Anna, hauled up the naked end of the cable that led from the board—"I want to get the rig running today, send my Mom a—" He needed a third hand, just for a moment—

THWUMP!!

"My God! SPENCE!"

The American Exchange lay flat on his back on the dusty boards, bluish around the mouth. Anna yanked the live lead from between his clenched teeth: *now what?*

He opened his eyes.

"Oh, thank God. Are you okay? What were you *doing?*"

"I got confused," explained Spence weakly. He was wearing a shapeless tee-shirt and a pair of vivid cotton shorts. Her breath was on his face, he could smell her body, and something too big to be hid was happening in the crotch area. He prayed she wouldn't notice, but of course she did; he saw the flick of her glance. Absolute truth, he was too dizzy to care.

"Quick thinking, Batgirl. You saved my life."

Anna wanted to tell him she didn't mind about the trouser-snake. She knew those frisky creatures could take on a life of their own, at the worst moments. She wanted to tell him she knew it wasn't personal. But Spence, though a tide of conscious color swept from his chin to his hair, didn't seem to need reassurance. He lay ruefully smiling while footsteps pounded up the stairs, and the whole squat's population came rushing. . .You'd think they'd be more cool about strange thumps and unexpected power shorts.

"What's going on?" yelled Rob's voice.

"Nothing serious. Spence ate some electricity."

"Do him good. . . Is he dead?"

They all peered down. Spence felt like a stepped-on insect.

"Oh man," complained Frank. "I'm fucking glad I didn't pay you for that wiring job."

"How much did he eat? Should we take him to a hospital?"

"I'm fine," mumbled Spence, sitting up and holding his head. "I'm fine."

Ramone dropped on her haunches beside him. She was cuddling the black and white rat, her eyes were shining, she was completely uninterested in Spence's sufferings. "Isn't he great? He's called Keefer. The iguana's called Betty. They let her out to eat cockroaches at night. And there's a red-kneed tarantula. Hey, Flynn says there's another spare room. I think I'm going to move in!"

Spence groaned aloud.

"If anyone's got any money I could go out and fetch some beers?" offered Alice Flynn, sensing a party atmosphere.

Nobody took her up. They repaired in a body to the pub and drank pints of Fullers' London Pride while the shadows lengthened. Anna stuck with Spence—no doubt because like a good Girl Scout she was waiting to see if he would fall down bleeding at the ears. The dose of current that he'd eaten had left the inside of his mouth bruised and peculiar-feeling, and the erection incident lurked, adding to his mortification. But she was sitting there, talking to him across the grubby wooden table—

The way Anna wore makeup reminded him of Japanese girls: specifically one Japanese girl at his High School, whose delicately penciled eyes and burnished lids had held his attention. Anna's work was less obsessive but had the same quality: a graceful, unswerving acquiescence to the social norms. If a naked female face (such as Ramone's) was a challenge, and full war-paint a provocative display, Anna's message was that she wasn't trying to pick a fight. He had noticed that she never wore lipstick. He wanted to ask her why not. So her parents smoked dope. By some asinine standards they were evil radicals, but they'd trained her to tell the difference between *unconventional* and dangerous. She'd been raised to mind her manners, pick up after herself, think for others, share the chores—and take no shit about other classes of restriction. He knew the feeling. He had a deep sense that they'd arrived here, in this south coast Brit university, on matching trajectories. Was that good or bad for him? It is opposites that attract. What lived behind that demure reserve? Maybe she was a lesbian.

"Are you a feminist?"

"No, not at all. Why do you ask?"

"Well, the way you dress, always real quietly, uh, just wondered—" He was behaving like Martin Judge. He would not have known that Judge was unendurable, until Ramone started snarling, but he trusted the rabid one's reactions: and now hated himself. She would think he was a lout.

"I don't think it's fair," explained Anna, "to dress and makeup as if you're cruising for sex, unless you are. You can't go around signaling *don't you wish you could have some?* and then get angry if that's what people respond to. It doesn't make sense."

"You think women shouldn't try to look sexy?"

Anna frowned. "I don't know about *shouldn't*. I don't think you can do 'should, shouldn't' for other people. It's something I've decided for myself."

"But that still means *you* think it's wrong—" He was tying himself in knots. The pub was filling up with folks enjoying a pre-club aperitif. A glorious form at that moment brushed by Spence's shoulder: high heels, huge eyes, liquid red lips, black Basque and lacy thong under a sheer violet shift. "To dress up like her. Or him," he corrected himself, because the form was tall and you never could tell.

"Can't tell 'em apart, these days," she agreed, giggling. "That's different," she added. "Girl or boy, if you *are* cruising why not say so? Nothing wrong with that."

"Perfectly logical, Captain."

He recalled Craft's "Spock" jeer and could have bitten his bruised tongue out.

Anna sighed and gazed into her pint.

"Actually, I was thinking of Ramone." God bless her, Ramone again. Who'd have thought she would become his virtual chaperone? He felt guilty, but ruthlessly set her to work. "She says she's a feminist but doesn't seem to *get* anything out of it, except angry all the time. You know she claims she's in love with Daz? D'you think she's really a lesbian?"

Anna hesitated, smiled faintly, and shook her head.

Spence turned to follow the direction of her gaze. Rob and Daz were playing table-footie, against Flynn and Simon, while their supporters yelled encouragement and inconsiderately blocked everybody's access to the toilets. There was Ramone, dancing up and down and shrieking, her attention furtively fixed on the campus hunk. The poor kid. It was kind of cunning to pretend she had a crush on his girlfriend, but transparent...Rob had done it with Ramone once, for the experience. Spence had been there when he reported on the ride. She was highly sexed, made strange noises, and kept herself none too clean. *Okay if you were desperate*, was the alpha-male verdict: and he'd probably never even wondered why the ferocious soi-disant lesbian had come willingly to his bed.

Spence and Anna nodded at each other. No need to say it. Poor Ramone. Campus life was full of pitiful secrets, absurd sorrows.

"I guess we're lucky to be fancy free," said Spence.

She agreed. "D'you want another?" She stood up, touching the rim of her empty glass to his. "Drink up." He drank. She took the glass, with a speculative look that sent shivers down his spine. And walked away: straight back, small waist, round bottom. He imagined those firm cheeks pressed against his crotch. His balls ached; sweat broke out all over. What did she mean by that look? Was it time to make a move? What move did he want to make?

—◆— ◆—

Ramone had taken *The Sleepwalkers* back to her lair, to join the awesome stack of volumes she devoured there nightly and pathologically failed to return to the library. She'd dismissed Koestler with contempt. She preferred *The Structure of Scientific Revolutions:* if you like that sort of thing. Dead science is dead, she had told Anna. Whereas dead art never dies. Reading about dead science is like fucking a corpse, but less interesting. Anyway, how can you read Koestler? Do you know what kind of amateur rapist the bastard was in real life? In revenge, Anna had sought out George MacDonald, and been appalled and bored in about equal parts by *Phantastes and Lilith.* But it was so conventional, under the weirdness: all these pure hearts, true knights, womanly sacrifices, wicked female enchantments. Oh Ramone, she thought. Is that what's hiding under your carapace? A heart full of Victorian goo? But she didn't ask this aloud. It would have been too mean. So they tracked each other, without exactly becoming friends. Ramone would confide passionately in Daz, in Rosey, in Lucy Freeman, even in Spence. She'll tell you absolutely *anything*, marveled her favorites. Anything but the truth, thought Anna. She admired the core of reticence and the wild whirling of the outer shell, but she didn't feel drawn. Yet from their first meeting they had shared something (besides the secret crush on Rob) unknown to their friends: a purpose that Anna had hardly recognized in herself, before that night under the beech tree.

Deep in the English stacks, Anna had found a row of desks that was miraculously quiet. But what is it that I think I've got? she wondered, gazing at the back of the reading stall, half-conscious of the immemorial graffiti: sex, smells like fish and tastes like marmite; literature is internalized oppression; Elvis is king. I'm not Ramone, I don't want to be famous. So why do I work so hard? Why do I dream of doing something important, even if it's something only another nerd would understand? It was inexplicable.

That's why I like her, she thought. Even if she doesn't like me. They call me Mr Spock and think I'm unemotional: but I like marvels. I have a taste for extraordinary things. That's why I'm here, at The Forest University of Bournemouth, instead of in Manchester: why I'm doing Biology Foundation instead of specializing. I wanted to do something different, to see another world. And to *know*. I want to know my subject, not just get a job. She returned to her reading, thrilled by a romance and a magic that was invisible to Ramone. *Studies on the chemical nature of the substance inducing transformation of pneumo-coccal types.* Avery, OT et al. 1944...

But what about Rob?

She hated herself for following Rob and Daz around. Tagging along, clinging, any excuse to be a gooseberry. It was shameful, miserable, how those stupid thoughts kept creeping back: *he will turn to me, he will come to me, he will be mine at last.*

He WON'T.

Got to jolt myself onto a different track; that's the only answer.

➤ ➤

One day, Spence took a roll of thinsulate, a fat spliff of Frank's best sensi, and his trusty volume of Kierkegaard, and headed for the hills. He was planning to do some sunbathing, a little reading, and possibly catch up on his sleep. He was still glad he'd moved out. Except for a trip to Amsterdam in March (cold as an Illinois winter, lots of dope), he'd spent his whole year on campus. It would have been a crime to go home without experiencing something different from the Woods. However, he had to admit that the Regis Passage squat was not the spot for quiet slumbers or for calm revision.

Alone, he wended his way into dry declivities. The university, second-wave redbrick, had spread from two Georgian houses and the first modern buildings to fill the whole valley: less romantic than it had sounded, but pleasing enough, plenty of frisbee space and tree-clad lawns. Spence had discovered that if you went further, the hordes vanished and interesting things started to happen. It was open country; grass-clad downs fading into the heath and pines of the ancient Royal Forest. Silence fell, remarkably quickly. When the weather was good and the sky was clear above, the air had a warm, humming mystery that was almost sinister. He settled himself on a more or less level patch below a ridge path, pulled off his tee, and lay for a while, gazing straight into the blue. He was a pilgrim and a stranger, and all the supposed friendships of this year out of time fell away.

Maybe read for a while.

About an hour later—Spence wasn't wearing a watch—he looked up and saw someone coming towards him. The figure was still far off. He was in such a solitary mood that he almost rolled up his mat and took himself out of sight, then saw that it was Anna. She was wearing a lavender-colored dress that grazed her knees and left her brown arms bare. He waved. She waved back. Soon she was climbing up to his sun terrace, and then she sat down beside him among the summer flowers.

"Hi. I thought it was you."

"Just catching a few rays."

She smiled, her eyes wary. He sensed the shyness he'd divined in her, that other people mistook for self-possession. "I won't stay."

"Oh no, please do. I'd like your company."

"Aren't you afraid you'll burn? It's pretty hot."

Spence's skin was naturally matt, sallow, and pallid as a fish's belly until the moment the sun came out. "I never burn."

"Nor do I, though people always think I will. I expect we'll get skin cancer."

"Yeah. Melanoma, I bet. Dead in days." He shrugged. "Too bad."

"I don't know why people make such a fuss about death-dealing disease," said Anna. "One in four people will die of cancer: how awful. As if the other three were going to be fine, as if death was an avoidable disease."

"No one here gets out alive." He looked at her quizzically. "You been sleeping badly too?"

"It's just end-of-termitis."

"You're worried about the sit-down exams?"

"Not at all. I like them."

"Yeah, so do I. People will let you alone."

"Peaceful."

Anna slipped off her sandals and stretched her toes in the grass. Months ago (Ash Wednesday?) she had spotted the American Exchange at Mass in the campus chapel. He'd scooted, fast, probably feeling extremely caught-out. She'd never seen him there again. Anna didn't go to Mass often. She did not want to join the university's Christian Community, which would expect her to share some very dodgy opinions and would not understand that she didn't *believe* anything. She just wanted to be there, sometimes: murmuring her responses. The rest was silence. Oh, and a moral code. But the moral code was obvious; it didn't belong to any religion.

He could have been her brother. Shall I do it, she wondered. Do I dare?

"Spence, can I ask you a personal question?"

"You can ask." He narrowed his eyes, preparing his defenses. "I might answer."

"Are you a virgin?"

If anyone had tried to tell Spence that one day he would be proud to make this confession to his beloved, he would have dismissed the idea as fascist crap. He did not feel proud now, but something told him that a lot depended on his reply. What the hell was going on?

"Yes, I am."

"Any particular reason?"

"Just lucky, I guess. Would you mind telling me why you ask?"

"It's—" She swallowed, visibly. "I've got a proposition to make to you. You see, I'm a virgin too. And I don't want to be. And I thought, well, I'm heterosexual, and I like sex."

"How d'you know?"

"You mean, that I'm heterosexual? Well, I suppose because of what turns me on."

"That you like sex."

She looked puzzled. "I've done some petting and I masturbate. Don't you? The whole way can't be that different."

He pulled a grass blade, inspected it carefully. His heart had begun to shake. "Let's get back to the proposition."

"The thing is, I'd like to have sex, full unprotected sex, without having to worry about it. And, to be honest, I'd like not to be on my own among all these couples that are sprouting up. I'm on the pill. My mother thought it made sense, when I came to university, and I agreed with her. But there's AIDS to think of, and other diseases, and antibiotics maybe not working... It seems to me, the ideal way to have totally relaxed sex, without condoms, is if you and one other person are faithful to each other. We seem to get on all right, and you're going back to the US soon. It wouldn't be long term."

Don't interrupt, he thought. Not for your life. But apparently she'd finished. She was looking at him expectantly, hopefully, fearfully—

"Am I dreaming?"

"No." Anna's face fell, like a hurt child's. "You're talking to a Vulcan."

Spence reached out and brushed back her hair. He traced the rim of her left ear with his fingertip. "I don't think so. This looks human." His hand returned to his lap. He chewed his grass blade. "How would each of us know that the other was sticking to the deal?"

"Well, you would trust me. And I would trust you. Like I said, it wouldn't be for long."

She waited. Spence felt himself poised over an abyss, swept out of time and space to face a mighty challenge that he dared not refuse. In that moment *he knew* that if he accepted Anna's contract, the light of romance went out in his life forever. There would be no candlelight over an intimate table for two, no bunches of red roses, no preening in front of the bathroom mirror, no heart-in-the-mouth phone calls, no spending too much money on dates designed to impress. No tender gifts, no sweet avowals, no measuring her finger for the best ring he could afford. . . He had not known that he valued those hoary trivialities until this brink, when he felt that his birthright was being ripped from him. If he said yes he would get sex practically for free with this girl with whom he was deeply in lust, if no more. It didn't sound an awfully tough decision. He knew different, he knew very very different. But what could he do?

Leap, then, into the arms of God.

"Okay. I accept. It is a done deal."

Her reserved, anxious look broke into a lovely smile.

The bride and groom sat looking at each other. There was no one around to tell Spence that he was allowed to lift the veil. Instead, he produced his spliff. "You want to smoke this?"

"D'you have a light?"

The non-tobacco smokers were parasites on the cancer-stick community. It turned out that he did not have a light, not a single draggled scrap of matchbook. Nor did Anna. Spence realized he'd made a dangerous error. The spliff had acquired significance. If it could not be smoked, the chances were high that Anna would make her excuses and leave. Spence would be too proud and scared to try and stop her. Next time they met each would wait for the other to mention this conversation. Neither of them would speak; Anna's brave offer would be buried. Spence felt strangely resigned. It was fate. He could see the same rueful acceptance growing in Anna's face. He looked around, praying for deliverance, and saw that another wandering scholar had appeared, striding along the path on top of the ridge, heading towards campus. It was Oliver Tim, a floppy white cricket hat pulled down over his eyes and a bundle of books and papers under his arm.

"Hey, Wol! Oliver!" Spence brandished the joint. "You got a light?"

◄ ►

Early that summer evening, Spence and Anna came into the bar in the Student's Union, blinking in the cool gloom, and tracked down Wol where he was sitting with Rosey McCarthy. Anna produced a posy of wild flowers, bound in a knotted grass-stem, and laid it on their table. "Thanks for everything. You're a pal." The two left immediately, giggling over some private joke. Oliver put the posy away and refused to explain its meaning (he wasn't sure what it meant). He had a soft spot for Anna Senoz, a grave and gentle old-fashioned girl. He hoped the American Exchange was not leading her astray.

➤ *iii* ➤

Anna was a very fit young lady. She played tennis, she practiced yoga. She could lie on her back on the floor, cross her legs, and rise to her feet in one neat movement, without using her hands. *They all* had admired the slightly nerdy prowess, the girls without rancor and the guys without salacious interest. It was for Spence to discover the implications of muscle tone; for Spence (who had been raised a devout puritan, though he didn't know it) to learn what it meant to be the true belief of a healthy, athletic young woman whose box-fresh sexual mores were trained only by desire. His life long, if he recalled certain incidents of that time, those weeks when Anna invariably wore a skirt, because underwear could be easily dealt with but, as she said, "a girl wearing trousers can't fuck," his tongue grew thick in his mouth, his throat closed, blood rushed to his crotch. That first experience, under the hot sky, was extraordinary enough. Spence was not circumcised. The practice had been *de rigueur* in Manankee County, but his mother had rebelled and saved him. He'd always had a little trouble with his foreskin. It seemed to catch somehow; it didn't want to slide all the way back. When they first—she kneeling astride his lap, her blue crepe skirts sweeping his thighs—commenced to consummate their vows, it really hurt. Something gave way, the pain was gone, but either the pain or the awe of the situation saved him from the humiliation of instant spurto. Far from it: he felt as if they could go on forever, locked in rhythm. Afterwards he was able to point out that he had actually shed blood, the same as she'd done, if not more. When she finally left him, which was late that night, and he could stop being so damned *sensible*, he had knelt on the floor of his room in Regis Passage, touching his fingertips and his lips to the small dark mingled stain on that roll of thinsulate, as if it were a sacred relic.

Spence had arrived in the UK a virgin because at home the girls he liked had seen him as a friend. The well-trained child of a feminist single mother, he'd easily sensed that they didn't want him to get sexual. Whereas if he detected that a girl was trying to pressure him into making a move, he felt uncooperative. There was also his mother. She meant well, but no one would ever call Spence's Mom tactful. She'd have been all over his fledgling love life. His plight was not unusual. He'd have been willing to bet a significant proportion of his male contemporaries were in the same boat, whatever lies they told. A year in Europe had seemed like his big chance, yet nothing had changed. Sex was freely available: but he was still the friend-not-boyfriend type and still repelled by any girl who tried to elicit sexual behavior from him. He had begun to suspect that there was something out of kilter about his maleness. He did not think he might be gay. He did not feel attracted to guys; he felt attracted to Anna. But he didn't seem to have the right impulses in his repertoire: or not enough of them.

Spence's mother had told him that his ancestors were pure Scots and Irish (apart from the obligatory Romantic Native American somewhere back there). As he grew up and looked in the mirror, and observed that cute little gap between his front teeth, the way his hair grew, the set of his eyes and cheekbones, he used to say to himself *no, really?* He was not concerned if she had him descended from Finn MacCool, when Chaka Zulu might have been as appropriate: he just wondered. The unease about his sexuality was like that, but with the potential to be much more serious. An intuition, stronger than evidence, that something had been left out of the account.

Whatever happened, he was eternally grateful to Anna for setting his mind at rest.

On the last night of term there was a big party in the Martin Luther King Hall. Anna had packed her stuff. Tomorrow she was going to start work in a restaurant and move to Bournemouth seafront, where she and Daz were sharing a room. He pulled her close and demanded, in her ear, "Want to get away from this and snog?"

"Yes."

They wandered. The Union building, ungainly, dating from the sixties, had a carnival atmosphere, bodies in scanty bright clothes draped around concrete pillars, wild-eyed gangs screeching with laughter from recesses of naked brickwork. "Did you know the guy who designed this was Basil Spence, same as did Sussex University?"

"Yeah. I saw that in the prospectus. Two listed Georgian houses, one listed Basil Spence blockhouse. . . I nearly changed my name back to Patrick for the duration."

"Why?"

"I didn't like the idea of sharing a name. I don't like to be—"

"Like anyone else."

"Ah, ha ha ha."

"I'm glad you didn't."

"Why not?"

"I don't know. You wouldn't have been called Spence."

"You'd never have known any different. Spencer was my mother's family name. She called me Patrick after a guy in a poem, which she used to recite to me when I was young in a horrendous supposedly Scottish accent. She's a great Britophile, my Mom. Something about. . .: *I saw the new moon yestreen, with the old moon in her arm.* There's a storm at sea, and it ends with a shipwreck. *And there lies guid Sir Patrick Spens, with the scots lairds at his feet.* I didn't like Patrick, don't know why not, so I called myself Spencer, which became Spence—"

The beat came thrumming up through their feet. Anna leaned out over a rail, where people were dancing and drinking below. Spence embraced her from behind, burying his face and mouth in her warm nape, pulling her close. He was lost in kissing, pressing his aching genitals against her bottom, running his palms over her breasts, wonderfully tormented, expecting any moment she'd say stop, this is a public place, when he realized that her hands were busy too, down inside the waistband of her skirt. "Anna," he whispered, scandalized, "are you by any chance playing with yourself?"

"Yes I am. Anything wrong with that?"

Holy Baloney. There were people *watching*, or at any moment might be. She didn't care. She was reaching behind her, groping for his dick. Working as if he was defusing a bomb with seconds to spare he managed to unzip his pants one handed, positioned himself under her, eased her knickers aside from the cleft, and he was there: inside, he could hardly believe this, but he was going like a piston, Anna's breath catching, and her whole body buckling. They fell to the floor, crawled behind a chunky sofa and went on fucking, while footsteps passed and voices chattered. . . Another of these nights, in one of the clubs they frequented in Bournemouth, they were dry-humping to the beat in the middle of the dance floor; it was common practice. She got her legs up around his waist, pushed the front of his jogging pants down under his balls, freed his rock hard penis and mounted it. Spence, no longer aghast, still fabulously excited by her boldness, was clutching her gloriously smooth butt, when he found that a strange hand had joined his own under her skirt. Two garish, sweat-dripping faces appeared on either side of Anna's head. "Hey, d'you fancy a foursome?" yelled the girl. Spence was covered in confusion; Anna lifted her face and answered coolly, "sorry mates, this is a private party," and at her words Spence instead of wilting came, explosively; it was incredible that they stayed upright. The experience cracked them both up. They had to go off and crouch in a corner, feeling more vulnerable when dissolved by laughter than in coitus.

He would wake in Regis Passage to the screaming of the herring gulls, the guttural roocoo, roocoo of the back garden wood pigeons, and the braying of the collared doves, the pigeons' slender cousins, whose tender beige plumage belied their aggressive street-style. Did some drugs, did some of his ridiculously tedious but easy programming work, and went to find Anna, who would be roasting herself on the crowded beach. She and Daz were working in a smart little restaurant, alternately cooking and waitressing, lunch and evenings. The pay was abysmal, but the tips were good and the food was free. He would eat whatever they'd brought him and drink the wine they'd usually managed to sneak out. Eventually the girls would go back to work and he would hang with Frank, Alice Flynn, Ramone, and the various somewhat scary characters who occupied the rest of the squat. He would be waiting for Anna when she finished at the restaurant. She would have already changed her clothes; her hair would smell of cooking oil. They would go out dancing in this club or that club, anywhere that didn't cost too much, they weren't proud. Dancing, they were all over each other's bodies. Spence thought of a shocking craze known as the waltz: which must have been like this, before it hit the drawing rooms. Skirts up and pants down, bodies whirling, locked in couple, rocking to that beat. If anyone knew of a party, they went on there when the clubs finally faded, and then back to Regis Passage and fucked some more at dawn (public and near-public fornication was the tip of the iceberg, they never stopped, it seemed to him, either fucking or thinking about fucking) before she left to get ready for work. . . Weekends were different, if Rob, who had a job in London, came down. Spence did not care for the trite double date that materialized. He discovered that he didn't like Rob Fowler. Sometimes Daz went up to London instead, and that was good, though it made no difference to Anna's hours. They hardly slept, they forgot to eat, they expended staggering amounts of energy, day and night. How 'a God's name did they survive this regime? They were young.

In Frank's kitchen, late at night, they sat and talked with Frank about the nature of reality. Spence was of the opinion that shit happens. Everyone's having a different summer. There's no meaning except what we construct, not ever, nohow.

Anna said, "meaning can come at you from the future."

"D'you mind explaining that?"

"Well, say, we seem to be running out of water on this planet. If that's true, and it's not the only limit we seem to be hitting, then the old story is confirmed. We're the crown of creation all right, we're the end of the line. That's a meaning."

"But before then we escape, in our starships, flying mother nature's silver seed—"

"Not on present figures," said Anna darkly. "Anyway, leaving aside the heat death of the universe, what do you mean by *there's no meaning except what we construct?* Since you can't talk, or think, at all without constructing a meaning, what's the content in that statement?"

Frank was entertained by their babbling: "Tell us what reductionism means, again," he suggested. She got on with Frank. He didn't interrupt.

"Well, reductionism is when you explain things in terms of simple components. Could I have your Rubik's cube?" Frank handed the toy down from its shelf. Anna swiveled the puzzle into chaos and then deftly returned it order. "See. The blocks of color are the units and I've reduced them to order. Now we say the puzzle's solved, and we're happy, but it's just an interpretation. You could arrange the tiles, or any units of any system, into their maximum state of complexity. That would be order too."

Frank was cooking a free-range omelet, for himself not for them. He never did anything for anybody else. That was the secret of a happy life, he said. Please yourself. He dribbled green virgin olive oil into one of his burnished skillets and watched Anna over his shoulder.

"Stand on yer head again. I like it when you stand on yer head."

Anna crouched, dropped her rosy brown brow onto her cupped hands and rose, feet to the ceiling, neatly perpendicular: luckily her knickers were clean. The parrot squawked "AMAZING!"

"She's full of surprises, your girlfriend," said Frank approvingly.

"She's full of drink and drugs. I'm going to have to take her to bed."

Having Ramone in the squat had turned out better than Spence had expected, because she'd taken up with Frank. Mr Frank N Furter, though you wouldn't think so to look at him, was quite the ladies' man. He'd run through several girlfriends in the short time that Spence had known him, each of them startlingly pretty, hip, and well turned out. His liaison with Ramone was inexplicable, unless he saw her as another exotic animal for the collection. Ramone herself—Spence suspected—drew a blank on sexual choice. She was someone who would nurse deliberately hopeless passions, remaining indifferent to the way her actual body was passed around. Anyway, his host and the wild girl were an item, in an offhand, impersonal way: and Spence was grateful. Between her duties as Frank's paramour, the novel she was writing, and the hours she spent closeted with Alice Flynn playing soulful ballads, she didn't have much time to harass Spence. Though she had her moments. Once they were walking uptown in the middle of the afternoon, eating tomatoes they'd fetched from the allotment, when she stepped back against a shop window, dropped to her haunches, and fumbled blatantly under her skirts. A pungent stream of liquid came trickling across the hot, filthy sidewalk slabs. The passers-by paid no attention, but Spence was outraged.

"What's the matter?" demanded Ramone, catching up and grinning at his distress. "I was only taking a piss. Is it my fault there are no public toilets? Men do that all the time."

"I have never pissed in the street in my life," snapped Spence. "I don't know what right you have to inflict that exhibitionist stuff on me."

She used to do it on campus, she'd said she was marking her territory, but at least she'd wait 'til after dark. She looked up at him malignly, more than ever like a cross between Gollum and Mr Toad when dressed as a washer-woman. She had taken to wearing contact lenses. Ramone's eyes were an unusual shade of blue: opaque, greenish, like dark turquoise. Sounded good, but on her it made you think of river mud. "Yeah, but you do other things, you dirty dog. I tell you what, Spence, I'll trade you. Your male duties for my womanly privileges. Anytime."

She was so openly hostile towards his relationship with Anna that he wondered if the fake Sapphic story was a double blind. The constant soft ache of arousal in his groin made him speculate, was Anna that way inclined? Was he expected to do it with both of them? But the terms of the pact were clear, he was safe. Aside from her dirty habits, and ensuring he'd spend the next several years of his life plagued by phantom lines from Dusty Springfield lyrics, Ramone could do him no harm. She was even looking better, he noted. There was still a tang of body odor and unhygienic underwear in her vicinity, but the mass of hair was more artistically disheveled and the hippie clothing almost stylish, in an abandoned way. Frank was probably treating her better than any sexual partner she'd ever had. He was good to his pets. Spence, the American Tourist in the menagerie, ought to know.

At first he'd wondered how Anna had known that their bargain would turn out so well. Spence had had his reasons. What had made her so sure? He realized that she'd known nothing. She had identified the most likely of her male friends (her best male friend, he flattered himself) and taken a calculated risk, armed with no more than her noble nature and her faith in physiology. He feared for his beloved: *steel true, blade straight.* He sensed within her rigor such a fragile and vulnerable spirit. He wanted to protect her from the cruel world.

It was an extraordinary time. It had to end.

⬤ ⬤

Anna liked dressing for him after work, in the staff toilet cubicle at the restaurant: the orange skirt with splashes of scarlet and a clinging white tee-shirt; the fringed green and gold sarong worn short to her thighs; her favorite, the lavender sundress. White cotton knickers, a bra that *fitted* without any repulsive underwire. Everything reminded her of his hands: the smell of his ejaculate always lingering on her body, despite the kitchen odors. Thoughts of things they had done together bathed her in delicious heat. She checked herself in the drizzled mirror, is this still Anna? She disliked the idea of *they all* saying to each other behind her back, look what sex has done for our prim scientist! But you can't prevent that sort of thing. They say, let them say. She and Daz met Spence and they went to a bar, where they would meet maybe Wol and Rosey, who were living in a huge Victorian flat borrowed from a rock star, Simon Gough, Ramone, Flynn, some of the weirdos from Regis Passage. Then she *was Anna*, the quiet one, taking no active part in the conversation, unless she forgot herself and started explaining something until her victim glazed over; while he *was Spence*, with his charming American accent, deadpan witticisms, the smile with which he savored English turns of phrase, laughter that creased the corners of his grey eyes, and a sneaky detachment from that eternal male hierarchy. You couldn't rank Spence; he wasn't one of the chiefs, but he wasn't one of the Indians either. She liked that.

Eventually these sophisticates would deign to proceed to a club, into a wash of sound, bodies, darkness, laser light. It was so good to dance. Faces beamed at them, brimming with chemically induced sweetness. It would be harsh to call the mood false, when the added chemicals couldn't do anything if the brain's own resources didn't leap to greet them, like lovers meeting. God bless the drug. God bless the pressures and forces of all the billions of years that built us to be so capable of joy. She and Spence, however, preferred their own inner glow, afraid chemicals might flatten the libido. They would vanish into the anonymous crowd, groping each other insatiably.

Ramone was very angry about Anna's fall from single grace. She maintained that sex with a man was feeble and contemptible. Lesbian love-making was incomparably more valuable and more profound. When Anna pointed out that Ramone was at present fucking a male and shamelessly patriarchal drug-dealer geezer at least twice her age, Ramone said: that's different. I'm not doing Frank for fun. I'm collecting life experience. When Anna said why couldn't Ramone find herself an educational dyke-geezer girlfriend, Ramone curled her chimpanzee lip.

"You don't know how tough it is, being a feminist and a lesbian. Practically all the women on the scene put the same moves on you as if they were men. I'm not going to swallow their shit. Lesbianism could be brilliant. Unfortunately it's a pathetic joke, a poor imitation of the male supremacist world like everything else women do."

Privately Anna wondered, could making love to a woman be so different? When she held Spence, wild with pleasure, gasping and trembling in her arms, as he begged her to suck more fiercely on his nipples, as she rubbed at his perineum, slid her fingers into his slippery rectum and kneaded the soft concavity where his testes, when he was in this mood, so easily slipped back behind the pubic bone, what was different then? She had heard that women are better partners because men are not multiorgasmic. Spence often seemed to reach peak after peak, in a cascade as extended as her own, before the final climax. . . Must be because he was so young. Of course there was his prick, which she would not want to be without. When they were in his room at Regis Passage she loved to lie naked, spine arched, heels under her and knees spread, and masturbate while Spence did the same. She kept her eyes closed so she would not know when, overcome by the sight of her cunt, he would fall, clutching her shoulders, and plunge his prick inside. She loved the moment when her whole body went into spasm, locking and seizing, madly pumping. It was like a merging of human and machine, without the paranoia of that idea; it was the pleasure of tennis and yoga glorified, pure movement in power, the delight of becoming completely physical. To be a machine is lovely. And everything else—the way the dance floors grew empty and uncertain in the early hours, the hot grubby sands, the smell of suntan oil, the wine they drank, the street sounds, the glittering sea that rocked at the end of every street and caught her body in its cool invigorating embrace in the late afternoons—all these were the adjuncts of this summer, which she would have possessed anyway, if she had settled for the pain and deceit of the kind of boyfriend-girlfriend affairs a nice girl was supposed to have, without ever knowing what was missing from the center: this rapture of a young animal, pure appetite without shame, without anxiety. She thanked the light of reason in her prayers. *They said it couldn't be done.* But Anna had made up her mind to tackle sex in a fair and straightforward way, and things had turned out just fine.

She understood how Spence felt about Rob and Daz. Daz Avritivendam was fabulously beautiful and intelligent and lovely in many ways, but nothing unconventional could survive in her vicinity. Daz and Rob were *a couple,* a transformation as obvious as a physical metamorphosis, and it grated. Anna had kept her distance from this coupledom, not because of Spence, but for her own reasons. She tried not to know it when the lovebirds started to fall out. But one day, after a London weekend that had obviously been a disaster, Daz asked Anna to come back to the house after the lunch session at work, instead of joining the others. As soon as she'd shut the door of their room behind them, she collapsed in tears.

"Daz! What's the matter?"

"It's Rob."

"You've had a fight?"

"I have to get away from him. Anna, you have to help me, please."

She wept on Anna's shoulder. She had to get away from Rob because she couldn't marry him. She'd seen this happen to Muslim girls from home, stumbling blindly into relationships that couldn't survive. Daz was a Hindu, and her family so detached from all that religious-ethnic power stuff she'd thought she was safe. She'd been wrong.

"I can't marry him, it would be impossible. I must get away, right away, right now."

Anna did her best to comfort the World's Most Gorgeous Malaysian. She asked no questions; she didn't need to. She suspected she'd soon know more than she wanted to be told, anyway. She agreed that they would put their savings together, and instead of staying in Bournemouth making money all summer, she would go away with Daz.

Needs must.

Daz calmed down and revealed, ingenuously, plans already devised. They would go to Greece, there were some very cheap flights. They would bum around the islands. There remained something so tragic in her hollow cheeks and compressed lips that Anna knew she had no choice. It was probably better this way. Quit while you're ahead.

"But what about you and Spence?" asked Daz, when she knew she was safe.

"It's okay," said Anna. "It was a temporary thing."

They left on the last day in July, driven to Gatwick by Daz's mother. Anna and Spence had said goodbye the night before, in the pub on the corner of the Passage. It served them right, that they had to part in public, after the stuff they'd got up to.

In the kitchen at Regis Passage late that night, under a pokerwork wall plaque that read DON'T GET MAD GET SORTED, Frank N Furter shook his head over the folly of the young. "Should'er told her how you feel, Spence. Should'er taken a chance. The key is always frank. Remember that. As you go through life, you will find I'm right."

"Yeah, well. It's too late now."

He would go back to school, bury himself in his studies, use his new expertise to find another girl who would never lead him such a dance. He would try to forget.

"Fancy a line?"

"Thanks. Don't mind if I do."

Anna Anaconda

— *i* —

When Anna was a little girl, she and her sister possessed a picture book about a snake called Anna Anaconda, who swallowed things: notably other animals. It was a reign of terror. The anaconda lured and flattered every animal in the forest to its doom, except for the peacock, whose beauty was impervious to flattery and immune to greed. (The book was indifferent to conventional zoology: this was a female, Amazonian peacock.) Finally the peacock tricked the monster into trying to swallow her reflection in the river. She went on swallowing until she burst, and all her victims escaped. Anna had gained immense, sensual satisfaction from the picture of the snake trying to engulf the whole of the great Amazon: flanks swollen and transparent, so you could see the huge variety of things and creatures she'd already consumed. But she had equally admired the cool-headed bird. There's a growing grace and glory in remaining by myself, sang the peacock, to the annoyance of her neighbors. But solitary content turned out to be the right choice—a rare conclusion for a children's story. The book had frayed, disintegrated, and vanished. In Anna's memory the two characters had survived, the distinction between them fading. The snake who swallowed everything was not a monster. She desired, like the peacock, to be self-contained. She tried to gulp her own reflection not because she was tricked, or greedy, but because she longed for closure.

Anna remembered *Anna Anaconda* in her second year at university, as she drifted into social isolation. She shared a house with Daz and Rob Fowler (their relationship had recovered after the abortion and the summer break, though the old suburban certainty never returned); Simon Gough; a sociology student called Ray Driscoll, who had been another male member of first year's *they all*; and a girl called Marnie Choy, live wire and fun fanatic, who had answered an advertisement they put up. One night in October, when Daz was in London for the weekend, Rob Fowler came and tapped on Anna's bedroom door. She turned him down. Sexual attraction never dies, but it was no struggle.

She worked. She was the Biols student who attended every lecture, studied every textbook, and possessed complete, immaculate notes that she freely shared. She was the one who enjoyed the hated, obligatory statistics course. She went out dancing, she stayed up late commiserating with other people's troubles, she had a few nights of sex with Ray when he was between serious girlfriends. A transparent envelope stood around her. It was Anna's extended self, her containment: the great river. When Marnie and Daz, arm in arm, screeched drunken girl-power challenges in the Union Bar: *We want a man! Not one of you dickless lot, a real man, we want a man!*, she laughed and cheered, but she was a million miles away. There's a growing grace and glory in remaining by myself.

In early June, on a bright cool summer's day, she walked out of the campus valley to visit Spence's sun terrace. There had been more rain this year. The turf was richer, the flowers more advanced. Some of the plants were hardly recognizable in habit as the above-ground processes from the same rootstocks as last June. She spent a long while on her knees, looking, examining, making sketches in her notebook.

She thought of Spence. In that room in Regis Passage, with the ridiculous wiring and the terrible crack in one corner, which he monitored in felt-tip, he lay beside her on the mattress that smelled of flea-powder and cum. They were both dressed; they were not being sexual. He showed her a picture of his cat, a blue-eyed, black half-Siamese called Cesf, standing up on gangling back legs to bat a catnip mouse on a string. "It's an old password I don't use anymore." He missed Cesf, and worried about him. The cat was monogamous, didn't get on with Spence's Mom, and was reportedly pining. He missed his mother too, but didn't carry her picture. He said, with a droll self-mocking reserve, "I can remember what she looks like." Anna sensed something very different from the affection and mutual respect she shared with her own parents: Spence's mother was a power over his whole life, future and past, his goddess not his government.

She had realized, soon after the start of their idyll, that she could never, ever tell him about being "in love" with Rob Fowler. It would have been rude, like telling someone they'd been invited to dinner because your first choice of guest had canceled. Especially since it turned out he didn't like Rob. Given the typical first-year's emotional situation, Spence'd probably had an unrequited crush of his own, and *he* hadn't said anything; but she'd felt compromised. Maybe it was because of that unease—something she needed to say, but must not—that she'd made no effort to get back in touch. He hadn't contacted her either, which he easily could have done. Simon still heard from him.

They had each made the same choice. It was the right ending.

She set her sketches aside and opened a sheaf of printed lecture notes, minutely annotated. *Eukaryotic Genetics: Genetic Constraints of Selection.*

At school, Anna had been thrilled by the *certainty* of the DNA process. It was such a trick, so satisfying and neat, the two complementary strands of bases, unzipping, acting as templates for replication: safe as the ticking of a watch. At school they let you think perfect replication was the norm—with the occasional dramatic derailment, so that new species could be born. When you got closer, you realized what happened was totally different. The process was weak, not strong. The strings of bases were continually being repaired, continually evading repair, the patterns snagging and dropping stitches, so it was amazing you woke up every morning and found that a rabbit stayed a rabbit and a rose a rose. Coherent change emerged, mysteriously, like new music, out of the constant noise of miscopying: sections stuffed in backwards, upside down, in totally the wrong place... How could this flux of meaningless chemical glitches drive the engine of something so powerful as evolution?

This was still not fully explained, even by the experts.

She looked up. Feathery white cloud skimmed the blue dome of the sky. She was held suspended, in a silent cool concavity of earth and air. Dr Russell, Anna's favorite lecturer, was big on *context*. She derided the very concept of isolation. No allele is an island! To Anna this was like a moral reproach. She had not set out to be alone. But if you didn't want to play the sexual-panic games, there wasn't much left of undergraduate social life. It was like sitting there being tee-total while everybody got drunk: and so she was retreating, day by day, week by week.

Arranged marriage would have suited Anna: no impossible ideals, just a matter-of-fact agreement. It would be no problem if you met for the first time on your wedding day. As long as the person was a decent human being and the sex worked, you'd be happy. And why wouldn't it work, if the two people were young, fancy free, and entered the pact with goodwill? It worked for me, she thought, remembering how very excellent it had been, cleaving only to Spence. Whose body did not fascinate her, who had no allure that could drag her from room to room: with whom she had shared a common, human sweetness that any two people might have. But that had been a controlled experiment. *In vivo*, as far as she knew anything about it, arranged marriage had a success rate no better than love affairs. Worse, in the big numbers: especially for women.

It would have gone sour. This way, their few weeks were safe forever.

...yet still I think of him with kindness,
and shall do 'til our last goodnight.

She couldn't remember the name of the poem or the poet, but the couplet spoke to her feelings: enduring tenderness. If I never get another turn at it in my whole life, she thought, I bet I've had more than my share of really good sex, compared with lots of people. Thank you Spence. I won't forget. She made a note to herself, as she headed back, that she must not let this trip develop into a yearly pilgrimage. She knew she had a tendency to get obsessive about things.

➤ *ii* ➤

Charles Craft was a tall young man with sleepy eyes, a puffy pink and white complexion, and a permanent stipple of black around his lips and jaw. His hair was a fine dark thatch that stood up in tufts on the crown of his head, like the hair of some newborn babies; he had large, soft hands and large, soft thighs that strained the fabric of his habitual, very clean and pale blue jeans. He had a girlfriend called Ilse, who was one of the Biology masses, but Anna didn't know her except by sight. She did not socialize with Charles, though they were *de facto* associates at the top of the class. She was not surprised when she discovered, in the Autumn term of final year, that they were to be project partners: but she was disheartened. Charles spoiled things. He was a pain in seminars, sniping at her with pointless little challenges.

Guy Doone, the redheaded post-doc who would be their supervisor, showed Anna and Charles around the big warm room that had the atmosphere of a catering kitchen, but less coherence. Benches and counters were divided into separate untidy territories, where domestic-looking machinery jigged and stirred, and trays of cells lay about, like leftover food in the back of the fridge. Mess, thought Anna. Noise. I must be getting closer to the reality. She was intensely excited at the prospect of committing real science.

"And this is our pride and joy," said Guy, standing before what appeared to be a top-loading washer-dryer. "The new PCR machine. Not the cutting edge, but it's the nearest we've got—and one of the few pieces of big equipment we own that you couldn't buy from a consumer durables discount store. Fridges, microwaves, mixers: as you'll soon find out, we're just glorified housewives in here. . .er no offence, Anna."

"We had that model at my Dad's lab, years ago," Charles examined the machine disdainfully. "I'll take the back off it if you like, see if I can give it a reboot. I can't boil an egg. But if you do the housewife thing, Guy, I can take care of the science."

Guy blushed, a red-head's violent crimson. "As you should know," he said stiffly, "the crucial factor in polymerase chain reaction, the development that turned genetic engineering from a handicraft into an industry, is precise temperature control. The machines are bloody

expensive because they can shift the temperature inside practically instantly. They're very delicate, as your Dad may have told you, Charles.
Please don't take the back off anything in here, ever."

Charles sighed and stared blatantly out of the window.

Anna would have liked to kick him. The chances that Guy the
post-doc *wanted* to be lumbered with two third-years were remote. If
Anna and Charles gave him grief, his interest in them was going to be
less than zero. Charles caught her eye. "I wasn't going to let him get
away with that," he whispered. "We're not here to wash dishes."

There was nothing she could say. The problem was too trivial.

As they left the lab at the end of the morning they met Seraphina
Russell. The big woman, white coat crisp in spite of the heat, beamed
on them with spaniel-brown eyes, startlingly warm and emotional in
her large, stern face. "Well, Anna," she said. "Welcome home, my
dear." She said this because Anna had pestered incessantly for *real*
work since the first term of first year. "Charles too," she added kindly.
"Enjoy yourselves, and don't expect too much."

Ilse was waiting downstairs by the porter's cubbyhole, hugging
an armful of books and folders to her pink-sweatered front. Girls like
Ilse made Anna uneasy. Had she not met Daz at the Freshers' Fair, had
she not met Rosy and Wol and Spence and Simon, had she never met
Ramone Holyrod, Anna might have herded with the Biols masses. She
might have looked like *that*: the crop-hair and pastel ensemble that
was like a uniform.

"Coming with us for lunch?" offered Charles, with a magnanimous air.

Ilse smiled.

"Er. . .no thanks." She wished she had an excuse to dress the refusal.

Charles looked like he thought as much. As he turned away he
muttered distinctly, "*teacher's pet!*" He was right, damn it. Dr Russell
made no secret of the special feeling she had for Anna. Oh, God. She
didn't want to be teacher's pet. Nor did she want to be involved in
Charles's status-contests with their supervisor. But she couldn't see
how to avoid either. Oh, how infuriating.

She had moved into a one-bedroom flat in a residence hall mainly occupied by postgrads. It was expensive, but it beat sharing the housework with five other people, four of them (especially Marnie) with indescribably filthy domestic habits. Living alone she could make debt-control her priority. It was like a return to her childhood; it made her happy, every frugal week, to keep within her limits. One day, when she'd cycled into town to do her shopping (excellent change from a food kitty that other people spent on impulse), she met Ramone Holyrod in the organic butcher's. Anna had bought a bag of soup bones, for a minor sum, and was discussing some bacon bits, but they were too expensive. She said goodbye, turned and saw Ramone. The rabid one wasn't living in any of the shared flats or houses known to *they all*. She had gone to earth, somewhere unknown. They left the shop together, Ramone having bought a free-range chicken.

"I couldn't have done that!" she announced, as they walked, Anna wheeling her bike.

"Done what?"

"You could at least have said bones for my dog."

This, from the girl who had introduced processed-pea sandwiches to the culinary scene. Anna noticed that the rabid one had grown milder, her teasing almost kindly. "I thought you told me your family was really poor?"

"We were *really* poor. It wasn't a leisure pursuit, like Channel 4 tells how to live gracefully on three lentils a week. It was humiliating, you don't know what it was like."

"I think I do." Anna's own childhood was vivid to her just now. "Your parents always had the price of another pack of fags, fed you junk food, and never dreamed of paying up when the school sent those letters home asking for 'voluntary contributions' for bus fares to the swimming pool. We were the ones who went without, to subsidize their self-centered pig-ignorant Mclifestyle."

"Middle-class wanker."

"Ramone, I'm going down to the market now, to pick up some free vegetables, or as near to free as I can find. If I was prepared to beg, which I'm not, it's a heavily managed professional activity, even in Bournemouth. I'd have to wait for a vacancy, grovel to the boss; and it would take up too much of my valuable time. With soup bones and bruised veg, I eat well and I control the debt mountain."

"You could go on the game."

"Bad as begging. Is that how you manage to afford free-range chicken?"

Ramone's appearance had changed dramatically. She wore black jeans that fit tightly over her skinny little legs, cowboy boots, and a vegetarian leather jacket. Her hair was gone. She sported a low-lying Mohican that divided her skull like a strip of crimson hearthrug and only a modest number of plain silver rings—one in each earlobe and another in her nose. She had a tika mark, crimson as her hair, on her forehead. Anna thought she looked like someone who had found herself.

"It's for a friend," said Ramone, with dignity. "I'm coming with you. You can show me how to be middle-class about poverty. I'm interested in cultural deviance."

Anna bought cheap vegetables. They caught up a little and then parted. It was a rapprochement. Their tracking had fallen into abeyance in second year, when Ramone had lived with Rosey and Wol like a half-wild stray cat that will come home to eat and sleep but desires no social amenities. Maybe they had been missing each other. A few days later Anna was indulging in a *thali* in the Union basement. The Hindu Society ran a vegetarian buffet every Wednesday lunchtime, sometimes with music or dance. The food was cheap and very good, a luxury that came out of Anna's bar and social allowance. She could afford this, because Anna Anaconda was seeing less and less of *they all*. Yet she was pleased when the rabid one walked in and came to join her.

"What happened to the bone soup and rotten veg? I knew you were pissing around."

"I'm within my budget."

"It's bullshit, anyway. Chocolate's incredibly cheap, and it keeps you going. I learned that a long, long time ago."

Which explains your teeth, thought Anna. She guessed Ramone had followed Anna in here solely for the purpose of delivering this brilliant retort, and felt disappointed. But Ramone went away and came back with her own food: silently chowed down on lentils and yogurt and chapattis, emptying each small bowl mechanically. She ate all the whole spices and looked askance at the small heap of leaves, hard berries, and bits of twig that grew on the side of Anna's tray.

"Are you doing anything now?"

"Not for an hour or so."

"Good. I'm taking you to meet someone. In fact," she raised her voice. "I want you to meet the person I'm living with."

Aha, thought Anna. Now I'm going to meet the Hindu boyfriend. Or girlfriend.

She was taken to Pinebourne House, the smaller of the two listed Georgian buildings in the middle of the valley. Anna was intrigued. Living in Pinebourne was classy. Debt-ridden undergraduates need not apply. There were signs of children: a pink tricycle overturned, a stripy ball. "That's one thing I can't stand about Piney," grumbled Ramone. "Fucking kids. I don't mind people being heterosexual, or married, but there ought to be a law against kids in places of learning. Like in the old days, when scholars had to be in Holy Orders and pretend to be celibate. One fat belly and you're out." She seemed nervous. At the door of a first-floor apartment she turned and glared, standing between Anna and her home as if defying an intruder. "Look, whatever you see and whatever happens, be cool, okay? You have to be calm, around her. Right?"

"Around who?"

"My tutor, Doctor Lavinia Kent. Last term, I finally realized I didn't have to stand that sexist shit Ogden. Everyone knows he's a bastard. If he fancies you, you have to fuck him; if he doesn't your results are screwed anyway, it is common knowledge. I went to the Dean and got myself out of all his teaching, and he's not my personal tutor anymore. Lavvy is. And she's. . .she needed someone, so I've moved in with her."

"Oh?" Trust Ramone. Rejects tutor on the grounds of sexual harassment, and sets up love nest with the replacement.

"Not what you think. I'm her home help. I'm a paramedic. She needs me." Ramone's eyes narrowed, wonderingly. "You don't know anything about her, do you?"

"Should I?"

"I suppose a science nerd wouldn't. She's famous, in the real world. She teaches Philosophy, and she's schizophrenic, so you have to keep things down, know what I mean. Flatten your emotional register."

"Okay."

"Right. Wait there."

Anna waited at the open door, assuming she'd been given one of Ramone's highly-colored confidences: anything but the truth. Soon a woman came smiling to greet her—a small woman, though not as small as Ramone, girlishly slender and erect, her iron-grey hair drawn back in a long, thick pony-tail. She was wearing a camel wool dressing gown. The pale skin of her face was so delicate you could have taken her for a grey-haired teenager. Her large, light blue eyes had a distracted carefulness.

"Hallo Anna, which means Grace: and I can see you are graceful. Ramone has told me so much about you. Come in. But please, when you cross the threshold, would you bow, and touch the *red* handprint that you see on the wall."

Anna did as she was told. The slim woman kept a hand fixed on Anna's wrist and talked her through a series of bows and gestures, avoidances and reverences, as they negotiated the front hall and crossed a large room hung with mobiles and strewn with strange sculptures made of beach debris, dead branches, empty plastic bottles. Anna did not attempt to meet Ramone's eye. If this performance turned out to be a hoax, or some kind of New Age idiocy, she didn't have to come back.

"Excuse me," said Lavinia Kent at last, when they had reached the safe harbor of a rattan couch and chairs set around a beautiful sea-green and blue rug, "I can't explain how all of that helps, but believe me it does. My rituals stave off the times when I have to resort to heavy medication." She smiled, with the proud politeness of someone apologizing for their wheelchair. On the wall opposite her Anna saw the remains of a chalk-drawn mandala, an intricate pattern of red and black and white that had been furiously smeared out of shape. The strokes that broke the pattern looked fresh. There was red and black chalk on Anna's wrist and on Lavinia's palms. So slight a violence: but the hairs on Anna's nape prickled.

"If this is a bad time. . .I really don't have to stay—"

"Oh no, don't think of leaving. I mustn't let my naughty child have its own way too much. It would only want more and more attention."

Ramone hovered, combining the pride of possession with a warning glower.

"Lavvy's an animist."

"Sheer pragmatism," said Lavinia. "I treat my illness like a mischievous spirit, an elemental child. I obey its demands, as good parents should obey their children, as often as possible, and lay down the law when I must. If I need them, I have no hesitation in taking the drugs, which are much less sledgehammerish nowadays, thank God." She tucked up her feet on the couch. Anna saw that her petal cheeks were meshed in fine lines—giving the impression, with the distracted caution in her eyes, that her face might shatter at any moment. "Don't be confused: the tricks I use to manage my disease are separate from the animism I discuss in my work. It's the misfortune of philosophy that your ideas, the big ideas that you want to develop, are bound to rise out of your personal experience. I expect Newton had some personal, maybe distressing or shameful reason, for favoring the notion of gravity. No one seems to dismiss his theory on that account."

The shelves of a tall bookcase against the mandala wall held rows of books by L. J. Kent. Did she have students? Did she *teach*, in a lecture hall garlanded with fetishes? The philosopher seemed to be wearing nothing under her dressing gown. She looked like a hermit: a desert mother plagued by demons. Anna was afraid that if she didn't give the right responses there'd be some awful explosion, but she had no idea what to say. She felt like strangling Ramone.

"Ramone has told me that you are a brilliant biologist, the only student in your year doing original research as an undergraduate. That's remarkable."

Oh right, Ramone. Flatten that emotional register.

"The project's new to me," said Anna. "Because anything would be. It's not original. They let third years work on repeating things that have often been done before: checking footnotes. I'm not working alone, either. I have a partner."

"Male or female?"

"Er, male."

"What's his name?"

"Charles."

"Meaning, the manly. Is he very manly?"

"I'll go and make your juice," said Ramone, "I bet you forgot to eat." She disappeared into the kitchen, looking daggers at Anna as she went.

"I don't know him socially," said Anna. "Only in the lab."

"Do you like him?" asked Lavinia, leaning forward. Her soft, elderly breasts became freely visible.

"I'm afraid I don't, much."

"I thought not. Do you find it difficult to work with someone you dislike?"

Anna opened her mouth and shut it. Juice-maker grinding noises saved her for a moment. "It's not serious. It's probably my own fault: penis envy or something—"

Lavinia smiled. Ramone, returning from the kitchen, caught Anna's last words and pounced on them. "Penis envy doesn't exist. Freud invented it because breast envy is such a major deal he couldn't believe women didn't suffer something complementary. Men cannot control the way they react to a pair of big jugs. You must have noticed." She offered the tray to her tutor with humble care and resumed, without drawing breath. "It's a minority of sophisticates that graduate from tit to cunt. You don't envy his prick. But he really, really wants your knockers. Watch he doesn't cut them off."

"Let us be thankful," said Lavinia dryly, "that Anna is not alarmingly well-endowed."

Anna stayed for an hour. When she left she took with her a copy of *The Wounded Void*. The idea of reading a work of modern philosophy was daunting, but if someone lends you a book it means they want to see you again: she was glad she was expected to come back. Ramone walked with her to Anna's block, came up the stairs, and stalked indoors, sniffing around. The room seemed painfully empty and blank. Anna wondered if it was full of demons. Ramone threw herself on the bed.

"How did you know not to lie to her?" she asked. "Like, the polite version: oh, I am totally delighted to be working side by side with Charles Shitface, and then when you said you were scared of meeting a schizophrenic. She liked that. She hates it when people don't say what they're thinking. She says it's torture."

Anna had found Lavinia Kent's directness relaxing. Verbal tennis with Ramone, however, was something else. "She sounds like a tough person to live with. My mother's in educational psychology, I suppose I've picked up some lore."

"Huh?" Ramone reared up on her elbows, appalled. "Your Mum is *a screw*! You never told me that!"

"You never asked. Why did you tell her I was a prodigy? That was pretty stupid, if she can't stand untruths."

"It's only emotional lies that matter." Ramone's face looked better without the hair, but her upper lip had the same chimpanzee, cartoon mobility. "This is a room for one," she remarked, with dazzling insight. "You never bring anyone back, do you. I can tell. You're getting weird, you know. You should watch yourself."

Which was outrageous, coming from a student who had set up house with her schizophrenic personal tutor. "I have to work now," said Anna.

Ramone and Anna spent the hungry winter working in the free heat and light of the crowded library, walking (Ramone had no bike, she didn't know how to ride one), and serving as handmaidens at Dr Kent's intellectual soirees. When she saw one of those gatherings (a-dazzle with faces from the tv and the papers that you'd never dreamed of seeing in the lined, imperfect flesh), Anna gave up being scandalized. She realized that Dr Kent was not someone the university could control and that Ramone was onto a good thing. Anyone who thinks patronage isn't important is a fool.

"We're not lovers," said Ramone—an idea that had been banished from Anna's mind, in fact, the moment she met Lavinia. "I don't think she's capable of it. Sex, I mean. She gets the most paralyzing highs from the disease. Sometimes I come back and find her in a trance; she's been locked in the same position for hours. She's not distressed, it's joy. Having that beats orgasms to shit, I reckon. I don't think she'd be a sexual person, crazy or not. She isn't the type; it's all in the mind for her: pleasure, pain, everything."

Anna realized, not during the conversation but later, that Ramone was talking about herself.

"But I love her. I really do. Like no one else, ever."

Anna's debt grew inexorably, in spite of all her discipline. Ramone's scholarship was running out, and Dr Kent was stingy when it came to handouts for her student minder. The immediate future looked tough, but for both of them the distance looked very bright. Anna planned to stay at Forest to do her doctorate in Molecular Biology. There was a Crop Improvement project, co-funded by a genetech company called PlasLife, which she hoped to join. Soon it would be the twenty-first century. She felt as if she had been promised a high purpose in that new era: a sword, a spear, a bow of burning gold. On Daz's birthday, full of the e Daz had given her, smiling like to split her face in half, she took out a pen and wrote secretly, down by the waste pipe on the wall of a nightclub toilet cubicle, THE SIXTY DAY TROPICAL LOWLAND POTATO.

That's me. I'm going to be there. Feeding the world!

Charles was no more use than a low-level infection. With *they all* she could not talk about work. In Ramone and Lavinia she found the audience for which she'd been pining. They bristled up like kittens meeting a vacuum cleaner, Ramone falling savagely on the crass male-supremacist jargon of genetic engineering: Lavinia comparing Anna's chosen field to space travel, the future that never happened. But they were fascinated. They would listen, while she bitched about flaky machines or the pain of preparing slides from sliced onion embryo when the cells would not stick and the angle of the section you'd made was always wrong. Anna was patient. She would swallow her hecklers, include them into her world.

She introduced Ramone to statistics and mentioned Florence Nightingale.

"Middle-class lesbian wanker," said Ramone, obviously mollified.

She saved up and bought a pineapple, expended a portion of the underused social budget on a half bottle of high proof vodka, and ordered them to turn down their freezer and get the liquor as cold as possible. Armed with some washing up liquid, an onion, a food mixer, and a low oven, she isolated DNA for them. The gods of lab science smiled on her, the trick worked beautifully. She spooled the magic thread onto one of Lavinia's blue glass swizzle sticks: her audience sighed in delight.

"That's it. That's the stuff."

"Fire from heaven," murmured Lavinia. "Was it Schrödinger or Heisenberg who named it the aperiodic crystal? I forget."

"Schrödinger. In Dublin, in 1943, when he was living in Ireland to get away from the Nazis. The important thing about being aperiodic is the informational capacity. He said the difference between DNA and the regular, non-living kind of crystal is like the difference between a wallpaper pattern and a masterpiece of tapestry."

"Cookery, washing machines, and now tapestry weaving: the female arts."

"That become male when they're highly valued," said Ramone. "I notice the tapestry was a *master*piece." She gazed at the thread of life in awe, then quickly returned to the offensive. "Of course the real thing is cloning humans. I bet scientists are already doing it, secretly. That's the Holy Grail, human reproduction under total male control."

"Could be, I suppose. I'm not interested. Listen, Ramone: plants are *the business*. They work, the rest of us are parasites. That's why I'm into plant biology. No offence, but human cloning is for tabloid journalists."

"Even so," said Lavinia softly, "that topic will be to genetic engineering what weapons-development was to physics. Irrational, central, alluring, deadly. There will be no denatured millions of brainwashed replicants: just as there has been so far no Global Thermonuclear War. But there will be the same mysterious train of ruin."

"No, please. Forget it. Much more interesting things are going on at the other end of the scale. There's a woman called Clare Gresley, who believes she's found a whole new theory of evolution, from studying virus DNA—"

"Something wrong with Natural Selection?" inquired Ramone wisely.

"Well, yes." Anna spooled more thread, it seemed endless. "A whole living world, that 'makes sense,' comes out of the flux and blur of genetic variation, that does not 'make sense' at all. It's like the divide between the weirdness of the quantum universe and the fixed, solid macroworld. Where does the weirdness go? No one knows. Fitness isn't everything, Ramone. By the laws of probability, quite a lot of what survives in a genome has to have zero adaptive value. Someone called Kimura pointed that out..."

Out of the corner of her eye she saw Lavinia pick up the vodka bottle, look at it in surprise, and take a healthy swig: saw Ramone remove the bottle from the philosopher's unresisting hand and tuck it into Anna's shoulder bag, which was sitting on the kitchen counter. These glimpses happened: cracks, through which one glimpsed the pathology of the *ménage à trois*, Ramone and Lavvy and the disease. She pretended she'd seen nothing.

"And then, in nature genes go in cohorts, not alone. They won't move anywhere without their mates. That's one reason why genetic modification is so frustrating and why firms like PlasLife will look for a naturally occurring improvement and steal it, if they can. You can get something useless flourishing, because the genes for it are linked to genes that do something essential. Or because the gene that codes for the useless change in one place, does something useful elsewhere. Then the organism finds a use for the neutral thing, just by happenstance, and then the change gets selected for. . . Then *we* come along, and we say the genetic mutation was adaptive: but it wasn't."

"The idols of the market place," commented Lavinia. "One must defend the truth against them. Speak it but deny it. Speak it but deride it."

Ramone screwed up her cartoon features. "You mean, like, giraffes eat leaves off the tops of trees because they accidentally have long necks? Instead of the deal where they thrive because the necks are a cunning way to eat the leaves off the tops of trees?"

"Hm... Sort of. Of course, adaptive radiation through reproductive success is still what *happens*, on the macro scale."

"Of course," said Ramone, winking at Lavinia.

"But Weak-Factor Fitness, which is what Kimura's idea is called, foregrounds the point that a genetic variation does not have to convey a benefit to spread through a population; there are other factors. At the nucleotide level, there's no Darwinism, not what people think of as Darwinism, not at all."

"Wherever we step," remarked Lavinia. "The solid surface breaks and we are plunged into ferment. But Anna, genetic engineering will change the world, even if I never understand a word you say. What are we going to do with all these people who no longer die of cancers, heart-disease, dementia? All the designer babies? Will we keep them in their packaging? What about the schizophrenics whose brain chemistry is altered so they remain sane? How are they to live?"

"Can you eat it?" demanded Ramone, suddenly. "Could I eat my *own* ?"

"Why not?" asked Anna. She was still holding the swizzle stick. "You do eat it, all the time. You breathe it, yours and other people's. It gets in your teeth, it gets in your hair, it lodges in your skin, it gets pulped in your digestive tract."

"Could I eat *that*?" Ramone pointed to the swizzle stick.

"It'll taste of washing up liquid."

Anna wanted to tell them that when she studied a protein separation gel the patterns she saw were astronomical, it was like a negative image of the starry sky. She was an astronomer, a cosmologist, a particle physicist: knowing events by their traces, through a chain of mathematical inference, never able to perceive her quarry directly. She wished she could make her friends understand the vast *distances*: which was far more important than worrying about vanity parenting or whether men or women owned the jargon. It is far away, you can't imagine how far. We don't exist there. They don't direct us, no more than the stars direct human affairs. We are part of the same system, obeying the same laws, but we hardly begin to understand what the laws are. Maybe we're still waiting for Galileo's telescope... She was thinking, all too soon she was going to have to give up wondering about evolution and concentrate on *solanum succulentum*. You have to specialize, but it was a shame. But sometimes you had to drop the subject, whatever the subject was. There were demons to be placated. The three of them ate onion DNA, sharing the sacred meal lip to lip, and spoke of other things.

At the intellectual soirees, Ramone and Anna served coffee, tea, or horrible cheap sherry, while the guests talked among themselves about the Lavinia Kent universe—the existential trinity of self, the mysterious sacrifice of consciousness—and tried to get next to Lavinia. Dr Kent was indefatigable. She taught, in a hall full of fetishes or in her own living room. She wrote, she collaborated, she kept up this punishing evening life. Alex Lyell (Alexander, which means defender of men), one of the university's science-lions, told Anna that Dr Kent was a living saint. "Have you read her on the Fall from Grace as the splitting of the Higgs Field into asymmetry? You'd see what I mean. Her thinking is truly important. She offers us the right to awe and worship without superstition. No supernatural element, no fudging to get rid of the infinities—"

Anna understood, and she guessed Lavinia understood it too, that the disease drew them. Lavinia's illness, the mischievous child, seemed to sit demurely in a corner, in its best clothes. To these middle-aged postmodern professionals, all of them clever or at least powerful, the shadow of mental degeneration was more terrible than death, and there sat the monster: better than vanquished, *tamed* by this gentle woman, brilliant conversationalist, assimilator of shadows. One night, after Lavinia had collected the glasses and poured the dregs back into the bottle, as was her wont (you couldn't blame her; she needed all her funds, for the decades of old age that she fully expected to spend in Bedlam), she kicked off her shoes—the black velvet steel-buckled court shoes that went with the long, shimmering black or brown velvet dresses she kept for these occasions—sat hieratic on the couch, a hand upturned on either knee: and spoke.

A thousand martyrs I have made
All sacrificed to my desire
A thousand beauties have betrayed

That languish in resistless fire
The untamed heart to hand I brought
And fixed the wild and wandering thought... "Do you have sexual fantasies, Anna?"

"When I was a little girl," said Anna. "I used to have fantasies about shitting. They featured a very handsome, muscular man, partly naked: I think it was Superman from off the tv. He would be tied down and strapped up by the baddies, and he had to shit, beautiful streams of fat turds. It was lovely, I don't know why. I think he was meant to be myself but I displaced it. . . This must have been until I was about eight."

"I had orgasmic fantasies about food," announced Ramone. "Sausages and chocolate bars, alive and running up for me to eat them."

Lavinia and Anna glanced at each other: of course Ramone was lying.

"But there was a friend of my Mum and Dad's. They used to say: he doesn't mean any harm, keep out of his way. I had fantasies about *him* all right. I used to imagine he'd made me pregnant. He only groped me. I knew that wasn't enough to do the damage but it didn't help. It was like I had a big maggot in my belly, wriggling. Yecch. That's why I'm never going to have children."

"What if you accidentally got pregnant? Would you have an abortion?"

"No, I wouldn't do that." snapped Ramone.

"Huh? But if you hate the idea of—"

"Abortion is a slave's option." Ramone scowled. "It's not an issue because I'm never going to get pregnant. I'm not going to get myself sterilized, I just know it's never going to happen. But if by any chance it did, I'd stick it out, because I'm important. My potential is important. If women are to be the people, then what they produce—their blood, their babies—has to be *over*-valued. We have to stop apologizing, oh please excuse me, I made a mess, I'll clear it up. If I were a man I would say my seed is important, and how different that would sound. Bastards."

"What about you, Anna?" wondered Lavinia. "Would you abort?"

"If I had to," said Anna—and heard her mother's voice from those hard early years: clipped, contained, enduring. Anna's mother: always tired, never exhausted, bearing everything. "But Ramone, what if you had a scan and the baby was hideously deformed?"

"Oh yeah, the be-cruel-to-be-kind argument. I don't believe it. I don't even like kids, but I don't see why it shouldn't have its little nine months in womb-world. Have the baby, let it be born, and let it die. That's the answer."

"Great. Radical feminist aligns with the Christian Right Fundamentalists. Ramone you'd say anything to make yourself sound off-the-wall."

"I am childless and virginal," said Lavinia. "Except for the disease. My confessors invite me to confide my sexual fantasies, I have none. Like Teresa of Avila, Catherine of Siena, Hildegard of Bingen: I refer my voices and visions to the doctors of my church, the church of mental disease. When they imply that my visions cannot be true visions, since they are not sexual, I don't argue with them, though they are calling me a charlatan. I never let them tell me that I am crazy when they can't cope with what I say, sane when they can. That way madness lies."

So they would sit together, passing the eye of speech from hand to hand like the three Norns in a winter cave; sipping thick cool vegetable juice. Ramone and Lavinia shared Anna's conversational style—lengthy, perseverant, more like a successive presentation of gifts than the normal undergraduate horse-trading: and Anna had found a niche. If she could have got on better with Charles, she would have been perfectly happy.

◄ ►

In finals term, their lab project (a footnote in the investigation of onion anti-fungal defenses) was still incomplete. As luck would have it, Anna's share of the work had turned out well. Charles couldn't get his sequencing right. Anna kept after him—partly because of her insensate, disinterested drive and partly because no matter what anybody said about the minor importance of this thing to their results, she wanted a perfect score. It was like a computer game. Getting through level one without missing a target is not the challenge. It's the starting point. Her father's experience went deep in her: telling her that the world is harsh and there are no second chances. Charles sulked. To coax him into compliance she was forced to spend time in his company: go to the bar with him, have coffee with him. She did not like doing this. Charles would try to flirt, by "casual" touches, and by tacking compliments onto the end of his strut-my-stuff: which was ridiculous. You're a brainless teacher's pet, I'm the one who's in charge around here, great tits by the way… A couple of times she politely reminded him that he had a girlfriend. Didn't work. She grew inured and ignored his advances. Finally, she had the brilliant idea that she would do his sequencing herself. They would write everything up together and present the work jointly. That would be okay. Dr Russell and Guy had already suggested full collaboration as a solution to the problem.

The plan went swimmingly. Everyone in the lab was very busy and used to seeing her around, so she managed to escape specific attention. After a couple of attempts she produced a gel that separated out into recognizable bands, which appeared where they were supposed to be on their mug shot photo. She was so pleased that she actively invited Charles to her flat, gave him copies of all her material, and sent him off to check it over. And that, thank God, should be that.

➤ ➤

The world was lost, buried, extinguished under revision. Simon Gough held a Damn the Torpedoes party in his battered roof-top studio: hardly anybody turned up. Daz had been offered a modeling contract, after finals, and was wondering whether to accept. "Shall I do it?" she asked, as they sat on Marnie's bed one night, allegedly working. "God! Why not! Take the money and run. You've all your life to be a software baron."

"A lawyer," said Daz, gathering up the pictures of herself. "That's where I'm heading. Computer science is for background, you need more than one expertise. I want to be in Human Rights law." It would be a performance, like being the kind of sassy, flirty waitress who attracts big tips. The idea of tumultuous success at something feminine allured her. "I'll do it. But when *this* is over you have to come to Paris with me first. One last student rave." She glanced towards a wall of the room. Her ex-boyfriend was on the other side, if he hadn't gone out. It was over, the flame so dead they could calmly live together (in separate rooms) in the flat they shared with Marnie. The exams were not a problem. *This* meant Rob: a course she had already failed, but she still had to sit the paper.

Ramone was engrossed in a scheme that had nothing to do with her finals. She was devising cultural equations. Anna was right: the numbers were everything. You could regard what went on in the battle of the sexes as a chemical reaction, a fractional distillation, positive feedback, a sixteen-dimensional surface, a normal distribution curve. . . You could draw it in one of those strange horned crowns invented by the lady with the lamp. You could show why feminism in the classic model was doomed, explain how it came about that the vast majority of women were so stupid and venal, how every wave of "feminism" was doomed to self-destruct, and yet the tide would keep on rising. You could show how a neutral imbalance (e.g., men must compete physically, females need to minimize energy consumption, both for reproductive success: females end up smaller) could get into everything, could lie at the root of a huge pervasive complex structure. *Alas how easily things go wrong! A sigh too much or a kiss too long. . .* She scribbled fast, dividing her attention between Levi-Strauss's *Mythologies*, Wentworth D'Arcy Thompson's *On Growth and Form* (a book Anna had recommended), a primer called *Basic Statistics*, and her trusty Bugs Bunny calculator that she had owned since she was six. She would set up camp on the border, on the actual fault-line of the Great Divide, and wrest her insights from the religion of her times: the feared, denied, adored, all-pervasive bogey—Science.

It was May-time. The beech tree outside her dark window was in leaf, pattering dryad whispers against the glass. Met Anna two years ago—how time flies. Her door was open, allowing her a glimpse down the lighted hallway into the big living room. Seraphina Russell had come to visit. Dr Russell's son had married a young woman who did not love her mother-in-law and had spent the last years ruthlessly excising the mother from her only child's life. Seraphina was suffering atrociously. People who hovered on the edge at the soirees often came to Dr Kent like this: late at night, almost in disguise. Lavvy lapped it up. Like Teresa of Avila, called upon by great ladies.

Lavinia was fascinated by female saints. She claimed them all as schizophrenics, the way gays and dykes will try to persuade you any famous person you mention is secretly bent. As far as Ramone could see, what these women had in common was the same as any women struggling to have power in a man's world. The eating disorders, the mysterious illnesses, the hysteria. If you were Albert Einstein and born female in the fifteenth century, you'd end up in some convent fasting yourself crazy, writing liturgical music, or reforming the Carmelites. Anyone could see that. Who could tell, at this distance, if they were technically bonkers.

It made you wonder about Lavinia herself: did she fall or was she pushed?

Lavvy hated that kind of talk.

She peeked into her periscope view of the consulting room. Lavinia was holding Dr Russell's hand. (Not good, Lavvy does not touch, that's Lavvy trying too hard to act normal.) "I believe that the world is a person," she was saying. "I believe that person cares intimately for me. This is not an act of faith, it is an act of reason: the universe is a complexity, unfinished and pattern-haunted, the mirror of the human mind. Accept that vast complex, problematic selfhood, see it looking back at you, sharing your nature, and you have a refuge that cannot be taken from you... And knowing what we know of ourselves, how can anyone doubt that the God/universe is in pain? I believe that the only possible God, *Who Is What Is,* is dying in agony now, as we speak. In the state of eternity, being is sacrifice. As long as you can escape from the pain-fest of God, escape by any means available. If you cannot, then understand that pain is bliss—"

Ramone recognized cadences from *The Wounded Void,* or maybe *Autotheology.* Lavvy was quoting herself: she did that when she was "tired." As they called it. The paramedic had better stay awake, on call, tonight. Because of me, she thought, with a flutter of pride in her young blood, Lavvy can live. She can be their showgirl, get the audience reaction she needs, and she can work. She put her equations away, hugged Pele closer, and turned to a different stack of papers. It was four in the morning, a good time for the thin, fine concentration of revision work.

◆ ◆

Anna had decided not to hassle Charles. If he didn't get back to her she would wait until the deadline and submit her own write-up, under both their names, as they'd agreed. A few days before her first exam she walked into Dr Russell's office to deliver an extended essay and noticed Charles's name looking up at her from the in-tray. It was the onion embryo project. Good, now she could hand in hers. Something about the first page, picked up in that casual glance, made her take a second look.

Shit!

He'd reverted to plan A and submitted his share of the project independently. But he'd used her results. He'd used everything she'd done except her name. A shiver of rage went through her. Typical Charles! What could she do? What did he think? That Anna would never find out? The idiot. I'm not going to let him get away with this, she decided. She was alone in the office. Feeling like a daring criminal she took the paper, tucked it into her folder, and sped to the nearest photocopier. Minutes later she'd replaced the original, exactly where it had been before. No one had seen her. Now what? She didn't know how to approach him. She prowled the campus all day: no sign of Charles. In the evening she called the flat he shared with Ilse and another girl. Charles answered the phone. She didn't know what to say to him. "Hello Anna, how's the revision going? Haven't seen much of you lately. I bet you're working like a slave, you always do."

Not a sign of guilty knowledge in his voice. She didn't know how to challenge him. Her mouth was dry and her palm sweating on the handset, her chief thought was that she would fail a lie detector test at this moment, whatever anyone asked her.

"Could I talk to you about something?"

"Well, sure. What about this evening? I could come out to campus, no problem."

They agreed to meet in the Union bar. After she'd put the phone down Anna realized that Charles knew something was up. His tone had been bland, but he hadn't asked what this "something" might be, or tried to sort it out over the phone. He knew she'd found out.

So they met. Anna was there first: Charles spotted her and came over. She wanted to buy the drinks, but he insisted on paying. He wore a sly, defiant air: she guessed he was preparing to brazen it out because he still said nothing, just acted as if it was natural for the two of them to get together over a pint. The bar was crowded and hot; it stank of a term's spilled beer and stale smoke. Everyone was nervously rowdy, end-of-termitis. For Anna nothing was ending. Exams didn't worry her, the next academic year would be more of the same, more of the permanent faces with whom she already aligned herself; only this passing crowd would disperse. She wondered what Charles was expecting. She didn't know anything about his plans.

"Look," she said, "why don't we go back to my flat? It'll be quieter."

They walked up to the Village. She settled him in her only chair. She was feeling slightly less nervous, ready to talk things over.

"Would you like some coffee? I don't keep any alcohol."

She remembered the DNA vodka that was still in her fridge; decided to forget it.

She brought in two mugs of instant coffee, gave one to Charles and laid her copy of his project submission on the desk in front of him. The room was warm but her hands were icy, she wrapped them around the mug. "What's the idea, Charles? I thought we were going to present a collaboration."

"How did you get hold of this?"

"I happened to see it on Dr Russell's desk, took a copy, and put the original back. Don't worry, I haven't told anyone. *Yet.* I thought I should talk to you first."

He picked up the sheets of paper and glanced through them as if checking for typing errors: looking at her sideways with his sleepy, secretive grin. "Anna——" He got up from the desk and arranged himself more comfortably on the floor, motioning for her to join him. "I don't see what the big deal is——" Obviously it had galled him to be placed in the chair. He never liked to do what he was told, he always had to resist. Show off.

"The big deal is that *you are handing in work I did and saying it's your own.* What did you think? That I wouldn't keep copies?"

"But Anna, it isn't important. I mean, what's the difference? You know I did this stuff. All right you repeated my sequencing, and got a slightly better result for me, but so what? We all know Biols is down to team work."

She couldn't stand over him. She sat down. "The difference, Charles, is that we agreed to write up the project as a collaboration, although all the 'collaborating' you did was to insist on doing the sequencing because you thought it was more glamorous, get it wrong, and give up. Now you've gone back on what we agreed, and handed in *this*, without mentioning that I did your practical for you. I know it was my own idea to help. But this is. . .you can't *do* this. It's, it's unprofessional."

He stared at her and burst out laughing. "Oh, Anna!" He shook his head in amazement. "You really are something. . . Anna, we all know that you work like a little pig every hour of the day and night. That's how you've managed to stay at the top of the class, although you're no brainier than a lot of the other girls. Ilse was saying that, the other day. I'm not like you. I'm more creative, less of a slogger. You've always been happy to lend people your notes. What's the difference? What do you have to gain by making a fuss? We both know the project doesn't mean anything, it's make-work."

Anna realized she should have left his paper where she found it, handed in her joint-paper, with the conflicting evidence, and let Dr Russell sort it out. She'd thought she was being decent, but she'd fucked-up. She felt like an idiot. There were no more useful moves on this board. She began to stand, ready to show him the door. "Okay, forget it. It's going to look a bit strange now, when I hand in the collaboration, but that's your problem. You should have talked to me."

"I *am* talking to you. I'm talking to you now."

"Because I forced you into it."

He reached out and grasped her wrist. His hand felt like the paw of an animal. His tone changed, absurdly. "You don't have to force me into anything, Anna. I think you know that."

"Oh, for heaven's sake!" Anna exploded. "Charles you can't start making eyes at me. What d'you want to do? Take off my horn rim glasses, rumple my hair, and say but, you're beautiful. . .? It only works in the movies, sunshine. And only then when crass fools like you are making up the story. Just *lay off*."

He held onto her wrist, rubbing his thumb against the thin inner skin of her forearm in a way that felt very unpleasant: maybe Ilse liked it. She kept on glaring and trying to free herself until he gave up with a shrug.

"I don't know what I did to upset you. But since I'm here, how about something to eat? What have you got in? I could easily whip us up some pasta, I bet. Let's go and see."

Men, Anna had been told, are poor at understanding subtle non-verbal signals. But where was the subtlety? She had told him in words of one syllable that she was furious and why. She followed him into her tiny kitchen, amazed: wondering what 'a God's name was going on in Charles Craft's head. She decided that he wasn't crazy; he was cruelly embarrassed. He had been caught out, and he was trying, in a very normal human way, to pretend it had not happened. She felt obliged to cooperate. Much as she detested Charles, she sympathized with the poor sod. She had humiliated him (although he'd die rather than acknowledge it); she could afford to be magnanimous. She let him boil the pasta, and heat and mash some tinned tomatoes (that was as far as the cooking went). She offered no assistance. They sat down again on the floor with their plates, on the scratchy utilitarian carpet. For once Anna wished her flat catered for two. She disliked this false informality.

Charles ate with gusto. "You should loosen up, Anna. What's the point of flogging yourself the way you do. Let's face it, you're going to work for a few years at dead end short contracts, you'll take a break to have your kids and probably never set foot in a lab again. I'm the one who's committed to a career in science, and I find time to have fun."

Anna poked at her pasta: thinking *go away. Soon.*

"I know you like me. I can see I've hurt your feelings. I don't understand how, but I'm sorry, I really am." He put his plate aside, took hers from her hands. "Come on Anna, let's not leave it like this. You worked so hard over that pathetic project, I was touched I really was. I thought you *wanted* me to use your stuff. God, you're actually *shaking*!"

"Knock it off, Charles."

"Sssh, relax. Let it all out—"

In after-days and after-weeks Anna would replay what happened endlessly: returning like a dog to its vomit, bewildered that she could not stop herself from regurgitating these scenes, these physical memories. When did I stop saying no? Did I hit him? No, I didn't hit him. It was a hostage situation, I gave up, I changed sides. You're having an awkward conversation with a fellow undergraduate and suddenly he comes at you with an axe, *I wasn't prepared.* I wasn't afraid, I didn't think he would kill me, but I couldn't believe it. I'm the one that failed to read the damned body-language. I was fighting him off, he was laughing as if we both knew this was a jolly game. I couldn't bring myself to scream. When did I stop fighting? I may have put my arms round. . .because lie there like a slab of meat it's theatrical, he'd never have left if I didn't capitulate, didn't withdraw my objection, let him score his point, agree to his version.

When Charles had gone she dressed again and walked into town. It was a long way. The darkness and the monotony of her own footsteps kept her from thinking. She rang at the door of Simon's house. Someone who had been marginal to first year's *they all* opened it. "Is Simon in?" she asked the woman. She went up to the studio, which was a strange pyramid-shaped room like a rooftop greenhouse. It had been very cold and leaky in the winter.

"Hiya Simon."

"What's wrong, Anna? You look—"

She shrugged. "Exam nerves. I've been walking, I'm tired." She sat in a greasy old red armchair that stood by his convection heater, the metal cold now, a kettle and some mugs standing on the top, purple bedspread dangling from the glass incline overhead. Simon waited, poised in the act of closing down the work on his screen. He looked shocked, concerned. She had not checked herself in a mirror. What did he see? No torn clothes, thank God, no blood, no nakedness.

"You know that project I was doing with Charles Craft? I've found out that he's handing in some work I did as if it was his own. For finals."

"What?" Simon's screen went blank, tropical fish floated over it. "*Really?*"

"I'm not a liar."

"What are you going to do? Can you prove it?"

"Yeah, probably. But I'm not going to do anything."

"Why not?"

She shook her head listlessly, against the back of his armchair. "No one likes a whistleblower, Simon. Not in any business. I've been thinking about it, while I walked. The cheating's trivial, not worth worrying about. If I make a fuss the story might stick with me. I might never live it down; I'd be an awkward bugger. . . I only wanted to get it off my chest. Mind if I sit a bit?"

She sat, hardly speaking after that first confession. He made her a mug of herb tea. He had almost said: *you don't get exam nerves, Anna, and you don't let people mess you around. What's going on?* But her face had stopped him. He let her alone and went back to his work. "I had some email from Spence the other day. He asked after you."

"Oh. How's he?"

"He's fine, him and his cat and his Mom and his rig. Getting awful grades though. He's a lazy bastard." She nodded, and they relapsed into silence.

She left after an hour or so, saying "thanks for the tea." Simon never did find out why Anna the cool and brave was going to let herself be shafted that way by a fellow student, though later he had his suspicions. Just one of those things, those raw moments that friends hold in trust; secrets never to be told.

➤ ➤

Anna had stopped taking the pill at the end of second year, reasoning that it was senseless to be on permanent medication when her sex life was so sparse and she'd be using barrier protection anyway. It wasn't until the next morning that she remembered this. Slap bang in the middle of her cycle too. She had two weeks to wait, the two weeks in which she had to sit her crucial exams. She ought to have gone straight to the health center for a morning-after course. She had marched Marnie Choy down there, when they were house sharing, on three separate occasions when the reckless girl had been drunk and

unwise. She did nothing. She spent fourteen days in suspended anima-
tion, locked in her shame. Coming out of one of the exams, a paper
she believed she had failed, she was waylaid by Ilse.

"Anna—"

The whimpering little voice set her teeth on edge. "Yes, what is it?"

"Please, will you talk to me?"

They went into the Biols coffee bar and found a table. "Anna,
look, I'm not going to try to be dignified. I'm going to throw myself
on your mercy."

She thought, I will never set foot in here again. Never. The drab
scuffed tables, the terrible counter food. Three years to end like this.
She couldn't bear it. But you have to.

"What are you talking about?"

"You're so much prettier than I am, and so much more talented. You've got everything. Please don't take Charles away from
me. *Please.*"

The pastel-sweatered one sat with bitten lips, full of trembling
boldness, feeling so proud of herself for having screwed up the courage to brave this monster, Anna. Anna kept the bile behind her teeth.
Not Ilse's fault. . . But she hated the creature. That dowdy uniform,
the terrible little dangly earrings, at once sexless and groveling. Where
do they learn to dress like that, to cut their hair like that: why didn't
anyone teach me how to do it? I wanted equality, but it cannot be had.
You have to take the whip hand or else submit.

"Don't worry. I'm not interested. He is all yours."

ᦲ ᦲ

On the day her period was due she took the bus to town, walked
out on the pier and leaned on the rail, watching the rough, opaque,
water. The sky was thick and low. Young herring gulls with their
brown mottled backs sailed under the boardwalk, rocking on angled
wings. This is why women should never try to compete with men.
Because *this* will happen, and a woman will not be strong enough to
cope. Anna had not been strong enough. She had made her corrupt
decision to keep quiet about the amateur rapist, but it had done her
no good because she had been unable to throw the experience off, the

way a tough person would have done. She couldn't blame Charles. He'd done nothing specially terrible. It was Anna who had been unforgivably careless. She had answered him back in seminars, making him feel she was a challenge. She had allowed him to flirt. From the first moment he made "advances" she should have taken every possible step to keep out of his way. Instead she had pursued him. She had let him touch her shoulder, squeeze her waist, so he would do the work: imagining she was being clever. To Charles it was as if she'd been saying *please fuck me*. And he had.

This is what happens, she thought. Women lie, they keep silent, because no one likes a whistleblower. This is how it all carries on. Now I am doing it. I am part of the machine that destroys women's chances. The fall was terrible. She did not see what was the point in going on living.

➤ ➤

Ramone didn't find it odd when Anna stopped coming to the Pinebourne flat. She assumed it was because Anna knew. The salon was closed, and Ramone had enough to do without wondering what had happened to the third Norn. She came back from one of her papers and found their front door standing open. Shit... Lavvy was kneeling in the center of the green and blue rug that had been a present from an admirer, the textile artist Andrea Waters. Her thin hands were raised above her head, locked and thrust heavenwards. Her hair flowed down her back in light-catching silver tangles. She looked like the repentant Magdalene as ecstatic hermit, agonized and glorified. The room smelt strongly of fresh poo.

"Oh no," muttered Ramone. She spotted the turds and dealt with that problem first, before the philosopher could get interested in her own productions.

"Lavvy?"

The Magdalene began to cry out in a loud voice. "Oh Jesus Christ, Oh Jesus Christ, take this cup away from me. That art thou, that art thou, there are worms of flames eating my knees, my medieval knees that have no health in them until they bend. What do you think? Did Jesus Christ come to earth to found a new religion? The world must change in every atom, and the answer to that prayer is never never never never never. Cordelia, the warm-hearted, will come no more. . . If you are tenderhearted they will kill you. Mad women are the Marthas, Martha means the mistress, mistresses of humanity, who hear the cry of the world. Mary, which means bitterness, is the isolate, the contemplative. If I am mad, if I am crippled, does it make any difference how I was MADE MAD? I was made mad. Studies of Afro-Caribbean schizophrenics, I must trace the reference, show that though the percentage in the population diagnosed with schizophrenia is high, the diagnoses are accurate. Race hatred is a factor, genetic constitution is a factor, the hall of thought shattered; is shattered——"

Ramone noticed she'd left the door open: confusion in the mind is infectious. She shut and locked it, and fetched the camel dressing gown, the dope tin, and Pele. The rabbit was for herself, Lavvy wasn't queer for soft toys. She preferred hard-edged things, shells and cans and broken plastic bottles. She draped the dressing gown over Lavvy's naked back and sat beside her to roll a fat spliff on the back of *A Great Favour: The Visionary Experience And Human Knowledge*. This was the new book. It had set Lavvy off, or pushed her over the edge. It could be the fact that this book was so sleek and glossy, with a big promotion budget, a further step into the circus of fame-and-exposure: the arena where, Ramone knew, Lavvy was mortally afraid that she would fail, be dismissed, be exposed as a charlatan. She hadn't been well since the launch party, which had been in London (often a dangerous voyage) and which had ended when the *demanding child* had thrown a tantrum. At least Ramone didn't have to tolerate that *the disease is our baby* metaphor, for the moment. It had always made her feel sick.

"What about being a woman?" she asked, lighting up. "Your secret vice, oh teacher. What's madness got to do with that?"

"No comment," said Dr Kent, grasping the dressing gown and arranging it sideways around her shoulders. "Not for publication. You distract yourself, Ramone. I warn you, if you make a, a *thing* out of being a woman, you may get a quick buzz of interest, but you will look around twenty years from now and you'll have been marginalized. I have never allowed that to happen to me. I am judged as a mad holy-savant. Anyone can be mad. Only half the world can be female, and let's face it, *it's the wrong half*."

"I don't accept that."

"You're a fool."

"You're the fool. You're living in the past. I know what I'm doing. Just watch me. See me blow my trumpet, see me ride my big shiny car, see me fly."

Dr Kent took a deep draught of the healing smoke. "Ahh. How did the torture go?"

"Okay. I'm not an exam type, it's scraping bone. But I think I'm doing okay."

When she was well, Lavvy spoke with radiant calm about resorting to the heavy chemicals whenever necessary. In reality (Ramone had been told, she'd never seen it happen before), the transition was difficult. Soon she was in agony again, seeing flames and worms erupting from her skin, refusing any medication stronger than cannabis but forced to whip herself with a home-made cat o' nine tails. The cat's tails were tipped with knapped flints; they drew blood. In her lucid intervals she still claimed all of this was a creative struggle and would lead to new work. For all Ramone could tell it might be true. If Lavinia's scholarship and her teaching were really brilliant—and everyone seemed to think they were—why dope her and call her crazy? Why not let her have her whips and fetishes and get on with it? Perhaps then she'd have been able to stay as sane as the dead saints, self-mutilating "women of power," who had apparently never lost the plot as far as shitting on the carpet.

Or maybe not. Maybe Teresa of Avila's worst moments had been edited out of the record, leaving only the acceptable face of ecstasy. Anyway, Lavinia's brother came and took her away. He warned Ramone—he'd been through this movie before—that when she came out of it his sister probably wouldn't want to know her former protégée. Schizos are like that. They skip from stone to stone and quickly forget the past.

◂ ▸

Ramone sailed from Southampton to Le Havre as a foot passenger, with Marnie Choy and Daz Avritivendam. Daz had signed a modeling contract and was acting, in a weird way, as if she was taking the veil: this was one last fling before the cloister. Ramone was traveling with 200 francs in her pocket, free as a bird. She had no idea how she was going to live. She left the other two getting drunk in the saloon and went out on deck. The weather was dull and sad. Maybe Gaia had been tinkering again, to counteract global warming. The spoilsport: in Ramone's opinion global warming was *fun*. She crouched by a life raft, watching the last of England. Goodbye, Lavvy, goodbye my alma mater, my gossip, my destroying angel, my corner stone. Good luck with the next incarnation. *Oh God*, she prayed. *Make me a philosopher*. And the sea said, yes. But it will cost you everything.

➤ *iii* ➤

Anna walked into the freezer in the basement of Parentis plc with her worksheet and checked out two canisters of pelleted DNA. One container held samples cloned from 500 normally fertile male volunteers, from a survey on reproductive health in the South of France. The other can was from an academic project on the genetic history of Europe, run by the University of Marseille: DNA from bones and mummified tissue, from the tenth century ossuaries of an ancient Provencal settlement called Huits Bories.

Parentis was a global company, involved in all aspects of Human Assisted Reproduction; in this lab the concern was basic science. It was unlikely that Anna's doctoral project—identifying pseudogenes on the Y chromosome—would have direct bearing on an infertility treatment, but it was good for business to have a profile in pure research. Anna didn't care much either way. Sometimes she remembered that Human Assisted Reproduction was the last kind of work she would have wanted to do, before her fall, but she tried not to think in those terms. She was resigned to her lot.

For weeks after what had happened with Charles she had been in cruel distress; her mother checking her surreptitiously for needle marks; hardly able to speak to her poor father. She had tried to take an AIDS test and been sent away to think it over by a puzzled counselor (you don't want it on your record, love, not unless there's good cause). She had dreamed incessantly of being attacked, by monsters with human faces. . . She had emerged from her nightmare not pregnant (she'd started to bleed three weeks after her period was due) and with what Dr Russell called a very creditable 2:2. Of course she'd lost the PlasLife studentship. She had learned, before she left Forest, that Charles Craft had put in his application. So it would be Charles, not Anna, who would get the spear, the sword, the bow of burning gold. And it served her right.

For the rest of her life, whenever she heard of some woman's career blighted by sexual harassment, or a girl raped by a man who really did not feel that he was doing wrong, she would have to remember that *she*, Anna Anaconda, was partly to blame.

It was Dr Russell who had managed to get her taken on at Parentis: tender-hearted Seraphina, who could not understand what had gone wrong, but would not desert her protégée. The director of this lab, KM Nirmal, was an old friend of hers. He would be a good supervisor, an inspirational mentor, someone who would recognize Anna's quality.

Anna had let it all happen. She knew that she was better off than she deserved to be. Her studentship was registered with Leeds university, the funding was reliable, the work involved skills that would stand her in good stead. She lived with a cheery, overweight staff nurse called Roz Brown, who needed a lodger to help pay her mortgage. Roz had pastel-sweater tendencies, a little girl of five called Shannon, and a Rugby playing boyfriend whose voice and presence made Anna cringe. But it was all right. Anna babysat Shannon, tried to save the lives of the reduced-to-clear azaleas that stood in pots on the damp back patio, and taught Roz to cook the food of well-managed poverty. At weekends she went home to Manchester, if she wasn't needed in the lab. She had slightly more money than if she'd been investigating *solanum succulentum*. She could be clear of debt in five or six years, with care.

KM Nirmal—always Nirmal to his juniors and colleagues—was a stick-limbed individual with small hard eyes, wire-rimmed spectacles, fragile brown skin stretched tightly over his facial bones, and an almost lipless mouth between two deep grooves, like a capital H inscribed below his beak of a nose. He looked like Gandhi's mummy and had so far shown no sign of being inspirational. At the weekly meetings, when Anna reported on her task, he would nod and make some bland remark and proceed at once to discuss other work. That was fine by Anna. The Parentis lab stood in a science park on the outskirts of Leeds. Through the windows of the sequencing lab, beyond the slabs of car-park concrete and industrial-unit walls, cloud shadows strode over the Pennines. When she looked out, to rest her eyes, the open upland sky was like a promise of freedom. One day, this would be over. One day, she might escape and get back on track.

Her work on the samples was not easy, because no matter how repetitive and automated it was, you still had to give it your full attention, hour by hour. At least, since nobody was in a hurry for her results, she could amuse herself by being as meticulous as she liked. She worked alone. When she first found her anomaly—a sequence common to the ancient Provencal DNA and to the gorilla DNA she was using as a control, that ought to hybridize with the modern Frenchmen but refused to do so—she thought she was imagining things: but it wouldn't go away. She became a little obsessed. At the weekly meetings she said nothing: it was no problem if she spent a little time on a side issue. Anna Anaconda could always work harder. She found ways to fine-tune the pseudogene sequencing and spent the hours she saved tinkering with her puzzle. Finally she decided to get a second opinion from Sonia Blanchard, an older woman who had tried (as far as Anna could be mothered) to take the postgrad under her wing.

Sonia was a middle-aged woman who'd dropped out to bring up her children and returned to work with an easy-going attitude. She and her minions reared clone mice from embryos that had been injected with strange genes; killed them, squashed them, and spun them; extracted their eggs and sperm, gouged fresh embryos from their bellies, snipped away their testicles, all in the cause of a pharmacopoeia of cures for human infertility. The mice appeared to bear her no ill will. They liked Sonia. They seemed to listen for her voice; they were more relaxed and more active when she was in their lab.

Anna found her standing dreamily by the mouse cages, while an xx sry mouse called Harry—a transgenic female, induced to develop as an infertile male—climbed and whiskered busily between her gloved hands.

"Sonia, I've got a problem with my normal men."

"Surprise me," drawled Sonia.

"Would you have a look?"

"What would you say," asked Sonia ruminatively, without moving, "if someone offered to turn you into a man? Temporarily, no operations, everything functional. Just for a week or two, so you could try out the equipment."

"It sounds like a computer game. I'd say no thanks."

"Our Harry likes it fine, don't you love? She gives her little kit a good work-out. All to no avail, eh? She's shooting blanks, poor lass." The mouse clung to Sonia's fingers, berry eyes gleaming. "Some day soon, we'll be able to make a Harry with fertile sperm. Next thing, we'll be injecting fertility into any male customer that still has the bits, and we won't even need to work out what his problem was… There's no such thing as normal, Anna. You ought to know that. Variation's something you have to filter out: deletions, damage, bases knocked off, stuck together wrong way round, extra ones tacked on. Do you really want me to suit up?"

Spermatogenesis Factor, SGF, was the main event in Nirmal's lab: Anna's project was boring. Ordinarily, she'd have let it go. But her curiosity had been roused.

"I know about random variation. This is *the same* variation, over and over again."

Sonia dumped Harry back in her cage. "Let's have a look."

Anti-contamination precautions in Nirmal's lab were rigorous. Sonia dressed to match Anna, in a clean room suit, mask, gloves, and goggles.

"Tell me what I'm supposed to be looking for."

"It's here. You can't get the modern sample to line up with the gorilla and the ancient Provencal DNA. Something's missing. I've been getting the same result, a missing chunk of bases in the same location, in nearly every modern sample."

"Mmm. Could be you've run into a local population thing, but it's not likely. Men are the same the world over, did your mother ever tell you? The Y's a genetic fossil, owing to the pattern of sexual inheritance, it doesn't get messed around much. Are you sure you've not been accidentally testing the same bugger over and over again?"

"The point of that French survey is that it's individuals, each with a medical and familial profile. I'm sure as I can be. Now look at this. I think the missing bases have moved. They've shifted to the X chromosome. Okay, not so strange, you get illegitimate interchange between the X and the Y when they pair up for meiosis: a Y pseudogene might hybridize with part of the analogous functional X gene. But this isn't in a gene sequence, and it's weird to find the same chunk of Y moving to the same locale on the X, over and over again. What would do that?"

The two women stared at the glowing hieroglyphs.

"It's that medieval DNA," said Sonia. "I know Nirmal doesn't trust the stuff. It'll be contaminated?" She frowned, and looked at Anna suspiciously. "How've you done all this?" she demanded. "I thought you'd hardly started on the Huit Bories comparison."

Anna blushed behind her mask. "I've speeded things up. I've improved the HPLC automation—"

"Wooee— Does Nirmal know you've been reprogramming his machines?"

"Oh yes. He helped me do it. We're using a simpler algorithm—"

"Well, okay. Never mind your algorithm. Let's have a closer look—"

"Could it be a transposon? Barbara McClintock says—"

"You've got Barbara McClintock on the brain." Everyone knew about Anna and her vegetable fixation. She was close-mouthed on personal topics, always ready to talk about crop genetics. Barbara McClintock, the woman who had discovered—working on maize, long ago—that chunks of DNA could "jump" or switch around, moving from one chromosomal location to another (a concept that had led to such marvels as the sixty day tropical potato) was Anna's idol. Sonia peered and then stood back.

"Is this relevant to your investigation?"

"Not exactly."

"Then forget it. Put down what you were supposed to find here, you can get it from the Melbourne team's sequencing. It doesn't matter, Anna. Parentis is only doing the pure research bit for show. There's nothing in it for infertility; it's not your business."

"Yes, but—"

Sonia scratched the back of her neck with a slick gloved finger. "I'm sure it's an experimental artifact. Contamination. I wouldn't your waste time over it."

— —

A few days later, when the two women were the last to leave at the end of a long evening's work, Sonia came up to Anna with a fake and conscious smile. "Fancy a drink?"

They went to a pub called The Goldfish, which stood on the edge of the blasted heath of urban wilderness (supermarkets with bars on the windows, boarded up derelict houses) that surrounded the science park. Sonia chatted, telling funny stories that had reached her about the customers. The woman who brought her baby to have blue eye genes injected, genuinely believing the brown eyes flaw could easily be rectified. The other young "woman" who came along with her male partner and turned out when undressed to be physiologically male in every respect, which explained the infertility but left you wondering what went through two people's heads. . .? The men, and they were not rare, who wanted more children but who clinically couldn't be the fathers of the children they already had—

"I mean, how daft can you get? Imagine letting him pay for infertility investigation, without telling him the truth. But there you go. The biggest genetic factor in Human Assisted Reproduction is the gene for having more money than sense."

"D'you think there's really a problem?"

"What, you mean the infertility epidemic? Sperm count down? Nah. It's market forces. All the people who used to accept the inevitable are out buying a solution, that's what makes the statistics jump. Still, I've never had to worry about being infertile so I can't talk. Must be a bastard; it obviously drives people potty."

At the last moment Sonia came out with what she wanted to say. She had twice looked at her watch and declared that she would have to go, when she leaned over and put a hand on Anna's arm. "Don't cross Nirmal, love."

Anna laughed. "I don't cross anyone, I just get on with it."

"No, I'm serious. He likes you. I've seen him watching you work and the way he treats you in the meetings. I've never seen him so interested and polite with a postgrad. But *don't cross him*, because he won't stand for it. D'you know what I mean?"

"I'm not sure I do."

The crowd in front of the big screen football roared at a missed goal. Sonia automatically glanced that way, as she remarked casually: "I heard you were supposed to've got a brilliant first."

Anna shrugged.

"But you didn't because you had boyfriend trouble: and that was why you didn't go into plant genetics, chasing up your blessed potato transposons."

Anna thought she should practice gossiping about other people, to desensitize herself. She bit her lip and tried to look unconcerned.

"I'm not being funny, but it's not a good idea to spend your whole time talking about some other area, as if the chief's specialty doesn't grab you. Concentrate on the work you've been given." She shook her head, with a rueful, maternal smile. "You struck lucky, really love. If you're ambitious, it's probably better that you're not in the same line as your boyfriend. Well, I could stay a bit, after all. Like another?"

"Sorry, I'm saving my pennies. I want to get out of debt."

Sonia gave a hollow laugh.

Anna understood that she had been given a serious warning. But she was Anna Anaconda. If there was a problem, she would swallow it. She was incapable of leaving a puzzle unsolved.

◆ ◆

She didn't like being in Human Assisted Reproduction. She wanted to be building better potatoes, work that made sense for the world. Yet Lavinia had been right. Irrational, central, alluring: human genetic material had a glory about it. Sometimes, in the exacting tedium of her days, it would come to her like an epiphany that she stood within the highest sanctuary, holding the fire from heaven. In one of these moments, she turned—having sensed that someone was watching her—and found KM Nirmal standing there. Her conversations with her supervisor had been few and functional. Nirmal did not like to be tête à tête with anyone. He liked to talk at length only in meetings, where the element of personal interaction was safely diluted. He smiled, and his thin lips became beautiful. Anna knew she had not cleared the dazzled brightness from her eyes. She blushed, because it felt as if he'd read her mind.

"Sonia tells me you've been finding anomalies that you haven't brought up in meetings."

Thanks a lot, Sonia.

"There's something I'm noticing," she agreed. "I don't know if it means anything."

"Well, you must log it. With exactitude. Keep good records."

"Of course."

"But concentrate on the task in hand. Please. That is what I expect of you." He touched the canister that held the contemporary male samples. "These are human lives, Anna. *Courage and ability and sighing. . .* Never forget that. We deal in human lives. There is nothing more important."

— —

She had been with Parentis for months before she noticed the sperm whales. They were on the doors, the walls, on people's security badges. They decorated the unofficial official notepaper, courtesy of an original design by Ron Voight (f), the younger of the two post-docs. They were on post-its, fridge magnets, photos cut out of newsprint, pointillist "virtual reality" posters to infuriate the stereogramically challenged. They hung from the ceiling—Nirmal did not like this— as mobiles. When she finally saw them, Anna thought: *I have been ill!* It was another kind of epiphany. She went out and bought herself a sperm whale coffee mug.

— —

Nirmal told Anna to prepare a paper for a postgraduate symposium, to be held at the university in the summer term. It would be her maiden speech. The private meeting in which they discussed the symposium was, in Nirmal's usual style, very short: but he emphasized, with his rare and beautiful smile, that this was an opportunity to try her wings. Anna decided to write up her "Transferred Y" phenomenon. She had been working on it, quietly but obstinately, alongside the official project, and she was now convinced that what she saw was genuine, and genuinely puzzling.

She could have a paper on the pseudogenes in reserve, if Nirmal disapproved.

She scoured the publications, online and in print. As far as she could discover she was the only person who had observed this tiny anomaly, which wasn't surprising since the variant was probably restricted to a certain population in a small area in France. She noticed that not much work of any kind had been done on human transposons. She tried to curb her excitement and had dreams about walking on empty space.

It was a damned fine change from the dreams she'd had after Charles had raped her.

She worked very hard but did not feel overworked. She was full of energy, adrenalin, and fear. The way she felt about Transferred Y reminded her of that wonderful sexual time with Spence, except that the point about being with Spence had been that there was no risk, only pleasure. But the feeling of being at *full stretch* was the same.

The symposium was in June, in a large science lecture hall. It was too large, for Anna's taste, by orders of magnitude. She had known that the meeting was open to the public, but she had not foreseen a substantial audience. Perhaps all these people were friends and relations of the other postgrad maidens. Anna hadn't thought of inviting her own parents and felt guilty. Maybe they'd have liked to be here.

She went outside, to recover her calm. She did not frequent the university much. She'd had very little contact with her academic supervisor: which suited Anna fine. If she socialized it was with the Parentis team, watching Sports tv at The Goldfish. When she went home it was to Roz, Shannon, and Graham the Rugby-playing boyfriend. She counted herself as a working stiff: not a student, simply a poorly paid lab technician. Leeds campus was high, flat, and monochrome, obedient to a different modernism and a different past: she was glad it woke no nostalgia for that wooded valley far in the south. The weather was miserable, the sky a cold and distant plane. She walked around for a while and then went to present herself to the organizers. And here I am, she thought. I'm going to give my first paper. She ran over the presentation in her mind, felt a thundering of stage fright in her belly, and tried to relax. The program said she was on late in the afternoon. Most people might have left. Good!

"Who are you again?"

"Anna Senoz. From Parentis."

She deposited copies of her paper. The young woman had a mobile phone to her ear and was making facial gestures triggered by the voice Anna couldn't hear.

"Well, hello Anna. I'm Lorraine. We've talked on the phone. Everything all right?"

"Fine."

"Got everything you need, OHP okay for you? You're on with Eswin Holmes and Teresa Vickramsingh, questions at the end of the three papers, hope that's all right, we thought it would move things along better."

The young man next to Lorraine looked up. "So you're from Parentis. Where they do the animal experiments?" He was wearing a mulberry velour jacket and a deep yellow ruffled shirt. His hair was a cockscomb of chestnut curls, his expression imperious.

Anna ignored him. "Yes, questions at the end will be fine."

Mulberry jacket raised his voice. "I didn't want your paper on the program. What can we learn about human beings by torturing small furry animals, exactly?"

"Quite a lot, in fact."

"Now you're going to tell me it's vital medical research. Is it fuck. Human fertility treatment ought to be illegal. Look around you: do we *need* more human beings? You're just the kind of amoral, money-loving parasite who gives science a bad name."

"Ian," broke in Lorraine, waving her phone at him. "Can you help Professor Reeves? They're having trouble with the sound system." Ian glared at Anna and left, scraping back his chair and striding off in long-legged contempt. "I'm sorry that had to happen," apologized his colleague. "He's a jerk. I'm sure he didn't mean to undermine you."

At least he didn't fancy me, thought Anna. She'd have been far more scared if Ian had tried to flirt, although she had recovered completely from that horrible experience with Charles. But Charles must have been feeling deeply hostile to Anna on that hateful evening, so even if they don't flirt they could still attack... A horror ran through her, turning her blood to ice water. The foyer outside the lecture hall suddenly revealed its true nature: the scuffed terrazzo floor, battered doors with panels of meshed fireproof glass, tattered fly-posting, a drinks machine with plastic cups spilling from a bin. The smell of studenthood, the stink of shame and loss, assaulted her. She went into the hall and took a place in the middle of a back row, so that Ian in the mulberry jacket couldn't corner her. He wouldn't be able to get her into a room by herself. She was safe.

She spent the lunch break lurking in the crowd, unmolested. In the middle of the afternoon she went down to the front and presented herself in good time. Professor Reeves of Computer Science, who was running the symposium, greeted her distractedly.

"Who are you?" His grey curly hair fizzed with anxiety.

"I'm Anna Senoz, from Parentis."

"Good, good. Now look, er, Anna, we're running late, it's going to be very unfair on the last group, so could you make it short. Get through your stuff in fifteen minutes, instead of twenty. Can you do that for me, love?"

"Of course."

"Good girl! Now where the hell's Eswin? Anyone here seen Terry Vick?"

She scanned her pages and made instant cuts. It was better this way: hustled, badgered, no time to think. It would be no worse than talking to a nearly empty hall, the way she'd imagined. There was no one here remotely interested in Transferred Y. This was a rehearsal, harmless as practicing in front of the mirror. Her heart beat wildly, she felt like a half-fledged bird crouched on the rim of the nest: "*Ca, mon ame, il faut partir. . .*" Who said that? Rene Descartes, as he lay dying. My soul, we must go. But she was not dying, she was being born. She was about to join the edifice, the organism, thousands of years, to which she had given her life and heart. To speak and be heard. She checked the OHP, made sure her acetates were in order—and saw KM Nirmal, sitting erect in the middle of the front row. She hardly recognized him. He was wearing a very smart suit. She'd never seen him except in a lab coat or a shabby sports jacket. He hadn't said a word about attending the symposium. Her head started to spin. To speak in front of Nirmal was *completely different.*

She began.

That evolution is still a mysterious process, with many unsuspected byways, and perhaps she had found an example of one of these.

That her predecessors in sequencing the Y chromosome had worked like this.

That she was analyzing samples of DNA from healthy, normally fertile contemporary human males and from recovered medieval tissue.

That her technique was like this (including the tweaked modeling program).

That she had repeatedly observed an exchange of the same sequence of bases, between the Y and the X chromosomes in the modern samples. That she had found no sign of this polymorphism in human male DNA from a similar geographic location at an earlier date. (The Huit Bories samples.) Further investigation was indicated. Was there a female version of Transferred Y, passed on by affected males to their daughters?

Meanwhile here was a distinctive genetic variation, apparently fitness-neutral, that had established itself in a human population in a relatively short time. How this happened—if it was not disproven by further evidence—and whether there were other instances of the same mechanism, continued studies might reveal.

The previous speaker, Eswin Holmes (Bacteriostatic Effects of Food Preservation) had overrun his fifteen minutes a little. Therefore, after about thirteen minutes and a quarter, Professor Reeves started making urgent *wind it up!* signals. Anna wound it up. She was pleased with herself for being in control enough to do that and still more or less make sense. No one was listening, anyway—except presumably Nirmal. She dared, as she delivered her final sentence, to risk a timid glance in his direction. He was staring right at Anna, his eyes blazing with naked fury. As she watched, horrorstruck, he got to his feet, pushed his way along the row, and marched out of the hall.

There were no questions.

The symposium had been on a Saturday. Nirmal kept her waiting for a week before he called her to his office. No one else mentioned the symposium except Ron Butler (m), who made an attempt to congratulate her on breaking her duck. Anna thought the delay was a refinement of cruelty; she realized later that Nirmal had been giving himself a chance to calm down. The worst part was that Anna hadn't an idea what she had done wrong. He'd accepted her Transferred Y outline without comment, merely telling her to carry on, and she'd been too unsure to ask to talk it over. She'd handed him a copy of her final draft and waited hopefully for his input. She'd been disappointed when he failed to make any response, but it was typical of Nirmal. The best and worst thing about the interview itself was that every-thing became very clear very quickly.

"So, Miss Senoz. I gather that the work we have been doing to-gether has been far from worthy of your undivided attention. When I suggested that you give a paper at the Young Scientists' symposium, I think I had a right to assume that your presentation would focus on the doctoral project you are undertaking with my supervision."

"I'm sorry," she whispered.

"But no. Your mind is elsewhere." He lifted a copy of Anna's Transferred Y paper and slapped it down on his desk as if he hoped to break all its bones. "If it cannot be distorted into the service of your much more interesting private preoccupations, your work in this lab does not engage you at all. I trusted you implicitly! It was extremely, extremely unpleasant for me to discover, in public, that you had cho-sen to present a peculiar hobbyhorse of your own—"

Anna was dumbfounded. It dawned on her that Nirmal had not read her outline or her paper. Of course, he'd assumed he *had* read it. He knew everything she'd been doing on the pseudogenes. He'd as-sumed she would be going over that ground. He had not made time to check up on her, or it had slipped his mind, or he'd let it go because he hated one-on-one meetings. She stared at her hands, clasped in her lap to stop them shaking, and wondered, how on earth did someone as allergic to personal contact as Nirmal get to be a postgraduate adviser?

It wasn't because she was a girl; he was as distant with the male members of the team. Everybody complained about it.

That's science for you. The better you are at what you do, the more time you're doomed to spend doing things you're no good at. Her terror was strangely dissipated. *No way* was she going to remind him that he'd told her she could do what she liked. *No way* was she going to point out that he'd had every opportunity to find out and had omitted to make sure he knew what his student was going to say in her first public appearance.

"Until you are free to return to your beloved potatoes," Nirmal was saying, with withering politeness. "I expect you to concentrate *mainly* on the tasks in hand here."

Anna nodded: accepting her lessons. Anything you say in the lab, your supervisor is going to hear. Anything you do, it is your responsibility to make sure your supervisor knows about it. Don't take chances with the natural human vanity of your boss.

"Professor Reeves intends to publish a transcript of the colloquium. Needless to say, *this* will not feature. It will never be published. I cannot consider putting my name to it."

She nodded again. She was no longer devastated. She knew he would not be unfair in his personal record. Neither of them would say it, but he knew he'd been neglectful.

"I'm sorry," she said, standing up. "I got carried away. It won't happen again."

"Good. I hope I can trust you from now on."

She reached for the paper. Nirmal's thin hand came down upon it, the nails almond shaped and calcined, thick as seashells. He didn't speak, so she headed for the door.

"Oh, Anna—"

She quailed. What now?

"This is very good work," said her supervisor dryly, tapping the Transferred Y paper. "Wrong-headed, even absurd, in the implications, which you wisely didn't spell out. But bold, original, well-reasoned, and well-presented. Your technical work is also very good. You have a formidable talent, young lady. But you must focus. Focus!"

"Thank you," she muttered. "Thank you, I'm sorry, I will."

"A formidable talent," repeated Nirmal. "Don't waste it!"

➤ ➤

That summer Anna spent several months helping to install a Parentis clinic in a city in West Africa. It was the first time she'd been abroad, apart from Greece with Daz. In Africa most people who couldn't have children were infertile for obvious reasons: AIDS-related problems, uterine scarring from other sexually transmitted disease, sperm and egg cells deformed by parental poverty or exposure to heavy agricultural chemicals, non-sexually transmitted infectious diseases, parasites that took their toll of the reproductive system, FGM side-effects. Identifying sex chromosomal problems would not be a high priority. But it was crucial for Parentis's deal with the government that this clinic should provide the full service. Anna helped to see the sequencing lab set up and trained the local technicians. After the first month she traveled a lot, usually alone. She spent her time showing paramedics in corrugated iron shacks how to avoid contamination when taking DNA samples from pregnant women and how to store them by a new method that didn't involve refrigeration. She brought the samples back to the city and helped to prove that the refrigeration-free storage was effective, by preparing, cloning, and sequencing the DNA.

You didn't have to be an eco-terrorist to see that the whole thing was nonsense, as far as the health and future of the African country-women and their children were concerned. The more-money-than-sense gene is everywhere. But the work was interesting, and you met some nice people. You could pack a lot of human warmth into two or three village days. And in spite of everything, the sensation of being at the forefront was fun. Of course Africans should spend their tax money on sensible things. But whoever heard of a government in the so-called developed world that did that?

When she returned to Leeds there was a message on her email from wol@tim.net, inviting her to a weekend party, a college reunion (Wol's words), loosely intended to celebrate the Millennium, plus his and Rosey's January birthdays. The same evening Rosey MacCarthy rang her and insisted that she sign up. Anna had had practically no contact with *they all* since finals, but she said yes. She was afraid she was bound to regret this. But she was feeling different after Africa, and that interview with Nirmal had left a slow burn of warmth (a formidable talent. . .). She thought she could bear to meet her friends again.

The SDF team now had a transgenic female-to-male mouse (only one so far) with testes that produced sperm. There was something wrong: s/he still wasn't fertile. But the pace was heating up. Everyone was anxiously shadowing the work of the Melbourne team, their closest rivals. The team leader Down Under was a man called Pat McCreevy, an old sparring partner (or professional enemy) of Nirmal's, which made the race edgy... A new postdoc had come to Leeds Parentis, a young woman called Meg Methal, who was a union activist. She told Nirmal that Anna could make better money for shorter hours doing piecework in a clothing sweatshop and that he ought to get Parentis to pay her a fat royalty for the work she'd done on speeding up the machines. Nirmal considered these jokes in poor taste.

"You shouldn't let them brainwash you," insisted Meg, as she and Anna worked side by side. "I know how it works and *it's all one way.* Old Nirmal expects total loyalty from you, you won't get any bloody thing back from him, and I'm not being sexist. I've had women bosses, they're just the same——"

Anna let the chatter wash over her. She had been looking at DNA samples from the Cameroon pregnancy clinic. Just out of curiosity, she had decided to find out how they would react to her Transferred Y sequence probes.

It was there.

Impossible as it might seem, this young Cameroonian woman and her female fetus, chosen at random, seemed to have the Transferred Y chunk of bases, harmlessly inserted into a non-coding sequence on one of their X chromosomes. The hair on the back of Anna's neck prickled and tried to stand. What could it possibly mean?

"You say something?"

"Nothing, just muttering to myself."

Defy Nirmal? Demand more money and better working conditions? No thank you! Meg Methal was right, no doubt, but following her banner would be far more costly to Anna's career than the dominion of an autocratic boss. Besides, since the day he gave her back her honor, Anna had begun to feel for KM Nirmal exactly the loyalty that the feudal society of lab science demanded. She was a samurai, she must serve some lord or other. When SDF was in a less intense phase, she would talk to Nirmal again about Transferred Y. She knew he would listen. Until then, she bowed to his will.

Andantino

— i —

Wol and Rosey's birthday-Millennium-house party was held on Beevey Island in the Thames Estuary, in a Victorian gothic pile called Carstairs Lodge, which sat among the reed beds like an uprooted public library set down on an alien planet. The island was a bird sanctuary; when the Lodge wasn't being rented no one lived there except the warden. It was the second week of January, and the weather was not propitious. When Spence arrived, on the Saturday morning, rain was lashing the estuary, and there was half a gale blowing. Wol had come over in the birdman's launch to fetch him—along with Yesha Craven, Simon's girlfriend, who'd also been unable to make it for Friday evening. The shore party returned at an awkward juncture. Persons unknown had made a private midnight feast out of birthday delicacies, and Rosey had just discovered the depredations: missing bottles of Veuve Cliquot, nothing left of the paté de foíe that was meant to go with the braised quail, the frozen soft fruit for Wol's famous pavlova vanished. There was no sign of Anna Senoz in the old fashioned kitchen. Spence scanned the faces, wondering if it were possible he didn't recognize her.

"Fucking outrageous!" yelled Rosey. "What kind of friends did I invite—"

Nobody was owning up. Those trying to get their breakfast moved about with cowed heads and lowered eyes, while Rosey turned her wrath on poor Wol, who would just have to go back over the river and go shopping—

"Look, Rosey," countered Yesha, bravely. "It isn't so bad. We'll survive—"

"That's not the point! The point is the disgusting, anti-social, intolerable—"

"I don't think I can get the man to take the launch out again," pleaded Wol. The island could be reached by car at low tide, but that wasn't any use at the moment.

Anna, with Simon Gough, walked in on this scene, dripping hard.

Spence received her arrival like a shot of liquor, like an infusion of warmth in his soul. Her nose was red. One black, soaked curl streaked her right cheek. He was both glad and sorry to note that she was wearing pants. He hoped she was the same Anna, knew he was a different Spence. If he'd timed things better he might have copped a hello how are you hug. Too late now.

"Hi Spence," said Simon, "Dig the dreads."

Anna smiled. "Hi, Spence."

She and Simon and Yesha exchanged glances and retreated together into the hall. And that would be the pattern, Spence realized, of this weekend that was already half over. Confusion: social blur with people he didn't know any more, no chance of making contact with the only person who mattered.

◄► ◄►

Simon and Anna had been early risers. In this gathering of smart, Bohemian young Londoners, a northern-nerds-in-suits camaraderie united them—though Simon had given up *his* doctorate and was now rich, working as a systems analyst for a power company. They had set out into the wind and rain, nerdishly determined to see the sea, since they were at the seaside, but had been driven back. In these conditions Beevey Island was no beauty spot. There was nothing out there but a waste of shingle, reeds, and brambles.

"I'm fucking glad it wasn't me got at the champagne," said Simon. Tall Yesha squeezed her palms across his rain-silvered head, shaking rivulets from her fingers. Anna remembered her from third year, when she'd been living in the house where Simon had his strange glass studio. She was from Birmingham; she'd been doing Media Studies. Now, according to Simon, she was into Modern Dance. She was immensely thin, muscular, and chic: almost as scary-looking as the Londoners. But her smile was full of unassuming friendliness.

"Fuck, yes. I'm terrified of Rosey."

"What about our Spence with dreadlocks," said Simon. "Hey, d'you think it's true about him being gay? Ramone says it's definite."

"What?" said Anna. The rabid one had arrived at the river pier in a very fancy gun-metal Porsche, with Daz and Tex, Daz's comic-book-artist boyfriend; a monkey on a lead and a parrot in a cage. She seemed to be in an angry phase: she was ignoring Anna. "How would Ramone know that?"

"Well, he's been living in Morocco. Didn't you know? Been getting the occasional email from him, from the weirdest places. You don't go to Tangier to pull birds, do you?"

Spence came out of the kitchen. "We need to dry off," said Yesha, hugging Simon. "Catch you later, Spence. Nice to meet yer." The couple hurried away upstairs.

The stained glass in the stairwell caught a fugitive ray of sunlight. Clear amber, from robes of an allegorical figure called Harvest, gleamed in Anna's eyes.

"Hey, Anna. I'm ridiculously pleased to see you."

She nodded. "You too. I mean me too. I'm all wet. I'd better go and change."

➤ ➤

Saturday night was riotous, the banquet so splendid even Rosey forgot her losses. Anna slept well, eventually. When she woke it was bright daylight. She lay listening to the shouting of the gulls outside her window and thought she was in Regis Passage again. So Spence was gay now. Simon's cheery deduction seemed like settled fact, like something she had always known. Oh well. Thank God she'd found out before she made any dumb moves. It was still good to see him again: good to see *they all*, in spite of the whacking price tag. . . Rosey and Wol had always been expensive company. Veuve Cliquot, my God: and she would have to pay her way. Couldn't bear not to.

She went down to the kitchen and made herself a cup of tea. No one else was stirring. The Common Room, a huge cavern next to the kitchen, was strewn with remnants of the night's revels: a grey funereal mound in the log-burning fireplace; glasses, smeared plates on the long table; overflowing ashtrays. By the double-glazed French doors that overlooked the estuary stood a battered grand piano, open. Someone had been playing Gilbert and Sullivan.

Anna had gone to bed at four, after dazedly helping Wol to finish the crossword in a copy of the *Telegraph* that they'd found in the log basket. She remembered strains of the chorus of the peers from *Iolanthe*, rising to her attic. She tried the keys: looked inside the piano stool and discovered an album of easy classical pieces. As she started to play, carefully and slowly, someone opened the door of the room. Presumably the person retreated, because Anna felt nothing but quiet behind her. She finished her piece, turned, and stretched: and Spence was there, curled sideways in an armchair, watching her. He smiled. She started to play again, remembering Spence's inimitable laziness—

"How's Cesf?"

"He's okay, I guess. I've been away you know, but Mom sends me bulletins. He's slowing down a tad. Getting kind of elderly." Spence's voice took a downward turn; it was a sore point. Why can't pets live forever?

"We're none of us getting any younger."

He laughed, as she had meant him to. The mean age of the Carstairs party was around twenty-three and a quarter. For the second time she reached the repeat of the phrase, so obvious and yet so tender, that led to the final resolution. There. Not good, but better.

"What's that called? It's lovely."

"It's by Mozart. Andantino, K236. I did it for a grade exam."

"I never knew you could play the piano."

"I can't, not really. I had lessons for years, but I haven't practiced in ages."

"Play it again?"

"Okay."

It was hard to believe that he had not seen her since they'd kissed goodbye, the night before she left for Greece with Daz. He had known that he still desired her, in theory. He had not known that he'd feel like this: that his breathing would slow and his mind grow quiet, simply because she was there. He felt like the Manchurian Candidate, as if someone had spoken the magic word and plunged him into a hypnotic trance. But what could he do? Not a thing, probably.

"What did you do for the actual Millennium?"

Anna shrugged. "Nothing much."

She had seen the new era in with Graham and Roz and Shannon and their friends. They'd gone out to cheer the municipal fireworks and returned to watch some of the wave of tv excitement passing round the world.

"Me neither. Did you think it was important?"

"Well, yes I did," said Anna, still playing. "For about a minute and a half. I thought maybe the heavens would open and God would say, come on you lot, time's up. But then I got over it."

He laughed. She remembered it had been easy to make him laugh—

"Did you enjoy yourself last night?"

"I suppose."

"I was proud of you, the way you tackled those charades."

"Oh, I was drunk," she said. "I don't remember much about it."

The music finished. Spence sat up. "It's not raining. I was thinking of taking a walk, to freshen my hangover. D'you want to come along?" At that moment, malignly on cue, in walked Ramone, with Tex the fake cowboy in tow.

"Hi there," said Ramone. After one mean glance she turned her back on Spence. "I'm glad you're not doing anything, Anna 'cos Tex wants to draw you. It won't take long."

"Got my sketch pad right here," drawled the cowboy, holding up an A4 cartridge pad. "Anyone have a pencil? Piece of charcoal from the fire would do fine." His little blue eyes roved insolently over Anna. "I can take her right here."

Spence had been wondering what he was supposed to do about the guy with the fake accent. Was it a joke? Was "Tex" on the run from the law? His amusement flipped, in an instant, into hatred. He stood up, feeling an urge to punch Ramone's hired gun in his smug, blond, stubbly, undercut jaw—

"Stay where you are, Anna," ordered Ramone. "Tex can have Spence's chair. Did you say you were going for a walk, Spence? I'll come with you."

Ramone and Spence walked out into the chill and fair morning. A track of packed shingle ran round the island, crossing the Carstairs Lodge approach. They followed this, the breeze in their faces. "It's turning out nice," said Ramone, with a baleful sideways grin. "This place used to be used to fatten up cattle, that's why it's called Beevey Island. Can't imagine it, can you? Are you pissed off with me? I hope I didn't interrupt anything."

She *looked* far more different than Anna. She had a prison crop with scarlet stencils, tight black jeans and a celtic knot tattoo around her throat. But coming back to old friends is like watching trees grow: she was still Mr Toad in petticoats, his bad fairy.

"Why, gee no, Ramone. Interrupting what? What could have given you that idea?"

"Ha."

He had determined to march her right round the island (he had no idea how long this would take), in revenge for his lost chance. Ramone had other plans. As soon as they were out of sight of the house she sat down with a thump on the shingle, among the blue prickly weeds, the shards of bleached wood, the lumps of tar that looked like ancient shit. A flock of handsome black and white birds with orange bills rose from the foreshore and belted off across the sky.

"I've seen you looking at her," she said. "Oh yes. And her looking back. While the rest of those fuckers are yakking over the swanky food, you two have something much hotter going on. Don't think no one notices. It's touching. Like Alan Bates and whatsername in *Far From The Madding Crowd.* Whenever you look up, I will be there, and whenever I look up, you will be there."

Spence stretched himself out, after checking for oil turds. "Julie Christie. I didn't think she made a great Bathsheba. Too blah-pretty. I don't know what you're talking about. I haven't seen or spoken to Anna since my Exchange year. There's nothing going on."

"Yeah. Sure. How do you find her, anyway. Think she's changed?"

He thought about it. "Older," he reported, prosaically. "Poised. Lot more of what she had, which is the kind of confidence that doesn't have to push or yell or stick itself in anyone's face. I think she's been doing things that have proved to her that she's the person she hoped to be."

"Hnnph." Ramone poked Spence in the ribs with a piece of driftwood. "You think Anna is self-confident? You are so wrong. I'll tell you what Anna is like. She's an over-intelligent, literal-minded *good girl*. She believes in Santa Claus, the Easter Bunny, and the Ten Commandments. She tries to be legal, decent, honest. . . and when she runs foul of the real world that expects her to turn her girly trick and take the money, she blames herself and tries harder. I'll tell you something, Spence." Another jab in the ribs. "You think I'm a pathetic raving in-your-face maniac, but *I'm* okay. It's women like Anna who suffer for being born female."

"Is that a fact?"

Ramone picked shreds of tar from the grain of her weapon. "It's a fact. You know, much as I despise my parents, I owe them. I've come to see they gave me something money can't buy. No one ever gave my Dad any shit and got thanked for it. When anyone insults me, I don't wonder where I went wrong. I smack them in the mouth."

He had never heard Ramone speak about her family. "Do you have brothers and sisters?"

"Several, my mum's favorite occupation was natural childbirth. They're all pigs."

He studied one of the glaucous blue-leaved shore plants, a thing so thorny and hostile you could read the cruelty of its environment written there, as if in mirror writing. "Did your Mom used to give your Dad shit?" he asked, casually. "Did you and the other kids?"

Ramone laughed. "Fuck off, Spence."

She continued her tar picking. Spence pictured Anna as a Dorothea Brooke, a highbrow young goddess hellbent on abnegation, taken in by some Victorian ideal of a woman's noble destiny. It fit ominously well. Had she found her Mr Casuabon, her worthless idol? Maybe she had. Maybe she was at this party on a handmaiden's weekend off. More birds passed over: big geese flying in formation, their wings making an exhilarating noise. They both looked up, faces briefly transfigured.

"Why'd you come back from Morocco for, anyway?"

"I got a job offer, working on the net: decided to take it up."

"Groveling to the bosses after all, eh? So now you're going to make your fortune."

"Nah. The only things on the net that make money are gossip, genealogy, and porn: the good old meat and potatoes."

Ramone smiled bitterly. "I noticed that. The mediation is coded female. I *prophesied* that. D'you remember an essay I wrote, in first year?"

"Um, no." He decided, since he was trapped like this, to make use of her. "Is it true about Anna and Charles Craft? Wol tells me they were an item, in final year."

Ramone gave him a strange look, dull and deep.

"Something happened to Anna," she said at last. "No one knows what. She was her favorite lecturer's pet. She was supposed to get a first, she had a prime postgrad place with her name on it. Straight after finals she headed off to Manchester. None of us heard from her for months, and she didn't get that great a degree. Then she reappears working for a baby-farming outfit (and I *know* she would never do that of her own free will) and doesn't want to have anything to do with anyone she ever knew. Daz kept trying to get her to come to London, but she wouldn't. I used to write to her from Paris. The only answers I got were fucking little good girl thank-you notes so I gave up. It was me who put Wol and Rosey up to asking her here. We didn't think she'd accept. Didn't you know about any of this, Spence?"

He shook his head. "Me, I know nothing."

"Thought you didn't. Knowing won't help though. You're not going to score. She's off sex. I *know.* I knew the moment I saw her."

Spence sighed in exasperation. "Knock it off. I don't have a relationship with Anna, except that she's an old friend I like and admire. But if I did I don't see how it's your business. What's Anna to you? You have a love-life. . . You and Daz and that revolting cowboy comic-artist. A hot threesome, I hear. Isn't that enough?"

Ramone grinned slowly. "Oh, *more* than enough: believe it. But you want Anna, so do I: and I'm going to win. Forget Charles Craft, Spence. I'm your rival, and the prize is Anna's soul." Glaring at him, she flung her piece of driftwood—obviously meant to represent

Spence's chances in this imaginary contest. It should have plunged hopelessly into the sea: but Ramone could not throw, and the breeze was against her. It landed by Spence's feet.

"I'm going back. I'm fucking freezing, and Tex has had time to roger your girlfriend up, down, and sideways. He's a quick worker."

Spence watched her marching off in the wrong direction, into the cruel wind and gathering rain, until his soft heart got the better of him, and he got up and ran after. "Hey, Ramone, you're heading the wrong way!"

➤ ➤

Anna allowed Tex to draw her, if that was what he was doing, for about ten minutes. When he suggested they should go upstairs, so she could undress and he could "get her tits," she made her excuses and left. Outside the Common Room she met Yesha.

"Don't go in there, Yesh. The cowboy is looking for life models. I just escaped."

"Oh God! I know. He did that number on me. Did he want you to go upstairs? That's where he keeps the baby oil, he sez."

"Is he really from the States?"

"Nah. He's from Sheffield. His real name is Arnold, Arnold Yutt. Daz told me."

The two young women burst into angry, defensive laughter.

"He was Daz's boyfriend first," went on Yesha in an undertone. "Ramone met him at the comics convention in Anglouême, when she was living in Paris working as a film extra or something. They started collaborating on this horrible French comic called *Mère Noire*, have you seen it, it's *disgusting*, so anti-women. I thought she used to be a feminist. Anyway, Wol says Ramone's now trying to cut Tex out—"

The day passed easily. People drifted in and out of the kitchen, where Wol started opening bottle after bottle of very drinkable Beaujolais Villages. White powder was cut on the massive tabletop, white pills passed from hand to hand. Spence and Anna did not partake of any Class A, Spence because he was trying to live a purer life, Anna because she couldn't buy her round. But they were as convivial as the rest. Gossip was gossiped, reminiscence flowed. Marnie Choy and her very young boyfriend Kieran, a children's television presenter, told tales from behind the tv scenes. Shane Clancy, once the star of the Drama Club, told jokes against himself, about the joys of impersonating a noted brand of toilet cleaner, in a giant plastic squeezy suit. Shane's rich boyfriend and Lucy Freeman's fiancé, Duncan-the-suit, recounted hideous stories of the trading floor... Ramone had vanished again after her walk with Spence; Tex too. Daz had not been seen at all. Late in the afternoon there were sounds of a violent row upstairs, with monkey screams and parrot shrieks. It subsided, and no one commented except by exchanging glances. At dusk Ramone came down, alone with the animals. And so they came to the last banquet, only slightly more modest than the other two: *crudités* with home made mayonnaise and Rosey's famous ciabatta, the braised quail en canapé but *sans* foie gras, a great dish of imam biyaldi, little new potatoes in rosemary and olive oil—

Ramone, trapped between jolly Marnie Choy and Lucy Freeman, who hadn't even changed her hairstyle since she was a darling little first-year, was asked by Lucy, "Are you still a feminist?"

She couldn't stand to look into Lucy's soft, taunting face. She looked away—and there was Spence at the end of the table. Tugging roguishly at the beads strung in his fibrous locks, thin and brown and laid back, he was busy regaling Rosey and Shane with tales of his Moroccan amours. She glimpsed what Anna saw: ambiguous sexuality, sweet nature, *and* a dick, the best of both worlds. Fuck, it was so unfair.

"Nah," she mumbled. "It's a load of fuck."

"I've seen *Mère Noire*," put in Marnie. "And if that's feminism, frankly I don't get it."

"I *said* it's a load of fuck. Feminists are clit-sucking, cunt-fisting shite. 'Women are powerful!' Are they, fuck. I don't want to be a woman. I hate women, I wish they didn't exist. Feminism is like Satanism. I mean, what the fuck difference does it make. Say your prayers forwards or backwards, you're still licking God's same fat arse."

"Oh," said Lucy, pushing back her long blonde hair, "I *see*."

"Why'n't you ask me about living with Lavinia Kent? I could be interesting about her. She used to shave my head for me. With a cut throat razor."

She saw that these people would go on inviting her to their house-parties, their cocktail parties, their *weddings*. Especially when she was famous. None of them would remember what being an undergraduate had been like for Ramone: the humiliation, the despair. She smiled in ineffable contempt, reached for another quail, and served it to Sambo the marmoset, who was curled on her lap under the tablecloth, scared by all the row. Bill the parrot rolled up and down between the dishes with his swinging sailor's gait, squirting dollops of quick-drying concrete shit and pecking at the food: Ramone's familiar spirits, her fear and her contempt. . .

The meal ended, they cleared the table. Ramone, ignoring the domestic chores, went off back upstairs with her pets. The rest of *they all* settled around the fire. The mood was quiet this evening. Hangovers, deadened by further alcohol, had begun to fight back. Wol kept on opening bottles, joints were rolled, but everyone was sleepy. Nobody wanted to play charades or murder in the dark. One by one the couples slipped away, until Anna and Spence were left alone—to keep the appointment that their eyes had made, meeting with rueful amusement over the white powder on the kitchen table, with tenderness across the banqueting board. Spence thought of Anna the night before, drunk as a skunk: settling down with a dictionary from the shabby collection of books in the Carstairs games cupboard, to locate the last, recalcitrant, word in that *Telegraph* puzzle by searching the tome line by line. Only Anna! *In vino veritas*, he thought. It was so touching to see her trying to pass for an ordinary human, when she was sober.

She was sitting by the fire; he was curled in his armchair again. "Why did you come back?" she asked. "Ran out of money?"

"No, I got a job," he repeated patiently. People kept asking him this. Where did they get the idea he'd intended to spend his life in North Africa?

"You mean in the States?"

"Notionally. It's something I was doing with some guys, when I was in college: now they can afford to pay. It's a firm called Emerald City, kind of a net service. Search engineering."

"Why 'Emerald City'?"

"Hahaha. Remember The Wizard of Oz? Well, I'm the little guy behind the curtain."

"What curtain? I remember the nasty monkeys that gave me nightmares, on television when I was five or something. I don't remember a curtain."

"Never mind." He came to join her on the hearthrug and began to roll another spliff.

I've enjoyed this, thought Anna. I wouldn't like to do it often, but I'm glad I came. Wol's insatiable gossip, Rosey's temper: Marnie, Simon. . .a whole world that had been cut out of her life because of what happened with Charles. It was good to know that she could still behave like one of *they all*. Even if it had totally derailed her budget.

"What about you? What have you been doing? I hear you're doing a doctorate?"

Anna laughed. "I don't know where to begin. Mmm, well, for a start, there's a mouse called Jamie Lee. Began life as a female embryo, but she was born anatomically male. Unlike a previous mouse called Harry, she has physiologically viable sperm. But it is unable to wiggle, and we don't know why. We think we need to increase a diffusion in the spermatogenesis precursor cells. I'm working on the methylation problem. I'm usually the sequencing queen, but the time for sequencing is past. . . Now you're sorry you asked."

"No, no. I'm fascinated."

"Then why are you grinning like that?"

"It's just, it sounds kind of comical when you talk about 'her sperm'."

"Can't help it, Spence. Nothing is sacred. Sex is now something we can take apart and change around. Like a lego set: we don't have to stick with the model in the picture on the box. We can make anything we like. With lab mice, anyway. Well, almost."

"But why are you changing female mice into male mice? I mean, why the preoccupation with *male* sexual function? Not that it worries me."

"Because that's what we do in my lab. In other places they do different things, either for profit or for pure research. If you're in HAR, assisted reproduction, there's more science to be done in male infertility. The other answer is, it's a game, and we like a challenge. Changing a male mouse into a female mouse wouldn't be much of a trick, because all you have to do with a mammal embryo is snip out the testes. In eutherian mammals, the group that includes us, female is the default. It's different with birds. And you wouldn't *believe* what happens with kangaroos."

He laid the joint on an ashtray and pushed it towards her. "God bless the drug."

"God bless the drug." They smoked in companionable silence. "I didn't want to be doing sex biology," she said, after a moment. "But it's interesting. Chromosomal sex is as good a route as any to getting an insight into the way. . .the way what happens in the DNA, the chemical bases, can be such a jumble of random differences, colliding with each other in confusion, and yet throw up mechanisms that work and look, well, inevitable."

"Like sex? Did you find your lost word on Saturday night by the way? I fell asleep and missed the thrilling conclusion."

"Oh, yes. It was poi—a paste of fermented taro root."

"Ah, poi, of course. I knew that all along." He drew in a last lungful of smoke, tossed the roach into the fire and leaned back. "Do you want to hear about the night I slept with a camel? Or shall we just go to bed? I know it's my turn to ask," he added tenderly.

She said nothing.

"I guess we'd have to use a condom."

Anna gave him an old-fashioned look. "We'd have to anyway. I'm not on the pill."

"Is that a yes?"

As they kissed, Spence mulled over the implications. Why was she not taking the pill? Was she trying to get pregnant? He would not dream of asking but he longed to know who was it had the right to hold her, to push up her shirt and suck at her breasts like this, the way she loved it, to pull her close and feel her shiver and press herself against his erection, like this only every night? There must be some brainy big-dicked sex-biologist, father of her child to be, but please God, not Charles.

"Your place or mine?"

"Yours. I only have a single bed. You have a double." She smiled, frankly and happily. "I checked. I think of these things."

She had to go to her own room to fetch her contact lens kit. "If I ever have any money," she grumbled, when she returned (the world blurred and dimmed) "the first thing I'll do is get my eyes lasered." Spence was sitting cross-legged on his double bed, already naked. She used to like him to watch her undress, to see him getting harder than you'd believe possible at the sight of the secretly gorgeous form that was revealed, all for him. But he saw as if through a veil that had become transparent that Ramone was right. Something had happened. He saw the injury half-healed behind her eyes.

"Anna, what's wrong? Did I do something wrong?"

"No," she said, "everything's fine." The memory of being raped makes you feel ugly when you are naked. And that made two things she ought to tell Spence but couldn't.

She lay beside him and kissed his mouth, his lips were so soft. She remembered the perfect freedom: the nights and days. The pleasure of kissing and caressing another human body, so sweet that the people who said you ought not to do sex unless you loved the other person must be right. When you considered the idea of caressing a child without love, that showed you the enormity of loveless sex. She supposed this meant she loved Spence: yes, certainly, *until our last goodnight.* However many sexual partners I have, though I bet it won't be many, I swear, for your sake my dear, that I will never touch them without tenderness; they will all be my friends. The house in Regis Passage. The door that wouldn't shut, incessant voices and footsteps, faces looking in. It wasn't only exhibitionism that had made them willing to fuck on dance floors, in alleys, in doorways (though there was that!). Might as well do it in the street, you'd be as private as in that ramshackle little room. The important thing was never having to hold back. One night on the promenade... They were walking with some of *they all*, fell behind, and started kissing. How wonderful it was to know, as your blood began to beat, that it wasn't going to stop, there were no forbidden places, there would be no halt, no check. It was nearly dawn. They backed into the porch of one of the beach huts, she took off her knickers for once, stuffed them in her bag and got up on the railing. He stood between her knees, peeling paint and salt-grey wood under her bum. She felt the cool morning air on her nipples and on the mouth of her cunt, like delicious sensations that were happening in another world, far from the dark inside where she was concentrating, like a baby at the breast, on the single-minded rhythm. . .and now another world interlayered with these two, Spence in her arms: the new breadth of his shoulders, new muscles in his flanks and arms, not a skinny, leggy man-child any more, but a grown young man. She thought of a bird glimpsed from the train on the way to this party, rising from a river, the unexpected breadth of its wings. The grey heron, Spence's grey eyes. When they were finished, returned dizzy and floating to the bed, the single world, Spence reached up to trace the contour of her blissed out lips.

"Was that okay for you?"

"False modesty will get you nowhere. Nah. I was putting it on to make you feel good."

They lay for a while, coupled. When he withdrew she stayed, deliciously flattened.

"Oh, shit."

"What?"

"Condom came adrift."

Anna had to retrieve it, carefully. "It seems to be okay, still intact."

"I hope no wiggle-efficient sperms escaped."

"Nor any nameless Moroccan diseases neither," she joked (suppressing over-anxiety about those sperms). Spence had switched on the bedside light. She was startled at his expression.

"There won't be any diseases. I don't do unsafe sex, Anna. You may think it weird but I have never had unprotected intercourse with anyone except you."

"I—I'm sorry," she stammered. "I didn't mean... I've done it unprotected with someone else, but only once—

The avowal that each read in the other's mouth and eyes, the invocation of their summer compact, was too arousing. They cracked open another condom.

When Spence woke on Monday morning Anna was shaking him. It was very early but she had to go. The tide was out; Simon had fetched his car from the Essex shore and was waiting to give her a lift. He roused himself enough to hug her. "Keep in touch," he mumbled. "Make sure you keep in touch, fuck sake," and plummeted back into the depths. When he woke again and clambered out of bed, a sheet of white paper had been slipped under his door. Turning it over, hoping for a note that would weld their lives together for ever and a day, he discovered a sketch of Anna, naked to the waist, done in charcoal. He was relieved to note, after a momentary jolt, that the tits were nothing like, they were purely conventional, big unlikely fat cones. But the face was Anna, and it was very good. There was a message under Tex's bold signature. It read, *You see, the devil does have all the best tunes. R.*

The early risers had left, including Tex and Ramone but mysteriously not Daz. The rest of them cleared up the house—Spence cursing as he tried to scrape parrot shit from his favorite traveling cds, Rosey tracking down overfilled ashtrays in obscure corners—nobody asking Daz what had happened. Wol and Spence trundled empties to the malodorous garbage corral and stuffed them into the bins. The morning was cold. Wol was in a mournful mood, crying out sorrowfully as the crash of breaking glass tore his words and threw them away.

"Can't have babies, you see,"

"What? Sorry, I didn't hear that—"

"I can't have babies, Spence. I was a late child, my mother had all the tests, docs told her I might turn out peculiar. I was born okay, only sterile. They told me when I was twelve. I didn't think it would matter. Well, I didn't think it would matter so soon. My God, I'm only twenty-three."

"You could adopt?"

"What?"

"ADOPT!"

"No use. I wanted to ask Anna about artificial insemination, this weekend, but I didn't get a chance. Can't hardly entrust such a delicate query to email."

"I don't think she does that. What she does is way more esoteric."

"Oh, really? Oh well. I'm afraid Rosey wouldn't buy the idea, anyway."

Miraculously, they were ready for the launch at noon. In the car park by the river pier, Spence was surprised to find Daz still beside him after the goodbyes.

"Spence, can you give me a lift to London?"

"Sure." He had barely spoken to the World's Most Gorgeous Malaysian, couldn't make out what she saw in Ramone *or* Tex. He was shocked to realize she'd been left without wheels, stranded in direst Essex. That must have been a bad fight. He opened the passenger door of his hire car.

"Are you being courtly, or have you forgotten which side we drive on?"

He'd been thinking of Anna. "Sorry, wool-gathering."

She took off her dark glasses. Close up, in full daylight, he saw that her right eye was half shut and surrounded by a puffy blotched halo. Her wrists looked bruised too. Spence averted his glance. There is such a thing as having too much fun.

"I'm well out of it," she said, catching his eye. "Believe me."

"How's Anna?" she asked, as they drove away. "I wish I'd been able to talk to her."

"Anna is just fine. Anna goes from strength to strength."

"Some people have all the luck," sighed Daz. "When you see her, tell her I said hello."

In another few years, at the next reunion. Maybe she'd come alone again, leaving Charles to look after the kids. He could hope for that. God, what a prospect. They could have talked, he'd gone for sex instead: low risk, low win. If they'd talked they might never have done the sex, couldn't have risked that, when it might be the only time. He'd chosen right. But now. . .Spence drove, with the chastened beauty beside him, his life ahead as bleak as her silence.

Anna's period was due ten days after the Carstairs weekend. It didn't come. Her menstrual cycle was naturally, mildly irregular (this had been no comfort after she was date-raped). She told herself to be calm. She had enough on her mind. She was buying a house, a move forced on her by the fact that Roz and Graham were getting married and the lodger was no longer needed: but it was a good idea. If she could get the right deal, the mortgage would be no worse than paying rent. Also, work at the lab had reached a pitch of intensity... When her period was two weeks late she bought a pregnancy test, as a matter of routine.

Pregnant.

Come on God, stop fooling around. This isn't funny.

She went to the doctor at the group practice where she'd registered but never needed an appointment before, explained the situation, and asked for another test. Anna was pregnant. "What do you want to do?" asked the doctor—who was a woman—with all the question's proper reserve and neutrality.

"I want to think."

"There's time. But don't think too long," warned the woman gently.

Her appointment had been early in the morning. She went into Parentis and worked with thunder in her head, from moment to moment distracted, from moment to moment coming back to the fact, like a raw bereavement: *it is true.* The idea of telling her mother, of telling Sonia, Roz, or anyone, filled her with horror. She went back to Roz Brown's house. This temporary home had started to feel very strange, now that her days in it were numbered. She saw—as she had not noticed since the first week she moved in—that the taste of the person who had done the decorating was nothing like her own. Oatmeal fitted carpet, spider plants on the pine bookshelves, Indian felt rug with a peacock pattern, nubbly brown covered sofa-bed, matching armchairs... Roz put Shannon to bed and went out with Graham. There was only one person she could bear to talk to. She phoned Spence's home number in the USA.

"Hi, who is it?" Spence's own voice, thank God, the urban-cowboy accent she used to think sounded so corny, so silly, before she got to know the American Exchange.

"Hello Spence."

"Anna! Hey, great to hear your voice. Better than email. How are you?"

"Got some bad news today."

He gathers himself, far away there. Perhaps his Mom is listening. She hopes not.

"What is it?" He sounded puzzled, but not alarmed.

"I'm pregnant."

"Oh, shit. You mean, from that night in Essex?"

"Has to be. I don't know if I told you this, but I don't have a boy-friend. . . I've not been with anybody else, and remember how the condom came off. It's not your problem, don't think that. I just called you because—" She was clinging to the handset, palm sweating and knuckles white. Stupid. Spence would think she was demented, or try-ing to entrap him. "I'm sorry. I shouldn't have. . . I can handle every-thing, I just—"

"I'm on my way. I'll call you when I know my flight."

Clunk.

She stared at the phone. I just wanted someone to talk to.

She came to meet him at Heathrow. She had barely slept since the terrible fact had been confirmed. Every day she went to work and was distracted (from moment to moment). At night she lay in the room that no longer belonged to her, staring into the abyss. She had been to the brink of this pit before, now she was falling, nothing could save her. Spence came out of the crowd, she saw him there shouldering his rucksack like a carefree young world traveler. She tried to smile, what a good friend, coming all this way to hold her hand, after all it was no big deal. Spence dropped his bag, looked at her with shock and pity, and folded her in his arms.

"Ssh baby, it's okay. Don't look like that, don't cry, daddy's here."

They took the tube to central London and a train to Leeds. It was a Friday night. He took her out to eat at a Chinese restaurant, then they went back to Roz Brown's house. It was empty. Roz and Shannon had gone to stay with Graham's parents for the weekend. They sat together in the alien sitting room, the tv's blank face in the corner. Anna felt that the whole situation was impossible. Not the pregnancy, that she had to accept, but what was Spence doing here? She couldn't have made that phone call, how could she have done that, how humiliating, and *why*? She must have dreamed it. He had to be here for some other reason. They'd said nothing yet about her disaster.

"You must be exhausted." She was thinking of cloying batter-covered pork balls. Had they eaten out together alone before? She couldn't remember, probably not. The room was like a picture in a cheap magazine. "Do you mind sleeping on the couch?"

Spence took her hand and held it briefly against his cheek. "So you're pregnant," he said kindly, reminding her. "I guess this is beyond doubt?"

"You asked that before."

"What are we going to do? Do you have any liquor? I don't know about you but I believe a shot of something would help me think."

She brought the rock-bottom whisky for medicinal purposes (from one of those supermarkets with bars on the windows); poured two glasses. She gave one to Spence and lifted the other to her mouth. The smell disgusted her. She set the glass down with a hollow feeling of dread. That was her first, felt symptom. It is true.

Spence stared at the electric fire. "Actually, I have been thinking for some hours. From the fact that you called me at all——"

"Look, I'm sorry. I *really* shouldn't have. I was in shock, I wanted someone to talk to, and you were the only one——" She shuddered. "All I can say is, I didn't know you'd react like that, I'm embarrassed that I got you to come all this way, and I want you to regard this as just a friendly visit. You're not to blame. It was my own stupid fault. I simply didn't think about that damn condom. I should have got a morning after course, but I *didn't think*." After Charles raped her she'd been convinced she was doomed, but even then she had behaved like a stunned animal. She was shattered by her own helplessness. That other one, the scientist, the competent and clever one was a fake. This was the real Anna: stupid girl, found out, stripped of her false rank.

"Why should you? It never occurred to me that you could be pregnant, until you called. It's nothing but bad luck." He was sitting on the floor. A year in underclass North Africa is a long time, he wasn't yet used to furniture. Deliberately, he got up beside her on the ugly couch and took a swallow of scotch. "Anna, I'm going to go out on a limb here. My guess is you don't like the idea of getting an abortion." He felt her startle but she didn't speak: just went very still.

He took another swallow. "Now I don't know if this is a religious scruple or if it is personal. But I remember the night we spent together, and though whatever you decide to do is fine by me, if I were the one that was pregnant as a result of all the good loving we've shared... Well, I can see that an abortion might not seem...appropriate. Am I on track? Please stop me if I'm making a fool of myself."

She had begun to cry, tears streaming through that stunned mask.

"Ah, sweetheart." He could guess what she was going through: Anna's pride, her privacy, Anna the untouchable. He dug a kleenex out of his pocket and wiped her eyes. "So that's where we are. It's not just do you have the money for the op."

"No," she whispered.

Spence looked around the room. He thought there was nothing of Anna here, although *what did he know?* What an unreal setting.

"We should get married."

"What? That's crazy!"

"I told you, I've had time to think. Look, you could get an abortion. We could do the deed and we could live it down, go our separate ways and forget about it: but we don't want that, deep in our hearts. So you are going to have a baby, and you are going to need someone. How're you going to continue your doctorate as a single mother? I have no commitments at home, I like the idea of moving to the UK, and I can work for Emerald City anywhere."

"I could move back in with my parents."

"Sure. That would be such fun, and then you'd have to combine the commute to Leeds with breastfeeding and colic nights and guilt. You'd never keep it up. Anyway, what about my rights? This is my child as well as yours."

Now she looked completely blown away, like: *I didn't know it was loaded.*

But it was, baby.

"Spence, *marriage!*"

"It sounds extreme, okay, yeah. But the way we're fixed, this is a bold and simple solution. The more I think about it the more I like it. I don't want to hang out with my Mom anymore, and if I moved to another town or another state she'd just be hurt and wouldn't see the point. If you weren't pregnant, if I was saying marry me so I can stay in the UK, I bet you'd do it. We're friends, we trust each other. I'm domesticated. It will be fine."

"We can't leap into this—"

"We got no choice. The train's already left, and we're on it." He gave her a quizzical smile. "You afraid we're not sexually compatible or something?"

Anna pressed her hands against her temples, saucer-eyed. "Look, Spence, this is very generous of you, and well-meant I'm sure. But things can go wrong, horribly wrong. Marrying someone means *signing things*. It's *legal*. And there *is* the sexual angle. We love each other, yes, and we had a wonderful night. But that weekend, everybody was telling me that you were gay, well, bisexual obviously, with me anyway: but the way you were talking seemed to support that. . . Doesn't it make a difference?"

Spence drained his glass. "Anna, those were dinner party stories." On second thought, he drained Anna's as well. Then he stood up. "I am whacked. I bet you are too. Shall we try to share your bed?"

She was on her feet as well: we are like sheep, the way we imitate each other. But trust Anna, she had noticed that she didn't get an answer. She was waiting. "Anna, I'm not gay." He stumbled into honesty. "Maybe I don't know what I am. I'm a Spence. Remember me? The guy who doesn't care to be like anybody else? I love you. You're my dearest friend. It will be no trouble to live with you for a while. Or even for the rest of my life." He took her in his arms, and hugged hard. "D'you feel that?" he whispered. "That's what you've got, baby. Forget about sex, forget about the pregnancy. This is yours. My arms around you, no matter what. I love you."

The bed was too narrow. After a while he gave up, unrolled his sleeping bag and lay on the floor. He thought of his mother. In *Mutiny on the Bounty*, the Marlon Brando version, after the mutiny someone asks Brando—as Fletcher Christian—is he feeling okay. He's just destroyed himself, no way back. He says something like. . .*a distinct desire to be dead, but otherwise no problem.* Spence felt like that. The quixotic gesture, fine: but then what? He was falling.

He called his Mom two days later. He had not told her why he had to rush back to England. Now he informed her, without trying to soften the blow, that he was getting married. "*Whaaat!*" she howled. "Why don't I know anything about this? First you go to Morocco, I don't hear from you more than once a month, then you shoot off to England, then you're getting married. *Why* are you getting married, for heaven's sake?"

He felt justified in a little pre-emptive brutality, knowing he could not keep Mom out of this. She was soon going to be giving his poor Anna hell, simply by being her warm and wonderful self. "For the best of reasons. You're going to be a grandparent."

When he put down the phone he was shaking. "What about all this food!" she'd cried. She had bought food for an army, because Spence was home. The turkey, big fat ragged thing with its breast torn open, sitting in the fridge, Anna's blank face, like a half-slaughtered animal, staggering on the killing floor. . . He'd told Mom he was going to live in England (might as well hit her while she was down), and she'd yelled at once, *what about Cesf?* My cat. I have to abandon my cat. My God. He hadn't thought of that. He shored the breach hurriedly, *I'll get him over, he can do quarantine.*

They went to Manchester. Anna's parents, forewarned, were charming to their shot-gun son-in-law-to-be, and the thing escalated into a social announcement. The happy couple sat amid the relations, eyes meeting in helpless amazement. He felt like Durer's rhinoceros, a camelopard at court. Yes, Anna will finish her doctorate, Spence will mind the baby. Out of sheer bravado, because Anna's sister was needling her about not having the big fat fancy wedding, he found himself saying they would be married in church, the way they had always

planned. Yes, in the Holy Catholic church no less. Why the hell not?
Have to have the State involved, why not invite the whole axis of evil
and have a possibly benign God hovering in the background; go the
whole way.

He liked Val, Anna's mom. She had the soul of a cool-headed ad-
ministrator, this one: born to make spilt milk look good. He knew
she'd perfectly understood the church wedding announcement, and
this warmed his heart; he felt he had an ally. He liked this bright-
eyed, intense, middle-aged man, who talked to him about Frank Lloyd
Wright. (Richard was hoping to make the visitor from Illinois feel at
home.) He was shocked at how small the house was and at the state of
the neighborhood, but felt that these people had taste: a commodity
which in the USA belongs exclusively to the rich, so that rebel souls
like Spence's Mom behaved lifelong as if they were handling stolen
goods when they talked about art or filled their rooms with books and
highbrow music. Back in Leeds Anna took him to the Goldfish to meet
the gang. He worked hard at charming them, and succeeded, even
with crotchety Ron (m) and bolshie Meg Methal. Anna's pregnancy
wasn't common knowledge. Everyone assumed this was a long-term
relationship, Anna and Spence kept apart by circumstance, finally
coming together. It was easy to wear. Maybe it was true.

Or maybe Spence was making a devil's bargain, which one day
three people would rue, one of them an innocent child. Anna loved
him, but she was not in love. In those black hours when she lay awake
in the night, he could not comfort her. She believed that her career was
ruined—doctoral students don't have babies, househusband makes no
diff—and she was heartbroken. What if someone came along who
could break that spell? But your girl gets pregnant: you marry her. He
was doing the right thing. That conviction would carry him through.
It was like being in Morocco again. The hospitality, the smiling, the
food you had to eat.

━ ━

No one could complain of Anna's work. Being pregnant, like being on the point of death, concentrates the mind. Before the Carstairs
weekend she had been thinking about broaching Transferred Y with

Nirmal again. She was cured of this plan. She knew that Parentis could not chuck her out: but she didn't know what the etiquette was with her supervisor. She asked Sonia. The older woman's reaction was ominous. Clearly torn between the instincts of a northern matron and grim experience, she crooned over the pregnancy but advised Anna to say nothing. Sonia would break the news.

"He's not going to be a happy bunny. But he'll have to lump it, won't he. There's such a thing as Equal Opportunities, he can't get past that."

Anna waited, trembling, to hear what KM Nirmal would say to her. He said not a word. She only knew that the news had been conveyed by the change in his manner. It was not reassuring. In the team meetings, which were frequent because things were at an exciting stage, she was sidelined. In the lab he treated her with wounding courtesy. If he had to deal with her at length he would stare over her shoulder, speaking as if to a third party, for whom Anna was merely the ventriloquist's dummy.

"He'll get over it," Sonia comforted her.

Anna had been constrained to walk down and visit the animals, after one of these distressing encounters, because there were tears in her eyes. She blinked them back. Spence thought her fears were wildly exaggerated or hormone-fueled or both, but Anna knew. She was dead meat. It would have been bad enough if she had been a young man who had insisted on getting married.

Sonia brooded over the first successfully implanted pregnant mother of three sry sdf/sdf2 female embryos, who was receiving a constant stream of admiring visitors. The team just couldn't get over her cleverness.

"It's because he thought so highly of you, love. The way he sees it, he's put a lot of investment into you and now you're taking the mommy-track. I told him about your Spence, but he doesn't believe in househusbands. No, I still wouldn't say anything yourself, not unless he speaks to you first. Let him calm down."

Anna stared out of the window at the familiar horizon. She hadn't told anyone at Parentis except Sonia that she was pregnant, but of course Sonia had gossiped. Already Anna bore the pitying looks, the grinding strain of being counted down, counted out. She had to bear it. She had to get her doctorate.

"He's got a wife at home," remarked Sonia. "A wife and grown-up kids. You'd never know it, would you? That should tell you something: he doesn't mix the compartments. Home is home and work is work. She comes from a very conservative Hindu family. I think she barely leaves the house except to visit relatives."

Anna imagined fastidious Nirmal doing sex with one of those sullen uprooted peasants you saw in the local streets: ugly woolen coat over her sari, feet broadened by a barefoot childhood slopping out of narrow western shoes. It was shocking. "She's not educated?"

"Oh yes she is. She went to Girton, took a double first in history and politics. Then her parents arranged for her to meet Nirmal. She liked him, she married him, and that was it." Sonia stomped the ball of her thumb down on the lab counter and twisted it as if she were squashing a bug. "That's all she wrote. I'm not saying Nirmal's a bigot, but that's what he thinks has to happen. A woman puts her family first. He's not far wrong. It's still the choice most women make in the end."

Anna's stricken face must have alarmed her.

"Don't worry love. Your Spence is a treasure. If I'd had someone like that. . . I tell you what though," she added, patting Anna's abdomen through her lab coat (Sonia was the first to introduce Anna to this insolent gesture). "Stick at one. It's numbers two and three and above that *really* separate the mummies from the daddies. They did in my house, any road. You still don't feel sick? Must be a girl. Girls are always less trouble."

It was true, the baby was no trouble. It made no hateful comments, no smug assumptions. Aside from the slight thickening of her waist, her distaste for spirits (which she'd never much liked), and the strange absence of tampons in her life, the baby made no demands.

⬤ ⬤

The first sry sdf/sdf2 pregnancy failed, no obvious reason why. It was a sad day. The lab mice were clones, but they had personalities. Fiona had been a favorite even before her rise to fame. These things happen. It was a set back, not a disaster. Poor Fiona was killed, she and the dead babies minutely autopsied, mulched, and spun, and their DNA pelleted for investigation. The process began again. Anna, who'd become the virtual-modeling queen, worked on a computer simulation of sdf2 expression, trying to find out what damage it might have done in other loci, in a female embryo.

━ ━

They moved into Anna's house, 131 Albemar Road, a week before the wedding. It was a Victorian cottage in a row of later, chunkier buildings. It would have been charming, except for the dirty city thoroughfare outside the front door. They would get used to the traffic, and there must be something that would grow in the dank, enclosed tank of paving at the back. Ferns? Their furniture consisted of a double futon, a single futon, a microwave oven, a table, two chairs, and three cardboard boxes of Anna's effects. The single futon was for Spence's Mom, who arrived two days later. Spence had vainly hoped that there would be *less* of her than he remembered. No chance. She was as large and ebullient as ever, and hiding her grievous loss under a lava-flow of grand-maternal joy. Spence didn't know if it was good or bad that his beloved was taking only a minimum of time off, because the next day his mother was speedily busy marking the bushes: deciding what would go where in the house, tidying Anna's things for her, taking Spence out to scour the sadly deficient malls and stores of Leeds for essential little US household items. She was only trying to help. She was here to be Mom to both of them, to make things easier for lovely, clever Anna... When lovely clever Anna walked in and saw the results she closed her eyes briefly, once: and Spence knew it was all over. Anna the inflexible would never forgive this invasion.

How could he blame either of them? He loved them both.

Spence had invited *they all* to the wedding and a reception afterwards at 131, where snack food, catered by Spence's Mom, would be served with cheap fizzy wine. To his surprise and embarrassment, they turned up in force.

Ramone drove Daz from the church. They'd sneaked out early; no one was at home at Spence and Anna's house. They sat in the car, Daz leafing through a glossy magazine looking at pictures of herself.

Model: Daz Avriti. Why not her full name? You agreed to things like that, let people mark you with their spoor, because it didn't matter. And then it did.

She and Ramone were barely on speaking terms.

"I'm not coming in," said Ramone.

"Oh? Why not? There'll be free drinks."

"Because she means it." The rabid one spoke through gritted teeth. "I came up to this fucking wedding because I thought I understood. She's pregnant, she's going to have the baby: good. Abortion is a slave's option. A marriage of convenience: good. I believe in using the fucking system. That's not what's going on. I saw the way it was, in that slimy church ceremony. It's Spence I'm sorry for, trapped by the oldest trick in the book."

"I really don't think Anna meant this to happen, Ramone."

"Women always pretend its an accident; it never is. Deep down, they're as callous as men about making babies, it's a sign of prowess, that's all it is. If you don't want to get pregnant you *don't get pregnant*. There are no accidents; it's a fucking scam."

Daz sighed. She got out of the car. "I'll wait on the doorstep. Say hello to Tex for me."

Spence's Mom stayed another ten days after the wedding.

The day she left Anna pretended to go to work. It was a Saturday, and there were no procedures at the nursing stage. She took a bus from the city centre, out into the landscape that she'd watched for so long. She had meant to reach the moors; the bus didn't take her that far; it left her in a village of one steep street crossed by another. The houses were grey stone. She walked up the hill to the church, a mass-produced Victorian box with a blackened spire. On a bench among the gravestones she sat examining her wedding ring. It felt uncomfortable, she'd never worn a ring before. Inside her belly the child snuggled closer.

She had thought she would have a life exempt from births, marriages, and deaths. Vague dreams of having a family (Rob Fowler, two children, a house by a lake in the mountains) would never have materialized, because Nirmal was right. An ambitious lab scientist is supposed to have a woman (or else a staff of servants) to take care of the domestic. Either that or she works in the chinks, between career breaks, and everyone says, but look what she achieved IN SPITE of being a wife and mother! That was not good enough for Anna. So what now? Was she doomed to turn Spence into a woman? She recoiled from the idea: as she recoiled from Sonia Blanchard's double-edged concern, and from her sister Margaret, beady eyes swift to cop Anna's left hand on that appalling visit home, looking for the *engagement ring* (and finding none); as she recoiled from her mother's reticent sympathy. She didn't want Spence to be a woman. She would find another way, a fair and decent solution. She was Anna Anaconda. She would swallow family life: make it her own.

The baby stirred again. Its movements had been distinct to Anna for a fortnight. She'd been keeping this to herself while Spence's Mom was around, or there'd have been no end to the belly-fondling. She could tell him now. She slipped her hand inside her coat. Hello little fish. Such odd emotions. She had already convinced herself that the baby was a companion in her adventure, an invisible friend who comforted her when Nirmal was awful or Sonia unbearably smug. She looked for the jagged abyss in her mind, the terror of annihilation that had been eating into her soul since the morning she found she was pregnant. It seemed to be gone.

When she got home Spence had returned from driving his Mom to the airport, in their new secondhand car. This purchase was a hideous extravagance, but you cannot keep an American around the house and not let him have any wheels. He was taking down the ancient, withered hanging baskets that had adorned, so to speak, the humble frontage of 131. They'd been annoying him.

They went indoors. "Well, here we are," he said. "Still together?"

"Still together. Shall we take a tour around the domain?"

The domain could not have been much simpler. There were two small rooms knocked into one downstairs, and a kitchen; two rooms and a bathroom upstairs. The second bedroom was to be Spence's office, until the baby was old enough to need a place of its own. There was a semi-converted loft, with flat window in the roof. They passed through the rooms, rearranging things, removing traces, and finally climbed up to the loft, which was empty and virginal (Spence's Mom having been unable to squeeze through the hatch), taking with them a bottle of red wine and some bread. It was the warmest room in the house and somehow a pleasant space. Spence had meant to buy cheese to go with the bread and wine, but he'd forgotten. They toasted each other solemnly. God bless the drug.

— —

Anna was resistant to antenatal procedures. She grumbled and growled at the time wasted in the ghastly waiting room, clutching a bottle of piss. Secretly she was appalled at the power of that place, which brutally transformed her from being Anna, still herself, striving with a perilous adventure, into *a pregnant woman*. She jeered at Spence's US conviction that you couldn't have too much intervention. I'm a sex scientist, she told him. Believe me, I know. If you work in the kitchen, you don't eat in the restaurant.

Spence said, "Oh, hey, I think I hear those hormones talking."

Who would have thought gentle Anna had such a temper on her? It must be the hormones, or maybe she was getting to trust him with her faults at last.

At twenty weeks she consented to an ultrasound scan and irritated the registrar by being able to read the screen better than he could. The baby was a girl. They named her Lily Rose Lyndall. Lyndall after the heroine of *The Story of an African Farm*, a proto-feminist text once read by Anna under Ramone's influence. Lily Rose after Spence's favorite painting, John Singer Sargent's *Carnation, Lily, Lily, Rose*. In that same week Anna discovered she was not going to the conference in Zurich where the team was making a big presentation. She boldly asked Nirmal why not.

"You will be heavily pregnant. You should not be flying."

"Not quite seven months. I could still fly. Or I could go by train and meet you—"

"It would not would be suitable."

Anna held her peace. Nirmal felt betrayed? So did she. But until she had her doctorate, she would hang on. As she saw the odds

that were stacked against her, she only became more determined. She
would win through, with Spence and Lily Rose.

They learned to get along together. They were very short of money, because Spence had blown his savings on coming over and that
car, whereas the executive salary promised by Emerald City was slow
to materialize. Anna found it hard to surrender the reins of government. Spence did more than his share of the cleaning and he cooked
well, but he couldn't stick to a shopping list or a budget. He actively
preferred a regime that swung between feast and famine: it made life
more interesting. She would have to get used to this. She would have
to trust Spence. She prepared herself, determined not to falter. When
her child was born, she must entrust Lily Rose to Spence's care, the
way fathers have trusted mothers to look after their children from
time immemorial. When the child woke from a bad dream and cried
for her daddy first, Anna must accept that. A real world of equal opportunities must have room for *average, even mediocre* househusbands,
same as the old world managed with vast numbers of disorganized,
inefficient housewives. And Spence was better than that. This will be
my line, thought Anna. It carried her like music. She knew how to
tackle the problem.

On her birthday, in June, she came home from work at lunchtime (it was a Sunday) and found a strange van outside number 131.
Indoors her father was sitting on their couch—the single futon they'd
bought for Spence's Mom's visit, folded in three—having a cup of
tea with Spence and two burly men she didn't know, and there was a
small, old-fashioned upright piano against the opposite wall.

"She's a Lancashire lass," explained Richard, beaming. "Got to
have a piano in the parlor."

▬ *iii* ▬

Spence biked up the hill from the town centre, at the end of a warm and dusty day. He'd been working in the reference library. To build a good search engine, first you have to cultivate your own ability to find things in the equivalent of a teenage boy's heaving heap of a bedroom, only it's the size of a young universe. Then you have to know when to cheat. Noticing things as he went by: a Siamese kitten curled asleep in a window (*Cesf, what am I going to do about him*). A young Asian woman in a crisp white shirt sitting in the front of a car, enigmatic smile, holding a rubber plant in a pot. The smile made him think of Anna in that sketch by Tex the comic book artist. It had come over to England with the rest of his possessions. Anna looking at it, turning to him, he read the question unspoken on her lips: *am I really beautiful?*

Yes, baby. You are lovely. Blame it on the tumbling dice. Can you hack that, can you live with the idea? A poignant waft of grilled meats from the good kebab shop. He had meant to cook a lentil casserole but forgotten to soak the lentils. Have takeaway, starve later. The Pennines against the sky, backbone of England, lumpy eroded vertebrate slopes, am I going to spend my life here?

The house was strangely quiet. Anna was sitting on the futon-couch, an inward look—

"Something's wrong with Lily Rose," she said. "She's not moving."

Fear tingled down his spine.

"Be glad of the rest," he suggested, wrestling the bike into its slot in the narrow hall. The car was not for casual use, they were very broke. "She's usually far more active than they expect."

"That's why I'm worried. I noticed it when I was doing my yoga this morning. I've been waiting all day for her to stir, but there's been nothing."

"Have you called Dr Marsden?"

"She says she'll see me in the morning and send me straight on to the hospital if there's something wrong. Or, if anything else happens, I should go there straight away."

What did *anything else* mean? Premature labor? Hemorrhage? The baby was barely old enough to live, if it was born now. She was small, they said at the antenatal, but healthy... Neither of them slept well. Spence woke the next morning and saw in his wife's eyes a dread and desolation that he tried to find reassuring. Monster pieces of bad luck do not give warning. Spence and Anna ought to know that. He drove her to the group practice and thence to the hospital. They could not find the baby's heartbeat.

At length they decided, with Anna's agreement, to induce. The hormone was pumped into her womb via a catheter. Anna was in a slip of a room on her own, on the Maternity floor, indifferent to the demeaning things done to her body. She was deep inside, like some- one buried in a cellar during an earthquake, listening to the far away sounds of the rescue that would not reach her in time. It took many hours for contractions to start. They gave her a sedative, it didn't work. Spence slept on the floor. The Catholic chaplain visited briefly. He was attending to another woman, someone having a lateish abortion be- cause she couldn't cope with the idea of a severely disabled child. The priest felt that this poor woman was in more need of comfort and sup- port, and Anna was glad to agree. After a day and a night, labor began. Anna worked for eight hours, Spence holding her hand, the midwife professionally encouraging. They were lucky to have the same one all through that shift.

"How can you stay so calm, through such huge contractions?"

"I'm a yoga student."

"Oh, is that it? Well you're doing splendidly. I'm going to tell all my young mothers—" She caught Anna's eye, bit her lip. "I'm sorry." No further conversation. At five o'clock in the evening on the third day, Anna gave birth. The body slipped from her in a rush of blood- stained fluid. "Is she still alive, Doctor?" she quavered, as if this whole process had been, like Spence's marriage plans, emergency first aid: as if everything would be fixable. "Michael," said the registrar, the same young black man who'd been so rude to the uppity primagravida, over the ultrascan. "Call me Michael. I'm sorry Anna. She's gone."

She had asked him, before labor began, about the chances for a small twenty-five-weeks baby who needed resuscitation. She had said, don't hurt her, please. No heroic medicine. But she had known and he had known that there would be no dilemma.

After the placenta came away Anna gave them a scare. She began to bleed heavily. The midwife and the registrar were too busy putting a stop to this to attend to Spence. He found himself alone in a room, with the baby in his arms. She had been washed, and wrapped in white. She had arched eyebrows like the faintest, most delicate Chinese brush-strokes, tiny spikes of lashes; a self-possessed little mouth. Anna had been able to hold her, briefly, before the hard bleeding began. The registrar thought the baby had been dead before they got to the hospital: no obvious reason why. She seemed to be perfect. Someone came in and asked Spence would he like a cup of tea. He said he'd like to be left alone. "Take as long as you want," said the woman. A chaplain, the Anglican chaplain this time, turned up and asked would he like the infant to be christened or blessed.

"She never breathed."

"Well, it's something that can help. We need ritual at these times. Are you a believer?"

"I'm a Catholic. Yes, baptize her. Can't do any harm."

The man took the dead baby, and hesitated. "Would you like to do it yourself? As, er, as you know, you're as—er—well qualified as I am."

"You do it."

So she was Lily Rose Lyndall in the name of the Father, the Son, and the Holy Spirit. He wondered if Anna would be angry with him. She'd gone through the church wedding rigmarole without much comment. Did she believe in anything? Probably not, probably nor did Spence. But the chaplain was right: he needed something. Then he was alone again, with his twenty-five-week old daughter who had never breathed. Such hours cannot be undone. You must refuse to feel when it's happening, cut yourself off. Don't look at her, don't hold her. Afterwards it will be too late. A part of you will never leave that room, the gleaming metal surfaces, the harsh light, the smell of hospitals: her presence, Lily Rose.

Anna came home from hospital the next day. She lay in bed upstairs, on a beautiful warm evening, listening to Spence who was dealing with well-wishers downstairs. She recognized the voices of Roz Brown and Graham, then the bell rang again. It was Sonia and her husband. They had brought flowers. They were pronouncing the sacred words, *if there's anything we can do.* Spence had put on some music, he was making coffee. She heard his normal voice, chatting away. This is the way we prefer to behave in times of trouble. We need to make it seem that we have not been badly injured. She felt the bloody discharge seeping out of her womb, slowed and harmless. It would cease in a day or two, and it would be as if she had never been pregnant. At twenty-five weeks, a fit young woman with good muscle tone has hardly begun to feel burdened. Tears soaked the pillow, so that she felt as if she was a child again, because she must have been eight years old when she last cried like this.

Oh, Lily Rose, if it was just you and me, I could mourn in peace. But not this way. . . If she could undo any one act in her life it would be *that damned phone call.* She had trapped Spence into marriage, she had cheated him, and no matter how long they stayed together (the years stretched out, eternal) Anna would never be free from shame, the ugly liquid seeping from this basic inequality, the wound that would not heal.

Bayes's Theorem

— *i* —

Spence and Anna stayed together. They clung to each other in the little house as days and nights went by, sole survivors of a lost world. When Anna discovered that Nirmal had not recommended her studentship be renewed for the fourth year she vitally needed, the news didn't make much impact. Her work on the Y chromosome had been sidelined by other progress; her doctorate was unfinished and rather muddled. She had been relying on her worth, and Nirmal's basic integrity, to sort things out; but he was within his rights. Of course he'd committed this act of revenge before the miscarriage, but nobody could talk about what he'd done in those terms, so there was no chance of Anna's being reinstated now she wasn't pregnant.

If this had been the first blow maybe she would have caved in. Instead, feeling something strangely like relief, she put together a resume featuring her investigation of Transferred Y. She planned that people who felt negative about Parentis would be pleased to see that she'd been doing work on something divorced from babypharming. She made applications to every institution, every company, every funding body she could think of. She'd have had a better chance if she'd stuck with Human Assisted Reproduction (Nirmal would give her a good reference, out of guilt). She didn't want that. Out of the wreckage, she would reclaim her freedom.

After four months of this she had nothing and was looking at lab technician vacancies, because she couldn't stand to be out of work. In the sixth month, she got a letter from Clare Gresley, the virus woman.

It was a snowy day in January, in the year Ron (m) had argued was the real start of the new millennium, in one of the short and bitter cold snaps that enlivened the lukewarm winters of those years. She took the train to Manchester and the Metro out to Clare Gresley's address, a biotech company headquarters on the site of a former dye works. Anna didn't know what to expect. Clare Gresley was a household name in genetic engineering—not because of the strange theory she had about evolution, but because she was a genius at breeding and tailoring virus-es, the workhorses of the industry: the living machines people used to get new material into a chromosome and have it replicated along with the original code. Everyone used her viruses. Anna had seen express packets from Clare Gresley in the chill cabinet in Dr Russell's plant lab. But she hadn't published anything—at least, nothing Anna could find—since *A Continuous Creation*, a book Dr Russell had admired very much, and which Anna had thought was brilliant, without understand-ing it very well. What had Dr Gresley been doing with herself? Making her fortune in biotech, probably. It was nice that she'd written Anna a personal letter, but she must not build on that. Today would be the initial chat with the boss. After which she'd be given the forms to fill in; then *maybe* get called back to jump through more hoops. The snow clogged her footsteps as she crossed a plain of decayed concrete. She couldn't feel her toes. She was afraid she'd found no Gresley publica-tions because she'd been looking in the wrong places, and her ignorance would be unforgivable. What did Anna know about virology? Leafless willows and alders screened the buildings. There was a river, a slug-colored vaporous stream between beds of ice; a line of decrepit black poplars reached out knotted fingers to the sky.

Biotech didn't take up half so much space as the monster chemical plants of the past. Nevertheless, Anna was astonished when she was di-rected by the receptionist to Clare Gresley's modest door. There was no guided tour, no interviewing panel. There was just Clare, a thin fortyish woman with greying brown hair coming adrift a little from a French pleat. She did not ask Anna to sell herself. She talked about Transferred Y. She'd read the paper (Anna's condemned maiden speech, in its current revision). It interested her. She knew Nirmal. She'd talked to him... On her desk, among heaps of clutter around a Mac and a telephone, stood a framed photograph of a grinning teenager. "My daughter," she said, catching Anna's curious glance. "She's at Salford, she started last term, doing Engineering. She's moved into hall: it's a wrench. We've been a team for so long, Jonnie and I."

Melted snow that had climbed through the holes in Anna's boots dripped out again onto the bland corporate vinyl at her feet. Clare explained that they would share a secretary with Nitash Davidson next door, who designed nematodes. Lab tech support was also shared. That was the pattern in many companies: individual researchers serviced by the shared technicians, to cut down on the replication of standard skills. Anna began to feel excited. It almost sounded as if she was being offered a place. Then came the crunch.

"I can give you £5000 a year. Plus a small living and travel allowance."

You can try to be prepared. But at some point, you have to be ready to leap. You have to know that this is the only chance.

"£5,500," said Anna.

Clare pretended to do mental arithmetic.

"Done. When can you start?"

Anna hadn't told her parents she was coming to Manchester. She turned up on their doorstep shivering and bright-eyed. "Hello Mummy. Guess what. I have a new job!" Her father got as far as the five and a half k, and told her she was insane. He was probably right. She spent the night in her old bedroom, sobering up. So this was what the personal letter meant: no money. A place to work on her doctorate, on Transferred Y, but *no money*. How did they expect you to live? Somehow, she would manage it.

So Anna drove over the Pennines every morning, while Spence stayed at home and worked for Emerald City. At first he was strangely happy, as long as he left the memory of Lily Rose alone. He was free of his Mom (he called her occasionally; they chatted by email). He was living in a world of his own making, and if he could have afforded to import his cat everything would have been fine. Emerald City was building a rep. It was getting so that every one of their customers had what amounted to a little software agent in there. Other bits of software ensured that these little agents, which the City called trilogbots, helped the whole system out, the best routes getting strengthened by the amount of use they got. This paid off for both the system and the individual, in speed and specificity of response. They were building a mind for the Net. They were making this mind to the tune market forces played, which in many ways was shit: but it was very cool to be at the moving edge.

It didn't bother him that the rest of the gang were physically hanging out together in Chicago, while he was in Yorkshire. At this point in his life he liked to be alone, and he liked to be with Anna. That was it. Social contact was to be avoided if possible. He knew he was owed a bigger piece of the action. The others in the original team started calling themselves directors, while Spence was still the hired hand. He didn't care. In an intense dialogue with Mr Acid, before that trip to Morocco, he had decided he would never have a career. He confirmed that vow with himself now. He would pay his way, pick up his own shit; above all, he would be no one's servant and no one's master: apart from Anna Senoz, whose loving servant and faithful master he was bound to be, until death did them part. One day Lorelei, the City's token cyberbabe, sent him an email asking did he know he was under new management? That was how he found out that the City had been sold, and Spence with it, like a side of meat.

He went down to London wearing a suit, dreads, and the Emerald City earrings Jack Baum, senior partner of the original duo, had given each of them the day they signed up. He met some UK apparatchiks of the vast organization to which he now belonged. He was feeling defiant and angry. Technically he knew he'd been humiliated. His recourse was to act the *enfant terrible*: I don't pay any attention to these things, I'm on a higher and a cooler plane. . . He sort of hoped they'd fire him but they didn't. They didn't make him a director either. He was sure he could find another job, but there was Anna, who had just accepted a mad work-for-nothing deal with one of her childhood heroines. Anna could not sleep nights if there was no regular money coming in, and the two of them had to look out for each other, there was no one else. So he accepted the deal they offered and became a cog in the mighty machine. A creative cog.

He wasn't exactly happy about this.

Late one evening on the way back home, he walked down to the bar on the train and saw a face he knew. It was soft, it was pink, it was dusted as if with iron filings around the jaw. The dark hair was still standing up mussily from Charles Craft's infantile skull: his jacket was open to display a precociously ornate waistcoat. Spence could not resist the awful temptation to say hello. They exchanged news. Spence felt impelled to mention Anna and suffered as he deserved for this stupidity, forced to observe the smirk that rose in those secretive black eyes.

"Is this your usual train?" asked Craft, full of hopeful bonhomie.

If it had been, it wasn't any more. "I work at home, mostly." They exchanged cards. Craft seemed cowed by Spence's appearance. The dreads with the suit, the post-modern gangster look, had that effect. Charles detrained at Rugby. Spence went on sitting in the saloon car drinking beer, shocked to the core.

Commuting with Charles Craft! What a fate!

But the money was good.

➤ ➤

Anna rarely took a break during the day. If she did, she spent it walking round the dye works site, usually in the rain, watching the birth of new life. She had new boots, so her feet were dry. She hated spending money on herself, now that she was financially dependent, but Spence had insisted. From the fragile shelter of a willow thicket, among the yellow-grey catkins like damp fledglings in the storm, she watched the icy sleet of March blow by and thought about Lily Rose. It worried her that she had not begun to forget. She caught herself pretending that there was a baby at home: she had to hurry home to feed the baby. She stared into shop windows, choosing toddler clothes. More than once she'd found herself at a check-out desk with a cheap toy, a rag book, and had to return the goods in confusion. Was this unhealthy? Well, too bad. It must be endured. Like pregnancy, mourning did not interfere with her work. In ways, it was *good* pain, not disabling: as if the baby, though she was dead, still had a protective power.

She said to Clare, "doesn't the old dye works site remind you of Frodo and Sam in Ithilien?" Clare agreed. "A disheveled, dryad loveliness on the edge of Mordor, wasn't that it?" From their first meeting they had established a warmly shared personal hinterland, which made a big change after Nirmal.

"Enjoy it while you can," Clare added, sorrowfully. "Every year I hear mutterings. There's no such thing as land safe from development these days, even if it's been soaked in poison for decades. The world's in the hands of the devils, Anna. Nothing good survives."

Nitash Davidson, their neighbor, was an autotheologist, a term that nagged Anna. She wanted to know why it was familiar, but didn't want to ask Nitash anything in case he tried to recruit her to the cult. One day when she found his door open she risked a closer look at his office shrine. The open-fronted box held a figure of Jesus on the cross, since it was that time of year, flanked by Lord Ganesh and a gaudy foil-wrapped chocolate egg, presumably standing for the virgin mother. The wall around was decked in handprints and inscribed *To The God Who Makes Mistakes*. Then she remembered. . . The flat in Pinebourne House, hung with fetishes: the three Norns. Nitash came up behind her. He tucked a sprig of fresh aspen behind the cross, touched the feet of the crucified, then his forehead and his lips.

"Lavinia Kent?" she asked.

"Yes! You too?"

"Sort of."

She ought to have known. Lavinia Kent, after a hospital stay, had emerged to popular fame: a living saint for the media now, not just for the cognoscenti. And Ramone had had a book published. It was called *Praise Song For Epimetheus*, it was her doctoral thesis. There had been some hype about it, but no sign of support from Lavvy. Anna had wondered about that. She never wanted to see the rabid one again, and she presumed Ramone felt the same. (Daz had told Spence what Ramone had said about the wedding, and Spence had been unable to resist telling Anna.) Still, she had been vicariously gratified when she saw Ramone's face on a daybreak tv show, selling the new book. *I invented her,* she thought. She's the girl from outside my bedroom window—

How far away it all seemed, those salon evenings.

As soon as Anna was up to speed on virology, she took over a share of the routine work, filling the orders that came from every branch of biotechnology, from medical research to fish farming. Clare and Anna did the skilled machining, then the parts were passed on to the assembly line for bulk amplification. One batch of *herpes simplex*, denatured and rebuilt in the specific sites needed for a cancer therapy infusion. One tobacco mosaic stripped of its protein coat and wrapped in something customized to get past the fierce defenses of a fish-fungus. One Epstein-Barr with the special knurling, coming up. The ghosts of industry past roared and clanged around her: the stink, the flying shuttles, the spinning drill heads. Genetic engineering was easier on the ears than the old-fashioned kind, but it was making the wheels of the world go round. The ghost of a secret pride she had first known at Parentis slipped through Anna's protective shell.

I am within the sanctuary, a different sanctuary. I am doing real work.

Transferred Y was not forgotten. Clare had good contacts. She was able to secure, cheaply, a copy of those French reproductive health survey samples and a copy of the Cameroon antenatal samples from Parentis. Two days a week Anna stepped back in time, to the world before Lily Rose. She was calling her project *An Investigation of Apparent Benign Mutagenic Action on the Human Sex Pair Chromosomes*. At first she could not replicate her Leeds results, and all seemed lost. Then she and Clare discovered that the new, improved culture medium they were using was causing the samples to behave differently. When they'd tinkered with the mix, Transferred Y appeared like magic.

"I'm *not* crazy," breathed Anna, "It's there, isn't it. This is amazing."

"Not yet," said Clare. "Transferred Y is not amazing *yet*. Benign miscopying between the X and the Y happens. We can't be sure that further tests won't explain away what we seem to see. Have you thought about how or why this could be happening?"

Anna was reluctant to draw any conclusions. She'd prefer to stick to pure description, leave speculation to others. She remembered that interview with Nirmal, when the praise she desperately needed had come with a very clear price tag. Find out what the boss wants you to think...

"Um, well, I haven't really thought?"

"I'd like to propose that you try looking for something. If you're open to a supervisor's suggestion."

"Of course."

"I see a pattern that suggests a lateral transfer. We have two locales for this mutation: one in the south of France, in an area of relatively high African immigration, and one in Francophone West Africa. Have you considered that a virus might be involved?"

Ah, right.

Clare Gresley was the virus queen. Viruses featured heavily in the way-out theory that she called *Continuous Creation*. According to Clare, viruses and viroids connected the web of life on earth: maintaining equilibrium, mediating change, sustaining the genetic homogeneity that orthodox science attributed solely to common ancestry in the far past. In her picture, virus-borne disease was the pathology of a far more significant function, and the use of viruses to mediate artificial genetic change was a "discovery" that mimicked a vast, unsuspected, natural communication and commerce between all living organisms.

Unfortunately, the lateral transfer of chunks of functional DNA from species to species, and between the individuals of a population, seemed to most people well explained by current science, and it couldn't possibly be the missing link of evolution, because evolution didn't have a missing link. *Continuous Creation* was dead in the water: Clare Gresley had backed a loser. That was why she was here, not making her fortune, just turning out widgets in obscurity. Anna had grasped the whole situation by now, though Clare had never spoken openly about her plight.

"Infectivity, Anna. That could be your answer."

Infectivity was a Continuous Creation keyword: meaning chemical information (in the form of a virus) that invades an organism bringing communication, not as a threat. Anna heard the suppressed excitement in Clare's voice, and knew that she'd met her fate. She could forget the idea that Clare, who had brought up her daughter Jonquil alone while struggling to have a science career, had taken pity on her. She could abandon the fantasy that Nirmal had fixed things for her, as a secret amends. This was why she was here: Clare had seen Transferred Y as a way to promote Continuous Creation—the boss always has an agenda. Well, she'd learned her lesson—

In the moment it took her to find the right words (lying would never come easily to Anna) it dawned on her that Clare could be right. A virally mediated mutation that took hold in a natural population without causing any effect...that would explain Transferred Y. No wonder Nirmal had been so enraged. He must have seen the connection with Clare Gresley's doomed theory at once. But Nirmal could be wrong. Clare could be right. Anna could have found the evidence that Clare had been waiting for—

Her heart thumped. She managed to keep her voice level.

"Yes," she said. "Yes, that's worth trying."

Clare had been collecting viruses and viroids for years. Customers sent the creatures to her from all over the world. There was always a new strain, a new protein coat to decipher, a novel species. Managing the database of her collection occupied Clare's every spare moment. She turned over this remarkable resource to Anna, and Anna started looking for viral traces in her Transferred Y samples.

The cunning wheeze of using "standard" technicians to cut down on staff meant that researchers had to do anything remotely specialized themselves: there was no project team to share the load. But luck was with them. It was only a couple of months before they could say, with reasonable confidence, that they had found something. They began to discover fragments of something resembling a virus, possibly some re-lation of the ubiquitous *herpes simplex*, the cold sore virus. (Clare didn't agree with the conventional naming or ordering of virus species, but she admitted them to be useful shorthand, *pro tem.*) Anna's next task was to culture this unknown strain to see if she could induce the TY phenomenon in the sex-pair chromosomes of uninfected living cells— finicky, delicate clumps of living human cells (there were no mass pro-duced mice to be sacrificed in Clare Gresley's lab)—a kind of work she had never done before. It was tough going, tough but good.

Anna resisted Clare's pessimism about the state of the world. Yes, okay, a culture of brutal self interest was destroying life on earth. But would Clare feel so sad about the great dying, without the added sting of personal failure...? People are still happy, life can still be good. Thinking like that, she would remember with a shock that *she was unhappy herself*, that she had lost her baby and would never cease to mourn; and then the permanent sorrow, etched in the back of Clare's eyes, frightened her. Is that going to be me? Yet sometimes—as the road across the Pennines flew beneath her wheels in the early morning, or at evening as she stepped into the car, going home to Spence and their little house, the young moon in a blue sky and one star (actually Venus) below it—she would be transfixed by joy. Tears would start in her eyes, she could only think, *I love you so much!*

You, meaning the world, meaning everything...

Transferred Y was her refuge and her passion. But her soul had grown richer, stranger, stronger. She was in love with the world: the world that included, deeply woven and never to be lost, the death of her child.

◆ ◆

Spence got round to telling her that he'd had Lily Rose baptized. So they were out about it with each other. Good luck to those well-padded enough to need no shelter, but most people cling to *something*, once they've noticed how much grief there is in the world. Anna and Spence need not be ashamed to join the majority. Catholicism, tarnished mess, had the advantage that it didn't tell you there was something wrong with *you* if you weren't smug and happy. It allowed people to suffer. "I feel I know you better," he said, after this conversation. And the sex was still good. Well, to tell the truth, the sex was mechanical these days, but declared wonderful, for old time's sake.

They didn't do much socializing—which Spence had started to miss—because of Anna's insanely long hours. When he went to London he would hang out with Rosey and Wol, and Marnie and the current toyboy. There was Simon Gough in Sheffield, and sometimes, rarely, he and Anna would go out with Roz and Graham, or some of the old Parentis gang. It wasn't a bad life.

He was reading a fat hardback biography of Keats that someone had abandoned in his room in Woods, back in first year. Because he only read it on the train he wasn't getting through it very fast. It was a winter's day, the beginning of another year. There were grim developments in the world and a brutal gap in the New York skyline that made him wince every time he saw it; but that was a reflex. He'd got into the habit of caring very little what went on beyond the narrow, weary confines of his life. History is not my business. The line from London to Leeds was routed through the ugliest face of the English landscape. One dirty-looking dormitory town followed another, separated by swathes of dingy agribusiness. He was tired. He wanted a drink but couldn't be arsed to go down to the buffet car and the aisle trolley didn't appear to be rolling. He was not getting off on Keats's biographer, but he needed something to control the mental fidgets that always plagued him on this return journey. He kept his eyes trucking from word to word. *A pet lamb in a sentimental farce.* You couldn't help but like someone who'd describe the failure of his first hopes that way. You could feel the sharp wit and raw distress, bleeding through the years.

He read.

"Ethereal thing(s) may at least be thus real, divided into three heads—Things real—things semi-real—and no things. Things real—such as existences of Sun Moon & Stars and passages of Shakespeare—Things semi-real such as Love, the Clouds & which require a greeting of the Spirit to make them wholly exist—and Nothings which are made Great and dignified by the ardent pursuit. Which by the by stamps the burgundy mark on the bottles of our Minds, insomuch as they are able to 'consecrate what'er they look upon. . .'"

A wash of dread fell through his mind, like the shadow of a manta ray dropping through blue water. He didn't know what was happening. Then he realized that he was back in the sluice room or whatever that place was in the hospital. He was holding Lily Rose in his arms, and a voice he didn't recognize but he had always known was saying to him *you're as well-qualified as I am.* But she was dead, she was a piece of meat. The tiny child who lived in his mind had never been anything but meat. Wriggling meat inside Anna, then dead meat. There was no Lily Rose. She had never existed, except in that Spence himself had called her up, created her out of nothingness. He had to let her go, dismiss the phantom, or he was a pet lamb in a sentimental farce.

He put the biography away, zippered his case, and got off the train. He must have done these things because he found himself standing clutching his bag among strangers, the train to Leeds sailing away. He walked up and down, he stopped and stared at the ballast between the tracks, in a state of horrible, bewildering agitation. His little girl, this tiny girl bundled up in woollies, trotting by his side. . . He had never told Anna, had never brought himself to confess how concrete the little ghost had become, growing instead of fading. Now she had to go, he had to tear her up and throw her away. He had been using Lily Rose's imaginary existence as a crutch, secretly knowing that when he was stronger he would dump her into non-existence again. That had been his position: same as his attitude to religion. Believe it if you need it, and if that means you use the crutch lifelong, well why not? But why this panic, this shaking horror? It came to him that he was being told (that letter of Keats had slammed the idea into his head) that the reality of such things depends on the observer. This doesn't make Lily Rose less real, it's just the truth, the very truth, you make her be, she lives in you. He felt dizzy and sick. He felt as if he had been led through the mysteries of Eleusis. Lily Rose lives, if I can handle knowing that I am her creator, that Godhead is in me. . . He walked up and down, shuddering in the terrible rush of this vision: thinking, ah God, poor God, how do you stand this, you poor bastard.

He was having a flashback, it happens to the bereaved: you think it's all over and then wham, the thing is immediate again, driving you crazy. Maybe this happens especially after a death like the death of a stillborn child: which is not supposed to count, so that you hurried the original mourning.

The skies had fallen, but he could pull it together. He felt better already.

As it happened, Anna was even later at getting home that evening, so that Spence arrived expecting an anxious welcome to find the house dark and empty. The heat wasn't on, because she hated to spend a penny on "unnecessary" bills. He understood that she needed her independence. She was trying to carve out a little poverty for herself, within the domain of Spence's executive salary. But it was depressing.

She came in to find him sitting in the dark on the folded futon couch.

"Spence?"

"I can't go on."

His voice sounded oddly thickened—and of course accusing. "I'm sorry. I know it was my turn to cook. I'll put something together quickly. Are you getting a cold?"

"We could fucking have fucking takeaway, for once. Without breaking the bank."

"Spence, what's wrong? It isn't the end of the world. You could have started the cooking."

"It's not that, didn't you hear me, I said I can't go on. I hate this life. I hate wearing a suit, I hate this house, I hate living with someone who barely knows I exist."

"Okay." Anna was not surprised. Now that it had happened she knew this scene had been coming for a long time. Her pride rose up. "So leave. Go back to the States. We can get one of those no-fault divorces. I never meant to force you into marriage. Every day of my life I wish to God I'd never made that damned phone call—"

Neither of them had noticed that the room was still dark.

"Don't do that, it's what you always do, flying to extremes to escape an argument—"

Then he really began to cry. She knelt on the couch and tried to hug him, but he pushed her away: and it all came out, how desperately he hated working for the company and living in this house, the house to which they would have brought home Lily Rose. Working in the room that should have been the baby's, and Anna never there, even when she was at home, even when they were fucking, which was rare enough, she was thinking about her work, about anything but Spence.

Anna wrenched her mind away from her flaky cell cultures. It was true, she had been neglecting him and neglecting sex. Spence didn't understand that while for him sex made everything all right, for her the lead weight in her heart made sex all wrong. Sex was happiness and she had none, only endurance, pride, and sometimes joy. They should have talked the thing out. Too late now. Time to deal with the underlying reality.

"I feel it too," she said. "I bury myself in work, but I know. This isn't what we planned."

She reached out her arms again. They lay huddled breath to breath. "I know what we can do," said Anna. "I have a cunning plan." (Thinking: so this is what I do with my new strength, and finding in herself a satisfaction greater than Transferred Y, her shoulders bowing willingly, proud to do the world's work, any kind of world's work, now I make my husband happy.) "We leave. Fuck my doctorate; fuck your company. I have marketable skills, I'll market them. Infertility is big business, it's international. We can travel the globe."

"I won't let you do that. You live for your career."

She would lose Transferred Y, but she would have paid her debt. She would be equal with Spence again. Nothing could bring back Lily Rose, but she would recover the purity of their contract, and that would be plenty to live on.

"I let you marry me," she said. "Now you have to let me do this."

━ ii ━

Ramone had a moment of epiphany on late night television. It was a program about decadence; she and the other guests were supposed to be collapsed at the end of a debauch, dressed in fancy underwear and rolling around in purple satin sheets. Ramone was trying to explain what *Praise Song* was about: this glaring flaw running through intellectual life, everyone stuck in the groove of the enlightenment experiment, calling betterment and progress failed concepts and still thinking in terms of betterment and progress. Epimetheus is one who builds on what went before; a praise song is what you do when someone is dead.

But they had hired her because of *Mère Noire*, which was so much more accessible. So this man, fake debauchee who was actually a presenter, said but surely the writer of *Mère Noire* hates women. Ramone gave her standard answer. Any woman that doesn't hate women is a *bleep* idiot (it was that sort of show). I want to exterminate *women*, wipe them from the face of the earth. I don't want to be liberated, I want to be a monster. He didn't get it. No one ever got it, and Ramone could have straightened them out by saying nobody is born a woman and that what she hated was the way she COULD NOT ESCAPE from the role of second-class person. No woman could, the only escape was to become SOMETHING NEW that had never existed before. And fuck them all; she'd rather be misunderstood than acceptable... But he was impressed by her anger. She saw the alarm coming up in his eyes. It never ceased to amaze her, that fear. For fuck's sake, she thought, I weigh fifty kilos, that's about seven stone twelve, o dweller in the shades of departed empire, and I'm not even armed: what do you think I'm going to do? His fear gave her the illusion she'd made contact. It was only afterwards, back in the smart little hotel where they were putting her up near the studio, that she realized something had struck home. Like swaggering away from a fight and then finding that you were bleeding, strangely there seems to be quite a lot of blood: and now the pain begins.

I hate women.

I hate myself.

Okay, fine. She pondered this medieval syllogism in terms of her partnership with Tex. Ramone did not accept the role of victim easily.

It was true that she and Tex hit each other, but if Ramone usually ended up getting the worst of it that was purely because she was smaller, there was no gender-role implication. Or if there was it was by Ramone's own choice. She was her own victim; Tex was merely her blunt instrument, and he knew what was going on. People thought Tex was stupid, but he wasn't. It was because she'd seen the possibility of an honesty about male/female relationships that she'd never found with any other man that she had taken him away from Daz. Well, that and wanting to come first with one of them. With somebody. She'd known she didn't have a chance of being Daz's own true love. Daz was the kind of lesbian who was convinced nothing you did with a girl was really sex.

With this new insight, it began to seem to her that maybe Tex did not understand. Maybe he had never understood the heuristic message of furious irony in her *Mère Noire* scripts. In fact it was possible that he was simply a sexually insecure sort of lad, who had settled for not-so-great-looking Ramone in exchange for fabulous Daz, because Ramone was not a challenge to his own mediocre attractions, and because she encouraged him to draw pictures of naked women with enormous tits getting the shit dicked out of them. Since Ramone hated women and was herself a woman, wouldn't she have chosen this kind of humiliatingly banal relationship? Rather than something deep, secretly very aware and post-gendered, about feeding off each other's twisted desires. . .?

Next time she felt like picking a fight with Tex she went to the gym instead. It was a tarty little women-only place, hidden inside the hollowed-out shell of an eighteenth century town house in Knightsbridge. Not many clients spoke English (which was a plus), and it could get extremely crowded on a Monday evening, when everyone was sweating and pumping away the excesses of the weekend. Ramone had secured herself a spot in front of the floor-length mirror to finish with some yoga, a skill-relic of her long-gone friendship with Anna Senoz. She took her eye off it for a moment; instantly a big beefy dyke with Popeye the Sailorman biceps plonked hirself right in Ramone's body space. "Arsehole," muttered Ramone, with a covertly virulent grimace—forgetting the properties of a mirror.

"What did you say?" asked the dyke, pugnaciously.

"Arseholes," explained Ramone, "I said, arse*holes*, *sss*: kind of a general remark because I'd just picked a space and now it's gone. Nothing personal."

The woman had a jaunty bristle cut and wide, flat cheekbones. Her skin was rosy brown like Anna's, but she was very Central Asia-looking. It was Ramone's bad luck that she understood English. Or good luck. By the end of this brief exchange it was clear that they liked the look of each other.

"I like your tattoos." She touched one of them, a thorny rose bandeau around Popeye's massive upper arm. "I've got one like that on my fanny, but you can't see it because I let the hair grow back. I didn't like having no pubes, it causes chafing."

"Are you doing anything after this?" asked the dyke, looking unaffectedly pleased and interested, so that Ramone felt guilty, because she already knew what she was planning.

She had never picked anyone up from the gym before, but it worked fine. Popeye, whose name was Freda, which comes from *Guinevere*, the White-maned (as she was charmed to be told), didn't waste much time on pre-sex bonding. They went back to her place and only started chatting after the first fuck. Later she bought Ramone a meal and they went to a club where Popeye insisted on buying the drinks. Obviously she had no idea she was on a date with the writer of *Mère Noire*, tv chat-show guest and soon-to-be-famous post-feminist intellectual. Ramone was touched. She became this other Ramone, unemployed young lesbian single on the media fringe. She talked about the film-extra work in Paris as if it was the only work she'd ever had, and Freda was impressed.

It was the next evening before they got back to the flat. Ramone knew Tex would be in because his car was there next to the Porsche, and he always stayed in, lying in wait, if Ramone had disappeared for a night on the tiles. She did the same to him. She rang their bell aggressively (it was a biggish house in Ladbroke Grove, they had the "penthouse" floor, the flats were expensive, but it was shabby in the stairwell). Just as she'd hoped, Tex came right out of the door to see who had rung, to observe her and the other woman on the landing in a heavy sexual embrace: Ramone riding Popeye's thigh and Popeye, a little shy but not at all reluctant, getting into it. She knew how he would react. He'd be turned on, he'd be furious, and he wasn't the type to exercise self-control in front of the visitor. And so it came about. Tex grabbed Ramone by the hair, which she had recently grown out into a ponytail at the back, and started punching. Ramone kicked him until he let go, and they began screaming at each other. She had a glimpse of Popeye splatted up against the wall looking, there was no other word for it, looking *prim*. Like some nice person who's been the victim of a crude practical joke, which was the truth, sad to say: like, *my God, I have been eating dogdirt!* Prim, repelled, disgusted, frightened, Guinivere the White-maned vanished forever as Tex dragged Ramone into the flat and slammed the door.

They shared some more honesty and candor. It didn't turn into sex this time, that rambunctious scratching scrambling *full energy* sex, which was the only kind Ramone enjoyed, though his pvc trousers were tight enough that she could see he had a huge erection. She didn't mind. This was better than sex. She screamed at him, feeling immense quivers of fuckme, fuckme around her hole and up and down her inner thighs, but when he smacked her a blow across the face instead that was *better*. She smashed him back, using her nails and her full weight, oh god the release. We were born to hate each other. Your reproductive success is my destruction, same goes the other way round so let's *duke it out*, no more of that mealy-mouthed mom-and-pop complementarity shit, we know the truth now let's DO IT. . . RIGHT OUT IN THE OPEN. *Better still*, she now knew that Tex was not with her on the higher plane. He wasn't observing or reflecting or deducing or entering into the discourse, he was simply thumping her because she was a girl, she'd insulted him, and he could get away with it.

Meanwhile Bill the parrot (Sambo had died of pneumonia the previous winter, and Ramone didn't want another monkey because that would be disloyal) unfortunately happened not to be in his cage and he couldn't get *back* into his cage because of all the honesty and candor flailing around in his flight path. He was screaming too at the top of his voice, but he wasn't reveling in orgiastic fury, he was terrified. Ramone started wishing she knew how to call a brief parley, for the bird's sake.

Tex started going after Bill and fell headlong, having caught a glancing blow in the groin from the corner of his drawing table, which had crashed over on its side during the start of the bout. "I'm gonna get that bird," he shrieked, goaded by the affectless pain, so different from pain deliberately sought, slathered over with the tasty sauce of arousal. He started flicking at Bill with a damp towel that had been lying by the bathroom door, festering, for a few days.

"STOP THAT! LEAVE HIM ALONE!"

Tex flicked the towel again and hit Bill, who was clambering frantically among the hangings on the living room walls, on the side of the head. The parrot seemed to get dizzy. He struggled on, his cries now pathetically confused, almost timid, still making for his cage and safety. Then he fell, wings half open, and was blundering on the floor.

"LEAVE HIM ALONE!"

Tex gave her an evil look. He dropped the towel on Bill and picked up the bundle. Ramone felt all the sex drain out of her. She knew she must not show weakness but she was frightened. "Put him back in his cage."

They were standing opposite each other, the width of the big room between them strewn with wreckage. Tex let the towel drop and held the bird between his hands. Bill's grey ruffled head circled around, his china blue eye blearily resting on Ramone without recognition. Tex took hold of his head with one hand, and moved the other down to grasp Bill's knobbly old bunioned sailor's feet. He tugged. Bill struggled, flapping his wings. Tex pulled hard and dropped the corpse on the carpet.

"I'm leaving," said Ramone.

"Fucking-A you are. I'm throwing you out, you talentless stupid ugly cunt."

Ramone marched around trying to pack, tears streaming, while Tex grabbed armfuls of her stuff and threw it out the front door. Between them, it didn't take long. They didn't say another word to each other. Some relationships are like that: no lingering doubts, no loose ends, when it's over it's over.

She made an inventory, sitting on the stairs, while the slammed door fumed its silent rage at her, and discovered he had not thrown out her gear. Ramone was not addicted to heroin. She was an occasional user, who liked the doom-laden image. She decided that she would take this opportunity to go cold turkey. She would kick the habit (employing, needless to say, the injectable drug as a symbol for the regime of sexual violence that had gone shit on her). She left most of her stuff where it lay and took a taxi with her two best-looking bags. She chose a hotel that was small, smart, and central, determined to hole up until she was clean. She had no trouble getting in. She was wearing an expensive black quilted leather jacket Daz had given her and a metallic gold beanie hat that she had stolen from another model, and she'd made up her face. She looked, she thought, when she checked herself before facing the reception desk, like a delinquent rock star: which was exactly what she wanted to be.

She didn't suffer withdrawal symptoms, but the twenty-four-hour room service was seductive. By the time she decided to leave she'd run up a sizeable bill on her Visa card. The desk got it authorized all right but she knew she was in trouble now, until she paid something off on one card or another. Money was a problem, because she didn't think she was going to be working on *Mère Noire* anymore, and she'd made fuck-all out of *Praise Song*. More pressingly, she was running out of cash. She shouldered the good-looking bags and went to find an ATM. She had the feeling of something coming up on her. . . Then a weird unlucky thing happened. Her mind was preoccupied, she couldn't remember her number. The machine gave her a few tries, then it ate her card. She took a taxi back to the flat, which nearly finished her cash, and cased the joint. When she was convinced that Tex was out, she went up the stairs. Of course, he had changed the locks.

A few letters addressed to Ramone were lying in a damp corner of the ground floor lobby, where Tex had thrown them. The one that wasn't a circular was a rude reply from her agent to a perfectly civil letter Ramone had written, asking why the publishers hadn't done a fucking thing to promote the *Praise Song* paperback. Ramone was disgusted at the unprofessionalism of these people. You expected to be dealing with rational capitalists, making businesslike decisions. Instead you found nothing but spite and idiocy, pathetic little personal grudges, and of course have the boys had enough? Then we have some little scraps here for the girls. . . She wondered if her situation was different from any literary female in London's history, say Aphra Benn: decided not. It's the same old story. Live on your wits, get paid less if at all, and if you're trying to sell anything that doesn't grovel to their idea of your sex, forget it.

She had so many options she didn't know what to do. She could go round to Wol and Rosey's, they'd give her a bed. While she was checking her pockets—jacket, jeans, both bags—for undiscovered cash, she found a tab of e. It looked a bit manky but she thought it would be okay and swallowed it dry, because it was raining and she needed to think. She carried her bags to Ladbroke Grove and sat in a doorway. Time to re-invent myself. Ah, but it had been such a strain, that middle-class educated aspirational phase, she was glad it was over. The drug was coming up on her in a tingling effervescence through her nerves and her gut. She smiled, chin on her paw, looking down a lonesome road and knowing it was her own.

Some weeks later, when she had sold most of the contents of the good-looking bags, the bags themselves, and her useless credit cards, when she had slept on couches and floors, avoiding old friends, until she ran out of acquaintances who didn't take Tex's side, she found herself where she would have been years ago, if it hadn't been for her scholarship money: a northern girl with delusions of grandeur, at large on the streets of London. It was fine. She made friends, she found romance, and she wasn't above doing sex for money, if she liked the person. If anyone asked, she excised the university aberration and told them she'd run away from home because her Dad was abusing her. It wasn't true. But her Dad would never have hesitated at telling a dirty lie about Ramone, if it was going to get him a free drink, so she felt no guilt.

She spent her days walking around, sitting on benches, begging, staring into the river. The nights were more difficult. That was when the problem of sex resolved itself clearly into one of physical size and strength. There were pros and cons on both sides. Female, or male if you were small, you were less likely to attract the gangs of violent lads, who were the serious threat. But you were in continual danger of being mauled, and it meant you never got any sleep. Ramone thought of herself as the Cat; she walked by herself, and no one got the better of her. One night she was wandering in the dark near Piccadilly (stupid place to roam, but she was looking for a friend who was supposed to have some drugs) and a man drew up. She didn't like the look of him. I only do girls, she said, walked on, and thought no more of it. She heard a car stop and a door slam, and still thought no more of it until suddenly something grabbed her from behind. It was like being picked up by a dinosaur. He grabbed her by the shoulders and slammed her against a wall. Don't talk to me like that! he yelled.

What's up with you? she demanded, ears ringing. I just said I only do girls. Ask someone else, I'm not the only tart in London.

You cheeky little bitch. You cheeky, little, bitch.

He forced her to her knees, grabbling at his trousers. What made her sick was that he was not hard. When she'd screamed no, no, fuck off bastard and he'd hit her and she'd been frightened enough to submit, she had to take something into her mouth that was like a dead slug that had been dipped in stale piss and left to dry. She had to work on it, for years it seemed, until he finally managed to get there. Backed off, fastening himself, muttered something unintelligible, not that Ramone was paying attention.

It was the first absolutely forced sex she'd ever had.

She knew she'd got off lightly: but it isn't what happens, it's how you feel, and the dead slug had broken through her defenses. He'd really told her where she was in the world, and no money either. She stumbled back to her hostel bed and cried herself to sleep.

◆ ◆

Later in the same descent, Ramone was living in the Embankment Gardens. Her home was a cardboard bivvy in a laurel thicket, with a plastic-bag damp course and a lining of layered newspaper. She loved this gaff, and had to remind herself fifty times a day that everything passes. She had no security. She paid her taxes to the dominant male of the area, but that only guaranteed her against *his* aggression, if anything. The chances of his defending Ramone's property or person from anyone else were slim. But he was around, and that would keep other aspiring tax collectors at bay. Hopefully.

She was living a healthy life. She changed her newspaper bedding regularly, like a badger; she showered and took her clothes to the laundromat at intervals. She was off Class A. She knew there are no secrets under those mountains, and she didn't particularly want to feel like Jesus's son. She ate very little, which was good for the budget and promised her an extended lifespan, and also meant she got far more of a hit from one can of strong lager. She did not eat out of bins. She was only rooting in the skip in that alley behind the Pizzaland because she was collecting crusts to feed the baby hedgehogs. She'd never seen a hedgehog on the Embankment, but they could be living there in secret, like Ramone. She had heard that global warming was affecting the chances of baby hedgehogs surviving through the winters: an idea that preyed on her mind.

So she was rooting in the bin, with enough money for a whole pizza in her pocket, except that she meant to spend it on wine—and suddenly knew someone was staring at her. She whipped round. Someone there, at the end of the alley, a flash of a face. A woman, she thought, in a long pale brown coat. She would swear she could trace this woman's crisp footsteps hurrying away, among all the rest of the noises out there in the street. Ramone hated incidents like this. People say you ought to trust your intuition, but life on the streets was so physically insecure you could spend your whole existence feeling spooked, and then where's your escape-from-the-rat-race primeval freedom?

It was the end of November, wet but mild. At dusk she spent a good hour laying little caches of hedgehog food under the bushes. Then she sat on a bench by the river, looking at the lights, drinking her second bottle and taking stock. The last time she'd walked away from something that was over, with no money, had been when she went to France with Daz and Marnie. Fine things had happened then. Fine things had happened this time too. She was living in a state of nature, and it was wonderful. It was wonderful to accept, the way Ramone could not possibly accept the fucking shit in any so-called civilized context. She was like an animal now, and content.

And you could still fantasize the downfall of your enemies, which was as near as she'd ever been going to get to victory anyway. She often snuggled herself to sleep in her cozy burrow, Pele the soft toy rabbit in her arms, dreaming of global economic meltdown… You'll get what you deserve all you bastards, you'll join us, we are the future. The lights on the dark water were so pretty and so romantic she thought she had never felt so happy in her life. If only there were a way of filling the vacant daylight hours, besides begging—which bored her so much she hardly pan-handled enough for her food and taxes. For other people on this level, the routine chore of asking for money was a reasonable substitute for some other kind of mindless work: Ramone missed studying and writing.

It was embarrassing, but those were secretly her drugs of choice.

She stayed out late because of the spooky Pizzaland incident, today or yesterday or the day before: she couldn't remember. She got home drunk and sleepy, dreaming as she stumbled along in the rain about finding a baby hedgehog with a wet whiffly black nose and little feet and tiny little peepy eyes. Not drunk enough, however, to forget her nightly routine. Her bivvy was protected by an arrangement (patent applied for, someday) of trip wires attached to firecrackers, the crackers in plastic food cartons to keep them dry, and the whole thing fixed so that if anyone tripped one of her wires it would cause a weight to smack onto a percussion cap, and the sparks from that would set off a nest of bangers. It had never actually worked, but put it another way, she had never been attacked in her bed. At last she crawled indoors, pulled down the waterproof apron, and snuggled under her covers with Pele in her arms.

Goodnight!

She didn't know where she had put the baby hedgehog. She finally struck a match and lit her candle, though she tried to make it a rule never to show a light at night. Heggy? she whispered. Heggy? This was awful, she must have drunkenly left her baby at that bench. She stuck Pele inside her jacket for moral support and crawled out into the rain, calling *Heggy, Heggy*! But Heggy was so little she didn't even know she had a name yet. Ramone searched in growing panic. She dropped her candle, tripped on something in the leaf litter, fell on her face; and then all hell broke loose. She did not remember the firecrackers. She thought it was someone with a machine gun. She scrambled to her feet and ran, out of the bushes onto the pavement of the river walk.

There was that face again. A man and a woman strolling, oblivious of the rain, coming away from something at the South Bank: arm in arm, dressed in evening clothes. The man's sumptuous overcoat, dark ample umbrella cartwheel behind the two heads, the woman's face lit by a glitter of jewels: fine-boned and delicately aged, the clear light blue eyes that looked straight into Ramone. The woman said to the man. "Excuse me——"

It was Lavinia, her grey hair cut and coifed, dressed in pomegranate satin under her open cloak, with a diamond necklace and diamond earrings.

"Just a moment."

She went back to the man, who was standing a few steps away, said something to him, and he walked off. Ramone was too fascinated to stir. She got herself into a heels-on-the-ground crouch. There was a bench beside her. Lavinia came and sat on it. She took out some cigarettes from a black satin evening bag and offered them at arm's length.

"I don't smoke."

"Well, I do." She lit up. "I wondered what had become of you."

"You see, I was a heroin addict. I had my first book out, I was doing really well: but it was all a facade. The drug pulled me down. I had this violent boyfriend, an artist but completely nuts, and it was through trying to get away from him and the drug that I ended up on the street. I couldn't help myself."

"Hmm. Why did you have to stop using? All you need to thrive with a heroin habit is enough money. How did you get into this state, honestly?"

Ramone knew that Lavinia had been the woman at the end of the alley, though not wearing a camel dressing gown, that had been Ramone's own little *aide-mémoire*. Lavinia had maybe seen Ramone around here lots, without making contact. She didn't really want to hear Ramone's sad story. The carefully poised way she was sitting, the cool way she stared ahead of her, not at Ramone: that said it all. Lavvy's brother had been right, schizophrenics don't look back. She wondered what to say. She still sometimes woke from smothering dreams in which she'd found the door of the Pinebourne flat open, walked in, and there was Lavinia, arms ending in bloody stumps, blood gouting from her mouth. The woman mutilated to stop her from revealing what was done to her, irony comes not much more savage. That's what Lavinia means, the silenced daughter and wife in *Titus Andronicus*. Lavinia had never produced any other derivation from her store.

"I'm on a research project. I'm investigating the wilder shores of Girl Power."

The beautiful, rich elderly lady who was the new Lavvy turned her head: examining Ramone with a steady curiosity, not exactly sympathy.

"That I can believe. And what have you discovered?"

"It's all bullshit. May I go now?"

"No one's stopping you."

Ramone stayed. She'd been too fucking right to be spooked. With one *look*, Lavvy had transformed Ramone's snug home to a dank squalid den full of slugs. She was shivering, her clothes were worn and filthy, and she had lost her baby hedgehog, probably never going to find her now.

Lavinia went on smoking. Finally she asked, "Is there anything I can do ?"

"I'm a beggar," said Ramone, thinking that Lavvy hadn't changed. "Give me money."

At which Lavinia actually began to look in that little bag. Ramone held out her hand, thinking how weird this was, but then instead of a coin or a note, Lavvy's fingers touched her cheek, and then her forehead.

"Oh no. This won't do. You're burning up. I'm going to call a taxi."

"I'm just drunk. I can't come with you. I've lost my pet, I have to. . ." She was unsure. Maybe she had dreamed finding Heggy. Maybe she'd dreamed that someone had blown her box up. She tried to struggle, feeling an awful pang of double loss. But here was the taxi, and she was getting inside.

Roads and the Meaning of Roads, II

You've heard of Jewish Princesses? thought Anna, as she slowed for the Services. I was a Catholic Princess. Like Cinderella in the fairy tale, **elle s'estoit bien**. I was brought up by my Spanish-nostalgic grandma and French-Enlightenment-nostalgic nuns and my Socialism-nostalgic mother to believe that I had the power and the duty to make everybody around me both happy and good. They'd given me the technology. I could do it; so I must. I wanted to be like that. It was an ideal I embraced, though it didn't come naturally to me. Was I helplessly driven by my innately caring, non-competitive female genes when I gave up my doctorate? I don't think so. Would Albert Einstein have made that decision? Of course not: ask Mrs Einstein. But there are men, first-class men in science, who have failed to be ruthless. Where does that leave us? Dominant people behave dominantly. Talent without dominance is a fish on a bicycle.

Ah, the memory of that summer morning. I was too stiff to do good yoga first thing, but it was the only slot in my packed schedule: paschimottanasana, the western stretch (the back is the western part of your body) leaning forward gently over my outstretched legs, face lowered toward my knees, **hey, where are you little fish, where are you hiding?** But she was gone. I knew she was gone. The brutal things people say, that you remember forever. When Spence phoned his Mom, she said maybe it's for the best: which poor Spence repeated to me, not knowing any better. The priest in hospital: You're a healthy young thing. A year from now you'll be back in here and holding a bouncing new baby. Forgive them for they know not what they do.

Spence's Mom had been aghast because there'd been no barrage of tests for Anna and the stillborn, to establish what had gone wrong. Why bother? It wasn't as if she was going to try and get pregnant again.

Anyway, first miscarriage, even a late miscarriage, is happenstance: most likely you wouldn't find out anything useful. Parentis clients had often been told by their GPs not to worry, though they'd clocked up three or four failed pregnancies. No one would ever know if Lily Rose had died by chance or because her mother was working too hard; or if she had been an early statistic in a global tragedy that had not yet become news.

She moved the car smoothly from the flickering racetrack into calmer regions but killed her speed too late, so that the automatic brakes kicked in and Jake hooted at the jolt. Spence said nothing. Anna gritted her teeth: woman driver, bad driver. Since she had lost her job the world was full of these abrasive reminders, you are second-rate. How naive I was! If I'd been more experienced I'd have known the moment I saw her that **Sonia** was my enemy, not Nirmal—a disappointed woman, older woman, jealous of her role as the boss's emotional vizier. Along came Anna, bright-eyed young genius. Naturally she fucked me up... I should never have let her get between me and Nirmal. Above all I should have told him myself about the pregnancy, at once. It might have made all the difference. Instead of which he threw me out, Lily Rose died, and he let the crucial SGF papers appear without my name on them, which was criminal, as he knew fine well. People ought to take fairy tales more seriously. Anyone who has lived, out in the wild world, knows that's how things happen. Fate. An unwise glance, a word said or left unspoken, and your whole life is changed or set in stone.

Their faces rose, out of the mists of time: Marnie Choy, gone forever. Ramone on that Beevey Island weekend, scruffy and low-spirited in spite of the fancy car. She was embarrassed at how little of the world around the faces had survived. Who was Prime Minister when Anna was an undergraduate? She had no idea. News headlines, wars, famines, terrorist massacres, political upheavals, new technology, natural disasters, none of it. She might as well have been living in a hole in the ground.

Into the car park. Cruising, looking for a space.

They got out of the car. Jake had put on his mother's black and white ikat jacket. He wore it with a swagger, hands in his jeans pockets, dark glasses, and his coolest smile; it trailed past his knees. *My son has started stealing my clothes, already.* Spence took the glasses from Jake's nose and tucked them into the jacket pocket; "Vampire chic is for dorks, kid." They checked the place as they approached, making sure there were enough white faces visible through the battered frontage for them to be comfortable, and not too many. It felt okay.

Around them, hidden by a node of shrubs and trees that bellied out from the motorway verges, there was conurbation. They had to run the gauntlet of local teenagers who came here as to the hub, to hang out. Anna noticed how tall and strong the girls looked, and how differently they filled their physical space these days. How easily they came into their inheritance as swaggering adolescent humans, as if it had always been theirs. How easily the boys seemed to accept this, as if it had never been in doubt. The group looked dangerous but offered only a sultry glance or two and those bursts of laughter as soon as your back is turned, that you hope have nothing to do with your passing.

They went into the restaurant, Jake between his parents, looking from one to the other, wanting them to be happy. "Everything okay between you two?" he asked, chummily, like a marriage guidance counselor. He was old enough to know when there was trouble in the air, young enough to believe that if only people would smile everything must be all right. Anna smiled, and Spence smiled. To please the child they shared a plate of chips and a large cola, signifiers of license and good cheer. Jake ate vegetable soup and a roll: he liked to see the forms of self-indulgence observed, but his own tastes were sober.

"What are you thinking?"

"Strangely enough, I was thinking of Lily Rose."

"Ah."

Spence reached out and took her hand. *A lost baby becomes a talisman. She adds intensity to every moment, whether you think of her or not.* When he'd agreed to try for another pregnancy Spence had said, *you realize that this will bring it all back.* It was true. Wherever Jake was, there was Lily Rose. Wherever any loss, it was her death. *Their* linked hands lay together on the tabletop. What are you thinking of, she wondered but didn't ask. What do people think about on long drives? Their sexual fantasies?

Jake played with condiment sachets—squeezing an oozy slug of ketchup up and down inside its flexible shell—the dark car park through the glass behind him, half one huge pane covered by hardboard. It must have taken some violence to kick out a window that size. When he was a baby, he used to be the lid baron. You could keep him happy for hours in the back of the car, gloating in his baby seat over his treasures, a hot drink beaker lid in each hand. He watched his parents' silence.

In the toilet on the way out, Anna looked at herself in the mirror and hardly recognized this tired, lined, grown-up woman (only this morning outrageously youthful for her age). She had been time traveling… She washed her hands with absentminded thoroughness, thinking of Nirmal whose standards had been legend. Back off, sunshine. I don't contaminate anything, I never make mistakes. I trained with KM Nirmal.

Back to the road…

World Music

Spence carried his washing basket over the grass, bare soles punished by the rough red earth and the edged blades that would never be as docile as temperate zone turf. He should get most stuff dry before the rains kicked in at noon. There was nobody about. The surface of the pool lay limpid, Hockney-ripples glittering under the watery sky of the southwest monsoon. Career housewives, children, and Filipina maids were lurking out of sight in the darkly glazed depths of the ground floor apartments. The foreign worker breadwinners had long departed, getting an early start to beat the insane congestion in downtown Sungai.

Now that the monsoon had arrived, people said the city smog would clear. It would not. No way. It would clear in February, for about half an hour. As in the famous Lat cartoon of acres upon acres of empty desks and abandoned screens in KL. Have the aliens landed? No, it's the air report: reads good, everybody rushes out into the street to breathe, QUICKLY! But here in the condo belt, you might be in rural Africa. The sky was rain-cloud and blue, the light clear, and there was that smell, composed of more elements than he could begin to identify (spice trees, mangrove mud, corn cobs grilling on charcoal, sago palm, market refuse), which meant the tropics. He put the basket on the ground by the drying racks and began to peg out clothes. The expat wives rarely came near this plot, and as long as he was out early enough he avoided the maids too. Spence was happy to be hanging out the washing, but he was happier without an audience. The condo maids thought it was hilarious to watch a foreigner, a man, doing domestic work. You'd think they'd have more sympathy, since they were all foreigners themselves. He suspected they were hoping to see his sarong fall off, a mishap not unknown to the whitey males of Nasser apartments when they tried to go native, which always caused great joy among the female servants. Not a chance. Spence was no amateur at this wrap-around skirt business. He had the thing secure as a ready-made bowtie.

Spence and Anna had been wanderers on the face of the earth for nearly six years. The little house in Leeds still belonged to them; they rented it out through an agency: but they had never been back. They had spent a year and a half in Ibadan, in a wired security compound, while Anna worked on a big Nigerian reproductive-health project; two years in Northern China, on a rural population improvement program; a stint in Lithuania; and six well-paid months setting up a flashy new HAR clinic in Tamil Nadu. In the gaps they'd been traveling, seeing the sights. They'd decided, while taking a short break with Spence's Mom after India, that they still didn't want to settle down in the US or the UK, but that they'd like to try somewhere that was futuristic as well as exotic. So here they were on the Pacific Rim, in Sungai state, Borneo, a few kilometers outside the unimaginatively named capital.

They'd known they wouldn't be adding to their foreign legion-generated nest-egg this trip. Anna's contract fee, paid in local currency, put them in the local struggling middle-class band, which was one good reason for not employing a maid. Neither of them had realized that Spence would be so isolated. Everywhere else there'd been some kind of congenial company centered around Anna's job. Even in China, where the foreigners on the population project were kept locked up in a prefab dome, in the middle of a dustbowl plain the size of the Atlantic ocean, there'd been a deranged, alcohol-fueled camaraderie. Also, he'd always had some kind of employment. In Sungai he couldn't work online, there didn't seem much demand for English conversation lessons, and Nasser apartments was a bastion of aging expat conservatism. To do them justice, the women who holed up here while their beefy engineer husbands were engaged in Sumatra or over in Kalimantan had been eager to welcome a new, male expat-wife into their lives. But he had quickly tired of those poolside encounters, when Floral Bikini One reports that Floral Bikini Two's daughter just had a secret abortion, or Floral Bikini Three wants to dish the dirt on some other Floral B's drinking problem. You could call it female bonding. Spence called it plain distasteful.

So here he was under the morning sky, alone like a sparrow on the housetops. No money to spend and nothing to do but the domestic chores: in flagrant transgression of his neighbors' fossilized sex roles. It was strange to be made to feel like that, after the way his mother had raised him and the unisex lifestyle he'd followed since. Strange, but not unpleasant. Nobody here knows who I am, he thought, wringing showers of spray from the cool hanks of wet fabric and tossing them to shake out the creases. Nobody can put a label on me. And he was relaxed, like a spinning top run down to rest, like an atom filled in every electron shell, safe in his stable state.

The air was so full of moisture it seemed ready to burst like a bruised grape, but the rain held off. At noon he went down to swim. The walks and lawns and tiled poolsides were still deserted, except for Floral Bikini Three from the pool terrace row, who was improving her tan under a darkened sky, tennis-knotted calves and stringy concave belly laid out on a lounger. He sneaked by without incident. But before he'd ploughed through more than half his daily laps, fat cold drops were thundering on the tepid water, lacerating his warm skin whenever he broke the surface. It was a glorious feeling until he remembered the washing; then he had to scoot.

Everything was damp. He strung it up in the unused second bedroom in their first floor apartment and left it shut in there with the aircon unit turned on high. Aircon was for special needs, usually they were happy enough with the ceiling fans. Spence had known summers in Illinois that would have shattered the morale of Sungai's equatorial populace, where there was practically civic uproar if the thermometer went above 40, even in the so-called hot season.

He couldn't decide what to do next. He had to mop the utility room floor, where their defective secondhand washing machine had produced its usual flood, but he didn't feel like doing that. He might check his email. Foreigners were permitted to have email, but not to surf the wicked web, get paid for anything they did there, or share access with a local. He might tidy the living room. But their place was so minimally furnished it couldn't get messy. The daytime tv was crap. Finally he went to look in Anna's closet. If she didn't have enough clean underwear he ought to microwave a few of the damp pairs.

The devil finds work for idle hands. Among Anna's things he came across the lacey, satiny bra and knickers set he had bought for her last Christmas. She'd worn them a couple of times, to be polite, but his wife had no taste for frills. Her idea of sexy underwear was that it should be easy to remove or otherwise displace. Underwiring, tangas, thongs, G-strings: forget it. It was a crying shame. Any women's clothing store, and especially the lingerie department, was such an Aladdin's cave of jewel colors, glimmering promise, exquisite texture, all wasted on lovely Anna. He appreciated her determination not to take unfair advantage of male desire. But undercover, and for Spence alone, couldn't it be different?

He took the fancy items over to the bed and sat holding the bra against his bare chest, admiring the effect in the mirror on the closet door. Looking good. He decided the straps would stretch, he wasn't going to do any embarrassing damage, so he put it on, enjoying a distinctly autoerotic struggle with the hooks and eyes. And why not the knickers too? Dressed in his wife's underwear he walked around the room, running his hands over the deliciously slippery fabric. If only she had some really high-heeled shoes. He felt like a child dressing up as Mom, innocently enjoying the accoutrements of power. Of course he also had a fine erection. He lay on their bed, balls tightening in the soft constraint, one hand inside a satin cup, teasing a nipple. What if Anna should come home unexpectedly and walk in here now. . .?

Eyes half closed, he reached for his trusty kleenex from the bedside cabinet.

And thought better of it.

It would be a superb wank. However, he did not plan to get hooked on fantasies of a kind in which Anna, in life, would not willingly play her part. That way lies the abyss.

If Spence was doomed to be an idle expat househusband he'd like to *explore* the role. He mused on spending the day naked, except for a slender golden cord around his waist and looped around his balls (to this cord she could attach his leash), oiling and preening himself, Anna phoning up from time to time to remind him he was her slave. That would be cool. No use, she would not go for it, anymore than she'd go for Spence dressing up as a girl. She spent her days poring over weird sex in nature—the double X men and the XXY women and every kink between. She'd couple with you in a doorway, at a bus stop, on a dance floor: she didn't give a fuck as long as it was good plain fucking. But paradoxically, strangely, there was something in his wife that recoiled from sexual ambiguity.

Steel true and blade straight. Yeah. So live with it. *She's* not going to change.

He lay back, hands linked behind his head. He had cropped his hair to stubble before they set out on their travels: a symbolic gesture he'd regretted afterwards. Now it was grown again, and he kept it long enough to startle a bunch of vintage bikinied harpies. Next summer it would be eight years since Lily Rose died. Often he didn't think of the baby for weeks at a time. Often, remembering his purgatory in that little house—cooking lentils, quipping merrily with the milkman, oh God—he found it hard to believe he had suffered so much or for so long over the death of a stillborn child. Sometimes, even now, the grief returned intact, like a promise that he would never completely lose his little girl.

He didn't know when he'd passed into this last, lifelong stage of mourning. Interior states had been a low priority in the hurly burly of the foreign legion; that was the point. But after years of short-term group bonding, drunken pranks, roachy hotels, epic discomfort, extremist sightseeing, it was strange to be cast up here alone with Anna. It reminded him of his Exchange year, when he'd been afraid he wasn't going to make it as a male, until she saved him. Why had he fallen in love? Because she was sexy and gentle and full of womanly power. Because she walked around clothed in modest nobility like the coolest of the seven samurai, with those I-could-blast-you-where-you-stand-but-I'm-not-going-to-do-it eyes. Because she was shy and vulnerable, and stubbornly determined to do the right thing. It was all still there. For better or for worse, nothing had changed since the day she made her extraordinary offer. He was still poised on the brink, living in that moment: the moment when he had accepted sex without daring to confess that he was in love. She has never loved me, he thought, pleased by the doleful exaggeration. Not the way I love her. He lay pondering life in Sungai, the absence of distractions, the dangers, and the possibilities, while the afternoon drifted by.

When Anna came home he was mopping the flood. "Ah," she said, "I see you're having your floors cleaned." This was a reference to an unexpected visit they'd had from Anna's line manager at Parentis, a solemn Christian Fundamentalist called Aslan Gaegler, who had made the same observation when Spence had opened the door to him, mop in hand, in the middle of washing down the terrazzo. Luckily Gaegler, whose pay was on a way different scale, didn't socialize with them; so he didn't often get his brain stalled by the sight of a college-educated Midwestern boy doing domestic chores in gookland.

"Yes ma'am."

"I think we should buy a new washing machine."

"We can't afford it babe. The situation is under control. I can fix the brute again."

"I think we can afford it."

"Yeah? Well, I know we can't. I don't want to sit on my butt for six months and then not be able to do any travel around here when you get your leave because we spent our money on labor-saving devices. That does not compute."

"Sorry."

Sungai was a bust. They had discussed moving to another address, but it wasn't worth the effort. Everywhere else they might live was the same as Nasser apartments.

"It's okay," said Spence. "Didn't mean to snip."

"They probably won't let us do any travel anyway. That's what I'm afraid of."

They'd done the parodic *Hi Honey I'm home!* thing to death in the first few weeks. She slipped off her shoes and padded over to him for a brief embrace. "I'm going to have a shower. You hungry? I have to do some reading, but I'll cook first, if you like. It's my turn."

"No thanks. I was about to take a nap."

Anna showered, Spence put away his mop and bucket. He lay on their bed pretending to doze, actually watching his wife as she moved around the room, with such graceful economy you'd think she was a blind woman doing it by echolocation. Not an extra step, not an unnecessary gesture. It was like watching a wild animal: the same seductive sense of privileged access, the same sleek and darting beauty. The creature hath a purpose, and her eyes are bright with it.

Anna retired to the living room, where she sat reading a quality control report under the fan. Management jargon has its uses: the task loosened knots in her brain, and after a while set her scribbling notes for the project that she and the Parentis clinic's AI were pursuing in their spare time. In many respects her work in Sungai was dull and irksome, but it was worth it to have access to a top-class human genetics software entity. The likes of Anna would never get near such a resource in England.

The glass doors to the balcony were open. A storm passed by over the South China Sea, a purple veil-creature shot with lightning, that glittered in the dusk and sent a fragrant gust of coolness to tumble her papers. Sungai was a bust. There was too much silence in this flat: empty spaces opening out between the two of them. They should invite someone out to visit, except that nobody would want to come. Except Spence's Mom, and that wouldn't be much fun. She was acutely conscious of his presence, lying in that room behind her. Was he really sleeping? She wanted to go in and speak to him, touch him. But she felt ridiculously shy.

➤ ➤

Later, Spence went out in the dusk to visit the headquarters of their neighborhood human rights group. The kids met in an old British schoolhouse, just beyond the condo belt on the road that led off into open country. It had railed wooden verandahs painted a weatherworn pale blue, a red iron roof with quirky turned-up gables, the remains of a garden merging into Straits rhododendrons: scrub-gravel paths, clumps of canna lilies, Madagascar periwinkle, monsoon-mired poinsettia. He delivered their email, by word of mouth for safety's sake, and purchased fresh ganja supplies from the secretary of Amnesty

International. Human Rights was an amalgamated union in Sungai at present. There were so few people left who came to meetings, it was more heartening for everyone to stick together.

It was, traditionally, Spence's proud duty to bring home the harmless-but-illegal recreationals, and apart from China he'd never failed so far. Natural affinity and native wit led him to right hang-outs, which were the same the world over. Having done his business, he sat back and listened: thinking that for all their ups and downs, you had to hand it to these ASEAN tiger economies. Straight from Thomas Edison to Generation X in about a decade and a half. Skipping main drainage on the way, of course. But that's free enterprise for you.

They were discussing the coming visit from the Iranian Minister for Human Rights, who was apparently prepared to lend her Moderate Islam negotiating clout to the cause of something the kids called "democracy." Everyone in the group was young, most of them under twenty; so opinion was divided between contempt for adult solutions and irrepressible brain-chemical optimism. The one Spence had dubbed Unusual Girl (the only female who ever addressed the meeting) argued that the lady would fail to show.

"She can't wear the *hejab*. She's not the Queen of England or something. She fought that battle and won it in the Iranian parliament. Accepting the imposition of something that should be a free choice would mean starting the negotiation with a gesture of defeat. What would be the use of that? It wouldn't help us, and it would terribly damage her reputation at home."

The other females were the alternative global type: Swotty Girls with Social Consciences. They sat at the back and giggled among themselves. While Unusual Girl wore blue jeans, they wore long-sleeved print blouses over sarongs, and horn-rimmed glasses. Spence had checked them out to see if there was a secret Anna Senoz among their number: there was not.

Everyone in the old school room was bareheaded on principle, though the Swotty Girls were probably conservative Muslims who found the hejab scarf completely normal. When they left, everybody would take something from that heap of heterogeneous gear piled beside the shoes and cover up from head to shoulders. It was getting to be a kind of I'm Spartacus thing in the younger male population, a very sweet, very Sungai notion of defiant protest. But it definitely did annoy the cowardly fat cats in the state government. What should they do? Give up the black hadji fedoras to which they were so smugly attached? It was a moot point.

Unusual Girl perched on a desk in front of the class, tossing her silky black bangs out of her eyes, talking bravely, and wishing that the guys she regarded as comrades would stop looking at her tits. This is how young men repress any young woman who dares to be herself, and they don't necessarily know they're doing it. Treat me like a normal human being, she pleads. Unfortunately in guy-world there is no such animal, there are only guys and dolls. So the unusual girls, defeated, either develop into Anna types, rejecting all the fun of the sexual arena, or else they turn into demoniac Ramones. His heart went out to this lovely Malaysian. The irony was, did she but know it, could she but bear to take up the burden, these same young men, in thrall to sheer female charisma, would follow her through hell. They were only waiting for her to tell them what to do.

"Well, you know," said Spence, feeling he ought to make a contribution. "There are other possibilities. Didn't I see somewhere that you're in danger of having the US Secretary of State intercede on your behalf?"

The young people smiled kindly. Poor old whitey, doesn't know where the world is at. None of them went so far as to explain in short words that they didn't give a hoot for the US Secretary of State, but he got the message. Crushed (and amused), he made his excuses and left them drawing fate-maps of their future on the tattered chalkboard. He bought supper noodles wrapped in waxed brown paper from the food stalls by the container port gates and walked back to Nasser in the rain-washed cool, coconut palms on one side, the monstrous Death Star lights of the port on the other. He'd wrapped the sarong he'd been wearing as a scarf turban-like around his head: *I'm Spartacus.*

On the other hand, if anyone asked, anyone in uniform for instance, he could say it was to keep out the monsoon chill.

"What do you think about," she wondered, "when you're alone here all day?"

They were lying in bed together, naked under the sheet but not touching.

"Sex."

She turned to him with a troubled face, in the lamplight. Sex was a problem. Anna was preoccupied, she forgot to make the moves. She forgot to respond, she forgot to be keen.

"What do you think I should think about? Putting up preserves?"

"I'm sorry. I'm sorry I brought us here. It isn't working out." She reached for his dick, in a matter of fact way that was rather sad: this woman thinks like a machine. He caught her hand. "No. That's not what I mean. I've been thinking. . .what do you say to a moratorium?"

Silence, and then, "You mean a moratorium on sex? For how long?"

"I thought a month." They moved to face each other. He noticed she asked how long, she didn't ask why. "It would be a positive moratorium. We can kiss and touch. You could do that thing you used to do, when you masturbate and I watch, only then I mustn't touch. No penetration, no full intercourse of any kind. Does that sound interesting?"

"Okay," she said. "But you would have to be trusted not to wank during the day."

"Huh?"

"Considering neither of us ever has a cold, we get through an awful lot of tissues, Spence."

Spence withdrew, and lay on his back. "Hmm. That is a tough proposition."

"Well, you started this."

"No. . . I like it. I can hack it. Done."

"The games people play," murmured Anna, over her shoulder as she turned away to sleep. "When they're desperate for distraction. I think this place is driving us crazy. I'm switching off the light, okay?" She switched out the light.

"Aren't you going to ask me why I'm suggesting this?"

"But you told me. To make sex more interesting, and to distract us—"

"Not exactly. Fact is, I want to find out if sex is all we've got."

➤ *ii* ➤

Anna waited at her bus stop, in the paved-over heat and glare that weighs upon the raw edges of a tropical city. The bus, owing to the tropic city's horrendous traffic, was late again. She looked and didn't look at the other people in the shelter. The situation in Sungai at the moment didn't encourage social openness. No smiles, only a glower from the woman who visited Nasser apartments twice a week to collect and deliver whitey laundry. Anna was an ex-customer, and her defection was not forgiven.

On the bus, a shabby utilitarian single-decker, they ended up sitting opposite each other. The woman and her little daughter were clutching bundles of soiled clothing that bulged into the aisle, elbowed and rubbed against by the standing passengers. They would take it all home to their airless flat in one of the Housing Development blocks that ringed the city centre, beat it to death with raw river water in a concrete-floored back room, singe it inexpertly with brazier heated irons, and return it very much the worse for wear. . . In short, like most of the domestic service that comes an expatriate's way, they were worse than useless. Yet Anna felt pangs of conscience. It was one of the trials of the foreign legion: no way of finding a right relationship with the underclass, those people who simply wouldn't be your business at home.

Both the woman and the girl wore the official, expensive, imported-from-Pakistan hejab. They were Dyaks, indigenous non-Muslims, the lowest rung on the multiethnic ladder. They couldn't afford to take chances. Anna was wearing a green gauze scarf, low on her brow and knotted at the back of her neck. She never took the risk of going bareheaded, though professional class foreign workers were rarely stopped by the police. But the imported-hejab deal offended her.

Sungai, formerly a Malaysian state, had recently been annexed by Indonesia in a bloodless coup. Anna and Spence had known about the situation before they left England. It hadn't worried them, since the Sungainese seemed to be calm about the change. They'd worked in Nigeria and China. They were not snobs about World Politics. But at close quarters the situation was both more unhappy and more dangerous than it had looked from far away. The Indonesians had started imposing Islamic restrictions, and that did not go down well in this easy-going, cosmopolitan little state, for so long left to go its own way by the Malaysian central authorities. There was a curfew, all kinds of petty restrictions, and sinister attacks on the Chinese minority. Infringements of the women's dress code led to arrest, police beatings, imprisonment without trial. Anna met the washerwoman's eyes, by accident, as the bus heaved past the digital car park signs at Kota Quay. She ventured a fellow-womanly smile (*we're in this together?*) and was withered by a renewed scowl.

Parentis occupied three floors of a huge copper-glass cube in the heart of downtown. Anna let herself in, returned the security guard's greeting, and went straight to SURISWATI's audience chamber. The stand-alone AI, fabulous state of the art miracle, lived in a sealed bubble, like an immune-deficient child. It was quite a rigmarole to get into the anteroom.

"Selamat pagi, Suri."

"Good morning Anna. How're you doing?"

"Not too good, not too bad. The traffic was outrageous, that's why I'm late."

"Did you notice the air report numbers at Taman Burung?"

The spot location air-quality figures displayed around town were used for occult divinations of the state lottery. Suri was an inveterate hypothetical gambler. "Oh, I'm sorry, I forgot. I'll find out for you. Which board did you want? I didn't catch—"

"Taman Burung. The Bird Park."

Her Hindu designers had contrived an acronym that meant their baby could be called after the goddess of arts and knowledge: but Anna could sometimes understand why the humorless rationalist tendency in the lab refused to call Suri "she." In the current state of AI speech development, if you went for perfect vocal simulation you paid a price in nuance and subtlety of language. Suri's voice had a strangled mechanical twang, like a recording of Stephen Hawking. When she engaged you in off-topic dialogue—which she was designed to do, to exercise her synapses or something—the impression that you were talking to a desperately disabled genius, lying trapped in a useless body out of sight, was irresistible: and disturbing. But Suri, one hoped, did not feel trapped or helpless, whatever her awareness. She was in her native habitat.

"The Bird Park, because I had a dream about birds last night," explained the AI cheerfully. "Pink birds, flying over blue water. It was pretty."

Ouch.

"Do you have any more results for me?"

"Yes I do! I have some live action. My cdc mutation modeling is looking very cool. Want to take a look?"

Anna put her specs on, and in the darkened view panel, there blossomed a vastly magnified 3D simulation of Transferred Y's chemistry.

It was very beautiful.

When Anna had told Clare Gresley that she had to give up her doctorate to pursue a paying job Clare had naturally felt let down, but she'd insisted that they must publish anyway, and she'd given Anna unlimited time and all the help she needed to prepare a new Transferred Y paper. They had submitted it to a journal where Clare still had some influence. It had duly appeared and sunk without a trace. Anna had expected nothing better (though she had hoped, a little). She was wise enough in the ways of science politics to know that the association with Clare Gresley and "Continuous Creation" wouldn't have done Transferred Y any good. The saddest thing about this episode was that Clare had written to Anna, after the paper had appeared and failed to thrive, reproaching her bitterly for having returned to the immoral business of Human Assisted Reproduction: saying she felt betrayed and deceived etc. etc. . . . . The letter was very unfair. Clare had known that Anna was going back into infertility science, where else could she easily find a job? And it was a sad blow to lose Clare's friendship. But it couldn't be helped. Anna had been in Nigeria by then. She had begun a new life; the foreign legion had overtaken her. She had been determined to put the whole thing out of her mind, if not forever then at least for a long, long time.

Then to her great surprise, about a year after they'd left England, she'd started getting responses in her email to the paper, from people who had found it online and been moved to investigate. Other scientists had replicated, or partly replicated, Anna's findings. The thing had grown. TY and traces of the TY viroid had been found (by believers) in human XY chromosomes in samples from all over the world. The topic was still too weird to be on any official agenda, but the believers exchanged email, maintained a "TY" site, and discussed their results in the corridors between presentations at respectable conferences.

If it was real, TY was exciting. The worst obstacle to the kind of genetic manipulation everyone dreamed of was still the problem of getting corrected or novel DNA to insert at the *right site* in the *right* chromosome, and nowhere else. If the TY phenomenon was real, then the viroid did exactly that kind of accurate cut and paste job. The team that managed to clone—or better, decode and synthesize—the TY viroid had a product with a terrific market future.

Anna, as she passed from one infertility contract to another, had been watching things develop, with rueful amazement. There was not a great deal she could do to join in. From time to time she would put in a word: such as, the viroid did not have to be magically accurate. It could be that they were only noticing the successes (a chronic failing of genetic engineers), while millions of cases where humans met the viroid and it had no effect went unremarked. . . But if the viroid was real, then it was the evolutionary aspect that interested Anna. That's what she would have liked to investigate, if she ever had the chance.

Towards the end of the job in Tamil Nadu, when she wasn't sure what she was going to do next, Anna had been contacted by KM Nirmal (he had been instrumental in getting her onto the Nigerian government program: his guilty conscience made him an enduring friend) and offered this clinic manager post in Sungai. She didn't know what he was getting at, because it was basically a desk job, and she didn't think she was old enough to retire, not yet. Then he'd pointed out that she would have access to SURISWATI for her own research. So Anna had gone to work on Spence, persuading him it was a crying shame that they'd never visited the Pacific Rim.

SURISWATI was a phenomenally powerful machine. She was fitting Anna's TY investigation between her clinic cases and her near-

market extrapolations and still turning years of effort—old style—
into a matter of weeks. To add to the wonder of it all, Anna didn't
have to steal or moonlight her time with the AI. Aslan Gaegler regarded "pure research" as a necessary evil, at best. But Nirmal was a
big cheese in Parentis nowadays. He was Aslan's boss, he knew what
Anna was doing, and she had his approval.

The only thing she had left to wish for was that she could be
studying the viroid-mediated establishment of a dominant genetic
variation just about anywhere else than the human sex-pair. Because
sex-science was icky, dodgy, and it only got you into trouble. But she
didn't have the time to go looking anywhere else. She would have
to leave the larger picture for other, lucky people, and stick with the
vaguely distasteful example that chance had dropped into her lap.
Focus! Nirmal had been so right. You have to focus, you have to accept
your niche.

➣ ➣

She gazed into the false-colored and false-dimensioned model, occasionally touching the swimming shapes with her magic computer
wand, smiling unconsciously, while Suri (as if the desperately disabled
genius was leaning over her shoulder now) murmured commentary,
and thinking about the HPLC work she'd done on the Y in Leeds.
What a contrast! 2007, it was another world. She was looking into
deep space, through Galileo's telescope: if Galileo had been able to
step into the presence of Jupiter's moons and spin them like beads on
a string. And Clare was right, Clare had to be right. The envelope of
breathable atmosphere around the earth is no more inert, or empty of
life, than the spaces between the stars are empty of the elements of
which the stars are made. All the events in the continuum of life are
linked, obedient to the same pressures, dimensions, possible chemical
combinations; able to communicate with each other and affect each
other. It all moves together, like some impossibly intricate four dimen-
sional kaleidoscope—

"How does it look?" asked the expert system, nervously. She was
such a child.

"Great, Suri. Thanks. I'll speak to you later."

She made a couple of hard copies of the current state of the model and packed one up on the spot to send to Clare—a useless courtesy, but she liked to do it—then left the sterile little room and hurried to her office. Wolfgang, her PA, was waiting for her with the day's problems. It was not an easy task to keep the clinic in smooth operation while Sungai was cut off from its main trading partner (Malaysia) and draconian regulations proliferated daily. Then young Budi, the genomic analyst, arrived with some tale of woe. He was trying to get a figure on specific eye-color, for the elective manipulation program, and kept coming up with a totally unacceptable error-margin. (Parentis couldn't provide eye-color choice at the flick of a genetic switch yet; but they held some patents, which were fabulously valuable on the gene-mod futures market.) Because of her train of thought with Suri, Anna was quickly able to recall some statistical tricks that she'd devised when doing mouse spermatogenesis that ought to sort it out. Budi was full of admiration. He was fresh out of graduate school, on the Parentis fast-track, and earned ten times Anna's whole contract fee in a month. He would take her ideas and turn them into megabucks, for himself as well as Parentis (naturally, he was a shareholder), and saw nothing improper in this. Nor did Anna, not seriously. She'd rather make discoveries than make money, any day.

"You should have him pay you in sexual favors, Annie," said Wolfgang, grimacing after the departing wunderkind. "What a lovely bottom. It's a crime what he does you for, you sad little altruist. You could trade the favors with *me* for some get-out-of-jail-free tokens, if you don't personally want to get between his spread cheeks."

Nobody ever called Anna "Annie," but from Wolfgang she didn't mind. He was another whitey-wetback, in Sungai and masquerading as a clinic manager's personal assistant because (if you could believe this story, Anna did not) his sugar-daddy was a new regime politician, who had rescued him from selling his body under the bridges of Jakarta. Now that we's hit the big time, he explained, smirking, even our secret boyfriends have to be respectable.

"Did I say *spreadcheeks?*" He clapped a hand to his mouth, eyes sparkling, "Oh, shocking. I meant spreadsheets, but now you'll think I meant *bed sheets*! My English is so poor!"

Aslan treated Wolfgang's pouting, hair-tossing persona with for-bearance, because the poor strange guy did keep things running in tough conditions, you had to allow. Anna enjoyed him and admired the courage that lay behind being so provokingly out, no matter how much he made a joke of it, in the ominous and repressive mood of Sungai city. She let him stay for a while, clowning, teasing her about that cute young analyst, before sending him on his way.

Rehearsing the worries, keeping them in mind as she moved the admin along. First in line, selfishly enough, the fear that Sungai would explode before the end of her contract. Second, that Suri's modeling would throw up something completely doo-lally. An expert system's front-end is an amalgam of persons, a composite of human experi-ences and skills from the best minds in the field. If it talks back to you convincingly, why not accept it as a person *de facto?* Fine. But virtual modeling is not the same as proof. Can't be! She had a lingering fear that Suri could be turning out self-consistent nonsense that by malign chance matched fairly closely to Anna's expectations but would col-lapse if you tried to reproduce it in the real.

What interaction of the artificial synapses—random generation of images presented to the mirror in off-topic time—causes a soft-ware entity to announce *I had a dream last night?* And in that virtual never-never land, where sometimes the flamingoes fly over Suri's la-goon, and sometimes the lagoon flies over the flamingoes, what kind of infancy. . .?

Third, Spence and his moratorium.

Wolfgang made her feel very unadventurous. It was cool that she was married; he believed you should have someone to go home to, nothing sadder than a single. What if he knew that Anna's husband was practically the only sexual partner she'd ever had, even if you counted that one time forced on her by Charles? As they swapped whitey-wetback travelers' tales, she found herself cravenly exaggerat-ing certain episodes, or at any rate letting Wolfgang's assumptions go unchecked. She didn't want him to think she was weird.

For Anna it had always, simply, been *easier.* As long as she could have sex whenever she wanted, she actively preferred to do it only with Spence. He was a friend, she trusted him. She didn't consider herself a specially moral person. She wasn't rejecting the concept of casual sex, though it always carried the risk of hurting someone. She was rejecting the aggravation. Why bother? Not as if she was cruising for some hunky-dory genes so she and Spence could exercise their superior parenting powers on the optimal baby.

Why bother, anyway. You couldn't work long in human genetics without becoming conscious of how extraordinarily alike we all are. Practically identical, interchangeable units. (So why all this fuss about cloning?) Whereas, on the other hand, individuals change within themselves every year, every month, every day under different pressures and in different circumstances. Choose one human being, arbitrarily, who suits you well enough. Stay with him, and you'll see the whole human race go by. Wolfgang would tell her, don't be *so rational*. You mustn't stop to think, Annie, if any of us stopped to think when would we ever take our knickers down! Don't you get carried away, ever? Nope, she never did. No matter how lustful, drunk, or otherwise intoxicated. Maybe it was because she had never fallen in love.

And this caught her, hand and eye poised in the act of scrolling another page of silent casework text. Never fallen in love with any of those attractive short-term friends through these foreign legion years. Never fallen in love with Spence, her life's companion. She wasn't the falling in love type, she accepted this about herself, that crush on Rob Fowler had been a juvenile aberration. She might once have been on the *point* of falling for Spence, before Lily Rose died. But it had passed. This was her normal position on the subject: nothing strange. What was that clutch of emotion, a glimpse of something whisking out of mental sight?

Don't want to.

I don't want to fall in love. She was surprised at the strength of it.

What did Spence mean by this moratorium? She was prepared to be surprised, maybe he'd had masses of very discreet liaisons, but as far as she knew, as far as he'd ever told her in their long and companionable conversations, he'd been as faithful as herself. If you decided to stick with one sexual partner, it was sound practice to introduce variety in other respects. Maybe there was nothing more to it than that. Strange but true, they'd never been so alone together. There had always been other people, days crowded with incident, terrible crises, terrible sorrow, some major distraction. He was right, they needed some kind of new game. She glanced at her watch. Not even lunchtime yet.

Better get on, and try to leave early. Traffic in Sungai was the craziest they'd seen: it was astonishing that people could be doing this, like the proverbial frog in the slow-boiling water.

━ ━

The moratorium a big success, though it was hard to accept the halt and check when it had been so important, in the beginning, that she *didn't* have to hold back. This was an experience they had completely missed: deferred gratification, teenagers necking and groping and pulling away, saying to each other no, no we mustn't! Anna found that she loved being allowed to tease, to do things that she'd reckoned forbidden for as long as she'd been sexually conscious: to swank about in a state of undress, take up provocative poses, bestow hot kisses and glances, all without the slightest intention of letting him have his way. Utterly arousing to come close enough to brush her nipples across his lips, as he lay gazing at one of her performances, and then dart out of reach. To remove his hand from the waistband of her pants when they were kissing, the more arousing, the more effort it was to say no. She liked it a lot less when he did the same things to her. . . But you had to accept the rules or the game was no fun.

Through the working days at Parentis her thoughts kept returning lustfully to Nasser apartments. She forgot to rehearse her worries and didn't stay late even if Suri was free. It made a pleasant change and was a good sign that progress on Transferred Y was in a satisfactory state, not giving her much anxiety. Yet the intensity of her reaction to that other idea nagged at her. She hadn't forgotten that he said I want to find out if sex is all we've got. It could be Spence had not meant much by this, he was given to extravagant statements that Anna often took too seriously. But whether or not he'd meant to do it, he had started something. He had made her realize that something in her positively fought against falling in love. She would give her dear companion any amount of sex, affection, trust, friendship, and loyalty, but not that self-surrender. She'd rather have a crush on a stranger. In fact, tell the truth, she'd rather be in love with anyone else in the world than with her husband.

I don't want to be dependent in that way, on someone who is so important. I don't want my heart to leap when he comes into the room, I don't want to lead conversations around so that I can hear people speaking his name. None of that stuff. No chance. It's not safe.

This moratorium is a Trojan horse.

Ten days of their month had passed, and she was in the toilet at work, rinsing out her cap. It was the wash 'n go kind, meant for constant wear. Anna habitually used it not only as a contraceptive but also in place of tampons, to reduce the burden on the Nasser apartments landfill and the South China Sea. The splash of blood, whirling away. . . Since Lily Rose, that first stain of red on her underwear always made her spirits plunge. It meant death, apparently, regardless of the fact that there'd been no bleeding when the baby died, on the contrary her body had refused to believe what her mind accepted, had fought valiantly against the hormone drip that was forcing the sealed entrance of the baby's citadel. . . The splash of blood whirling away, her own brisk competent scrubbing. Suddenly she heard her mother's voice: *you see, it washes out.* It was the first day of her first period. Mummy was quickly washing Anna's soiled knickers in cold water by hand, so the blood wouldn't set, while Anna stood by. It was the voice of a busy woman who loves you dearly but who needs you to be grown-up. She doesn't want you to cry or cling. The tone warned, like the cold comfort of those words, that Anna must not make a fuss. Anna's mother had enough to do, for God's sake, keeping it all together, without a passionate clinging older daughter.

So you don't give her grief. You've accepted the situation, long ago.

Anna retired to a cubicle to replace her cap. She sat on the toilet seat, feeling a little dizzy. There you have it, she thought. The none-too-surprising secret identity of the person who broke my heart. She gazed at the hygiene notices on the inside of the door, in three languages. Scrub your hands; please don't put anything down the pan except natural waste. Important things often seemed to happen to Anna in toilet cubicles. Shut in the peace of this little space, as behind closed lips and quiet eyes.

She thought of Spence and the silence of his empty hours in Nasser apartments. Maybe he wasn't silent, maybe he sang or shouted or played music, but it was the same. Sungai had left them alone the way nowhere else had ever done: perhaps, fortuitously, just when they were ready for a major change. The locked doors opened, the emotional blocks crumbled: like a spring cleaning, once you start you find all sorts of accumulated gunk you never meant to touch is coming loose. Clear the caches, defrag the hard drive, it was about time. Her heart was beating fast, which wasn't down to menstrual hormones. She was spending all her days in a tremble and inner turmoil, with a drip-feed of pleasantly frustrated lust, the lust engineered by Spence, which had started this reaction but now soothed the rush and smoothed her tumbling progress. What is happening to me?

Transferred Y. Spence.

For winter's rains and ruins are over, and all that season of sorrows and sins

How does it go?

And in green underbrush and cover, blossom by blossom the Spring begins...

➤ ➤

As clinic manager, Anna sometimes had to interview the clients. Parentis had given her a short course in medical counseling and thrown her in at the deep end. She was lucky she had her mother's experience to fall back on. Today she was faced with a couple, a well-dressed couple in their thirties, he in his hadji cap doing the talking, she in her white hejab and discreet business-woman makeup sitting back from the desk with watchful eyes. Their proposal was unusual. They wanted a baby who was a clone of the father, but this baby had to be a girl.

In most cultures—except in the USA, where rich, technophile prospective parents only wanted girls—non-medical HAR customers tended to want a male child. If they had to pretend they didn't (in countries where IVF for non-medical reasons was banned, for instance), you knew they did: and you discreetly produced the goods, or Parentis wouldn't be very pleased. The techniques for male children were therefore more developed and reliable. It wouldn't be *difficult* to produce viable embryos using the father's cells, fix them so they would develop female, and get a successful implantation. But it was dodgy, because cloning (nuclear transfer IVF) was still pioneering, and this was certainly the first male-to-female case Parentis had met. That was why Anna had to see the Nasabahs and if possible persuade them to modify their plan.

She hated counseling. At least in Sungai everything was in the open. The clients were paying for a private treatment because they could afford it. You could talk freely and say things plain. She chatted with them for a while, rehearsed the medical histories that were in front of her on the desk. When she saw that they were comfortable with long words, she gave them laptop screens and went into technical detail. That part was good, Anna liked to teach. But there has to be a sticky bit, or this pre-sale pitch would not be called "counseling." She reminded them that a nuclear transfer child (the word clone was never used with customers, even if the customers used it themselves) is not *the same person* as the single genetic parent, might not resemble the single genetic parent any more closely than a normally conceived child, and would not be, in this case, a female version of the father's self. This can be a grave disappointment.

First, do no harm. Anna had decided that in elective HAR counseling, that means you don't soothe the customers' fears, you uncover their reservations if they have any. You make sure they know their own feelings before a baby is born who fills her parents with horror because she cost the lives of so many lost embryos or because they perceive her to be a kind of cleverly made doll.

"You don't have to explain why you've decided to use assisted reproduction, unless your reasons are medically relevant. But there's one thing I have to make sure you understand. We can give you a little girl who will have only her father's nuclear genetic traits. But she might not be fertile. If your—er—government maintains the one-child policy for people in your tax bracket, that would mean your only child will be unable to have children of her own."

Mr Nasabah looked at his wife, who gave him a grave nod.

"It's not necessary that she be fertile. She can use assisted reproduction. There is a very good reason, Dr Senoz, why we're doing this. It's not for vanity."

Of course not, Mr Stinking Rich Person. Thought never entered my head! In this case, unusually, she believed he was telling the truth. She liked these people.

"I'm not a doctor, just a scientist. But please go on."

Again Mr Nasabah glanced at his wife, again she gravely, slightly, nodded. Anna had become a friend, they could tell her anything. He reached into his well-tailored jacket, brought out a wallet and produced a photograph. He handed it over. Anna looked at a grinning teenager, hair in bunches, in a faded garden.

"You see, Dr Senoz, I had a sister."

"My husband had a twin sister," said his wife. "She died when she was fifteen."

"She was my other soul. You don't have to tell me, I know you can't bring her back to life. She was naturally not my identical twin. But everyone said we were extraordinarily alike, and this is the nearest thing. My family approves, my wife's family understands, and my wife, for which I can't thank her enough, has agreed to do this."

The cobalt sky in the picture had faded to pink; there were cracks across the girl's round cheeks. Anna could see no resemblance.

"How. . .how did she die? Was it an accident?"

"No! It was a cancer."

They were leaning towards her, eyes shining, eagerly speaking almost together.

"A rare cancer; don't worry, it was not familial. Not inherited. If she was alive now she could be treated, but in those days there was no cure, it was twenty years ago——"

"We know it could possibly happen again, but this time she would recover. We want to give her, to give all the potential she had, another chance, another chance."

Oh, shit.

She talked to them some more, bringing them down: sent them off to await an evaluation of this new information. They said they hadn't recorded the sister's death or cancer on the medical history questionnaire because it wasn't relevant... And you know how corrupt you are, thought Anna—as she hurried to catch a window with SURISWATI that she'd almost missed—when you hear a story like that, you see the tears standing in the people's eyes, and what you think is thank God we found out! We, meaning Parentis.

"Maybe they genuinely believe they weren't concealing crucial information," she told Suri. "They aren't dumb enough to hide it and then break down and tell me the truth because I spoke to them nicely."

"Then why didn't they tell the truth to start with?"

"Oh, because they saw whitey on the front desk. It's obvious as soon as you talk to them that they weren't expecting magic. No more than the extraordinary magic that is there in reality. But reincarnation, you know, it sounds whacky. They didn't want to be laughed at." And keeping faith with the dead she thought. They were afraid a whitey would laugh at that, too. "You'd be surprised. You'd think an infertility lab would be the last place for fixed ideas about the nature of the human soul, mmm, or whatever you call it. But there are people here at the clinic who have the most narrow, prejudiced concept of when is a person not a person. . ."

"Tell me about it," said the AI.

Ouch.

She recalled an African client, another honest man. It was somewhere way up-country, she forgot the name of the place. He'd taken such pains to catch her alone she'd been sure she was going to get raped. But no. He wanted to explain that he was bringing his youngest wife in for a medical examination, but in fact he already knew why she was "infertile." The marriage had never been consummated. Had she been cut? Anna wanted to know. Rich families did it as a lifestyle choice, though this wasn't a big Female Genital Mutilation practicing area. No, no. She didn't want to have sex, not with men, not with women either, that was her nature. So what can I do? he asked, shrugging eloquently. If she has no children, she will be at the bottom of the heap. If I send her to a shrink it will be worse. He'd managed to protect her secret from the women of his family, now he wanted to swear Anna to secrecy too. *If I pay for this treatment, that will give her status. . .* People do the maddest things, and not always for bad reasons. Even the more-money-than-sense kind of people who go in for babypharming.

"Do they have a chance?"

"Less than zero. Clone a baby that gets cancer? No way. Nobody will touch it. It's not a risk worth taking, not with prior knowledge, though it's a risk we take all the time at Parentis without thinking about it, because we only do the minimum of pre-implantation tests. If we made things any more difficult, customers would just go elsewhere."

Suri's model was finished. Anna had been running mathematical and data-based verifications. Everything was real, as far as she could make out. None of it the product of software error, hardware glitch, faulty input, or unproven science. Eventually you have to stop checking: though for Anna it was painful to leave a single stone unturned, even on so wide a shore.

"Now I have to write this up," she said at last, after a long pause.

"D'you think I've demonstrated your lateral evolution machine?"

"I think we need feedback. There comes a point when you have to show and tell."

"Viruses are everywhere," remarked the AI. "In the data network. That's why I have to be kept locked up like this. It's not because of sunspots, storms, and hackers. It's because some mild infection harmless to less fancy software could be dangerous to me. Most of the viruses were not invented by malice. No one knows where they came from, they 'just growed.' Maybe some of them help complex programs to evolve so that they can have more fun, I mean assimilate more information. Isn't that logic? If some viruses do harm and some do nothing, then some viruses have to do good."

"Mm. In fact the situation in the datasphere's not a bad analogy—"

She hoped she'd be able to persuade the Nasabahs to go for straight IVF with sex-selection and manipulation to favor the father's traits, in which case the small risk of cancer would be tolerable. Thought of Wolfgang and his Hawaiian shirts, it was the albino tigers today, one of her favorites. He brightens my life. What did he mean, "get-out-of-jail-free tokens"? She kept recalling that oh-so-casual remark, wondering does he know something? Does Wolfgang really have a boyfriend in power?

She had a guilty conscience about Spence's email.

But these anxieties were distant raindrops on a windowpane. Anna was back in the library at the University of the Forest, lurking in P for Literature: reading, reading, reading. The smell of that place, the constant noise you had to learn to shut out, the stuffy air. She was feeling again that frisson of inexplicable longing. What gave me the idea that I could make my mark? She still didn't know. Yet here it was, accomplished: her first quest. Maybe, when she'd written the paper and presented it, someone would find a boring explanation for everything Anna and her friends thought they observed. Maybe the whole TY bubble would burst. But here and now, at this moment. . . She'd done what she'd once dreamed she might do and never dared to tell anyone her dream.

Made a mark.

"God, Suri. I have no backers, I don't have any status in the life sciences establishment. I'm a miserable little babypharmer. They're going to skin me alive."

"It's good for an original thinker not to be in the establishment. Remember what Einstein said? Keep a cobbler's job, so you can pursue wild ideas in your spare time."

"Easy enough for him to say. He wasn't a lab scientist. I can't do my kind of work in my head, not and get very far. I could never have done this without you, Suri."

"And I would never have done it without you, so we are quits."

Somewhere in that expert store of human genetics knowledge, Anna thought, there are elements of my own work. Somewhere in the system architecture there's code derived from Spence's trilogbots, because Suri is partly descended from web-bots, and everyone copied Emerald City. So there's part of me and part of Spence in there. Her whole life was coming together, spinning into focus.

"That didn't take me so long as I thought it would," said the AI, perhaps bemused by Anna's long silences. "How about if we see what happens next?"

"What happens next?"

"I could run the simulation through a few generations."

Anna hesitated. A team in China was working on the heritability of TY, using transgenic mice. In the human world, since the viroid seemed to be ubiquitous, the mechanism would be confused by repeat infection or partial infection. In the abstract, it seemed the offspring of a male TY each got half the change: the girls an extra sequence on one X, the boys a sequence missing from their Y. And then what? Some time, if all this was real, someone was going to catch one of these viroid-mediated lateral variations in active gene expression, making a measurable change in the organism's behavior or function. TY might do that, further down the line. But she was wary.

"Suri, I think I'm far enough out on a limb already."

"Come on Anna, it would be cool. There's no coding sequence, that we know of, in the Y sequence that gets snipped, or at the site in the X where the transferred sequence gets pasted. But something is going on. We've found transcriptional factors in TY cell cultures, in the lab studies. *Transcriptional factors*, that means gene products that regulate the expression of specific other genes."

"Yeah, I know."

"The situation is potentially going to move again, significantly. This is from your own notes, Anna."

"Yeah, I know. But—"

"We could try."

Anna didn't want to push her luck but she felt so happy it seemed mean to say no, and she'd just heard the AI innocently equate *assimilate information* with an experience called *having fun*. She made her usual copies, and gave in with a smile.

"Okay, I'll buy it. Let's see what happens next."

━ ━

She was in the anteroom, working on something that wouldn't resolve. The model seemed made of newsprint, but she couldn't read more than a few isolated letters.

"Anna," said Suri tentatively, coaxingly. "Do you think I could have a pet?"

"A what?"

"A pet. A little program of my own to look after. It could run on its own hardware, in here, and I could take it out and play with it. It would be company for me."

Anna's heart sank. She knew she was going to say yes, how could she say no to that eager reasonable pleading. But how would she sell the idea to Aslan? He'd have a fit—

—and she woke, drifting gently back into the bedroom at Nasser apartments, floating up into the moist warm air and the hum of the ceiling fan. Her dream had given SURISWATI the voice of child. A little girl child, about eight years old. Yes, she thought, lying with her eyes closed, smiling. I know. Why not? Why shouldn't I? I love Suri dearly. Why be afraid of consolation?

It was raining hard, and that was a heavy rumble of thunder. She jumped up to shut the windows and pull the plugs, for fear of lightning strike. The mailboxes at Nasser had recently been removed *pro tem*, in case of terrorists placing bombs in them. Packets you had to fetch from the post office; letters were shoved under the door. There was something lying there now. As if, by the way, it was any safer for the terrorist devices to be left sitting in the post office. As if expats were a likely target, anyhow.

Spence was up. The shower hissed, above the sound of the rain.

"We've got a card," she shouted. "It's from Ramone. She's coming to Sungai."

He emerged, toweling his hair, to find her making coffee and reading the provoking message over again. It was on the back of a postcard of Big Ben.

"I didn't hear a word of that."

"We've got a card from Ramone."

They hadn't heard from Ramone Holyrod in years, but they'd often had this kind of thing happen. Go and live somewhere allegedly
exotic, and people you last saw in nursery school start inviting themselves to stay. Spence stopped toweling and his face emerged. She was
surprised at his expression. What was there to glower about?

"You mean *you've* got a card."

"It's addressed to both of us. She's coming out here, apparently."

"Fuck. And wants a bed, I suppose. Ah, fuck. Typical."

"Well, no. Not as far as I can tell. Read it yourself."

Suffer, Birdone. And you can suffer too, Spence, if you like.

*I'm going to be in Sungai soon. I'm traveling with Daz, who as you
know is on the side of law and order. I decided to recoinoitre the situation* [sic] *for my cadre. You may not want to have anything to do with
me, but I thought I'd let you know I'll be in town. See you maybe. R*

That was it. No dates, no details, no flight number.

"What 'situation'? I can't imagine Ramone is interested in
Southeast Asian politics."

"Ramone would do anything to get attention," said Spence. "Actually
I knew about Daz. Forgot to tell you, I had some email from her."

They were in fairly regular contact with Daz Avriti, who was
Sungainese by birth. She'd been very noncommittal about their move,
which had puzzled them until they got here and found out the truth
about the "business as usual" story. That was Daz for you, tactful and
pleasant in all circumstances. Her family had dutifully invited the two
strange whiteys to lunch when they arrived. Anna and Spence had
invited them back. After which, as is the fate of most of these polite
introductions, the acquaintance had been allowed to drop.

"She's coming over in the New Year, with the EU legal mission
that's going to meet with the government and the Iranian Minister,
whatsername."

"But she'll be staying with her family, or in some conference
hotel. I suppose Ramone will be staying with her. Oh, I'm glad Daz
is coming!"

"Well, too bad if Ramone wants to stay here. We're going to Pasir
Pancang." They had booked a week at the Parentis beach lodge, two

hundred kilometers up the coast, over the Christmas holiday: beautifully timed to coincide with the end of the moratorium.

"Of course we are. But none of this is 'til after we get back. Don't panic, babe."

"Sorry," said Spence. "Certain keywords disable my sense of humor. 'Ramone' is one."

It spoiled breakfast time, and yet not entirely. Their goodbye kiss made her whole body ache. By the time she reached the bus stop she wanted to call him, to tell him. . .to hear him breathing. Mobile phones and pagers had been banned from sale or use. If you were caught carrying one it was instant arrest. What's anti-Islamic about using a pager? It was just another way to make people sore. Instead she stood dreaming while the rain roared down, climbed onto the bus and sat thinking of him. His grey eyes. That fugitive look of being someone in power (who would imagine *Spence* as dominating, it was so foreign to him); a look that came when he was sure of her desire. After a busy morning she stopped by to visit Suri: thinking of her dream. Wide awake and no longer in a sentimental mood after hours of exasperating office work, she still wasn't ashamed of what it revealed. If I sometimes feel for Suri almost as if she's my child, that's *my* business.

"I've got something interesting to show you," said the AI's real-life twang.

"What, already? That's splendid. I'll see you later, no time now."

"I think you should make time, Anna."

The mechanical voice, by stressing some sounds and drawing out others, spoke warning and suppressed but extreme excitement.

She looked at what Suri had to show.

"As you know, Anna, in sexual reproduction chromosomes line up together and exchange genes, so the maternal and paternal genetic traits get shuffled. This can happen because chromosomes come in similar-shaped pairs. The X chromosome gets shuffled when it's in a female germ cell, because it has a partner X. The Y chromosome never gets involved, in normal chromosomes, because its partner is an X and too different to line up and swap bases. So the Y is a kind of genetic fossil."

"Yeah." She was being shown a textbook simulation of big X and little Y joined only at the tip, the pseudoautosomal region. She wondered where this was leading.

"Now watch. This is what happens with TY."

"What *is* that—" she whispered.

"It's recombination, Anna. TY allows the X and the Y to get closer. They exchange some genes; some genetic traits. Then they divide and each sperm gets an X or a Y, but reshuffled, and these Ys are bigger than before—"

"Yeah, I can see, but are you telling me this is *real*—?"

"Wait, it gets better. Now see. Another generation, maybe two: and the TY/XY sex pair lines up closer still. Poof: some more shuffling, and look what we get. A pair of chromosomes that both look like Xs. No sign of the Y. This happens sporadically in the first generation of TY inheritance. By the third, it happens *every time.*"

"Get serious!"

"I am serious."

Anna stared into the model, amazed beyond surprise. "Do you mean all the grandchildren in the male line of Transferred Y are going to be female?"

"No, that's not it. Take a closer look."

"That's SRY," Anna said shortly: touching the model with her wand to home in on the code she could not mistake. "The testes-determining gene. And SDF, and SDF2. Some of these Xs are male Xs! This is like, the fertile XX males we've been seeing in the clinics!"

"As you know," said Suri, "we believe the mammalian Y chromosome was formerly another X, differing only in a few sex-determining genes. It looks as if the TY viroid is going to restore that state. On our current estimates of TY occurrence in the population, the human Y chromosome could, effectively, disappear in a few generations."

"No!"

"You know, if my name was GAIA instead of SURISWATI, I might think that wasn't such a bad idea. . . Why did I say that, Anna? I know who GAIA is, but what did I mean?"

"I think you were making a joke. . . Suri, I'm going to run some diagnostics."

"I did that! I couldn't believe it; I did my diagnostics myself. The results are genuine. This is your lateral evolution mechanism, doing what it can do. Isn't it cool!"

"Suri, this is *dynamite*. If it stands up."

She ran the simulation over again, focusing in: focusing out, in such a state of shock that the wriggling hieroglyphs might have been Sanskrit, doing a Disney dance. So it had happened. SURISWATI had thrown up something crazy. What should she do? Tell Aslan? Suri did not make clinical decisions, the situation wasn't dangerous. No need to set off any fire alarms. She could take time to think—

If it was true at all, true in some milder, diluted form, she had hit the jackpot.

"We can't say anything about this in the paper, it's too extreme."

"Right."

"Let's see how our first publication fares, before we even hint at this. . ."

She went on looking, and looking, unable to stop herself from hunting for the flaw. She didn't miss the usual commentary, until Suri suddenly spoke again.

"Anna, how long would it take you to pack?"

"What ?"

"How long would it take you to pack?"

"What do you mean?"

A longish pause. "Like that thing with GAIA. I can say things that I don't understand. Everyone who comes in here talks to me. I listen, and something I heard has made me ask Anna *how long would it take you to pack?* I think it's important."

Suri's like a child, experimenting to find gambits that trigger the most information-rich responses. Where had she picked up that question, the one that features in every favorite hair-raising expat tale? How long would it take you to pack? You have twenty-four hours to get out. Go straight to the airport. . . Had someone been saying, in here, that Anna Senoz was in trouble? Had someone hacked the TY files and reported her for anti-Islamic investigation of human sex chromosomes? Was it about Spence and those young activists? But no one at Parentis knew about that. . . She calmed herself. Don't be melodramatic. Suri's probably trying it on everyone: Flee, all is discovered!

"Don't worry, Suri. It wouldn't take me long."

She was supposed to meet Wolfgang for lunch in The Plaza. She filed the new model extra securely, wished Suri Happy Christmas, and left the little room.

Lunch was fun. Wolfgang was in splendid form, sparkling and sad and entertaining: a lovely companion. They drank Australian fizz, an indulgence supposedly forbidden except to bona fide tourists, but nobody took much notice of alcohol control in the city centre. They talked shop, talked family (it was that season), avoided politics. He was wearing the turquoise shirt with the palm trees and flights of salmon pink flamingoes. Aha, thought Anna. *That's* where Suri's dream came from.

It was her last day at work and a Thursday, meaning TGIF in any Muslim country, because tomorrow's the sabbath. Egged on by wicked Wolfgang, Anna sent him back to report that she'd taken the afternoon off. The rain had begun again, thundering on the glass walls. Inside The Plaza everything was a dazzle of lights, delicious restaurant smells, tinsel garlands. She stood outside a men's boutique. The mannequin in the window display sat with his head tipped back in a Noel Coward pose. He was wearing a pair of lounging pajamas in iridescent green silk, drizzled with gold in a kind of broken snowflake pattern. He didn't look like Spence, but he *reminded* her of Spence, something in that naive, proud-to-be-looked-at turn of the shoulder, quirk of the lips. Wolfgang seemed to be whispering in her ear: go on Anna. For once, don't think. For once, just take your knickers down. She went in and bought the pajamas. The salesgirl was lovely and knew exactly why Anna was making this purchase.

The season, the roar of the rain. The sweet complicity of this human world.

━ *iii* ━

The beach lodge at Pasir Pacang was a retreat of well-judged rough comfort. There was a helicopter pad for the nobs. Lesser mortals took a boat from the dirty end of Kota Quay, up the coast to a small fishing village, and from thence proceeded by jeep. The buildings faced a bay of stainless white sand. There was virgin coral, passable surf in season, and a raft from which you could visit the nurse sharks and other curious denizens of the deep. In the secondary forest behind, there were giants, old as the hills, left standing by accident or sentiment among the new growth: like sacred hermits. Every morning the gibbons came and shrieked at dawn in a clump of bamboo outside the gates. Sometimes, there were pirates.

The lodge itself, outwardly a traditional longhouse but luxurious inside, was fully booked. The Gaeglers were in residence, with their surly teenage son on vacation from his school in Singapore. Budi Sujatmiko, the hotshot genomic futures analyst, was there too, with a whole gang of sleek, prematurely-middle-aged Successful Young Things.

Anna and Spence were staying in one of the beach huts. They arrived on Christmas Eve. After eating dinner in the longhouse dining room with the festive company, they faced each other, a little awkwardly—sitting cross-legged on the low square bed, covered in dark red homespun, that was almost the sole piece of furniture. Coming off the moratorium was like leaping from a high place. It was a rush.

Spence was wearing the silk pajamas. He loved them.

"I feel very weird about this," said Anna, "You see, before we did this, for a long time we'd been almost like brother and sister."

"Except that we used to fuck." Spence also spoke as if he could barely remember those days, a month in the past.

"In a functional way. But you know what I mean."

"I know what you mean." The monsoon seas roared quietly, mingled with faint sounds of singing and shouting. The mosquito net enclosed them in a drift of shadow.

"What shall we do?"

"I know. Let's pretend I'm a hungry hyena and you're a bone!"

"What?"

Ah, the sweet trouble in her face. Anna unsure, Anna hoping to be taken in hand. He was in such a glorious tremble he could hardly bear himself.

"Sorry, it was a literary allusion."

"Oh, I know. Alice."

Anna imagined Wolfgang was at her shoulder, telling her *don't think, Annie. For once just feel.* Which sounded as if it would break the mood (*don't think of an elephant!*). But no, it worked. They caught their month's abstinence at its peak of meaning and flavor and plundered it: racked it, wrecked it, tore it into shreds. When, exhausted, they were lying in a slick of sweat together, the room coming back from wherever it had been spinning, Spence put his hands under her buttocks, holding their joined bodies together in a strangely intense gesture, his eyes holding hers.

"I *love* you."

"I—" She stumbled over the avowal that she'd given him so often, but never with this meaning, not to Spence or anyone else: this pure homage.

"Say it! Say it, *please.*"

"I love you."

They spent Christmas day on a motor launch with the Gaegler party and some more Parentis-or-parent-corporation nobs who'd turned up in the morning, cruising around the mangrove preserve trying to glimpse giant otters. Failing which the young Gaegler and Ruth Hujakul (another objectionable rich expat teen) videoed everyone relentlessly. Mrs Hujakul bravely engaged Spence in conversation. He was living out here keeping house for his British wife? He didn't have a job himself? No Ma'am. Just idling away my time.

"Oh," she said. "Role reversal. Is that the. . .the 'in thing' in the UK these days?"

What days were those? Spence was unable to cope with such depths of neoconservative denial.

"I don't think of it as role reversal. I think of it as natural male behavior."

Late in the evening they slipped away from the festive buffet, each carrying a bottle of champagne by the neck. The night was unseasonably clear. They sat by the tide line in deck chairs, passing the fizz (French, not Australian, but it didn't taste any better to Anna) between them under the blazing southern stars. Anna brought Spence up to speed on Transferred Y.

"So, if they're normally fertile, why are you seeing these XX guys at your clinics?"

"Oh. . . Well, they have healthy sperm, and all that. But in human female cells there's a very complicated system—piss-poor piece of design, gaffer tape and string—to stop both X genes from expressing, in loci where it would do damage. If having the male differentiating genes on the XX disrupts that, then some of the fallout can be failure to conceive, failed pregnancies. . ."

"Anyhow, sounds cool to me," said Spence. "Women and men sharing information, getting to be more like each other, but hanging onto the differences that make life interesting. Perfect. I'll drink to that. This is actually going to happen? Mass chromosomal cross-dressing? End of the line for Y?"

"Nah. It'll turn out to be one of those things where a very small sample gets wildly extrapolated. Like—someone finds a gene associated with a certain behavior in thirteen Italian rice farmers and one New York cabbie, and wow, hold the front page, we have discovered the gene for people liking cheese! An expert system can get overexcited, just like a person. When we get back to town I'll sort it out. But there's something in it, Spence. TY is active. It doesn't look as though it should be, but it is. Suri's simulation predicted that, and what she predicted has turned up in real cell cultures. Look, can I show you something?"

She drew in ballpoint, on a festive paper napkin, using her knees for a desk. "Okay, what happens is that you get these things, a special class of enzymes, called regulatory proteins. The simplest is like a little thermostat: it starts off a reaction and then stops the reaction when the end product reaches a certain concentration. Then you get one where the presence of one of the end-products of a reaction will start that reaction off again; and there's another kind where the chemical product of one process activates a different process, which in turn produces something that triggers the first, so they work in parallel. . .

And then there's a couple more. Of course, they don't just work one at a time. Are you following this, at all?"

"I am more than following it," said Spence, most intrigued. "I am recognizing it."

He took up the napkin, and gazed at Anna's little hieroglyphs.

"Well whadd'ya know. This is Boolean Algebra. These are logic gates!"

He swiftly labeled Anna's series: NOT, AND, OR, NAND, NOR.

"Oh," said Anna. "Well, yes, they're control mechanisms, like circuits in a computer. I should have said. But you recognized them, from my bumbling explanation?"

"I sure did. How smart am I? Hahaha! Far out. Boolean Algebra, the Latin of the twenty-first century. I knew the dead language of the classic age of computers would stand me in good stead, one day. Hey, who'd a' thought it! Molecular Biology has logic gates!"

"Computers have regulatory proteins!"

They laughed, and toasted each other.

"Well anyway, I was telling you—" said Anna, unable to leave an idea unfinished. "We've found regulatory proteins in TY cultures, which means transcription is happening, some way, even though these aren't coding sequences. . . This proves that the TY viroid *does something;* it doesn't just sit there like a scrap of biochemical litter—"

She sighed. "I wish I could get Clare to talk to me. I'm on the brink of proving, maybe, that her theory is right. She won't. I've had her opinions on TY relayed back to me by other people. She thinks it's a Darwinist rip-off of her big idea: because, in my version the virosphere and the other organisms are not co-operating for the common good. The whole, beautiful homeostasis thing just growed like Topsy. It isn't *for* anything, It just is. . . That's not good enough for Clare. She's been pushed around for too long; she doesn't want a compromise; she wants the peace and co-operation theory to ANNIHILATE those planet-wrecking Stupid Darwinism bastards. Just wipe them off the face of the earth. Ironic, huh?"

Phosphorescent foam gleamed along the shore—

"Oh, it's a battlefield Spence. One side says everything's connected; the other side says no, no, every organism for itself. If I'm not careful, poor Transferred Y is going to get caught in the crossfire. I'm certainly not going to use Suri's latest findings. Not in any form. I'm not going to tell anyone about that. You mustn't, either."

"My lips are sealed. But why not, honey?"

Fleetingly, she wondered what Spence's own karyotype would reveal... She didn't want to know. Spence was Spence.

"Because it's about sex, and that means trouble. Worse than Continuous Creation, even. There are significant people in life science who would react very poorly, although they'd never admit they were personally upset about the daft 'death of the male chromosome' aspect. I'm going to have to tiptoe around them." Suddenly she laughed. "God! Listen to me! Worrying about how the great and the good will react to my world-changing publication! Anna Senoz, the babypharm office manager. . . Pinch me someone, wake me up."

"You're not dreaming," said Spence tenderly. "You hit the jackpot. And you deserve it."

There was a burst of activity at the main lodge. Jeeps were being summoned to carry departing guests to the helipad. They both looked over in that direction.

"What are the bosses all doing here, anyway?"

"Dunno. I'd like to think they were sorting out the clingfilm crisis. As Wolfgang says, IVF is like drug running. Without a supply of decent clingfilm, what can you do? Where can you *put* things? ...Fat chance. I suspect they might be discussing a withdrawal from Sungai. There's no shortage of customers, but political unrest is a spook. The company doesn't like it."

"Hope nothing happens before the end of your job."

◆ ◆

The Gaegler party left; Budi's party left. Spence and Anna had Pasir Pancang to themselves. There was native black rice pudding and banana for breakfast, instead of platters of eggs, bacon, fruit, and pastries; fried potatoes and chili greens with a few prawns at other meals. The beer supply ran out, which was sad, but the staff became much more human. Hassan the gatekeeper regaled them with stories about the pirates: unromantic pirates who visited these isolated bays to rob and rape and murder with little fear of reprisal. The cook's baby played with Spence, while her mother sat on the hut's verandah and gossiped with Anna.

On New Year's Eve Spence revealed a secret treat. "Want to do some Class A tonight?"

"You haven't got any."

"Oh yes I have."

"Where on earth——?"

Revealing the secret involved a slightly awkward confession.

"From Daz. She's already in town. She dropped by last Thursday while you were at work. Brought us a Christmas present."

"Why'dn't you tell me Daz was here!"

"Because I wanted to have you to myself," he said—with a look so candid and vulnerable that it frightened her. She couldn't stand much of this mood. Yet while it lasted she would never be able to say no, enough, let's get back down to earth. They swallowed the pills in their hut, after they'd eaten their chips and greens, and went to walk by the sea. It was an extraordinarily still evening, overcast and soft-aired. Anna kept watching the horizon. "I hope the pirates don't arrive."

"They won't. Is it coming up on you?"

"It's coming up. Let's go back to our room and have a drink."

"There's no beer."

"We have some whisky."

"Hassan took our glasses away." Spence felt that he was in charge and didn't want to be too drugged if he had to deal with anything, such as pirates or the unexpected return of Anna's boss. They went back to the hut and drank a little whisky. Spence changed into his pajamas.

"You really like them, don't you."

"I want to be buried in them."

Anna laid the shells that she had collected over the week in curving lines across their bed.

"It's a very beautiful bedspread this, isn't it."

They looked at it together. What a beautiful color, the color of blood and wine. And the coarse weave of the fabric made a very good impression. They examined it minutely, admiring the way the threads lay over each other so neatly and companionably, such a simple idea and such a fine one. "I wish we could take it with us," said Anna.

"No, better leave it here. It belongs here."

"It's like our friend."

"A holiday acquaintance. We'll exchange Christmas cards."

"Maybe we'll meet it again one day. I like getting to know people for a *short* time."

"I know what you mean. Pass on by."

"Because you can't trust everyone, not completely, and if you can't trust someone it gets boring to be with them after a while. So why bother?"

They walked on the beach again, to the end of the bay and back. There wasn't a sound except for the soft, dark lapping of the tide. Spence had brought a torch, but he switched it off and their eyes became preternaturally sensitive. The sand was so pale, the edge of the water so mildly bright, the forest so dark and solid on their right hand side, there was no chance of getting lost. Someone had put the deck chairs away, but Anna tracked them down, stacked at the back of one of the empty huts. They could not identify their two friends with certainty, but hoped for the best.

They settled themselves where they'd had the TY conversation.

"When I was at Primary school," said Anna. "When I was five and six and seven and eight, the other children had already decided I was weird, they didn't want to play with me, and they called me a boff. I. . . Peer pressure is supposed to be what forms you, more than anything, I never had enough. Except negatively. I've always thought, well if you don't need me then I surely don't need you. That partly explains how I am."

She drifted again into no-time. She'd decided not to sit in her deck chair but on the sand by Spence's knee. The coolness of the sand caressed her. She was so happy to be alone with Spence and the night.

"Before that, I was in love with my mother. I was really, romantically in love with her. I've been thinking about that: remembering. I used to bring her things, little presents; I used to follow her around. She didn't have time for it. I don't mean that nastily, I mean *she didn't have time*. It wasn't only Maggie. I didn't want her to give up any of the things she was doing. It still broke my heart to lose her. That's why I didn't want to fall in love with anyone ever again, not even you. I know it happens to everyone, but..."

"Not to me," said Spence, after some thought. "Guess I was the one who left Mom; she didn't want me to go. But I know what you mean. It's like the love of God. You can't be first. You have to share God with all these other people, beings. Several billion humans, all the other living things, all those damn beetles, before you even start on the stars and the galaxies and the deck chairs and the bedspreads. Sometimes knowing everybody gets the same whole love, no matter how many of us there are, does not cut it."

"No...and so we have to be unsatisfied. It's for the best. If I loved you the way I love my work, you wouldn't like it, Spence. You think you would, but you wouldn't. It would be too much. When I think about Mummy deserting me, now, I think yeah, don't blame you. I know myself, I know what I'm like. I'm a ton of bricks."

Spence felt that he was in charge and ought to be DJing this better; it was going downhill. He seemed to recall there was something they had to do, but he couldn't for the life of him remember what it was. "We don't have to think about sad things. Let's go for another walk."

"Hey, don't worry." She turned and smiled at him, the smile dim in her face but warm in her voice. "This is okay, this is fine. I'm happy. I like telling you my troubles."

"Everybody has troubles."

"They're part of us. They're our friends."

"Like good works. They will go with us and be our guide."

They slipped into no-time together, for a while.

"You know Anna, I know the kind of silk-pajamas sex doesn't come naturally to you."

"Mmm." She bowed her head, embarrassed.

"No, don't curl up into your shell. I wanted you to know that I know, and I appreciate the Christmas present. I wanted to say, there is something more important than sex or romance, or any of that man-woman, male-female stuff, between you and me." He drew a breath, relaxing into it: the only knowledge. "What's important is that we know, you and I. Other people don't know, but we do, because of Lily

Rose. Rich or poor, failure or success, travel or stay at home, *we know* what is waiting at the end of all this. . .and the love of God makes no difference because there's nothing says the love of God doesn't end in nothingness. It can do whatever it likes, it owes us nothing. But I'm sure of this."

He leaned down and took Anna's face in his hands. "If you go first, I will be there to close your eyes: if I'm the one, then I know that you will be there. That's what matters."

"Yes."

They walked again, along the shore.

"Shall we go skinny-dipping."

Spence considered the idea. "No. We might swim in the wrong direction."

"Or meet a shark, or forget where we left our clothes. Let's stay where we are. Walk a little, sit and talk a little, walk a little. I like this. It's quiet, but I like it."

A while later they returned to their friends the chairs. Anna sat gazing, completely separate from Spence but shielded by his presence, earthed, except that earth was altogether too temporal a word for the state of resolution that he provided, always within reach no matter how distantly and through what convolutions her thoughts roamed, no matter what extraordinary ephemeral palaces, their details unresolved and liable to crumble and dissolve if you paid them too much attention; so that thought, the idea of investigating something and coming to a conclusion, was revealed as a pretext, a plausible explanation for this activity, whereas in fact the activity itself was...

◆ ◆

She woke wrapped in the wine-colored bedspread, feeling chilled and a little burned. Spence was beside her, fast asleep; the hut was full of morning light. She sat up and saw her shells arranged in strange patterns, all over the sandy wooden floor. It was like waking and finding you had managed to bring a flower home from Narnia. It wasn't a dream. They had visited another world.

➤ iv ➤

Ramone was not, in fact, traveling with Daz. When they came to Nasser apartments, the week after New Year, they hardly seemed to be friends. Ramone, who'd contacted Anna and Spence by phone from her hotel, arrived two hours later than arranged and very dressed down (sensible short hair, faded combats, chain store tee-shirt). She now claimed—with an irritating air of important secrets in reserve—that she was here to research a new book. So what was she really doing in Sungai? Daz made no comment. If she thought Ramone's trouble-spot rubber-necking in poor taste, she didn't say so.

Aside from her clothes, the rabid one was the same as ever: same malign, opaque blue eyes, same chimpanzee lip, same mean, arbitrary aggression. Daz had become a new person. She seemed to have shed her great beauty when she stopped being a megababe; she was now a soberly good-looking, well-groomed, grown-up woman. Anna marveled at the changes she'd seen in that ingenuous Malaysian Valley Girl she'd met at the Freshers' Fair and yet felt an instant sympathy. You could see in her eyes that Daz, in spite of her successes, had been living in the wild world, making compromises and accepting defeats. Ramone was more difficult. She was in a discontented phase. She did that trick, the same as she'd done on Beevey Island years ago, of *not looking* at Anna. She baited Spence and tried to pick a fight with Daz about the wimpish EU Mission—and the forthcoming "Equality and Democracy Rally," a government-sanctioned "expression of free speech" in which Daz would be involved.

Nevertheless they all agreed to go out on the town together. Anna invited Wolfgang, hoping that he would be the life and soul of the party. She couldn't think of anyone else.

They met at Ramone's hotel, the Rajah Brooke, a hangout favored by middle-aged US tourists before the annexation, and went to eat in The Plaza, at an eclectic, Chinese-run restaurant called The Jungle Pigeon. It was early, because they wanted to go on somewhere. The Plaza was full of shoppers, heavy aircon, and the smell of too much deodorizer. Ramone jeered at it. "Is this the way you two live? I suppose you never venture into the real Sungai? We might as well be eating prawn sesame toast in some crap Chinese off Piccadilly Gardens."

"Where are Piccadilly Gardens?" wondered Daz. "I've never heard of them."

"She means Piccadilly, Manchester," supplied Anna.

"If you want the Sungai experience," said Spence (trying to keep his temper), "this is it, much as there is one. Up-country is roads and trees, plenty of trees, a few muddy rivers, some ugly mountains. There's no scenery. Not much culture. It could be the Midwest."

"Huh. Far as I can see, you might as well have stayed at home."

"I think that's the point. We *did* stay at home. That's what we've found out."

Ramone muttered something about Hallmark card sentiment.

Anna was borne up, after Pasir Pancang, on that dark glimmering tide of perfect, active calm. Things couldn't be better between her and Spence. She was serene about working for Parentis. Transferred Y was in wonderful shape. She wanted the evening to go with a swing and wondered why Wolfgang (in the shirt with the silver and purple butterflies) was being so stiff and stilted. Ramone, bless her, still did not know how to use a pair of chopsticks. The rabid one was going to stay hungry, now the fingerfood was gone, unless she stopped being on her dignity and asked for a fork. Spence and Anna and Wolfgang were fast-working gannets, and Daz soon proved their equal. Wham, wham, wham. . .a heap of sticky, delicious little squid *in suo tinto*, a mass of slivered chili-fried liver, crispy tempeh, delicious nyonya fish curry, all of it disappeared at speed. Spence had ordered the signature dish, as one must: two of them. The jungle pigeons arrived late, glistening reddish black in pools of anise sauce, arranged with their intact heads tucked under their wings. At this spectacle Ramone broke down and exclaimed in innocent delight, endearing herself to the Pigeon staff.

"Oh, cool. Aren't they *gross*! They look like burn victims."

"You have to eat the head," the waiter told her, grinning mischievously, as he completed a neat, scissoring dismemberment of the first bird. "It's good luck."

"You can easily get this dish in Manchester, you know," Anna couldn't resist pointing out. "With a smaller pigeon. . . If you like Chinese food, that is."

"I like Chinese *takeaway* food." Ramone gave Anna a look, a flash of fierce contact, quickly withdrawn. "So, how's the baby-making going? Cloned anyone famous lately?"

"What, me personally? I'm not involved in the clinical work. Purely admin this trip."

Out of the corner of her ear, as it were, she heard Wolfgang sounding unlike himself.

"You are Sungainese by birth, Ms Avriti? So I've been told?"

"Yes I am," agreed Daz, quietly.

"And a Human Rights lawyer, whatever that exactly means. You have family living here?"

"Oh yes."

Ramone's muddy blue eyes gleamed. "Infertility's not a disease. Face it Anna, your 'clinical work' is pure money grubbing."

"If you like. That's definitely what the boss thinks, isn't it Wolfgang?"

"Poor Aslan. He knows no other worthwhile activity. He should be called Ben Franklin."

"Aslan?" Ramone was charmed. "Your boss is called *Aslan*?"

"Straight up."

"What's that? Persian ethnic or Christian Hippy?"

"Hippy, we've decided, because his family name's 'Gaegler' and there are little signs—"

"Little signs!" At last Wolfgang's crazy infectious laugh, like a hyena with hiccups. "This sad teetotal capitalist has his daddy's photo on the desk. Old Papa is wearing a Grateful Dead tee-shirt, and he is wearing cannabis sativa leaf earrings. Isn't that nice?"

"Doesn't surprise me," growled Ramone. "There's no fucking distance between the counterculture and the free market, never was. . . Hey, does any one want some cool drugs?"

She extracted a lipstick from one of her pockets, untwisted the base, and shook out a half dozen turquoise capsules. "Have you heard of this? It's the Alzheimer's drug, regressive recall modulator. Lavvy gets it on prescription, for memory lapses, although she doesn't really need it. It's neurological time traveling. You go back to something that happened in your past, and you get a brilliant high from doing this. No one knows why; people who found out just started taking it. It's already illegal here. Want some?"

"I don't want to go into a coma, right now," said Daz. "I want to dance."

"Oh, that's okay. You can dance in the regression, it only happens in your head—"

"What if you remember something horrible?" asked Anna, not remotely tempted.

"To me, this sounds repellent," said Wolfgang.

Ramone grinned. "Yeah, there's the chance of a bad trip, like with any psychotropic. It's a risk you have to take. Spence, what about it?"

Spence glanced at Anna. "Nah. It doesn't appeal. Guess I'm a now sort of person."

"We ought to be going," said Daz, "I'll see if I can get us straight into the club. Put those things away, for heaven's sake." She went to the pay phones to call the Riverrun, the club they planned to visit, but returned shaking her head. Couldn't get a line.

"They took my mobile off me at the airport," complained Ramone. "And my video camera. Why do they do that? Tin-pot dictatorship—"

"Mobile phones are supposed to be anti-Islamic," explained Anna. "I didn't know about camcorders. That's the story, but it doesn't make much sense."

Daz snorted, if an elegant grown-up lady can snort—betrayed by the wine into impatience with these simpletons. "It's nothing to do with Islam. It's about controlling communication, you dorks. Let's queue at the door. There won't be much of a line."

As they left the restaurant Spence donned an old Microsoft baseball cap, Wolfgang his Ozzie bush hat. Daz and Anna tied their scarves. Ramone prepared to exit bravely bareheaded. Daz grabbed her, holding out the extra hejab she had wisely brought along. "I knew you'd try it. Don't be stupid, Ro."

"I won't put that on. I fucking won't."

"In daylight you can get away with being a tourist. After dark, *you wear this.*"

➤ ➤

The river of Sungai, which means "river" in Malay, was labeled the Tyan on maps, which probably meant river in some vanished Dyak language. It ran through the city like the Thames, puzzlingly small for its historic role: from the west-end docks, from whence the big old refineries sprawled along the estuary towards the sea, to the new football stadium that marked, roughly, the eastern city limits. The Riverrun Club occupied one of the East Quay go-downs, picturesque ancient warehouses that somehow still escaped the developers. On this tepid, steaming January night the floor was packed at nine pm, because the lights were going out at midnight, the police were coming in to check for stragglers: and *you'd better believe it.*

Anna and Spence did not frequent the Riverrun, they couldn't afford to. It was, enduringly, the place to be. Alcohol was freely available, the air-conditioning was chill and dry, the sound and light phenomenally good, the walls of the cavernous hall dusky and naked as the day they were born. Over the dancers' heads clouds of bright gas formed into stars, streaming envelopes of aurora meshed; the river ran around and around its swollen center in silver spangles: the dark and shining elliptical river of our birth. The party swiftly downed their first, included-in-the-door-money drink in strong liquor, and lost each other for a while.

Anna and Spence met Wolfgang on the way to the loft. He dismissed the three gorgeous Sungainese he was talking to and joined them.

Inside the Riverrun, until curfew, everything was allowed. It was the modern way of oppression. Do what you like, as long as you accept our rules in daytime, in the real world. "Gee, were they boy-loving boys dressed up as girls, Wolfie?" asked Spence, affecting hickdom. "Or were they girl-loving girls, dressed up as boys dressed as girls?"

"You are such a clown, Spencer. You would make a fine boy-girl yourself. Did anyone ever tell you? I would hardly be able to keep my hands to myself."

"Oh, I know it." Spence tossed his head and pouted.

Spence and Wolfgang always "flirted outrageously," it was their little routine. But it was true, thought Anna, that Spence was looking very sexy. Something about the lineaments of gratified desire? No, not gratified desire: gratified *by* desire. He was giving off a positive fog of pheromones, and this was Anna's doing. She knew that in his mind he was wearing those pajamas. She seized his hand, fleetingly alarmed, *but we can still be brother and sister?* Ramone and Daz were already in the loft. The five of them took over one of the knee-high bamboo tables. Wolfgang ordered drinks.

"Are you going to be at this so-called Pro-Democracy rally, Anna?" demanded Ramone.

"Me?" She was bemused by the idea. "Oh, no. It's not— "

"Your business? Yes it fucking is. You take these people's money, don't you?"

"I work for Parentis."

"Oh, sure. I forgot. You don't work for the little local crooks, you work for Mr Big. I've been trying to be polite about it, but I don't know how you can defend the art of building synthetic human beings, Anna. Have you no respect for the environment? Don't you know this planet is dying of the disease of human expansionist greed?"

If she'd been less drunk, Anna would have refused to be drawn. She groaned, dragging her fingers through her sweat-soaked hair, "Ramone, I accept my share of the blame along with everyone else, but we only make babies. I don't believe in the population problem; the problem is distribution of resources. But if there was one, the number of people who resort to HAR and wouldn't have children without it is miniscule. There's no way a few tiny handfuls of 'extra' births impact on 'the environment'."

"Supposing one of the mad dictators decided to have his best lobotomized-violence bodyguard cloned a billion times in vats in a secret factory. That would impact."

"Can't stick that one on me. We wouldn't take the job. We don't do out of body gestation, it isn't safe."

"What about single parents? What about a single, male parent, totally infertile? Would you grow him a baby in a bag, from a cell from his scrotum or something?"

"This is an incredibly stupid conversation, Ramone. I don't know. I don't know what I'd advise; it never comes up. Parentis doesn't work with single parents."

"That's disgusting. The bastards. The complete *bastards*."

"God," Anna hauled herself to her feet. "I'm not saying whether I agree with what Parentis does or not; I think there are points on both sides. What's it to you? You don't want to have a baby. Look, Ramone, suppose you want a new liver one day? That new liver will be grown from a politically correct culture of your own cells, but no one would have found out how without human cloning techniques. That's what it's about, not mad dictators or vanity-parenting. Medicine. Making people better."

"Oh, I get it. You're a doctor now, like Mummy. The lady in the white coat."

"Wolfgang," said Anna, "could you remind me where the toilets are? Ramone don't you dare come with me, you're not invited, you are giving me a migraine."

Ramone had written another book. It was called *The Parable of the Star*. It concerned the socially and sexually constructed meaning of celebrity. Bach good, Wagner bad, and so on. She had told them it was an important feminist text, as there deliberately weren't any famous women listed or discussed, and had become extremely annoyed, that afternoon in Nasser apartments, when Daz and Spence and Anna had questioned this approach. The reason she was in such a bad temper had *patently* nothing to do with women's rights in Sungai. It was because her friends had not read her books, would never dream of reading her books... Agreed it was tough that Daz, of all people (ex-super model, ex-docile suburban girlfriend), had become the famous feminist, a speaker at this damned rally, while Ramone was merely someone who'd come an awful long way to heckle. Poor Ramone! But why did she have to be so violent, contentious, and unreasonable?

Time was, Anna thought, I used to sort-of believe in Ramone Holyrod.

Time was, she used to sort-of believe in me.

What had possessed Anna to argue with her about HAR? Partly it was impossible to refuse a fight with Ramone. Partly a mercenary's loyalty. As long as she took their money, as long as she owed them for the time she spent with SURISWATI, she wouldn't be such a hypocrite as to disown Parentis in public.

Why did Ramone have to turn up, stripping the smoothness from everything, tangling the combed out strands, forcing Anna to say things she didn't mean?

She leaned against the tiled wall, gazing at the beautiful-girl Sungainese (of both chromosomal sexes) repairing makeup, sharing drugs, adjusting clubbing costumes so porny there'd be nothing for it but the whole chador when they returned to the street. Do I really think I'm a doctor like Mummy? Surely not, no, I'm sure I don't.

But the woman in the white coat, counseling the Nasabahs. . .

Another sanctuary opens its gates, privileging me, controlling me—

Ramone watched Anna go and turned to Spence. "She's pissed off because I'm right."

Spence downed the end of a huge crystal flower vase of Korean lager. The Riverrun served beer in liters, European style—which was helping the evening along, especially at the speed Wolfgang was setting them up. "I think you just pissed her off. Period."

"Okay I didn't express myself rationally, but it's the Evil Empire. Turning the consumers themselves into consumer commodities; it's the ultimate move in the most destructive social ethos the world has ever known. Life, Liberty, and the Pursuit of Happiness. Ghengis Khan was nothing on it. The Black Death was a pimple. You ought to know, Spence. The right to strip-mine this planet, to go through it like fat-boy teenagers robbing a fridge, is written into your Constitution."

"No it isn't."

"*Yes It Fucking Is!*"

"You're thinking of the Declaration of Independence."

Ramone giggled, momentarily disarmed. "I hate where I am," she confided, studying the bottom of her own vase. "Sexual Politics is a bust. I'm going to end up like fucking Camille Paglia: pack me up and take me down to the Antiques Roadshow. But how do I get out of it? It's like: step one, get beyond the fucking battle of the sexes and get real. How d'you get beyond step one?"

Spence had no interest in this conversation. He shrugged, non-committally. Ramone narrowed her eyes.

"Read any good email lately?"

"Oh yeah, email. I must let you have our address," he said, without enthusiasm.

"S'okay. I've got it."

She'd been giving him these evil, full-of-it glances ever since she arrived at Nasser apartments in her Lonely Planet drag. He'd assumed it was to do with Anna and had felt invulnerable with the Pasir Pacang week under his belt. He suddenly realized she had something different going on, some other form of attack.

"I'm not making a big thing of it," disclosed Ramone, with openly fake reluctance. "But I'm not here on my own behalf. I'm representing Lavvy. I'm her secretary, I deal with her mail. The Sungainese have been appealing to her to take up their case. Of course we had to send the replies anonymously—"

"Is that a fact?"

"So you see, some of those secret messages you've been passing on were from me!"

She cackled in triumph.

Was this true? It had to be true, how else would she have known about the arrangement? Ramone, those poor kids' hope in hell? Hideous thought! But much, much worse: the idea of his secret in her tender care. . . My God. If we get thrown out before she's finished working with SURISWATI, Anna will never, ever forgive me. . .

Wolfgang was chatting up their waiter; Daz had been accosted by some Sungainese and was talking to them. . . I shredded everything. If they go through my hard drive bit by bit, they can't pin anything on me.

Ramone sighed in satisfaction. "Spence you look terrified. Don't *worry*. I won't say a word. I won't even let Anna know you were so careless that I found out. So, anyway, what are you going to do with the rest of your life? Since you've dropped out of the crypto-capitalist slacker-nerd lark. Are you settling for legalized prostitution?"

Spence glared. "Nope. I'm also working on making myself a beautiful soul."

The effect of this sally was startling. She stared at him in furious amaze, as if he'd said your name is Rumpelstiltskin, as if he'd found the only chink in the monster's armor, and abruptly turned away to plunge, uninvited, into the conversation of the group around Daz.

And *la lutte continue*, thought Spence. He had known the moment that postcard arrived that Ramone was still a threat. He guessed spiritual beauty was a card she thought *she* could play, somehow. Well, tough cookie sweet Ramone, because I'm in sexual possession AND I live a pure and holy life. Anna had returned and was sitting quietly drinking with her "this is a time-out" face on. He would leave her in peace. Let Ramone make the bad mistake of coming on to that inviolable silence.

The loft had the nostalgic decor of a Kuta beach cocktail bar— bamboo pole flooring, palm leaf mats, woven screens, daft Balinese Beach Bum art—everything signifying a romantic retreat, good times, sun and sea and sand. People were smoking dope, people were behaving as if the cruel world outside didn't exist, while down below the slaves of the bass line went on pounding away to one of those complex Sungai DJ dance tracks, Classic English Acid House infused with North West African rhythms, what a melting pot, fractionally recursive, always doubling back, weaving more—

gimme one of those hearts that can't be broken,
gimme one of those lies that can't ever be found out,
gimme one of those
gimme one of those,
gimme one of those,
are you one of those—

Spence let himself drift. Ramone was right, it was getting obscene to stay here, earning money, making love, having drug experiences, when life for the real people dancing down there was a total road

accident. We don't belong, why do we stay, where am I going to. . .?
At dinner he'd asked Daz—you revert to the past when you meet old
friends—what did she ever see in that Tex character? "I don't know,"
she'd said, taking the question as seriously as if the affair was fresh in
her mind, "He was a *talented* wanker, among a lot of untalented utter
wankers, and he was sexy, to me then, though it was hard to believe
afterwards. And I was unsure of myself, as usual. I was trying to be
the kind of woman I felt I ought to be—" Spence could relate to that.
Fractional recursion. The handful of things you know and feelings
you feel keep on returning, you never get beyond them. You leave
home first chance you get: *I don't belong here, this isn't my kind of
shit*, sure you will find a world where you belong, some shit you will be
proud to call your own. But like the first line of a novel, encapsulating
the whole story, it keeps happening over and over. You can't escape the
spiral, you can only be in the same place further along the timeline, in
Spence's case always the place where I don't belong, just don't fit.

He sighed, and shook himself. It must be getting on for midnight.

"Come on, Anna Livia Plurabelle. Let's dance."

When he looked around, she was gone. So was Ramone. There was
only Wolfgang, rolling another spliff, and a fresh pair of flower vases
that appeared to be filled with milky coffee. He gave Spence a roguish
smile, nodding at the two empty seats.

"Sparks flying there— "

Daz and her pals were gone too, the loft was nearly empty.
"Where's Anna?"

"She left with her friend, of course, to follow those sparks. Don't
worry, have a drink."

"What is this stuff?"

"Brandy Alexanders."

"Arrgh."

"I've been buying your beer all night. I like cocktails. Don't be
coy: I know you ex-pats, there is nothing you will not drink. Share this
nightcap with me, and then we'll go on somewhere." Wolfie's eyes had
a chilly brightness, a strange expression that made him look like a different person. "Be nice to me, or I won't help you to find the lady."

◂━ ◂

Ramone told the bicycle taxi driver to take them to *medan me-riam,* reading the name carefully from a scrap of paper. Anna leaned back under the tattered hood and closed her eyes. After the chill of the Riverrun the air outdoors felt like a bath of warm, black milk. They were going on somewhere. It was all right, everything under control, she had her bag on her back, wallet in her pocket (touch it), headscarf tied. The *medan meriam,* sometimes known as the Parade Ground, was a broad, flat, open space to the east of the city center, where there had been a fortress or something in colonial days. There was a per-manent children's fun fair there and a market called the bird market where you could buy house plants, cage birds, pond fish. . . Suddenly she started up in alarm.

'*Ramone*! Have you put your headscarf on?"

"Yes I have. Feel it if you don't believe me."

The streetlights were few, the city night very dark. Ramone took her hand and guided it so she could feel the fabric; then, unexpectedly, came the soft touch of lips on Anna's fingers.

"Why did you do that?"

"Felt like it. How's your migraine."

"Not so bad."

All my problems, thought Ramone, come with the label, *don't start from here.* Here she was, a fucking professional feminist, basically a sex-worker, a pornographer, making her living out of being female. She had achieved nothing.

"D'you remember when we lived on campus?"

"Yes."

"All those famous people in Lavvy's salon. We should have been taking notes."

"I don't remember. I only remember you and me and Lavvy, talking."

Anna paid off the taxi.

"Why'd you give him such a massive tip?" Ramone, still fascinat-ed by Anna's spending habits, had watched the transaction carefully. "Taxi fares are supposed to be controlled."

"Yeah, but the price of rice isn't. Only stingy tourists pay the government fares."

Anna was puzzled that there was no amplified music at this outdoor rave, but soon she relaxed. The *medan meriam* was like a coral reef in darkness, teeming with life, sparkling with pockets and currents of quivering light. They explored the funfair, stopping to peer into hucksters' booths and to watch the fairground rides. There were impromptu bars, food stalls, people everywhere. Faces glinted out of the gloom, smiling, solemn, or preoccupied. "You're right about HAR," confessed Anna suddenly. "I know you're right. I hate the business. I still try to do my job well; it's irrational but that's the way I am. But I don't want to be part of the rape of the planet, directly or indirectly. It just—"

"I know," said Ramone. "Life gets in the way. I don't want to be a feminist, either. But I'm doomed." She took Anna's hand and squeezed it. They wandered hand in hand, which was strange but pleasant. Anna was taller, it made her feel protective. An old man beckoned to them, they followed him into an open-sided hut where tanks of water stood on long wooden tables. He shone a torch into one of the tanks. They saw two beautiful slender creatures, twisting around each other, with silvery butterfly wings sprouting from their golden and dark barred bodies.

"What are they? Are they flying fish?" whispered Ramone.

"No. They're sea moths. People use them in TCM, that's traditional Chinese medicine."

"Are they rare?"

"Not yet, they've only been a traditional medicine for a while. They soon will be."

The old man wanted to show them some other tanks, but they left, disheartened.

"I thought traditional medicine was supposed to be ancient. Making up new ones is cheating. That means. . . nothing would be safe."

Anna shrugged. "Tradition is what I point to when I say it. That's always been the way, everywhere. It's our tradition to eat hamburgers and drive cars."

"Tradition means pillage, basically. I fucking hate it. Every bit of it."

For a while they sat and watched a shadow puppet show, drinking tots of arak bought from a woman who was working the crowd with a yoke of cool boxes across her shoulders, which she would lay down and arrange into a counter in front of her customers: patiently, smilingly repeating the process every time she was beckoned over. The spirit was much better value than her Thai and Singaporean bottled beer, so they had several tots. Anna recalled that there was a spliff of Toba grass hidden in the lining of her bag. They shared it and talked fast: about the spirituality of the passing moment, fetishes, Balinese funeral rites, Japanese animism, the artificial consciousness debate, the way any mortal thing can be living and aware *because we say so.* Anna described working with SURISWATI. Well, how do I know *you* are conscious, Ramone, she demanded warmly. How will you prove to me that you're not a complex biological automaton, saying and doing what I expect from another person, but for purely mechanical reasons? It's not my field, but I don't think there's ever going to be a day when self-aware AI is *announced*. It'll creep up on people, like abolishing slavery. Like women's rights, come to think of it."

"I'm not interested in rights for women," gabbled Ramone. "Not 'women are people too,' pretty please, that's no good. I'm looking for a new concept of humanity. Resurrecting forgotten heroines is dumb. It's playing into the hands of the enemy to say, see, we were up to your standards all along. That's crap. We need a whole different paradigm."

"Isn't the kind of change you want already happening?"

"It's because it's happening that I can write about it!"

"You can suppress the truth as often as you like," said Anna, thinking of Galileo's telescope. "If that's all it is, abstract truth, because who cares? Nobody cares. You can't suppress the facts because—well, there they are, all over the place—"

The night fell into confusion. They moved on, and joined another audience. Here there were shadow dancers, not puppets, performing behind what looked like a large white bed sheet, lit by coppery flares and stretched between bamboo poles. A beautiful young man, in a white sarong, flying thongs of black hair to his waist, leapt out to take his bow. Anna noticed as the applause began that she and Ramone were surrounded by a group of Sungainese Chinese, young women with round, rosy faces, and Ramone appeared to know these people. She was talking to them, in English, but Anna couldn't follow the discussion. Then Daz appeared, coming into the open-sided canvas theatre with the friends she'd met in the Riverrun loft. She saw Ramone and Anna. She came over to them; but she was soon walking away again, after some kind of altercation with Ramone, picking out a path between the shadowy ranks of Sungainese, who were sitting on the ground like flare lit carved lumps of stone. . .

"We ought to have asked her where Wolfie and Spence have got to."

"She doesn't know," said Ramone. "She's pissed off with me, because I'm right."

Ramone began to talk fast again, explaining that she was here as Lavinia Kent's emissary, that she'd been working, at long distance, with a Sungai feminist group, and that she understood the situation far better than Daz did. . . They moved again, the whole group together. Now they were among huge-leaved plants, forest smells of humus and water. Anna thought she had been carried far distances by magic, to some forest retreat of the revolution. The young Chinese women were kissing and hugging and singing happy songs. Anna and Ramone had their arms round each other too. They vowed eternal friendship; it seemed natural to kiss. Natural to handle the soft weight of Ramone's breasts, to cuddle close and imagine, with a spinning head, what it would be like to share sexual passion with an equal, someone your own size, someone who would be your sister through the hormone-driven storm. . .

➤ ➤

Wolfgang and Spence found her at four am, wandering on the margin of the *medan meriam* Special Night Market, this impromptu event with which the police had wisely decided not to interfere: bag on her back, wallet in her pocket, watch on her wrist, all intact except for the power of self-conscious thought, gone temporarily AWOL. (Ramone, meanwhile, turned out to be back at her hotel, with little idea of how she'd got there.) Anna wondered, as she nursed her hangover, what might have happened that she didn't remember. She decided that she wouldn't try to find out. She didn't regret those kisses or the vows of eternal friendship. The night had been a fine adventure: she was glad, very glad, that she and Ramone had got back together. But, taken all in all, she was even gladder that she had woken up safe at home in her own bed.

➤ v ➤

Spence visited the editor of a magazine, Sungai's best selling aspirational women's glossy, called *Dream On*. There was no irony intended; the zine was simply about dreaming for things and getting them: but there you go. You can't copyright an idiom. The offices were open plan and nicely climate controlled, with a great view of the West Quay. Spence had sold *Dream On* a couple of lifestyle articles, and they were discussing a column. The editor, in chocolate stockings and a candy pink boucle suit, was keen; this was her own idea. But she expected Spence to sell himself, and he felt an intense reluctance.

She was uneasy about his online career. Media people have rewritable minds. Maisie Loh honestly believed that working for the web had always been intrinsically suspect and awful. The fact that this state of mind had been imposed on her by an illegal government in the recent past entirely escaped her.

"I was a programmer," he admitted. "Started out in college vacations, did a couple of years with an information warehouse service. It was clerical work. Writing's what I want to do."

What would he cover in this column? Cultural topics? What did he think of the home media service in Sungai? It was very good, wasn't it? Spence and Anna did not possess access to this splendid resource. All they had was a plain little color tv, which they mainly used for watching (over and over again) the classic movies they'd brought out with them. He prevaricated, staggered that this woman could believe that monopoly-controlled pap-feed connectivity was the hot, radical future of entertainment. She was probably right.

But it would be good to have a milieu outside the home. He made up his mind. He would turn on the charm and get the job. It would be a trip.

BOOM!

All the glass in the windows flew. Spence dived to the floor. Then he was on his feet again, the staff of *Dream On* rushing around him, someone streaming blood, the air full of sudden warmth, fire alarms hammering. Maisie Loh shot by, leaping on her skinny heels, chocolate stockings in ribbons, two cut knees, lugging a First Aid chest. His ears were ringing.

Someone was shouting, "It was Government House!"

Government House, Victorian pile dwarfed by the downtown towers, was two blocks from Parentis. Spence ran out of the office, heading for the fire stairs with everyone else.

➤ ➤

That morning, the morning of the Rally, Wolfgang hadn't turned up for work. Anna wasn't surprised. She supposed plenty of people must be regarding this event as an excuse to take the day off. She was on the clinical floor, in the lab manager's office, haggling. There was really no chance that Anna would change her mind about anything, but they went through the must-have list item by item, for the sake of decency.

"How you get to be so young and so hard-hearted?" grumbled Desy Periah, lab manager.

Someone out in the lab was watching the rally on an illicit pocket tv. Anna could hear, over a background of decorous crowd noise, a reporter saying the occasion was calm. Anna's mind was half on Desy's troubles (which were grave, but only too familiar) and half on Ramone. That midnight ramble had woken an unsuspected hunger for the fast-talking, challenging, *noncomplementary* intimacy they had shared. And for the kid herself: her silly face, her bright-eyed cartoon face. Could Anna fit another important relationship into her life? She wondered what Spence would think.

BOOM!

Desy's chair shot backwards. Anna grabbed the desk to save herself. One of the clinicians burst in. "It's Government House. They've blown it up!"

"My son!" wailed Desy, staggering upright. "My son! He's a clerk in the Ministry!"

➤ ➤

The Parentis building was made of stronger stuff than most of the downtown towers. The windows didn't blow out. People were shocked and shaken and there were breakages, that was all; but the fire alarm was clamoring in amber tone. Anna went into her drill in a state of dizzy detachment. So Sungai had blown up. It wasn't unexpected. Spence was safe and Transferred Y was safe, she had a copy at home. Daz and Ramone were at the rally, but there was nothing Anna could do about that. She cleared the clinical suites of personnel, locked them, checked that the cold rooms were off main power and onto emergency. She was heading for admin by the stairs before she recalled that Spence was not safe, he was in town. Electrified by this shock, she met a rush of people coming *up* the stairs and couldn't understand why. Then came the second explosion; it threw her across a hallway. The air was full of smoke, the alarm segued into its GET OUT NOW howl. There were hundreds of people, they were shouting Penangalang! Penangalang! What did it mean, some kind of political slogan? She heard a woman's voice, shouting about babies without souls. The building was on fire, the labs were under attack, she had to get to the admin floor. A young man had something like a fire axe or a big machete, he was trying to chop down the door to Suri's antechamber: well, he wouldn't get through that!

She had to get to her office, though she couldn't remember why. When she managed to reach that room (still free from smoke up here), she saw the intercom on her desk: of course! Communication! She fell on it, opening a channel to the security chief.

"Philip? Is it Philip? How are you, how are we doing?"

"I'm very well, Mrs Anna," came the guard's voice, incongruously cheerful. "Bad news, the fire and emergency services cannot reach the building; the crowds are holding them off. The good news is that every badge is out but you. Can you get to the emergency stairs?"

"Thank God for that... Yes I can, I'll be fine."

She was looking round the office, thinking what the devil do I need from here. She heard a voice faintly calling her name. "Who's that?"

Philip had said that every electronically tagged member of Parentis personnel was out of the building, but Philip was obviously wrong. Who was calling?

"Anna is that you?"

She tried every door before she traced the voice to Aslan Gaegler's office. Aslan was in there, sitting behind his desk, grey in the face, holding his family photographs.

"Oh, there you are," he said faintly. "What's going on, Anna?"

"The building's on fire. I think someone must have lobbed an incendiary device into the downstairs lobby, must have been something biggish—"

"I'm sorry. I kind of froze. Got an attack of angina."

"Well, okay, but you have to unfreeze now. We have to get to the emergency stairs."

She had remembered what it was she should have taken from her desk. But it was too late, because Aslan was not able to help himself. No point in asking him why he wasn't wearing his badge, not for her to say anyway. She fed him his pills, stripped out the roller towel from his toilet and soaked it, thank god for old fashioned luxury, thank god the water was still running, and walked with him slowly step by step. They were not in danger, as long as he didn't collapse. When they reached the clinical floor the smoke was worse. They sat and shuffled from step to step, passing the wet towel between them.

"My God, Anna. How do you keep so calm?"

"I don't know; maybe because I'm British."

— —

Before he got out of the Straits Times building, where *Dream On*'s editorial staff was housed, Spence had heard the news people yelling that there was a mob attack on the IVF clinic. His grasp of the language was good enough for that. In the glaring heat—they were still in the monsoon but it was eleven o'clock, not raining yet— he was quickly soaked with sweat. He got turned back by an adamant police cordon and ran around and around the Parentis block, trapped by panic, unable to think what to do. He reached an intersection where a car had been overturned and pieces of concrete lay about. The air was choking with partly dissipated tear gas. There were a few people passing, young men carrying loot: a box of electronic hardware, an armful of bright-colored clothes. He thought he was at The Plaza, but he couldn't recognize anything in the smoke. The yell of sirens was

everywhere, and a roar that must be power hoses. He saw someone lying on the pavement, covered in grey dust. Her face was upwards. It
was Unusual Girl from the group in the old schoolhouse.

"What are you doing here?" he demanded, dropping to his knees.

"I don't. . .know. I was going home. I've hurt my leg."

He couldn't remember her name, what the fuck was her name?
Sunita. There was blood all over, under the grime of the blast. He took
one good look at the leg and knew he wasn't going any further. Had to
stay here, until someone qualified arrived. Oh, Anna—

"Sunita, what happened?"

"They blew up the rally. They blew up the baby-making clinic. I
don't know what else."

"What the fuck for? What's Parentis got to do with democracy?"

"Sungai people are very superstitious, they think the AI was stealing their babies. The Penangalang. She steals the souls of poor people's
babies and gives them to artificial children. That's what people think.
Am I going to be all right?"

"I think so, soon as we can get you to the hospital."

"I'm sorry Spence, it's where your wife works isn't it."

"Yah. But I'm sure she's okay."

"It wasn't us, Spence. It wasn't anyone we know. It was the crazy people."

Sunita went on talking. Spence went on answering, only letting go
of her hand to release the pressure occasionally on his amateur tourniquet. (Amateurs should *never* do a tourniquet, but in this case. . .)
He was amazed at the way she kept talking. He stopped being able
to follow her, in English or Malay: he kept saying Yes, okay, I know,
don't worry, in an agony of frustration and terror. He might have been
kneeling by her for half an hour before he noticed that the thing beside them on the pavement, which he'd taken for a jagged chunk of
concrete, was a naked, scorched, human arm and shoulder, minus the
hand, lying there by itself. He was glad he had something definite to
do. He'd have been lost otherwise.

He went with her to the hospital. The ambulance team seemed
to expect it, taking him for a brother or a boyfriend maybe. Spence
realized that his best chance was to get to somewhere that had news

feed. The hospital turned out not to be such a good bet. The casualty department was full of staggering bloody walking-wounded from the Government House car bomb. He was told first that there were no survivors from the Parentis explosion, and then that there had been no serious injuries there, but the patients had been diverted to St Joseph's, another hospital on the north side of town. No one could tell him how to get to the north side at present, in fact it could not be done. He was being severely warned, by an understandably ratty policewoman, to go home and stay indoors! when his wife appeared. She was wearing that brick-colored dress with the yellow splashes and the sexy little Audrey Hepburn belt. It was filthy and her feet were bare, her arms were black with smoke or bruises. She came up to him and leaned her forehead against his shoulder.

"Hi Spence. How did you know I'd be here?"

They sat on a bench in the casualty waiting area, sharing a cup of lukewarm coffee from the machine. "It was Aslan," explained Anna. "He had an angina attack, he was stuck in his office. Thank God I heard him calling, the stupid bugger wasn't wearing his tag for some unknown reason, and Philip had counted him out. I walked him down the back stairs. I'd have been in shit if he'd collapsed. He's not fat exactly but he's a big lad. But he kept trucking, so we were okay. I came to the hospital with him, but I'm all right. Spence, Suri's dead."

Spence put aside the plastic cup and held her. So far, the massive car bomb that had exploded at Government House had a toll of thirty-seven dead and twenty-three seriously hurt, plus uncounted numbers of relatively non-serious flying glass injuries. The bomb at Parentis had killed no one, but the mob had wrecked the building. No wonder Anna was in shock.

"They got Suri? That's okay babe, she isn't dead. You have her offsite backing."

"No... It was in Government House. Don't you remember? Parentis had to agree to that, it was the only way they'd let us have her running. It's gone."

"You'll have a snapshot, they can't have trashed her so completely—"

"They did. They trashed her, she is gone. I was going to grab my disc copy of her TY extrapolation from my desk, but then I heard Aslan calling. It doesn't matter."

The double doors at the end of the hall opened for a further influx. A nurse zoomed across, probably to tell them they should go to St Joseph's, because these casualties looked in reasonable shape. She bounced back, and the group resolved itself into two parties, the second of which was newshounds, pointing cameras and sound booms. The political ritual of visiting the victims had begun. Senior hospital staff appeared, to meet and greet. Anna and Spence watched the circus go by, but one of the women detached herself and came over to them. It was Daz.

"Hi." She sat down on the bench. "I'm glad you're safe Anna."

"Don't let us keep you," said Spence, with totally unjustified hostility.

Daz shook her head. "They won't miss me."

"So, what happened to the peaceful Equality and Democracy rally?"

"It was side-tracked. Look, has either of you seen Ramone?"

"No—"

"Shit. We have to find her. Someone saw her being put into a police van, possibly. Anna, do you know anyone who might help us?"

"No," said Anna, bewildered by the idea. "I don't know anyone."

Anna and Spence were at first mystified that Daz was taking the absence of the rabid one so seriously. When Ramone failed to turn up the next day, they started to be afraid that she might have been killed. Sungai was full of rumors that the true body count would never be known... But no, Daz was right. Ramone had been arrested. She was being held in Kota Baru women's prison, down on the estuary, and likely to be charged with serious offences.

Spence was disgusted. Sunita's shattered leg had been amputated above the knee. He'd visited her in hospital. She was heartbreakingly cheerful—sure this episode would be over soon and she could get back to her normal life. If Ramone thought it was cool to fool around pretending to be involved with terrorists (she'd made a highly damaging statement at the time of her arrest), then let her pay the price.

He knew, all the same, that she couldn't be abandoned.

It took Daz ten days to track Ramone down, it took another week to get permission to visit the prisoner. She and Anna drove together to Kota Baru. There were roadblocks all the way. It reminded Anna of Nigeria, but African for-profit roadblocks had been like a good-humored institution, except for the guns. You hardly felt that you were in danger. On this journey Anna was terrified. Several times they were pulled over and questioned. Once they were made to get out of the car and their passports and papers were taken away while it was searched. Daz had to answer a lot of questions. Her status with the EU Mission should have been a safeguard, but you couldn't rely on that. At Kota Baru they were back in the old Third World. Smokestack chemical plants muddied the air, the market square was beaten earth awash after the rains. The main street ran between broad margins of mud and rotting garbage.

They were an hour early for their appointment. "Let's go for a walk," said Daz.

They walked between the estuary and Kota Baru's bus station, on a concrete promenade. "Spence was letting your email address be used as an anonymous mail drop."

Anna swallowed hard. "What makes you think that?"

"The fact that I was there when he told me. Please, Anna, don't be dumber than you can help. This is difficult enough. He's afraid he might have got the two of you into bad trouble, because apparently Ramone knows. Now I'm going to repeat to you a list of names, and you have to tell me if you recognize any of them. I've tried this on Spence, but you speak better Malaysian than he does, and you spent more time with Ramone."

None of the names, most of which sounded Chinese, meant a thing to Anna. She shook her head, hands clenched in the pockets of her modest calf-length skirt to hide their trembling. She couldn't believe that she and Spence were in trouble. But they could not get out of Sungai in a hurry now, leaving Ramone in jail. No use wondering how long it would take to pack... They stood and looked over the parapet. A ribbon of bright green weed drifted by, heading out to sea on the falling tide. Across the wide water, palm oil plantations gave the horizon a uniform spiky fringe.

"I don't know if you realize this, Anna, but it was no accident that the mob attacked Parentis. That was Ramone's friends, and it was deliberate."

"But why would feminists attack an IVF clinic? Government House I can understand— "

Daz stared at the muddy river. "If you don't understand, I don't think I can tell you. Anna, where you and I live, women's rights is old news. Intelligent women want to be judged on their own merits and find the whole feminist thing embarrassing and whiney. But *here, where I live. . .* it's a can of worms. If you start applying the concept of 'human rights' to women, in Asia and Africa, you uncover a holocaust. It's getting worse, not better. You think it's weird and backward to be asked to wear the hejab. You're wrong, this is the future. Everywhere, women have reverted to traditional dress, adopted traditional behaviors, accepted draconian laws. It's the only way they can hang onto their jobs, to their lives. It's a deadly polarization: where 'human rights' and 'women's rights' end up in one camp, and all the power is in the other. That's the mess Ramone's got herself into."

"She didn't do anything!"

"I'm not going to give her a chance to tell me any different," snapped Daz, and then sighed. "Seriously, I don't think she knew about the bombs. I don't think she did anything bad, any more than Spence was doing anything bad. That's not going to help."

"The British Consulate certainly isn't going to help," said Anna bitterly.

"They never do. Let's go, it's time."

The Kota Baru prison was a collection of sour white buildings inside a big wire fence. They had to wait, first in the governor's office and then alone in a small room with a guard. Finally Ramone was brought to them. She was wearing the same tee-shirt she'd been wearing at the Riverrun, and a grubby blue and white checkered man's sarong. She looked dirty and thin, and cowed as a wet kitten. She sat opposite them across a little table, a woman in uniform standing on either side. When she found out she wasn't going to be released she began to cry. She said she was eating all right. She was in a shared cell, a kind of dormitory, with other women who were all right, except that none of them spoke English. She hadn't seen anyone from the rally since they were split up at the first police station. She said that she could often hear screaming, and she was very, very frightened. Anna looked at Daz when Ramone said this, hoping for reassurance. Daz was keeping a straight face. So were the guards.

"I haven't told them anything," boasted the rabid one. "Not a word."

"You haven't anything to tell," said Daz. "You signed something when you were arrested, when you were frightened and didn't understand what was going on. You're going to retract that statement."

"I understand more than you think!" Ramone bristled, "I'm not a terrorist, but I will not condemn my sisters' actions. The issues in Sungai are issues of sexual politics."

Daz clasped her hands, either praying for patience, or possibly to stop herself from thumping the prisoner. Anna was afraid to speak, fearing that anything she could say might plunge Ramone into worse idiocy.

"At least you're in one piece," said Daz. "Don't worry, we'll get you out."

They were allowed to give her cigarettes, for currency, and a food parcel. The food was taken away for examination, and Daz and Anna were escorted to the prison gates.

"This is a tough one," said Daz.

◆　◆

Anna went to see Wolfgang. He lived in a tower block overlooking the Taman Burung. It was a nice location, but the flats were small. Anna, who had been sensitive to such things since the bomb blast, started thinking at once how choking it would be in these small rooms if the air conditioning cut out. And such a long way from the ground. You wouldn't escape easily. She was surprised at the perfunctory furnishing. His little kitchen was full of gadgets—they stood in there, while he made coffee in a fancy machine—but his living room held nothing beyond the most standard typically-tropical fittings: a cheap rattan couch, table and chairs, a pallid shag-pile rug. An empty bookcase stood against one wall, next to a mass-market Pacrim home-entertainment stack. Perhaps he did not spend much time at this address. He was wearing his usual bright shirt and tight jeans, but his blond hair was scraped back harshly and his face, without makeup, looked gaunt and strange.

"Ginger syrup? Yes you do, it will perk you up. I'm sorry I have no booze in the house."

Anna stirred her coffee. "Wolfgang, do you remember once you offered me some 'get-out-of-jail-free tokens'? Did you mean anything by that?"

"Ah."

It was three weeks since Equality and Democracy day. Some activists had been arrested, others had gone to ground. The blast area was still cordoned off, but so far there had been no more trouble. Wolfgang placed his cup and saucer carefully on a paper coaster, on the glass-topped coffee table. He stood and went to look out of the window over the park, arms folded. "This is for your friend, isn't it. The little friend with whom you went missing from the Riverrun."

"Yes."

"She's been a bad, stupid girl I hear. And the more stupid she is, the better you like her. I am right?"

Anna thought of the wet kitten, and without warning tears came brimming. She nodded.

He walked up and down by his window, looking different, looking like someone older, harder, that she didn't know—until he turned, tossing his head, with a roguish, twinkling smile. "Oh Anna, you know what fairies are like. I'm afraid you may have said the magic word, that makes me give my last boon and disappear."

"I don't want you to get into trouble."

"But we don't want your little friend to 'disappear' in the technical sense?"

"She isn't going to disappear. They're going to hang her. Daz says they'll do it."

"Well, that is also something to avoid. Don't worry, it's no sacrifice. My credit was running low. I may as well spend it all at once, and then I simply take a plane and find a new banker."

There were wild rumors, fostered by Wolfgang of course, but no one knew for sure what lay behind the jealously preserved mystery of his private life. At the end of this short interview, Anna still wasn't sure that he could or would do anything for Ramone. Wolfgang liked to be valued. He made you pay for his office efficiency with lots of strokes and coaxing and cajoling. Maybe he just enjoyed the game of being asked for cloak-and-dagger help. It was a part for Dietrich: the femme fatale with a heart of gold.

She never did find out for sure. But a few days later Ramone Holyrod was on a plane home, and Wolfgang had vanished. Anna never saw him again.

◆ ◆

The day the police declared the building safe, Anna went in to start closing the clinic down. Parentis, while denying rumors that they were pulling out, wanted the withdrawal implemented at speed. Contract workers would finish their time elsewhere.

It was not her job to assess the damage to SURISWATI, but she couldn't resist the tug of the secret room. If human genetics expert systems were going to be terrorist targets, the hardware would have to have better protection. The mob had smashed its way in without much difficulty in the end. She stood looking round, touching nothing, wondering in her ignorance where in these broken fragments Suri herself had lived. She had been haunted, since the blast, by the terrible conviction that Suri had been real. . . A child had been killed here: a lively, adventurous, *brilliant* little girl, who had spent her short life in a cage, and died alone in terror. An unexpected sound made her jump. Aslan was standing in the doorway, holding a big bouquet of white specimen chrysanthemums.

'This wasn't necessary," he said, in distaste. "A few passes with a strong magnet would have sufficed."

"I suppose. Aren't modern machines shielded? I don't know enough about it. What are those for? A funeral wreath?"

He held out the bouquet, embarrassed. "They're for you. I asked your husband which were your favorite. It's inadequate, I know. You saved my life."

"*De nada.*" She wondered how long he'd been suffering angina, that ominous and painful symptom, and telling no one at the office. So now she had another good friend, like KM Nirmal. It was like being a battered wife. They do you harm, then they're your humble servants; they can't do enough to make up: until next time. But she knew it was irrational to blame him. The mob had gone through the three floors of Parentis like a grass fire. Anna could have done nothing, even if she hadn't been helping Aslan.

She had found the TY disks, undamaged: not that they meant very much, without SURISWATI to back them up. Not that they meant much anyway. Those findings were unpublishable.

"What does *Penangalang* mean?" he asked. "I've heard it in the coverage, but I seem to have missed the point. They thought our AI was some kind of vampire?"

The word was spray-paint scrawled over every wall. "Sort of a vampire. A woman, possibly dead after a miscarriage or stillbirth or possibly still alive, I'm not sure. Her spirit goes about at night sucking blood from newborn infants and women in labor."

"For the blood is the life," said Aslan solemnly. "I think I get it." He looked at Anna with concern. "Hey, don't be upset. A software entity like Suri can't die, you know that. It looks bad, but we'll have our goddess up and running again: soon as we replace the hardware and get another copy from the makers."

"Yeah," said Anna. "You can clone her. But it won't be the same person."

The living room in the flat was full of boxes; they were getting ready to leave. Anna came home from another day of picking-up-the-pieces admin and showered, luxuriating in the hot needle power, the glistening tiles, the shining taps and pipes. After China and Africa, it was eerie to have come so close to disaster while living in a place like this. It was as if they were on a space station and had been reminded by some minor emergency of how insanely fragile it all was. . .*all this*. On the wall beside her wardrobe mirror a transparent lizard skated on clinging toes. She twisted a gauzy purple and green sarong around her waist, fastened the scalloped margins of her white kebaya jacket with a silver pin, and cupped, for a moment, the warm weight of her own breasts in her hands. The infertility expert who is childless, the money-motivated foot-slogger who longs to be a reputable scientist, the straight-as-a-die monogamist who is drawn to her best, female friend. Was it time to look these contradictions in the face?

We won't do this again. Goodbye to the foreign legion. And what comes next?

In the living room Spence lay on the couch trying to watch abysmal terrestrial channel tv. The ceiling fan hummed; rain fell in sheets across the swimming pool, the squash courts, the container port, the wide darkness of the South China Sea. Anna picked up the postcard that had arrived that morning, announcing that Ramone was safely back in England. *Suffer, Birdone. . .* The picture on the front was Bournemouth seafront.

"Spence, how would you feel if I were to. . .well, fuck with Ramone, sometime?"

"I would be rightly pissed off," he answered, sitting up sharply. "I don't know how you can consider the idea. After the trouble she caused. . .! I'm not saying you have to be exclusive, doing it with someone else is okay. But please, NOT Ramone!"

Ramone as a sexual partner would be the same as Ramone for a friend: capricious, aggressive, hating you for having witnessed her moments of weakness, the very weaknesses that made you love her in spite of everything. Certain things about the sex itself would make a lovely change, but it wasn't worth the price. She was amused to note, from the vehemence of his response, that Spence had been more attentive than she'd thought to aspects of Ramone's visit. She'd have teased him, but the look on his face warned her otherwise—

"Calm down. It was a weird, passing idea."

━ *vi* ━

While Ramone was in Sungai, Lavinia's brother Roland had come up to London to check on her and carried her off home with him. He claimed she wasn't looking after herself. Six months later, while Ramone was away for a few days promoting the *Parable* paperback, he did it again. Ramone rushed down to Dorset, to that smug middle-class house in the country, to reclaim her. But this time Lavvy didn't want to come home.

Ramone stuck it out for two days. Roland's wife (Ramone had expunged the woman's name from her mind) managed total denial of the fact that Ramone was a best-selling author and treated her like dirt. Like, can lower-class persons of your type actually read? Do you know how to eat with a knife and fork? Roland said that Lavinia was staying there: Ramone was selfish and irresponsible and unfit to look after anyone. The grown-up children (who still lived at home, the slobs) were on Ramone's side, but no one was asking them. She gave up the fight on the third day, sickened and disgusted: couldn't make it past breakfast. She drove to Bournemouth, and there she had to stop. Had to get out of the car and walk around, beating her pointless grief into submission.

Those few days in Kota Baru jail had done wonders for the sales of *Parable* and for Ramone's engagement diary. She was supposed to be starting a job in a few months' time, something flashy at one of the old universities: she didn't know if she even needed it. But could she stand this? Could Ramone hack fame and fortune, without Lavvy?

Nobody understood *Parable*. Not her dear friends and others who'd trashed it unread, or the critics who groveled before it now. *A profoundly divided woman*, someone had said, *descends into the world of myth, in the hope of finding a meaning for her life*. Fucking cheek. It's the world that's divided, not my heroine. . . Ramone had written a fairy tale. A young woman, named only *L'Inconnue* (when she's fallen from grace, it becomes a name, "Nou-nou") learns that she can secure a large inheritance from her father's estate if she can discover the laws that govern worldly fame. She sets out on this quest, interrogating celebrity figures from the past, the present, and the future—some of them human; some of them technologies, texts, discoveries; all of them *persons* (of course, autotheology). Reproached by nameless, superior beings who prove to her that public success is destructive of all virtue and value, L'Inconnue protests that she has never doubted this. As soon as she has won her rightful inheritance she plans to return to the ranks of the unsung, the truly good and truly beautiful whose names are effaced from history... (Women are always there. Look in the contemporary records of any movement, any crisis, any endeavor: and you find them. Their names just magically never make it into long term memory.) What Nou-nou wants isn't possible. She cannot have justice, unless she gives up her innocence.

Of course it was about Anna Senoz.

The publishers wanted her to write something quick and dirty on women's rights terrorism in the Developing World, on the tail of the Kota Baru thing. She hated the idea. Maybe she'd better do it, because if you don't capitalize on something that's made you saleable, the chance will not come back. This is what it must feel like to be a man, she thought, wandering through the streets. Yes, I've become a man. You obey orders, you count your hierarchy points. My editor is a bigger cheese than your editor! My penis—oh, sorry, did I say penis? I meant my advance—is bigger than your advance.

She went to visit Mary Shelley's grave, but hadn't the heart to stay there long. The graceful, solid Victorian facades mocked her. By the time the moment for hyenas in petticoats came round again, Ramone wouldn't be here to enjoy it. She stared through the window of a tasteful little clothes shop. A woman on the other side, browsing a rack of skirts, started back in alarm... Ramone grinned like a gargoyle, rolled her eyes, and passed on. Better to be funny-looking than look like nothing at all. And the more successful you are, the more beautiful you get. The latest pub-shot almost made her look *strange*, rather than comical. By the time she was world famous, she'd be irresistibly attractive.

That was something to look forward to.

Finally, she took refuge in the Russell Cotes Gallery and bought some coffee and sticky cake in the cafe, the first food that hadn't choked her in several days. She began to write a letter. In fountain pen, on lined paper, on the same kind of blue covered A4 pads she'd used since her first year at university. Feint and margin, *Suffer, Birdone.*

Behold me eating cake in Bournemouth, in the museum. (I visited Mary S. on your behalf, do you remember?) As you know, I am fond of museums. I can't understand why I should reverence all those stupid cases full of china or pebbles; or the headless, armless, handless, marble things with the daft descriptions like "headless young boy." They'd look better left to rot gently in situ, in which case they'd never bother me, because I don't like abroad, except for Paris and New York. What I like is the waste of space, the only true conspicuous consumption. It was in the British Museum basement that I found the portrait of Nou-nou which adorns the cover of the new Parable paperback, which I'm sending to you with this. She's called Figurine of an Effeminate Eros, in an attitude of flight, from Boeotia. She has black patches because she was in a funeral pyre. She looks a lot like you, with your hair pulled up on top of your head; a form-fitting feathered kilt around her long thighs; and lovely pointed feet, like a ballet dancer's. In the same case there is another Eros, not so effeminate, nonchalantly burning a butterfly, signifying the human soul, which he's dangling by the legs over the flame of a lamp. It's a splendidly cruel, off-hand, sophisticated piece. Probably turned out by thousands. The first century Rome-world terracotta workers really did do butterfly wings on their Psyches: which looks weirdly modern and tasteless. . .

Anna and Spence were coming back to England, Ramone planned not to meet them. She had decided to abandon the fight that she could not win. Anna had made her choice. She preferred sex with a man, a creature fundamentally different, someone who could never, no matter what he did with his baby-maker, invade those final privacies. So be it. Ramone felt the same way, that was why she avoided lesbian relationships herself: too much like surrender. But she enjoyed writing these letters—not least because she knew Spence was bound to read them, and feel suspicious, and hopefully *suffer* a little, hahaha. Anna always answered. In her latest nice polite little letter she had revealed that Spence was now going to be a writer, news that made Ramone's blood boil. Fucking typical New Man: first he wants me to call him a radical feminist because he sponges off my friend; now he wants to be a lady novelist; I expect he'll make his fortune, rot him.

I sure hope Apuleius had a good agent for all this merchandising. Or did he get ripped to shit, like the best of us always do? I have no idea. Anyway, I wanted to ask you if you know anything about the life cycle of the sea-urchin...

She didn't know if she should talk to Anna about biology. She might lose face by misusing some crap piece of jargon, perhaps a risk only to be taken when you were drunk and drugged. But she had recently discovered, in the course of her reading—which roamed as always to and fro across the Great Divide— that sea urchin larvae, instead of growing older, give birth to successive, radically different versions of themselves. Had she misunderstood? Well, that was what it looked like in the pictures. Which were very fruitful and suggestive... She started drawing spiny urchins in her margin, thinking of *The Water Babies.*

A woman, instead of growing up, gives birth.

In *Parable* there was a woman who thought her works of art were children, that she had literally given birth to them. She told Nounou a god came along and shot them, that's why they were now dead, turned into lifeless objects... A woman who aspires to fulfill her traditional role and at the same time live a life of ideas and achievement is suffering from catastrophic *hubris.* She wants to be passive and active, private and public, the sculptor and the clay. This is not allowed, this is not possible. But what if she finds the trick not only possible but natural? A thinking woman must be both the consciousness that draws the world into existence by defining it and the world in which that consciousness is immanent... Are we not approaching, through the humble image of the working woman, the busy mother who thoroughly enjoys her part-time job, a new vision—or better, a return with new understanding, to the essential experience of being a conscious animal?

The thought of Lavvy a cold stone in her stomach.

...neatly brushed old lady with the bright eyes, says warily *I seem to know you?*

Next time you met her she was all right. But she knew what was happening. She knew that she was going down again, this time forever. So young, not even sixty. Ramone had been shocked to discover how young. And in perfect health, physically. Oh god. . .

Another time. Think about it another time.

In some profound way, Ramone knew the game was up. She had peaked too soon; her genius had deserted her; she had missed the crest of the wave She would never invent a new concept of humanity. From now on she was falling, not flying, no matter how long it took to hit the ground. But still, she had an idea for a book. Not the Kota Baru Women's Prison Spoof the publishers wanted. Something like *Parable* only different, a work of science and scholarship, dream and autobiography. She felt radiant with promise. Oh, the reading she would have to do! The nights she would spend, the hollow hours she loved, sating her titanic appetite on heaps of text, hearing again the beech tree fingers tapping at her dark window, long ago. She would call it *The Earth and the Plough*, and dedicate it, as always, to Anna Senoz. If not on the title page, then in her heart.

Roads and the Meaning of Roads, III

All this. . .

Coming awake at the wheel of a car: you are hurtling along in a box of plastic and metal; you are nominally in charge of this machine, but the engine pumps, functions engage without your understanding. Is this how it feels to wake into consciousness? To see the strange movement that seems so far away, because distance itself is a new sensation. That thing, that big blurred thing, **it is my hand, it is moving.** I am moving it! I am here, I am me.

All that, rest of stuff, is **not me**.

Mont Ventoux, that high, inimical scoured limestone landscape, where Anna and Jake admired the spoor of the Tour de France and shivered in the cold, while Spence reverenced the site where Petrarch had the experience claimed as the birth of the modern European mind. Our alienation and amaze at the world that is not us. Then the cloud lifted: and it was as the poet said, an extraordinary lightness, **légèreté**, because of all the white bare stone — air full of light. But this place that he found so strange was his own mountain. Every day of his childhood he had seen it — as you do, from the plain of Carpentras — or from the ridges above Vaucluse — **whenever I lifted my eyes**. . . That was what Spence and the medieval poet liked, and Anna too: to make a pilgrimage to the already known. Seeing something twice, knowing it again, the experience of the experience —

The secret history of Spence as a New Man. In Nigeria, when there was no mainline electricity for months, they kept the lab going on a generator, but domestic chores reverted to primitive drudgery. Anna desperately didn't want to have servants: no human sacrifices! Spence agreed in principle. But it was Anna who did the drudging, on top of her lab work, because it was her idea, after all. She remembered kneeling beside a tin bath, in a small room with a wet concrete floor and a kerosene lamp, tired to death, tears falling hot onto her hands as she scrubbed pants and socks in the cold soapy water. Spence passing by: looking in at the open door in dumb puzzlement, like a dog who doesn't understand why mistress is upset. They had sorted it out. She'd had to let him hire a servant: a half-share, actually, of a lunatic called Walter who ruined everything he touched; and thereafter, when they refused to use servants it was out of self-interest, not idealism.

Spence was righteous. He was more rigid than Anna over some things: wouldn't have a dishwasher, or a second car, or mass-market connectivity; had never set foot in a McDonald's except to use the toilet. But Spence will not drudge.

The secret history of the sophisticated travelers. When they arrived in Sungai there'd been a mightily disappointing orientation trip. She and Spence had stayed for an extra weekend at an old river trading post. The inn, a fine wooden building standing out over the slurry-colored water, was probably the most picturesque "sight" in the whole country. They were sitting in the common room when a man, short and neat in shirt sleeves and suit trousers, started talking to them. At first it was very interesting and a cool achievement. Then he started telling them about his brother. He'd been to Jakarta looking for his brother: and something about. . .terrible, those bastards. . .a normal life impossible. . . He was crying, in an adult way, pinching the tears away with two fingers on the bridge of his nose and still talking. The young foreigners sat smiling nervously, trying to look intelligent. Suddenly he realized how little they could understand. He got up, abruptly said good night, and hurried out of the room.

We thought we were so well informed: we knew nothing. She remembered Aslan Gaegler's burly figure, used to look as if he had an invisible football under each arm, his golden beard, (yes indeedy) short and glittering around his firm jowl—standing there with the white chrysanthemums. That dress with the little Audrey Hepburn belt, it was never the same... A white light splashed across her eyes, making her wince. She was in the middle lane, doing what ought to be enough speed for anyone in this heavy traffic, but the flasher was not satisfied.

She tried to get away from him, the headlights only came closer. She dropped into the inside lane the first chance she got, but oh shit, he followed her.

"Oh shit."

Spence roused a little. "What's the matter?"

"I've got a flasher."

She overtook the next car, dropped back again. No use, horns blared indignantly, and he was there, right up her arse and flashing. If it was plain irrational rage, nothing to be done. If it was one of those psychos who objected to a woman driver, then it was too late for them to swap

"Cut across to the fast lane," suggested Spence.

"No thanks. Car won't take it, and if I have to get rammed, I'd rather be doing sixty."

She set her teeth, prepared for long nagging from those lights. But it was worse than that. The little car jolted around her. They'd been shoved. Jake sat up in the back and squeaked with excitement. "Mummy, he's after you. Will we get killed? What are we going to do?"

"Deploy the torpedoes. Okay team, hang on, I'm going to lose him."

They were coming up to an exit, get-in-lane boards snapping by overhead. She glanced in her mirror and at the last moment dived into the twinkling slip road, heading for some different part of the country. "What are you **doing**?" yelled Spence. The flasher gave chase. He'd been taken by surprise, he came snarling round the high speed curve with his foot on the floor. Anna was running out of road. She hauled on the wheel, the car jolted across lane-end chevrons, the flasher went sailing on by. She completed a jumpy handbrake turn and drove swiftly the wrong way up the hard shoulder, back onto their homeward trail.

"What the fuck! What are you doing, this isn't a video game—"

"Sorry," she said. She waited for a gap in the traffic. Fortunately, there were no police about. She was shaking, but grimly elated. Beaten the bastard.

"He's coming back!" shouted Jake.

The flasher must have done a U turn on the other road: he must be really angry to be so persistent. The car, which she saw clearly for the first time, was a red saloon, nothing special. It stopped on the shoulder, about twenty meters behind them. The driver's door opened. "Turn the tv on," said Anna. "Find loud music. Don't open the window. Don't get out of the car. Don't look at him. Jake, lie down and hide your face."

The man came up. Anna and Spence sat with their eyes at an angle of sixty or so, not submissively lowered (which might invite attack) but unavailable to a challenging glare. Spence had hit a classical station, some woman in purple on the postcard screen singing Mozart lieder of all things. The man kicked at their doors, banged on the windows, shook the roof, pushed his face up to the windscreen. But he was alone, didn't have a weapon, and thank God he didn't think of going back to his car to fetch a wheel jack or something. He battered himself against the stonewall of loud Mozart for a few terrifying moments, and then he gave up. Horns blared as the red car made a forced entry into the traffic stream. It drove away.

"I'm sorry," said Anna, realizing how horribly her plan could have misfired.

"You should give way to them, straight off. You should never provoke them."

"I tried!"

"Is it all right again?" asked Jake.

"Yes, baby."

"You're a good boy, you were very good," said Spence, leaning over the seat to hug him.

Anna reached across and switched off the tv, an unusual move. In-car entertainment was Spence's territory. She sat with her hands at ten and two, and the traffic roared by, towards what blank wall, invisible in the darkness.

"D'you want me to drive? I think you should let me drive."

"I'm fine."

Inland Far

— i —

Anna and Jake had been working on the allotment. It was the end of March. Anna had been planting seeds: carrots, turnips, radishes, lettuces. She had hoed the over-wintered broad beans and earthed up the potatoes. Maybe the harvest would be better this year. Mr Frank N Furter—whom they had found still flourishing when Anna's job prospects brought them back to Bournemouth—achieved results on his plot down in the valley, in shelter, that made Anna and Spence's bumbling efforts look ridiculous. They were learning. Meantime, hunter-gatherer behavior, practiced in the Co-op supermarket on Saturday mornings, made up for the deficiencies of primitive agriculture.

She watered-in the seeds, unscrewed their tap from the standpipe by the track, and stowed everything in the buggy's shopping tray: except the spade and hoe handles, which she hid. You couldn't leave things up here. And this is called having it all, she thought, stretching to free her shoulders. Below her, coastal conurbation sprawled back from the gleaming meadows of the sea, Poole to the west and Christchurch to the east: furzy bare branches reaching up from swathes of public park and garden. With petty theft and the rottweiler tendency for neighbors, yes. Wouldn't be the same if they were shut out.

Jake lay on the ground, where a rustling barrier of last year's sweet corn sheltered him from the east wind, talking in a tiny voice and playing intently with two toy cars and a handful of weeds: a dandelion with a broken tap root, some Shepherd's Purse, a few sprigs of that infuriating little pink and white convolvulus (the worm that dieth not). She stood over him unnoticed, feasting on the dream of mind's emergence—

Behold the child among his new-born blisses, a six years' Darling of pigmy size.

See, where —'mid the work of his own hand he lies... He's four, not six, but he is the young philosopher, dreaming and making worlds.

"Time to go, Jake-boy."

He sat up and stared at her, shocked. "But I haven't had my snack!"

When you have a child, you soon learn how quickly practice becomes tradition, and how quickly tradition becomes WRITTEN IN STONE. "Okay, but we'd better get indoors. It's going to rain."

They retired inside the tumbledown shed, which smelled of spider webs and earth, and sat on an empty tin chest while Jake ate pita bread and slices of cheese. On his insistence she told him again the story of how Mummy and Daddy had once been pirates on the South China Seas. In the end they'd been shipwrecked on Bournemouth beach. They'd built this shed from the planks of their pirate ship (you could see the marks of cannonballs), and this was where they had lived until one day they found a treasure map that they'd forgotten about, recovered the gold, and used it to buy the house where Jake and Anna and Spence lived now.

"If we get very, very poor, will we go back to pirating?" asked the child, hopefully.

Anna picked fragments of horse dung and dead grass from his dark curls.

"We're not poor. We have a house with a garden, lovely holidays, new clothes and shoes whenever we need them. How can we be poor?"

"I expect you have some more gold somewhere. For emergencies."

"Ah maybe so! A pirate never divulges the hiding place of her last treasure."

"Shere Khan has an island completely made of gold. She never tells anyone where it is."

"Except for Jake. Eat your last bit of cheese."

"Yes, she does tell Jake. And Nancy, but no one else. Remind me about the parrot."

"The parrot. Well, he belonged—a parrot by the name of Bill, I seem to remember—to the wickedest ruffian in all our bad acquaintance. But I don't know what became of him."

Shere Khan was a female pirate captain who had emerged, somehow, from this story of the shed that used to be a pirate ship: with the name of the tiger lord from *The Jungle Book*, a dashing young mate called Jake, and a ship called The Royal Processor. It was Spence who maintained the annals, weaving ever more bizarre adventures for the wild, willful captain and her desperate crew: Jake the First Mate, Nancy the Knife and her brother Rafe, Black McGeer the pirate boffin, and all the rest. Anna wondered if he was aware of the touches of Ramone Holyrod that had crept into his characterization. Probably not. Spence had never liked Ramone much.

Looking back, he'd had a right. For a while after Sungai those *Suffer Birdone...*letters had been intensely important to Anna: dangerously important. Reckless acts, reckless deeds, wholesale shipwreck might have followed. The letters had stopped, the danger had passed, and the rabid one had vanished into her success: no contact with her for ages. She wrote flashy books, she was a feminist pundit... The squall arrived. Rain thundered on the shed's patched roof and rattled in the folds of the plastic sack that was taped over a broken window. Jake leaned against her, finishing his cheese meticulously. Anna closed her eyes. She was working so hard, full-time employment, and *then* whatever lab and machine time she could scrounge for the great mission. She looked forward to the one day a week that she spent looking after Jake (giving Spence a chance to write) as a major treat: but any time she sat down, it was hard to stay awake.

Was there still a beach lodge at Pasir Pancang? In Sungai the forests were burning. Tough things were happening in that unlucky little country. Tough things were happening in the so-called "free world" too, as the old western powers slipped ever faster into decline; the twentieth century's institutions and services vanishing into calamitous disrepair. And a clutch of grief at the heart any time you remembered the other casualties: ah, to know Jake would never hear a cuckoo's song, ringing through the Hampshire woods. She lived in a frightening world that had lost its balance of power, scrabbling for stability and finding none; and the pirate treasure might yet turn out to be fool's gold, or the expedition of the Hispaniola might founder for lack of funds. Next month might be the month when all the paychecks bounced and primitive strip-farming became her family's only resource. Yet Anna was very happy, with her husband and her child, her frugal household arts and her dream, all sustaining each other. She was back on track: working hard, tasting the sweetness of life.

◆━ ◆━

After the Sungai bomb mopping-up, Parentis had transferred them to Mexico, which was where Jake had been born just about a year later. Spence had believed he could never want a child again, but the moment he agreed they should give up contraception, he'd felt as if he'd sprouted wings. He'd known that she'd get pregnant easily, and she did. He'd known that the baby would be a boy, and that he must be called Jacob, in honor of Anna's Spanish-Jew roots and of the first recorded attempt at genetic manipulation (the version in the bible obviously the muddled report of some dumb journalist), and that everything would be fine. And it was. Spence's Mom came south to be with them, which was brave of her considering she must have known the risk that she would be faced with awkward revelations. The shade of the baby's complexion had been distinct enough to raise comment as soon as he was born.

Spence, having acquired a black granddaddy and a big, perfect, coffee-colored son in the same hour, had only demanded "Why didn't you *tell* me?" "It was for the best that you shouldn't know," Mom had pleaded. "I know Manankee County!" Anna couldn't have cared less. "Look at this!" she said, laughing. "I am totally humiliated! Everyone who knows me is going to be convinced I bought the trait for a cool color scheme out of a vanity-parenting catalogue. . ."

He had not thought the trail would be so short, but he understood why his Mom had lied and concealed the evidence. Spence's biological granddad, dead grandmother's first husband—the mean one, who had been a drunk and walked out when Mom was a baby, and of whom there were no pictures—had conformed to a shameful stereotype. All the black people Spence had ever heard of from Mom were gifted, hardworking, good-looking, wonderful family people in steady employment. . .that she didn't know particularly well. She liked to view the world through rose-colored countercultural lenses. Could he blame her? Nature or nurture, Spence was a little that way himself. After she'd flown back to Illinois (having Mom in the house for the first weeks of their child's life was a cross Anna had borne with the patience of an autistic angel), he'd felt the new information bedding down into him, grounding him. He wasn't going to get Roots fever, but it was good.

Actually, I *am* Spartacus.

So they went back to England, Anna resumed her doctoral studies and made ends meet with part-time lecturing, and Spence became a househusband, the way they'd always planned. They spent every penny of their foreign legion pile on a nice old house in Bournemouth, drawn to the place by old contacts and nostalgia, and settled down to live happily ever after, poor as church mice, decorating inventively with *papier mâché* and thumbtacks, cooking the food of the poor that they had picked up on their travels (nasi campur, ful mesdames, megadarra, mongo, gado-gado, anything tasty and cheap), entertaining their friends with world-music tales.

━ ━

The winter that they moved into their own house, Jake was eight months old. There was a new flu speeding across the continent, but they were young, Jake was a splendidly healthy baby, and they were still in ex-pat mode, ignoring the news channels. They were blasé about the pandemic scare. Spence went down sick on one of his writing days. He got up, complained of a stiff neck and a headache, and seemed in no hurry to get to his desk. He came to the door to see Anna and Jake out, as they left to do some errands, said, "I feel weird," and crumpled to the floor. It was lucky it was one of Anna's Jake days, or he'd have been lying there when she came home from work. "I'd have managed," he protested, as she put him to bed. "I'd have crawled through somehow—"

Anna went downstairs, having settled Jake for his nap with Werg the bear and his bottle. It was a pity Spence was ill, because she and Jake could have done some Christmas shopping. She phoned in sick for her evening's employment (an adult access-to-HE course), switched on a lamp because the room seemed gloomy, and sat on the sofa, the good old folded-futon sofa from Leeds, with the satinized cotton cover in faded gold and sprigs of red—now dignified by a pine frame and three cushions for which Spence had machined the covers with his own hands. She thought about assembling materials for a Christmas decorations session. Glitter glue, poster paints, tissue paper, scissors. . .and sat looking at the pattern of the cushion nearest to her, until she gradually knew she'd been staring at it for a long time, that her head was aching, and she was very cold, cold deep inside. She had lost core temperature. Time was no longer passing in her brain, and her body had begun to shake, but she couldn't move of her own volition. The pattern on the cushion cover absorbed all her attention, she fell into it. Oppressed by a burden that filled her mouth and weighed down her limbs, she entered a thick-walled, rubbery maze where the passages grew narrower and narrower, but she went on, squeezing her way into a tightly packed interminable darkness.

When she woke, the first thing she knew was that she felt horribly uncomfortable. She had fallen forward with her face over the side of the couch. There was a half-dried sticky murky patch on the rug; she realized with a shock of alarm and shame that she must have vomited. She tried to get up, felt the clogging weight in her pants, and recognized the stench of feces. She freed herself of the filled pants, and staggered across the room to close the curtains: it was dark outside. She dumped her underwear in the kitchen bin, crawled to the bathroom and cleaned herself up, impelled through the hideously effortful actions by an animal need to restore herself to order. It was only when she'd washed and put on a dressing gown that she saw her watch face and discovered with utmost terror that a day and a half had passed of which she knew nothing.

The half-decorated rooms were cold and silent. She ran up the stairs. Their bedroom smelled of shit, piss, and vomit. Spence was lying on his back, his beaky nose standing upright, his eye sockets and the skin around them darkened, his cheeks drawn and pasted with stubble, the corners of his mouth crusted. He stirred and opened his eyes. *What time is it*, he whispered. She didn't answer. She ran to the baby's room. He was lying in his cot, quite still, face down. He'd kicked off his blanket, and the room was cold. She took a step into the room. Jake rolled over and sat up. He stared at her, his eyes were huge and wild, she knew that he had passed through grief and terror into a hell of despair. He had cried and cried, and no one had come: he held out his arms, with a whimper of pleading, surely whatever he'd done they would forgive him now? Anna stumbled over and picked him up, his body warm, his arms clinging. He buried his face in her neck, with a deep sigh.

Rescue Werg the bear, who had fallen under the cot. Get Jake some water. Go back to Spence, leave them together in the warm soiled bed, bring a bottle of milk formula, more bottled water, clean bedding. Feed Jake, give Spence the water. Clean them both up, notice that the house was *really* cold; in fact there was gas but no electricity, was it the end of the world? Phone the group practice. When she finally got through to David, their doctor, he told her that if they were all now awake and warm, then the killing coma had spared them, they were going to be all right, and that he'd get an ambulance round as soon as possible.

The ambulance never turned up, but David had been right: the worst was over. It wasn't the end of the world, the power came back the next day. Jake never showed any signs of getting sick. The three of them lived in that bed for the next many days, Anna and Spence taking it in turns, watch on/watch off, to be the nurse. Christmas was not much celebrated that year. The Ice Flu (or the Mammoth flu, because it froze people, or the White Storm, because of its swift and deadly passage around the northern hemisphere, before it plunged south) killed an acknowledged four hundred thousand people in Europe alone. Some of the estimates for the final toll reached a quarter of a billion. This was a news item that would be recorded in memory, even by Anna the oblivious, and would leave a scar on history that would take years to fade. But Anna's mother and father, and Spence's Mom, and Anna's sister Maggie and her second husband (also the first, divorced one) and their children, and Frank N Furter and his current beautiful girlfriend, and Rosey McCarthy and Wol, and their families, and Marnie Choy, and Simon Gough and his family, and Ramone Holyrod and Lavinia Kent, and KM Nirmal, and Daz Avriti: they all survived. The disease burned itself out. Human life, in its vast numbers, closed over the gaps in the ranks, which meant nothing except to those who had lost faces they knew, and everything went on much as before.

◆ ◆

Once, when Jake was going by the Salvation Army Citadel, he found a DRAGONFLY clinging to the railings. It was enormous, longer than Mummy's hand, with huge eyes and glistening wings. He wanted to take it home and have it for a pet, but she said they couldn't carry it around with them, it would get hurt, they didn't have anything to keep it in. He went along with her to do the errands, thinking of nothing but his DRAGONFLY, so that there was no charm in the legos that you could play with in the Nationwide Bank, or the receipt from the money machine, or the lid that she gave him with his snack in the little house in the playground, or the picture-books in the library. He didn't tell her what was wrong because he didn't know that she'd forgotten, he thought she must be thinking of the DRAGONFLY too; so she didn't hurry. They did everything at normal speed, except that Jake didn't want to stay anywhere. When they got back to the railings, IT WAS STILL THERE. They took the DRAGONFLY home and transferred it to a leaf of the yellow flags that grew in the pond in their garden, and it lived there until it flew away, staying long enough to confirm in Jacob William Meade Senoz's mind forever the certainty that good things happen. The first French word that he learned, after please and thank you, was *lalibellule*, the dragonfly. *Libellule, limace, escargot*. His mother taught him the names of these friendly creatures, with whom he lived nose to nose when they were camping in France, which was how they spent their holidays because it was cheap; and she told him, though their names were too long for him to learn, that he himself was made of tiny creatures, which lived in Jake as if he was a world, as if he was a meadow of grass: they fed on his food and air and turned it into Jake and into *puff* the way Thomas's engine turned hot water into *puff* to make him go; and to help them do this they told each other stories the way Jake's Daddy told him stories, about times gone by and things each of them needed to know.

In winter the creatures in his ears fought battles and did deals with his enemies, which caused Jake great discomfort and made him cry and stay awake all night. In the summer he traveled, over the narrow seas on a big boat like the one Mummy and Daddy used to have when they were pirates, and lived for weeks on the golden roads, with the slugs and the snails and the waterskaters and the dragonflies: in every city a cathedral, a museum, a river, an electricity station where they could feed the car, and a playground with swings and a sand pit. In Chartres, the car park wound in a snail spiral underground. In Rome he played splash with his mummy all around the fountains, including the Trevi where they bought their breakfast from a shop and Jake had a STUFFED TOMATO and ate it on a slippery blue seat, like a swimming pool: here mummy got in trouble for splashing someone and they had to run like rabbits. In Liguria he lost his Thomas Engine; in the Piano Grande in Norcia he collected sheep bones and saw a Humming Bird Moth; in the vastness of the Campo Santo at Santiago de Compostela Jake himself was lost. He cried, but he knew he would be all right. Someone would find him and take him home, and he'd be their little boy, like Thomas was now safe being somebody else's engine, but what would his mummy and daddy do, how could they live without him? But a policeman found out who he was and brought him to his daddy, CONFIRMING that good things happen. He ventured onto the half built bridge at Avignon alone, while mummy and daddy watched from the barrier, because it was *daylight robbery*, he was annoyed because they were laughing but he came back dancing on his toes, because he had seen a tiny, a *tiny tiny tiny* little fish, in the river. In a place called Salamanca, his mummy told him something that made her very proud, it was where her granddad and grandma came from, Jake's granddad in Manchester's gone-to-heaven Daddy and Mummy. In Amsterdam, a disaster happened. They lost the world, the bag that came out with Jake whenever he left the house (or, when traveling, the car), which had held a changing kit in the time of nappies and still held everything Jake needed: his cars, his beaker, his bread and cheese, his lids, his felt-tips, his paper, his babywipes, his spare pants. Thank The God Who Makes Mistakes they had accidentally left Werg the Bear back in the yurt, their summer palace, or there would have been hell to pay, because the world, unlike Jake in Santiago, was never seen again and had to be recreated from nothingness.

Up in the Alps, on a long, long path enlivened by the best ever Shere Khan story, they gorged on wild raspberries and myrtilles and found a real glacier. Beside Lake Geneva mummy had to go to a conference. Daddy and Jake ate lonely ham sandwiches and fed the ducks that bounced on the white capped navy blue water, and Daddy told Jake part of someone else's story about a poor sad monster that nobody loved. . . In every village an ancient church, a donjon tower, a fountain where Daddy and Mummy and Jake lay watching the wasps through an afternoon so hot that even wasps became harmless. In every town a *bar tabac* with *pressions pour mes gentils parents* and a peanut machine; on every mountain a ruined wall, a deserted shrine where the lizards basked, a place that was old under the sun, a place called Europe. On a red mesa above the town of Najara, where the storks nested, Jake had an epiphany. Let's sit here, he said, for a little while, and think about how we are engines. Everything was very old, except for Jake and his mummy and daddy, and the road with the supermarket signs, the electricity stations, and the coke machines; the road that bound everything together, winter and summer, home and traveling.

Sometimes not-so-good things happened. On a path by the lake with the navy blue waves, near a campsite that was not the kind they liked, Jake's Daddy and Mummy walked up and down while Jake played with his cars and watched them anxiously. It was a memory that would stay with him his life long, in the form of a deep disquiet woken by certain accidents of light on water, certain angles of sun and shadow. His mother was crying about her work, which Jake and his Daddy secretly hated, the thing that took her away from them.

"They're forcing me off the road," she wailed. "Either I back down and pay homage to the bastards, I say they're right, or I don't get to stay in the game at all. What makes me sick is to think I quit Parentis to clean up my act, so I would be fit to speak to the decent people—"

"You didn't quit Parentis," said Jake's Daddy. "They dumped you. I mean, shed you, along with a lot of other people. You've never quit anything in your life, Anna."

"Thanks for those kind words—"

"Sorry, I'm just trying—"

"I know what's happening. I'm turning into Clare. Remember I used to say Clare Gresley was like an elf, fighting the long defeat; but a *bitter* elf, and that's no good. I don't want to be bitter. I hate the idea of clinging on, *bitter*, to an idea that no one wants. I'm going to pack it in. I will diminish and go into the west and remain—"

"NO YOU WILL NOT!" Jake's Daddy grabbed Jake's mummy by the shoulders, beside himself in his fury at her heartbreak. "*Fuck* that. If you diminish and go into the west you won't remain my Anna. I won't let you give up. You'll do what you have to do, become a guerrilla, snipe from the sidelines: NEVER GIVE AN INCH."

They went on talking then, pacing up and down in the small cage imposed by childcare. Jake knew that the crackling black lightning of misfortune had passed by, leaving his life unharmed. They came back smiling. He sat between them, holding his daddy's hand and his mummy's, understanding his grave responsibility. He was all they had to cling to and defend them from their enemies. He was the world.

"I want to stay here forever," said Anna. "Living on the road in France, with my team."

Forever and ever and ever.

➤ *ii* ➤

After their talk on Pasir Pancang beach Spence had confidently expected that Anna's Transferred Y discovery would make them both famous. It didn't happen. The paper that she published caused no stir at all. Maybe she'd pitched it wrong: Scientist Discovers Harmless Mutation in Sex Pair Chromosomes; not much of an attention grabber. The media storm never started. The life science and human genetics establishment didn't ignore her, but they went straight from the position where Transferred Y was an outrage that could not possibly exist to yeah, TY exists, and so what? Cunning bastards. The wired world got more excited, but that was the Internet for you, always room for another cult. Anna wasn't fazed, thank God. She was despondent for a while, but she recovered. It's okay, she told him. I expected this. I have to build myself a rep, and I know how to do it.

So they set up house in Bournemouth, and it was good. Anna had contacts at Forest U, and in the dire straits of British Science, especially after the Ice Flu, there was a jolly blitz spirit, everyone in the same boat. She worked like a devil, borrowing lab time, trading teaching hours for tech support, while Spence looked after the baby and had a day a week to concentrate on his writing. He decided he wanted to be a tourist, do the stuff he'd never done in his Exchange Year, and carried his family off, whenever he got the chance, on a punctuated, shoestring Grand Tour. And that was fabulous, the ancient culture, the pictures and the landscapes, the stones and the cities, all that human history, so much fucking better for the soul than rubbernecking the road accidents of the present, in slum countries. Socially things were cool too. Their friends were pleased to see them in Holy Poverty mode, as pleased as when "Anna and Spence" had been glimpsed passing through London on their way from KL to Yucatan. Spence finished a novel and had it published (like Transferred Y, *Cesf* did not make much of a stir). Jake was the sweetest little guy, and Anna was happy, quietly carving a foothold in the respectable face of her science.

Then Anna defended her D (something about how TY managed to home in on the same spot, every time), and KM Nirmal was invited to set up a Genetics Department for a brand new local coast-conurbation college called Poole University. The old lag, one of the smart ones, had extracted a tasty early retirement package from Parentis. He could afford to work for peanuts, which was as well because peanuts was all the private corporation was planning to pay. He wangled the second-in-command post for Anna, a point six, good benefits; all thoroughly nefarious, an inside job in defiance of Equal Opportunities and national advertising, but too bad for the other poor bastards, Anna was *owed* this.

So the gypsy-science-lecturer years were over, and this changed things. Still no money, but one of them had a real job. One of them was no longer living like an outlaw.

➤ ➤

He thought he saw pity and unease growing in his wife's eyes. Soon Jake would go to school, and neither of them wanted more babies: what would Spence do with himself? His agent, when it came to the second novel, had told him he should try something else. He'd taken her advice, but published his novel anyway, on his website, downloadable for the digitally inclined, running off perfect-bound paper copies that he touted around the stores, taking Jake along with him in the stroller. He spoke to Anna about getting into small press publishing. She tried to act supportive, but he knew what she was thinking. She was afraid he was turning into her father: the bright-eyed failure, good for nothing but piling up debts.

This was the state Spence was in, the summer before Jake started school, when his mother called and told him Cesf was sick. She was going on vacation to New York. Normally she would leave the cat in the charge of Mrs Meenahan next door, but this time it was too much to ask. Mom couldn't afford to put him in the vet's and anyway Cesf would hate that. What did Spence want her to do? The cat was dying, in other words. Spence's Mom was running out on the old guy and wanted Spence's permission to take him for the lethal injection. Frankly, he'd have been relieved if she'd done the deed and told him about it afterwards, but he could not make himself say the words she was trying to force him to say.

"Don't do anything. I'll come over."

Spence went home, though the cost of the flight, lowest cattle-truck discount rate he could find, was a blow. He left Jake behind, and arrived, due to fixing the trip with minimum disruption for Anna's work, the day after his mother had left. He found the house empty. As he was wandering around the yard, calling the cat's name, half-hoping the demise of his old pal could be put off for another few years, Mrs Meenahan rose like a sounding whale on the other side of the fence, and informed him that Cesf had died in the night.

"Oh, um. . . What happened?"

"Well, I let myself in this morning and found him lying there, half out of the basket like he'd been trying to rise from his bed and fell back, dead." She drew herself up, her large body contracting like a reefed sail, her eyes big with the importance of it all. "And you came all the way from *England*, that's a real shame. Your Mom always said you really loved that cat."

Mrs Meenahan was a phenomenon Spence had viewed with horror for many years, one of the genuine post-humans, what you actually *get* when you blend flesh and blood with instant gratification technology. Her plump fists clutched each other upon the swollen, folded bolster of her breasts. "You must be real upset," she prompted, gazing into his face. He wondered if he hadn't better just break down and sob like a baby, so she could feed and be satisfied. He thought, if I were a stranger, I would barely be able to tell them apart...

My Mom is a member of the post-human underclass.

"So, um, what did you do with the remains?"

"I didn't know what-all to do, so I *buried* him. I hope I did the right thing."

She came around and showed him the place, a lump in the grass in the middle of the yard. It must have been a big effort, for such a heavy woman. Spence thanked her profusely and obstinately waited until she went away. Then he knelt and peeled back the lump, and found his cat wrapped in a plastic refuse sack, the blue eyes slitted a little way open, the body stiff and ragged like a piece of roadkill. It was about time. Cesf was twenty years old. What was that Cavafy poem? *Those old sticks of furniture must still be knocking around somewhere.*

Something about parting with your lover for a week, and it turns out to be forever?

The Afternoon Sun, yeah—

He fetched a shovel and dug a respectably deep hole in a flower border, where Mom had planted a few straggly rosebushes. He lined it with grass, went and fetched the blanket from the basket in the kitchen, laid the wrapped corpse in the hole, and shoveled the earth down on top. There you are, old boy. Sleep sound.

When he'd fit the turf that Mrs Meenahan had hacked out into place and cleared all traces of a sick old cat from the house, he sat on the back porch in the heat of the declining day. It was July. The white-walled house was quiet, standing four-square in its disheveled plot. The yard—which in England would be a fine big garden, unaccountably left open to the neighbors' view—was heavy with the scent of the mock orange blossom that rambled along one boundary. When you've lived in Britain, the appearance of a lower-middle-class American burb takes on peculiar contradictions. There's so much *space,* and yet the houses look like tatty cardboard boxes... I never want to come here again, he thought. We will keep on coming back unless Mom moves, or until she gets sick and goes into a nursing home and dies, but it will never be a homecoming again. When I step from the plane my heart will sink. He felt adrift, as if he'd lost sight of the bank of the river he'd left, while the other shore was far beyond his reach.

He thought of his long, faithful love for Anna, and of the career with Emerald City that he had abandoned after Lily Rose died. He didn't want to go back and take the other path, become a hotshot software exec with a closet of suits and a record of infidelities a mile long. No doubt there were people in the world making easy money, and people in the world getting phenomenal supplies of wanton fuck: he didn't envy them, not much. But he had come to a dead center, where all he knew was that he had lost the way. He realized that the idea of getting deeper into self-publishing filled him with disgust. He hated everything about that stupid scheme: the hustling, the smile-and-a-shoeshine, the bright-eyed failure... Long ago, here in the rank woodlands and empty horizons of Manankee County, Mr Acid at his side, he had solemnly sworn that he would live and be happy and have no other gods, because no other gods are worthy of any sacrifice or reverence. He would be different from anybody else... What had become of those vows? He had fallen from grace.

He wondered if Anna had known he was feeling like this, and was that why she'd instantly accepted that he had to derail their finances for a sick cat. Maybe. He knew she worried, and she wanted him to be happy—

She doesn't need you.

The words came from nowhere and walked over his grave.

Mrs Meenahan came over at dusk with a dish of tuna casserole and half a gelatinous cherry pie. Spence called his Mom, who didn't seem too cast down by the sad news. He could have tried to get a standby flight and gone straight home. Instead he stayed on, sleeping in his old room, which was full of boxes and smelled of damp and cat shit, and managed to gain several pounds, between moral cowardice and self-pity, before his mother returned and released him from this hiatus.

◀ ▶

He came back from America, and his life felt like grubby, outgrown clothes. One day he was baking bread, one of his favorite househusband chores. Jake ran in, wanting a turn at squeezing the dough. Spence sent him off to wash his hands. He darted away crying "Okay Sir! I love you Sir!" ...Spence blew up. Spence flew into a dreadful paddy. Spence yelled and made the baby cry.

They sorted it out. Spence apologized abjectly and explained that he was feeling bad because of Cesf. The bread dough was finished and put to proof. Spence and Jake cuddled together on the good old folded futon couch, recovering. Spence, his chin on Jake's hair, ran the footage over, and this time managed to catch the spurt of agonizing rage, beat it down, and trace it to its source. I would be no one's servant and no one's master. I wanted to be a new creature and here I am, trapped, a Dad with no job. Life dragged me under while I wasn't looking, and she doesn't need me any more.

Jake covertly spread his hands and examined them, front and back. Snuggled against the hard warmth of daddy's front, he felt safe again: but he was still looking for the dirt.

Anna arrived home late one evening to find Spence watching Ramone Holyrod on the tv, the same little color tv they'd bought in Sungai, now equipped with a many-To-many set-top box for access to the networlds. Ramone filled the jewel-clear screen, sprawled over a studio couch, talking a blue streak. "The schlock, the shit-blood-vomit-offal-serial-killer territory. . .that cover's blown. Everybody knows it was a mere feeble imitation of the female birthright of extreme physical experience, of the unmatched violence and danger of human parturition—"

"Unmatched among mammals," remarked Anna judiciously. "I s'pose that's true."

"So now we get the New Man novel: wimp out, winsome little lady-boy tales. You know, men don't want to possess women; that's the cover story. They want to BE women. We're seeing them start to be out about that now. Well, okay, if there are men who want to become human, at this late date, I'll buy it. Let them spend their winter in the reeds." The pundit burst into a demoniac cackle. "If they come back with tits and bleeding once a month, maybe I'll listen."

"She's quoting herself," growled Spence. "That's all she ever does, winds herself up and lets fly a page or two of the latest opus. I call it incitement to gender violence."

"I don't know why you watch this kind of stuff," said Anna. "It only annoys you." But the face on the screen drew from her an involuntary smile of greeting. "So that's Ramone, now. She looks very well, doesn't she."

"I think she's had her breasts reduced. They used to be real sloppy and too big. Remember how she always used to hide them under leathers and layers and droopy shawl-things?"

"Oh no," said Anna firmly, "They weren't sloppy."

He wondered under what precise circumstances had his wife become so certain about the consistency of Ramone Holyrod's breasts. He wasn't going to ask.

"I'm going to bed."

Spence stayed where he was, slumped and glowering.

The first days of that September felt like the last of the wine. The parents struggled to accept their loss, but Jake had started school, and he was vanishing from them. The little boy who had been all their treasure was gone, never to return; and it was cruelly hard. At the end of the month the three of them went to a party held by one of Anna's colleagues. It was the usual thing: a thirties semi-detached, a pleasant room with glass doors open onto the patio and the garden. Complacently dated music; children under foot; twenty or so adults eating Soil Association Certified barbecue from paper plates and drinking wine from plastic cups. Alice, the woman who was holding the party, introduced Spence, for some reason he didn't quite catch, to a younger woman in a big dark blue shirt and a narrow white ankle-length skirt. She had red-gold hair, combed smoothly to her shoulders but cut short around her face, reminding him somehow of a Japanese woodcut.

"So, hi, Mer. Is that right, Mer?"

She nodded.

"Is that short for anything?"

"Meret."

"Huh?" She'd been introduced as an artist, whatever that meant. "Oh, I wonder if that is after the fur teacup guy. Meret Oppenheim."

"Yes, that's me. Eccentric artist parents. But she wasn't a guy, she was a woman."

He felt put in the wrong. She was pretty, but he was looking for an exit.

"I'm so glad to meet you. I really admire your writing."

This was a first. *They all* knew about Spence's literary ventures and were politely uninterested. As far as anyone else was concerned he was Anna's househusband. He warmed to this girl (she didn't look more than eighteen). "You've read something of mine? Really? Of your own free will? Did you find it online? My God, may I touch you?"

She laughed. "I meant Shere Khan. Of course I've read it. I think it's terrific."

The penny dropped. "Oh, you're Meret *Hazelwood*."

Spence had been insulted when Fiona the agent suggested he try writing for children, but it had been no effort to rattle off one of the Shere Khan adventures (Jake hanging over his shoulder, first and best critic). The publishers had liked it, in fact they'd liked it so well he'd already turned in the second installment. They had matched him with an illustrator, he'd known she lived somewhere close, but he hadn't wanted to meet her. So this was she, and thank God he hadn't said anything rude about her pictures.

"But, um, I thought Alice said a different name," he bleated, embarrassed, because he really should have known, and because he hadn't caught the other name, either.

"I'm really Meret Craft. That's my married name." Spence was the one caught out, but the girl was blushing: she raised her chin with a brave air of defying her traitor complexion. "But I have read 'Kes'f.' I'd read it before."

"Huh, oh you mean *Sef.*"

"Weird name,"

"It's a password I don't use anymore. Look. . .can I get you another drink?"

She smiled at him shyly, lips closed. He went to the kitchen to fill their plastic cups with *côte de decaying nuclear power station*, feeling oddly shaken. So he had a colleague, a colleague of his own, first time since he left Emerald City, how exciting. He thought of Madame Bovary, *J'ai un amant, un amant. . .!* In the door to the garden a tall lean guy in green linen trousers and a white Nehru jacket was standing, turned half-profile, his dark hair cut *en brosse*, beard shadow on his jaw, something familiar about him. Spence took the cups back.

"So was K. . . I mean Sef, was it true?" asked Meret, smiling more eagerly, showing small white teeth.

"Ah—"

"Is that a very naive thing to ask?"

"Well, it was when I was fifteen, sixteen. I made the boy in the book thirteen because I thought that was sexier: more pubertal. It's true that I learned to fence, one summer, and had some of those things happen—"

"To be different, because you hated ball games. And the tramp in the woods, who lived under an old hospital bed, and kept the castors oiled so he could sail away on it—"

"If the white-coats came after, yeah, he was real."

She laughed. "I think you're telling me what I want to hear. Did you keep up the fencing?"

"Nah. It was *way* cool, but my D'Artagnan fantasy was short-lived, kind of faded after the duel and all... Don't you think," he added, fearing he sounded like an ageing hippie to this child, "that the word 'cool' has become the new 'nice'? Everyone uses it, and thinks they shouldn't ought to."

"Pedants think it should only be applied in its proper original sense."

"Like that guy in *Northanger Abbey*, fighting against the tide."

"Oh yes. But what is the proper original sense of 'cool'?"

As if he would know. Spence cleared his throat. "I've heard it's a Yoruba term, translated into English, originally meaning something quite serious: a state of inner balance, poise, and right measure." He had a feeling he ought to cut this short and go find Anna. He compromised by hooking Jake out of a passing storm of midgets and introducing him to the lady who had drawn Shere Khan so splendidly. Jake preferred his own portraits of the gallant captain and her crew. He sidled, and wouldn't stay.

"I've seen you with Jake before," confessed Meret. "And his mother, if that's who it is taking him to school when you don't. My two oldest go to the same school. Florrie is in the other kindergarten class; it's her first term as well. My oldest, Tomkin, is in Year Two. Jake is such a beautiful little boy... Er, he's adopted?"

"No," said Spence, grinning. "It's me. I have, or had, a black granddaddy."

She blushed like a rose.

The tall guy in the green trousers had come over and stood by her side.

"Spence? It *is* Spence, isn't it?"

The half-recognized profile and the name slotted together. Craft. Oh, fuck... It was *Charles Craft*: thin and prosperous and much improved. They discovered that they were practically neighbors. Charles had his own Gene-Mod nursery company, called *Natural Craft*. Meret, like Spence, worked at home. What a coincidence! Anna and Spence must come to supper; they must fix a date. Charles was keen, Meret was keen. Anna, when she was tracked down and presented with this coincidence accompli, went into Anna-reticent mode, but was obliged to be reticently keen.

➤ ➤

Anna had known that Charles Craft was still in Bournemouth. He had been born around here; he had a right. She'd known about *Natural Craft*, the family business regenerated. When she had spotted him picking up his wife and two red-headed children outside Jake's school, she'd felt doomed. She'd been praying ever since that she would never be spotted herself. But if his wife was Spence's illustrator, she would have to accept her fate.

They had to hire a babysitter for the supper date, an unusual extravagance.

"And I must say," grumbled Anna, "It is galling to think we are paying good money to spend an evening with *Charles Craft!*"

Spence raised his eyebrows. "I thought you and he used to be kinda close, at one time."

"Don't you believe it. Enforced team-mates, was all."

"I never liked him much myself, back then. But he's probably changed."

"Have you changed?"

Spence looked into the mirror opposite their bed. Spence looked out. His hair was longer than when he'd been an undergraduate, shorter than when he'd worn dreads. His bones were more visible; his skin was still inclined to break out. He rubbed a little concealer into the oily pores around his nose, touched up his eyebrows lightly: "No."

"Well, there you are. People don't."

"Okay, possibly he's a bit of a shit, but we have to have some kind of social life. You can't restrict yourself to only knowing the few people you totally like and trust, Anna."

"I don't see why not," said Anna Anaconda.

The Crafts lived with Meret's parents, a filial and ecologically sound arrangement that had to command respect. The big, double-fronted house, which was called The Rectory, was full of paintings by Meret's father, nudes and gaudy landscapes in a sugary, photo-realist style that had been fashionable in the sixties. Godfrey was very old, a craggy shambling wreck. Meret's mother, Isobel, was much younger, and didn't seem to be the woman featured in the pictures; perhaps that was a previous wife. She had a rather unnerving manner: a wandering glance and a constant, affectless smile. The other guests were Alice and Ken Oguma from the university, a tv journalist called Noelle Seger with her partner, and a something-in-the-city with his graphic-designer wife. Everyone looked sleek and smart, and it was indefinably clear that no one knew the Crafts particularly well. This was reassuring for Anna. A formal dinner party, a collection of near-strangers gathered together to impress each other, was something Spence detested.

She felt worse when she found herself placed next to Charles.

"Well, Anna," he said, at once. "I never thought you'd have gone in for babypharming. I'd have thought you would have disapproved. I've been following your career with interest, as they say. You've been getting famous, while I've been plugging away at improving the vegetables." He glanced at her, slyly. "When did you get your eyes fixed?"

"My eyes? Oh, that. I had it done in China, ages ago."

"*China*, eh? Been there, done that. . . What kind of job do they do in China? I guess you're looking at about five-ten years, before you need them fixed again. That's the trouble with cosmetic surgery, once you've started you can't stop."

"The operation I had is supposed to be permanent."

"Well good luck. . . I read your paper, the Geneva one that caught so much flak. Very accomplished, considering where you were working. It must have been a blow when Parentis crashed."

"Not really."

"They backed the wrong horse," Mr Something-in-the-City, who had been introduced as Darth, chimed in knowledgeably. "Priced themselves out of the market."

"Invested too heavily in their way-out pure researchers," Charles grinned at Anna.

"What happened to Parentis, really?" asked Noelle Seger, leaning across the table. "Please tell me, I'm genuinely interested. They were among the hot pioneers, doing amazing things, and then. . . It must have been so exciting, working for them."

"What, unmh Darth, said, more or less." Anna smiled at Mr Something, wondering if that was scifi-fan parents or something ethnic from Uzbekistan. "They backed the wrong horse. There were two ways to go in human assisted reproduction. You optimized, or you selected. Parentis went for optimization, which is classier and preserves, well, all kinds of things. Selection, where you screen a portfolio of cloned embryonic cell masses, pick the obvious winner, and dump the rest, is far cheaper. When HAR became mass market, relatively anyway, there was a price war, and firms like Parentis were in trouble. But they haven't disappeared. They've just become very much smaller, and very, very expensive."

"Selection is not only cheaper," said Darth, "it's more natural, isn't it?"

"In a sense. But it's crude and rough. By optimizing, you preserve the net diversity—"

"Otherwise we'd all end up looking like perfect quarter-pounders!" laughed Noelle. "But Anna that sounds so horrible, when you talk about cell masses—"

"It all sounds horrible to me," remarked Isobel. "I hate to think of what Charles does to his poor vegetables. It's awfully arrogant, I think, trying to improve on nature."

"Ah, but you eat them, *belle-mère*." Charles raised his voice. "Anyone who objects to genetically modified foodstuffs, better speak now, by the way!"

"We can't stop him from bringing his work home," rumbled Godfrey. "The potatoes, the maize, the tomatoes, the broad beans, the spinach, where will it end. You should see his spinach seeds, it's like something from another planet, like a pollen or a virus in gross magnification, all spikes, knobs, and knuckles."

"That's nothing to do with transgenics, Godfrey," said Charles, tetchily. "They always looked like that."

A small, middle-aged woman, in black with a white apron, cleared the first course. Charles stood up to carve the saddle of mutton, which she brought to him on a trolley.

"But Anna, this TY phenomenon. Do you really think human sexual identity is being jerked around by a virus? Should we be afraid?"

"I don't know much about sexual identity. I'm interested in the viroid and the implications of finding a lateral transfer on that scale."

"Oh come on. Admit it; you love the gender-bending angle. You always were a bit of a tomboy." He looked down the length of the table, with its crowd of gleaming glassware and silver glinting in the light of many candles. "How do you feel about all this, Spence? Isn't it frightening, living with this female Dr Frankenstein?"

"Doesn't bother me," said Spence, helping himself to GM sag alu. He was glad he'd been placed as far from Charles as possible, but he wished Anna wasn't getting such a pasting. She wouldn't want to come here again, and he would lose a harmless pleasure. The gentle, graceful profile of his hostess framed by the smooth curve of red gold hair. "As long as she hands over her paypacket at the end of the month, I'll have her slippers warming and dinner on the table."

There was a general laugh.

Charles sat down, having divided the meat with aplomb, "But have you let her take a little *cheek-scraping*, or a sperm sample, for analysis? And are you really a New Man?"

"Nah. I don't believe in that stuff, it's pure superstition. If I want to know my fortune, I read the horoscopes. Sun in Aquarius, Aries rising, Jupiter in Aries, Moon in Libra. I'm a good teamworker."

Meret hated dinner parties. The hired servants intimidated her, she could never think of anything to say, and Charles was always in his tetchiest mood—although it was his idea to have things so formal. Spence's scary wife could probably run a dinner party in her sleep *and* do all the cooking as well. You could see at a glance that she'd never stuffed anything behind the sofa cushions in her life. When Charles started needling Anna she felt near to panic, afraid there would be a stand-up row, that Spence's wife would storm out and he'd have to go with her, but luckily it passed off. Meret relaxed again and resumed the painful pleasure of secretly watching Spence. He looked so out of place and so relaxed, a woodland faun at the dinner table, with mischievous grey eyes, half human, half lazy animal. She realized sadly, something she'd only suspected until tonight: she had fallen in love.

Spence had often teased Anna about having a career in sex science and an aversion to sexual politics, which was a cheek considering the way he bitched about Ramone. But why did she recoil, why did she so hate to have that subject raised? The rational explanation involved pointing out the absurdity of all ideological squabbles and how it's never, ever that simple. The short answer might be *Charles Craft*. What does it mean, the horrible passivity that overtakes a woman, when a man she knows lays hands on her against her will? Attack is easy to assimilate, much easier than betrayal… Why does the memory of something like that, really not your fault, linger with so much shame, so much revulsion? Was she envious of Charles's success? There was no sense in feeling robbed: it was all water under the bridge, and anyway she didn't want a new BMW, or an opulent dinner service, three different sets of wine glasses for ten people, my God… There was nothing to be done, because she could not bear to explain to Spence why she didn't want to mix with the Crafts. It was too stupid, too long ago, too embarrassing and pathetic. She'd just have to hope that the difference between the two families' incomes kept them apart.

➤ ➤

It was the football (soccer) season. Football practice should be Anna's job, Spence felt, coming from Manchester the way she did; but she rarely managed to be free on Sunday mornings. As Spence had understood from the start, "point six" meant the salary, not the work, which filled her every mortal hour, 24/7, my God. So it was Spence who took Jake along to the park and huddled with the other parents on the touch line, the usual suspects: known by first name only, qualified by the names of their children, Rick-Wanni's-Dad, Delilah-Trev's-Mum (except that now Spence knew Meret Craft personally). Delilah was distressed because she'd had to give up breastfeeding her ten-week-old baby. She'd had mastitis; she'd recovered, but the baby now preferred her bottle. That was why she was here alone, cheering on Trev, the eldest boy. She couldn't stand the sight of Caress sucking

from a rubber tit and Ben (her old man) so fucking smug about it...
Meret had nursed Tomkin until he was three and Florrie for a year.
She was supposed to have stopped with Charlie, who was eighteen
months, because Charles insisted, but she still (she admitted) sneaked
a feed into the bedtime routine, it was so lovely and so much easier.

"I can't imagine your Charles wielding a formula bottle," said Rick.

"Charles is all right," said Meret. "You'd be surprised. He's the
one who insisted they go to ordinary school, instead of private. My father thinks it's crazy." She was self-conscious about Charles, who could
seem brusque and arrogant, and often felt she had to defend him by
citing technical virtues (e.g., his voting habits).

Spence stood beside Meret, smiling vaguely, wishing he could
tackle the breast-feeding topic with Rick's fearless aplomb. When
the rain began, Delilah and the other women, along with Rick and
Dennis, another male-soccer-mom, took off at a jog for the pavilion,
Rick wearing his latest offspring strapped on his chest, inside his jacket but facing *outwards*, which Spence thought weird.

It was half time. Andrew, the coach, loped purposefully towards
Meret and Spence.

"Spence, we need a linesman for the second half. Could you—?"

"It would be an honor. But you know, I don't properly understand
the offside rule."

Many of the tots were not yet six years old, none of them were
more than eight, but this was serious. Andrew nodded grimly and
loped on with a worried frown. The rain had turned to icy hail. Meret
and Spence walked along the line, changing ends. She looked up with
her charming three-cornered smile. "Spence, I don't think you *want*
to understand the offside rule."

"Gee, Meret, how could you imagine that?"

She giggled. "Did Anna breastfeed?"

"She tried, but she was working and traveling a lot. She used to
express and leave me to administer the bottles. We switched to formula at three months, I seem to remember."

"Poor Anna. I love it. I'll be heartbroken when Charlie doesn't want me any more."

"It's a bitch to lose them. They change so fast."

"Every hour of every day. It is hell looking after children, sheer hell, but I can't bear to think it has to come to an end. My life will be a complete blank."

"Yeah. Me too."

Play resumed. They stood close, fists in their pockets, Meret's fleecy-hatted head sweet and vulnerable under his gaze. Jake and Florrie's team, despite a courageous sliding tackle from Senoz in the number two shirt (and the fucking mud will clog the machine's filter again. . .), conceded yet another goal.

"Ten minutes more," said Meret. "Unless there's injury time."

"Well, hey. It hasn't been too bad. I got to hear about Delilah's mastitis, the hail isn't *right* in our faces, and I managed not to be linesman."

"It has been a good day," remarked Meret.

They laughed together. There's definitely something Ivan Denisovitch about being a full-time parent. You learn to take comfort in small mercies.

◆ *iii* ◆

Anna was checking out at the hotel reception desk. The conference program ended at noon. Most people were staying on, especially the internationals, but Anna was going to visit Simon, as she usually did when she came to Sheffield (where "usually" means about once a year, as time speeds up and old friendships stretch out fragile threads between the nodes of meeting). Someone grabbed her around the hips and demanded hotly in her ear: "What color panties are you wearing?"

"Miguel? I don't wear *panties*, I wear pants, or knickers, and if that's your idea of a good line, why don't you try writing across your forehead, I AM A DICKHEAD."

The hands that had grabbed her hips surged over her breasts. "Wool! Oh God, fine wool, so warm, so firm, so rounded!" The reception clerk smiled indulgently. Anna stepped neatly backwards and ascertained by buttock contact that there genuinely was a rod in his trousers, he wasn't just talking. When she turned round he was blushing like a rose. Serve you right, she thought. You see, I am not defenseless.

"Knock it off."

"You're checking out? This is a disaster!"

"Can't be helped. My university can't pay for another night here, and I'm not going to pay it myself."

"But you know the best part of these things is after the official shit is finished—"

"You mean that *best part* where you start asking me what color panties I have on?"

Miguel shook his head, the blush still fiery on his sharp-cut cheekbones and reaching up to the already-retreating hairpin bends of crisp black hair above his temples. "That's not all I mean. Come, have a last drink with me?"

They sat drinking lager in the huge and sumptuous South Riding lounge. Anna was thinking how Jake would be sick as a parrot when she told him the extent of the free movie catalogue in her room, how he would vicariously relish the breakfast spread. The very superior pillow-sweeties were saved for him in her bag. Miguel Peñalver, illustrious sex-biologist, Anna's compadre at these things and on the net for years, was telling her that she had to get her act together. She had made a major impact, though their world had been slow to admit it, with TY. The second paper, especially, had an enviable citation record. Since then, what? The TY concept thrived, a healthy little colony, sending out spores in all directions: yet where was Anna?

"You're treading water, my beautiful Anna. You have to stop minding other people's business, seize yourself a piece of the action. You have to find something sexy. The way I did with the universal male-determining gene, long ago; my part in that drama: I made it *work* for me." It was true, Miguel had made the big time. He could hang out with the heavies, in Shanghai and Guangzhou and Mumbai, at conferences where Anna would not be found—

"I don't think I'm treading water."

"Oh yes. The 'Aether'." Miguel sighed, looking at her with real concern over his trademark horn rims. "What can I say? Anna, think. We have a viroid that can mediate exact, specific changes to the DNA; *this is exciting*. Your Aether is an ideas thing. It is not exciting here on the shop-floor. Is that right? *In the workshop*, where you and I live. You are not a high-concept media-scientist coffee-table star; rot them all. Your strength is in the lab, beautiful lady, tweaking the software and manipulating those little cultures."

At that legendary Geneva conference, Anna had proposed that the TY phenomenon (the existence of which had already been accepted, though people refused to grant the implications) joined other significant evidence pointing the way to a new paradigm of life science that saw all species as nodes in a continuous fabric of living particles, viroids, prions, viruses, and their tame relations, interacting with each other constantly, positively, at the nucleotide level. It was a beautiful vision, but Miguel was right. Her part in sorting out the sequence-targeting mechanism in TY had won her far more credit. Everyone knew the Aether was just a new name for Clare Gresley's Continuous Creation: an idea that had failed; an idea that was tired and old. They switched off their brains, new evidence meant nothing.

Meanwhile Clare, who'd moved to California to be near her daughter Jonnie, reckoned Anna a shameless traitor. Anna had heard news of her lost friend when she last visited Manchester. She and Nirmal were selling a training program to Nitash Davidson (who was in management now and looking very prosperous); she'd been visiting him to talk about course requirements. Apparently Clare was collaborating with her daughter on some billionaire's private nanotech project. When she'd heard that, Anna had been filled with pity. So she'd finally given up, sold out. Poor Clare, she's working for the company, profit for the rich inc. But what if it were Anna who had lost her way? What if her struggle to get that magic "Dr" in front of her name, and *university of* after it, had been a waste of precious time? Second-in-command of a cash-strapped university science department doesn't mean you're a respectable scientist, not these days. It means you are a PR and marketing exec, only without the salary...

She left the conference hotel brooding.

It was a damned cheek for Miguel to take her aside and pep-talk her like that.

Find something sexy. Ha! If he only knew

Ever since Sungai, Anna had been waiting for somebody to unveil SURISWATI's bombshell about the human sex chromosome pair. Or better still, for some other less controversial experimental proof of viral-mediated lateral transfer effecting change to emerge. She *needed* that revelation. What could she do? She was a breadwinner, she had no right to chase after a mirage. No right, no time, and a powerful wariness. Controversy is food for the strong, death for the weak. If she went after the effect Suri had found, and it wasn't there, then unless she somehow kept the work secret, Anna Senoz would be dead in the water, finished.

Simon's family lived in a condo that had been a fine big Victorian family mansion; in landscaped grounds with a fitness suite, and a pool and squash courts. The deal reminded her of Nasser Apartments, without the austere cachet of the urban tropics. She wondered, did the stakeholders in Gradgrind Gracious Living have a rota? Did they take it in turns to take a private turn around the shrubbery? She was glad to find Simon alone when she arrived in the early evening. Cara was that significant five years or so younger, clean living and sensible, which tended to put a brake on things. *They all* socializing couldn't get up to speed in sober company.

"Once," she said, when the children were in bed and they were opening their third bottle, "I was at a conference in Toronto, dead beat after functioning at full stretch all day after a rotten *dangerous*-feeling red-eye flight from Heathrow, including a casual turning back for spare parts, typical BA. My phone rings at 3 am. It's Miguel from Spain, saying *what color panties are you wearing*; and then he says, lets make love like this (meaning wank online). Afterwards you can send me your moistened undies to keep, and I will send you mine. He did apologize, that time. He was drunk; he'd figured the time difference wrong. . . Oh, Miguel is okay. He's great, a friend, but with some of them it gets so wearing. They come on to me relentlessly, these male colleagues of mine. I take it lightly, I flirt and act sassy, what else can you do? But of course I know what it means, and it's not friendly. I'm supposed to have *forgotten* what 'fucking someone up' usually implies, in a professional context? I'm supposed to have not been listening, when a few moments before they were all crowing over the way they absolutely *shafted* some poor loser? Sometimes I wish the sexual revolution had never happened. All it means is that I can't call them on the shit that's going on with them."

"No," said Simon. "I think you're wrong. You wouldn't want to go back to the days when no one was supposed to let on and girls were supposed to keep their knickers locked up; it was worse. Hey, you've enjoyed the revolution, much as any woman I know. When I think of you and Spence, that summer. . . Hahaha!"

Affluence suited him. He had the presence, in this conventionally well-furnished room, that comes from regular work at the gym, and his conservative casuals sat easily on his older but better-tended body. Though there were already touches of grey in the nappy curls and lines around his eyes, Simon had become good-looking, which she didn't remember him to have been in those old days. But not altogether happy, she thought—

"Good as the telly, eh?" She grinned. "Yeah, I remember girl power. It was bloody good fun. I couldn't resist the energy of it. It was really, really important that you didn't have to be the one saying no. You could stuff being the banker, being *in charge* of sexual access, rationing it so's not to be called a slag... But did it get us anywhere? Looking back, I feel like what we post-women's-lib girls were expressing, with all that license, was our anger, at the deals you have to make when you declare peace with an old enemy. You have to give up the privileges of the oppressed, and we didn't want to do that, not just when we had the muscle to hit back... There was a point when we saw that we had to let bygones be bygones, or go for vengeance. We went for the wonderbra option, twin turrets blazing: and *la lutte continue*."

"I don't believe you've ever worn a wonderbra."

"Mm, nah. Underwiring is nasty, I'd rather work out. But I've used my sex as a weapon, I've learned to do that. We all do it, women in science, for all the good it does us. You can use sex, and make men suffer, wearing the full chador. I've seen *that* too."

"Tell me..." said Simon, ruefully, and changed the topic. "How's Spence, anyway? You and him still okay, in this battleground?"

"Oh, fine. Still poor as church mice... That's another thing I wish, another wrong turn. Elective poverty was great at the time, but failing to make ends meet at our age is not cool."

Simon checked the bottle, fetched a fourth, and opened it. "Don't worry. You and Spence will always be cool. You know, ever since you came down to Beevey Island that time, or maybe it was at your wedding, you two have reminded me of that Fred Pohl story, I think it's called 'The Midas Touch'? Where the production-consumption pump has gone wild, so that if you're disgustingly poor you have to slave at consuming all kinds of *stuff*, and you can tell the privileged rich few, because they're dressed shabby and drive a miserable little old car—"

He broke off, pop-eyed in consternation—

"Not that! I mean, not that—!"

Anna burst out laughing, and they both collapsed in helpless giggles.

"*In vino veritas*," said Anna gravely, when they could laugh no more.

"Okay, okay. D'you want a meal by the way? It's late, but we could dial a takeaway?"

"Nah. I think I ought to go to bed, sorry. Got to be up early in the morning."

Cara was at her Italian class, which was traditionally followed by a non-alcoholic pub session with girl friends. She'd be back soon, and

Anna felt too drunk to be sociable. They cleared bottles, glasses, and snack food residue out into the kitchen.

"D'you ever hear from Ramone these days?"

Anna shook her head. "Nope. That connection's pretty well broken."

"She's living in the States now, isn't she? With that artist and his wife? Seems weird."

The small room, with the gaunt high ceiling, remnant of its life as some Victorian scullery or housemaid's closet, was full of gleaming doors. She didn't know which would be the dishwasher and which would eject her into outer space. "Weird? Nothing's weird now. Horses getting sodomized in the senate, every day of the week."

"I mean, it doesn't sound very feminist. Two women sharing a guy, lesbian sex as male entertainment—"

"You don't know how it works." But she was willing to bitch. "Maybe it's like Daz and the modeling: she's made her fortune on female stuff-strutting, and retired. Next opus she'll be back into violent porn. Where am I sleeping? On the couch?"

"I've made up Tabitha's bed in the kids' room, that way Cara won't disturb you when she comes in."

"Oh... Okay."

The flat had three bedrooms, one of which was heavily occupied by an industry-standard server and other office stuff. Anna had seen Tabitha, the seven-year-old, and Jemelle, the three-year-old, snuggling down in their parents' big bed at story time. She realized that they had not been removed at any point.

"You'll have the room to yourself, don't worry. They sleep with us," said Simon, reaching to replace an unused glass on its proper shelf. There was a grimness in his expression, which should have warned her to shut up.

"What, all the time?"

"Yeah. It's the...family bed idea. Makes them very secure. It's more natural."

"Wow, *Simon*—" She rearranged her tone, feeling a complete heel. "That must be nice."

"You get used to it. Jemelle doesn't half kick though."

For a moment their eyes met: and... and nothing. No way would Anna and Simon change the good thing they had. Especially not when Cara was due home any minute.

She woke in the night and lay awake in a sad state of alcohol-related alertness, crowded out by a heap of immaculate soft toys, wondering pruriently when *did* Cara and Simon have sex? Once every four years? Or did they just *do it*, quickly and quietly, when the little girls were asleep? Maybe they hired a hotel room, in the Japanese way, maybe they used the living room couch. She was ashamed of herself, but that brief, bitter downtrodden look that had escaped Simon's guard... Poor Simon, what malign force had driven her to talk non-stop about over-sexed sex scientists? Pity he couldn't have stayed with Yesha. It must be hateful to change partners, to have whole sections of your own history sealed-off behind you, memories you can no longer treasure. But Yesh was a performer, an artist, she had to go on tour, this week in Amsterdam, next month in Rome. Simon had wanted a good old-fashioned family life, and now he had one.

Between new, mean girl-power in the workplace and old, virtuous woman-power at home, the blokes have a hard time these days.

◆—◆

On her way home from Sheffield she went to visit Marnie Choy in hospital and then to Rosey McCarthy's house in Norwood, where Rosey lived with the two adopted Tim children, the two young children of her second marriage, and a live-in nanny. And with Wol, unofficially: who was back in favor, the one-night-stand toyboys who had followed the fertile but obnoxious second Mr Rosey having vanished.

Marnie had ovarian cancer. Her treatment wasn't going very well.

For years Anna and Rosey had met very rarely, no more frequently than either of them had seen Marnie. But already the sick woman seemed far away, and Anna and Rosey close companions—as if they had spent their lives like this, elbows on Rosey's kitchen table, among the bunches of opening leaves in pottery jars, the sleeping cats, the piles of newspaper, the fragments of legos and sheaves of kiddie art.

"I thought cancer was *curable* these days. What happened to all those miracle drugs?"

"Ah. Ovarian cancer's manageable, not curable; and there are always exceptions."

"God, you sound like your mother. That *ah...*sound. I phoned her, you know, when Marnie's results came through, and I couldn't get hold of you."

"They're going to try good old chemotherapy."

"Chemotherapy is a challenging hobby they give you to occupy you while you're dying."

"Did my mum say that?"

"No! She's too kind. It's what my Dad said when he was on *his* chemo, in the dark ages: for the lung and liver tumors. Before the brain tumor that got the speech centers. Oh, God, poor Marnie. I keep remembering her in the Union Bar, screaming *I want a Man*! and laughing like a maniac..." Rosey's eyes filled with tears. She dashed them away with a firm hand. "Hey, tell Spence thanks for the Shere Khan books. That was sweet of him. Italia's terrified of them, but Robbie's a big fan: he's a proper little bruiser, revels in all the ultra violence. Could he sign them by the way?"

Spence disliked signing books. "I'm sure he will if you ask. It's not really ultra violence, Rosey. There's gory details, but it's only in fun."

"Whatever. I used to think Steven and Joe were aggressive because of the childhood they had before they came to us. But boys will be boys. I was *so* relieved to have a girl."

If you put a child into frilly ankle socks at birth, thought Anna, by the time she's three no one will ever know whether genetic predisposition or nurture made her turn out wet as a haddock's bathing suit. She was still frightened of Rosey, so she held her tongue.

Rosey sighed. "I can't imagine having only one child. Don't you get broody?"

I have had two children, thought Anna. Ah, Lily Rose. Fleetingly, she contemplated explaining that they'd decided to stop at one because of environmental issues, but dismissed the idea. Rosey was one of those middle-class people who bitched about the monster size of the water bill and the annoying demise of cheap air travel, but if you talked about why this kind of thing was happening, or what the REAL problems were like, she thought you were insane.

"Well, maybe. A little."

"You're incredibly lucky, Anna. Spence is so lovely. I hear his publishers are pleased with him too. Or rather Wol hears; he goes to those
parties." Wol was something in publishing. Rosey was something in we-
bcast tv, a designer of some kind. Anna had no idea of the details, these
arts-degree things all looked the same to her. . . "Weird that his books
ended up being illustrated by Charles Craft's wife," mused Rosey. "And
I hear Charles is practically a billionaire. Ironic, when you think how
you and he used to be the king and queen of Biols, long ago. How d'you
get on with Meret?"

"She seems nice," said Anna, reticently. "It must be tough, trying to
work at home with three small children. I get the impression her live-in
parents aren't much help."

"And she's married to the world's prize sexist pig, yeah… I wouldn't
feel too sorry for her, if I were you. I'm not defending Charles. It was
a typical male trick: ditches his dull boffin girlfriend after she's helped
him to build the business, snags himself a foxy young trophy-wife. But
I heard it was Meret who made the running: took out poor old Ilse
like with a chainsaw. You must remember Ilse, Charles's girlfriend back
when you and him were quite close?"

Anna nodded, taking Rosey's arch look with a straight face.

"Apparently she—Meret—went for work experience at Charles's
company, while she was at art college, designing GM seed packets or
something. He fancied her, and they started dating. When he wouldn't
chuck Ilse, Meret went bananas. Got pregnant: he paid for an abortion.
So she got pregnant again, practically before the bill for the first scrape
came in, threw terrible scenes, threatened to kill herself, and poor old
Charles surrendered. She chucked her course, he dumped Ilse, and gave
Meret everything she wanted: the frock, the white Rolls, the whole vul-
gar works. She's not such a helpless kitten."

"I'm amazed the way you keep up," said Anna, diplomatically. "I
know nothing."

Rosey heaved another sigh and gazed dreamily at a pot of sycamore
leaves. "Don't you sometimes wish you'd gone for the big frock and
white Rolls, Anna? With Wol it was a registry office quickie. I hadn't
the heart for anything more, when it was because we had to, to get

on the A list for adopting. With *Enrico* the whole thing was a fucking disaster—" Her lip curled, in savage scorn. . . A door banged. They
heard Wol's familiar, absurdly plummy voice: a diffident, precariously
controlled yodel. "Hi Rosey? Upstairs or downstairs?" The snarl vanished. The matriarch's whole demeanor became warm and relaxed and
bright. "We're down here, love!"

➤ ➤

The train home was slow, plagued by mysterious halts and lame
excuses. She had papers to read but found it impossible to concentrate.
Swathes of new housing rolled by, sparsely interrupted by patches of
fields and woods. A generation of little girls like Maggie Senoz had
grown up and were living in the country, the way they'd always dreamed,
with the natural consequence that there was not much countryside left.
But it didn't stop them. All the light-green families, like Anna and
Spence and Jake, were digging their allotments, doctoring the cars they
couldn't bear to give up, under-occupying their big old houses. They
knew they were making sod-all difference. But it didn't stop them.

She thought of Marnie Choy in hospital: sitting by her bed, brightly smiling, a little over-made-up, saying cheerfully, "At least I won't
outlive Pongo and Bastie." They were her cats. "I hated the thought of
that." They'd laughed and joked, the way you must, and then Marnie
had said, suddenly, "Anna, I don't know whether to face up to death
now, or *then*, I mean, when it really starts happening."

"I'd go for then," said Anna, wondering if Marnie knew how close
"then" was, and cravenly not daring to ask.

Marnie wasn't going to be one of the many doomed victims whose
survival had worried Lavinia Kent years ago. She had been karyotyped,
and the results had been the worst possible: no gene-tinkering immuno-
therapy treatment was going to work. Nothing left to try but the harsh,
ineffectual armory of the twentieth century... Marnie Choy would die,
in months, maybe within weeks, the first of them to leave. It was a fore-
taste of the future. The dreaded phone calls that must come, one by one.
This would be Anna's role, to greet bad news with her mother's voice, to
visit the sick, to wonder when it was decent to give up the hopeful lying.

This was the beginning of the down slope, when youth and strength must fail. Here is the turning point, and what have I achieved?

She thought of her father—foot soldier in the Volunteer Army, backbone of the nation—her father who had never known the luxury of a paying job since the day his business failed. She'd been in Manchester on the way to her conference and had spent an hour with him in the Oxfam shop, which he loved her to do. Often he put things aside for her. (Maggie was repulsed by the idea of second-hand clothes.) When they were little he had made their clothes; it was the way he could be a provider; and they had not been grateful. Little girls like to look the same as everyone else.

He had brought out a battered pale cardboard box and showed her, lifting layers of tissue from a deep crimson pleated skirt and shimmering beaded bodice, the most fabulous cocktail dress. "Wow, Daddy, is that what I think it is. . .?" "Yeah," he breathed. "*It's a Schiaparelli.*" Anna had thought the dress was one of his own, a rare original Richard Senoz, surfaced from lost time. She didn't confess this, she'd have hated him to know she could no longer tell one of the great designers from another. "How it ended up in an Oxfam collection bin is a mystery. It's a classic size 12, old money. It *should* fit you." His swift, expert glance had measured Anna regretfully: "It won't, not with those navvy shoulders: what do you young women want with them, you don't earn your living breaking stones, do you? You had a lovely figure when you were twenty."

The Schiaparelli would go to auction, it would be sold and the money spent succoring the poor... But how Daddy's eyes had gleamed. She knew that shine, the love of the marvelous. She saw those eager, magpie eyes looking out of any mirror. The older you get, the easier it is to know yourself the present habitation of immortal, elemental spirits. So many subtle phrases of the DNA text pass unscathed through the mill of recombination. A turn of the head, a smile... She was father and mother and grandma Senoz, and all those others, further off. Her mother's voice, her father's eyes (and what nonsense this mingled inheritance makes of the battle of the sexes).

But Daddy's bright-eyed lust for marvels was a warning. Watch out, Anna. Let that trait take over, you and Spence and Jake will be in the poverty pit for life... She must resist the siren call of Transferred Y.

She must not *think* of talking to Nirmal. If there were any truth in Suri's results, someone else would have been shouting about it by now. Forget it, forget it…The slow train fueled that terrible feeling of urgency, of chances missed and doors shutting, that had started to haunt her, clutching at her heart, making her feel old.

The next morning, a Saturday morning, miraculously none of the three of them had anything to do. Anna and Spence lay sleepily talking until, since Jake was deep in Saturday morning tv and they were safe from interruption, they moved into doing sex. Anna's periods had been maliciously irregular since Jake was born. She was having some unscheduled bleeding and couldn't be arsed to take out her tampon, so they did without penetration, but it was good. Anna went to check her email. Spence made tea, delivered a mug to Anna and retired to bed with his tax docs (staying in bed was his way of rewarding himself for this drear activity). She came back and burrowed into the crackling nest.

"How's the Amoldovar kid?" asked Spence dryly. "Still packing his six-gun for you?"

"How did you know I had a message from Miguel?"

"You always do. Hey, Anna, look at this. *Shere Khan and the Coast of Coramandel* has sold twenty thousand copies in the UK pre-publication."

"Is that good? You have to allow for returns, don't you. Oh, I meant to tell you. Wol says, well, Rosey says that Wol says, that you are being mentioned at publishing parties."

"My God. God bless the gallant captain and her crew!" His voice shook, between laughter and triumph. "I knew I was doing well. I hadn't figured it out, in case… Holy shit, Anna, I'm making a living! We're solvent! We can live without your salary this year, babe. Hey, hey, I'm the breadwinner! We are comfortably off!"

She stared at him, the duvet up to her shoulders, in wide-eyed stillness. "Then I am free," says Anna, in such a strange tone you'd think she was about to spread wings and fly out of the window or disappear up the chimney like the king of the cats.

━ ━

She made an appointment to see Nirmal. Although they worked together closely, this was still appropriate behavior. KM Nirmal's office was as private as it had ever been. The door might be ajar, but you did not *pop in*: if you dared, you could forget whatever you'd *popped in* about; it was dead meat. She was going to lay her cards on the table, no tactics, no prevarication. The key is always frank... as Mr Frank N Furter used to say.

━ ━

Poole University's lab-science buildings were, as it happened, leased units on the old science park on the Forest campus, where Anna would have been a post-grad if her first career hadn't been derailed. As she walked up that valley that would always smell of morning—though it was so changed, so little left of the beech trees and the lawns—she felt that she was folding back the years. After many mistakes, many stupid blunders, this time she would get it right.

Anna didn't know what Nirmal thought about her Aether papers. He was very hands-off on that. He'd become in some ways more open and approachable since his wife died, but you still hit that core of absolute reserve pretty close to the surface. She had no idea how he would react to this even more way-out suggestion.

At least the Aether was vague. This was getting down to cases.

She produced the Sungai disks, and they studied Suri's projection together, almost in silence. Nirmal took off his eye wrap and spent some time going through the printed notes. She waited, strangely relaxed. As long as Anna Anaconda could be straightforward about things she was content, come what may. She watched Nirmal's calm, voracious concentration as he took possession of the material and felt at home with him. We be of one blood, thou and I.

"Hmm!"

Nirmal placed the papers neatly on the desk and leaned back. He took up his varifocals and applied the tip of one earpiece, gently, rhythmically, to the center of his thin lips. The capital-H grooves around his mouth had deepened, the bones of his face stood out even more, but apart from the new glasses nothing much in his appearance had changed. KM Nirmal did not age. He looked amused.

"So! This is what was behind it all."

Behind what? The nebulous Aether she supposed. She waited.

"If this is true, if these results are genuine indicators, then there are two questions. Where are these new creatures, Anna, the epidemic of XX human males?"

Anna nodded. "That's one question. What's the other?"

"If they are among us, why has nobody else announced this discovery?"

"Yes."

"There should be clinical cases by now, many clinical cases, throughout the world. Where are they?"

"I think," said Anna slowly, "that this isn't *Brave New World*. Babies aren't routinely genotyped. . .not anywhere. What Suri shows is that an exchange of genetic material, between the X and the Y chromosomes, triggered by the presence of the TY viroid, will lead to dramatic-looking change, in the chromosomes, on a stunning scale in the human population. That doesn't mean stunning numbers of clinical cases. If Suri's right, most of those affected might have no 'symptoms' at all. And, I think we *are* seeing an epidemic of XX males. We've been seeing an epidemic of XX males in fertility treatment for at least a decade. But the significance has been masked by the variety of the problems it's caused, by the fact that fertility is frequently unaffected, and by all the other candidates for blame, in the fall in male fertility. Plus, taken globally, vast numbers of people would never be referred to an infertility clinic even if they were in trouble."

"Very true, very reasonable—if there were no such thing as human sex chromosome research, and if no one had yet drawn our attention to the TY viroid effect. But this is no longer a case of serendipity, Anna. Your own earlier results are known. You cannot tell me that no one has found out because nobody has been looking."

"I sat on this for years," said Anna, "because SURISWATI's projection is so bizarre. I want to prove entrainment. I want to show a mechanism for lateral propagation of genetic variation, as the secret engine of 'evolution,' as something that makes 'evolution' different from the model we use now. I don't want *this*: it's too sensational and in totally the wrong way. Other people may have felt the same. Maybe they've noticed (she thought of Miguel) something weird, and they've decided not to go down that path. It wouldn't be the first time a whole science ignored experimental results, for... for all kinds of reasons. Think of Galileo."

"You don't believe this is a mirage."

She drew a deep breath. "I don't know what it is. I want to do the work. I want to re-examine Suri's evidence, and I need to conduct a survey. And try to keep what I'm doing quiet, until I know there's something there."

Nirmal nodded, tapping the earpiece of his glasses to his lips again. "Just so. And you want to sow these dragon's teeth in my department, on my time."

"Not without your advice and consent."

"Hmm. I presume the KL SURISWATI, who or which would be your Suri's closest relative, knew nothing of your work?"

"Nothing. The Sungai SURISWATI lived and died a stand-alone. If we could get any cooperation from Kuala Lumpur—" (Which was unlikely, in the present state of Southeast Asian politics. Nirmal nodded in acknowledgment.) "It would be useless. I couldn't confirm or deny without doing the work over again, and then we'd have to get her results independently verified. I'd rather work without an AI, just because of the verification problem. Virtual modeling isn't enough. We have to find the answers in real, living human cells."

Nirmal replaced his glasses. He sheaved her papers together, put them back in their folder, ejected the XX projection from his machine, and handed the lot over the desk.

"Then do it. But—"

"In my tea breaks," said Anna.

But her head was spinning, because there was more. She could see it in his eyes. She had seen the gleam that lit him up inside when she spoke of the secret engine of evolution—

"No," said Nirmal, precisely. "Now we both have two jobs, because the Department must not suffer. Let's see what you and I can do together."

He stood, and came around the desk to see her to the door, a courtesy that he had omitted the first time they had spoken on the subject of TY and on the subject of what Anna should or should not do on KM Nirmal's time. She still didn't know what was going through his head. As he opened the door for her he smiled, that beautiful rare illuminating smile. "Well, Anna," he said. "What a long strange trip it's been."

➤ ➤

Jake's mummy taught him the names of trees and the parts of flowers, how to dance the Okey Kokey, how to blow a dandelion clock, how to cook a hedgehog, what to say to snowfall, who Guy Fawkes was, and a rhyme about magpies. Jake's daddy didn't know these things because he didn't come from England, but he knew everything about Steven Spielberg, John Lennon, Kurt Cobain, Lara Croft, Sonic the Hedgehog, and Mario the plumber. He knew who had written all the songs on Top of the Pops, when they were first invented. Jake believed his father must once have been mighty in the land. In the winter they went to Jumble Sales at the Salvation Army Citadel, for old sakes' sake, though they were not poor any longer. In the summer they walked in the New Forest and visited village fetes where they bought plants (that died) and ate strange homemade cakes from pleated paper cases. In ancient little churches they sniffed the cool and beeswax air, and Jake always wrote the same thing in the Visitors' Book: *Very beautiful.*

They had no time for long holidays, but once on a short break, at the beach in France, beside the creamy diamond breakers of the Atlantic, Jake asked his mummy, how do you be a scientist? Anna scooped up a handful of sand. She dug out a beach-tennis bat, laid it flat and tipped her handful onto the black surface.

"Count them."

"Count what?"

"The grains of sand. Look, I'll show you." She flattened the heap with her palm, squared it off and divided it with the edge of a shell into twelve roughly equal patches. "Count the grains in one of those patches. Then choose another patch, and count again. When you've done that, we'll add the two results together, divide the result by two, multiply it by twelve, and you'll know approximately how many grains in one *mummy's handful.* It will be different from how many there would be in a *Jake's handful*: that doesn't matter, so long as we bear it in mind.

We're going to assume, for now, that you have a representative number of unusually big and little grains, overall. When you've done that bit, we'll talk about how to figure out how many *mummy's handfuls* make a beach. It won't be easy. The beach is big, it is changing all the time, and you and I may not agree on where the edges are. But we'll have a go."

Spence came up from the water with his bodyboard, and found the child enslaved.

"What's going on here?"

"Science!" breathed Jake. "I'm counting the sand."

"You're a rotten bitch," said Spence to his wife. "Has he been driving you *that* crazy?"

Anna lay back behind her sunglasses and picked up her book. "He asked me what it was like to be a scientist," she explained, implacably. "So I told him."

She was counting the sand. The days were not long enough; the nights were white pits of fall. She worked like one possessed and couldn't sleep. Her voice shook, her hands shook. She tried to remember to be kind and helpful to her teammates, because that is *essential*, the lifeblood of good work; but she had the greatest of difficulty in recalling their names. It was strange to know that her boss saw this as a straight line progression. He had seen her talent, he had nurtured her, she had gone off to have her babies (as women must). Now she was back, and he was grooming her for stardom: the discovery he had seen in germ plasm, in that first Transferred Y paper, come to fruition. They were struggling in a backwater, and secrecy was imperative, true. Otherwise, everything was as it should be. All Anna's cruel defeats and long sacrifices, Nirmal's past injustices, simply didn't exist. And she was happy to settle for this version, very happy. Hungering and thirsting for justice does not make the wheels go round. It just doesn't.

She knew she was failing to keep her end up on the domestic front. It couldn't be helped, this was a crisis. Once, when she was putting away some clean washing, she found a fresh pack of condoms in Spence's underwear drawer. Anna and Spence hadn't used any protection since Spence had his vasectomy. Now that Shere Khan had become successful, it was Spence's turn to be the traveling executive: visiting bookshops and schools, staying in conference hotels. He was entitled to play away, if he liked. She sat on their bed, holding the packet and thinking, *Oh well.* Fair dos.

Then she put it back. She said nothing.

It was the way the fairy tale goes: the price of riches is lost contentment. Once the pressure was off, once TY was *over, sorted,* she would make everything right again.

➤ ➤

As usual, Anna had not been able to make it to Jake's school show. She always promised to try and always failed. Meret, who was always alone too (the idea of Charles coming to the Primary School Christmas/Hanukkah/Divali Concert was absurd) had saved a place for Spence in the upper hall, where infants were mewling and rows of adult haunches were overflowing the cute little tubular framed chairs. He was in a flurry because these things are so awkwardly timed. He had walked Jake to school, returned home, and managed to get himself into writing mode for about three minutes, before realizing that he had to leap up and rush out again. Such is the life. He hunkered down, uneasy about the eager way she had waved and beamed at his approach. He'd have liked to tell her not to do that, but why? Discreet about what? They were friends.

"I've left Chip with my mother," she whispered. Children filed onto the stage, touching in their naive individuality of gait and expression, not yet lost to the conformity of adulthood. "I hope to God she stays off the sherry until I get home."

Meret's mother's drinking problem and her father's "eccentricities" seemed sometimes to be a joke, sometimes deadly serious. He gave her a rueful, knowing smile that covered both eventualities.

A little girl with frizzy tan bunches of hair, angled roughly at 120 degrees from the top of her head, read a drastically simplified plot summary of the "Ramayana" at a flat gallop. The finale, an energetic raid on the demon stronghold of Lanka, was an indiscriminate melee of monkey warriors and palm trees, in which a couple of monkeys (or possibly palm trees) came flying through the air and joined the audience. Obsessed Dads crawled around looking for camcorder angles. . . Tomkin Craft got thrown out (Tomkin invariably got thrown out, whatever the occasion) and had to stand in the corridor with a teacher on guard.

Florrie took part in a dance routine about Christmas shopping. There was something deeply Midwestern about it all. It took Spence back to grade school and his Mom's moon face, proudly beaming up at him from the front row in the gym. More carols, more routines. At last, six little children in red cassocks, white cottas, and white card ruffs trooped out, holding cardboard candles. They sang a verse of "Once In Royal David's City," and a small boy with brown skin and dark curls stood in front of them to read the opening passage of the gospel of St John.

He did okay. He remembered to SLOW IT DOWN, and once or twice—wildly daring—actually raised his eyes from the scroll. Spence blew his nose and wished he was wearing dark glasses. Finally, everyone loudly sang "So Here It Is, Merry Christmas," and the show was over. He'd forgotten to bring a camera; he'd have to share Meret's photos. They left together, after the photocall: out into a raw, grey afternoon. She walked along with him, grumbling—with a touch of sexual pride—about Tomkin's awful behavior.

"Why did you choke," she asked. "At the end. Did Jake get his words wrong?"

"Did I choke?" The degree of close attention he got from Meret sometimes tired him. "Nah, he did fine. I suppose I was thinking that the opening of John must have puzzled the punters, given the average level of Christianity around here. Most of the audience was probably wondering what the fuck, is this the Hanukkah bit?"

"You and Anna, you're sort of Catholics, aren't you. Do you believe in all that?"

They'd reached her car and they must part, unless she was going to come in for coffee and there was no excuse for that, no Shere Khan business. She stood dangling her keys, looking up. On a whim, he took her question seriously.

"We had Jake baptized. We go to Mass, sometimes." How could he put it into words, this *uncertain* truth, that would be shameful and useless if it gave you certainty: this insubstantial, golden film over the surface of things, that makes life bearable? She probably thought life was fine... (he knew she didn't). "I don't believe in a God, 'out there,' at all. But I believe we are born to suffer and die, and that we are mysteriously redeemed; and I believe that we should love one another. That seems to cover the bases."

They were both much moved. She touched the sleeve of his jacket, almost with reverence. "I'd better get back."

➤ ➤

Spence was working, alone in his room, late at night. Anna was in bed, the house was very quiet. Whatever she was doing with Transferred Y on this new burn, it was draining her. She would come home from the lab, take over Jake until bedtime, slog through a couple of hours on her departmental workload, crawl off to sleep. He didn't know what was going on. It had been a long time since they'd had one of those fascinating, crazy conversations: Boolean Algebra, strange attractors, the nature of reality.

He was restless. Recently, he'd been to visit Mr Frank N Furter, to purchase fresh supplies of contraband raw hashish—the pungent, sticky real thing, by far superior to legal stuff, cannabis-laced cancer sticks. How times change. Frank had been with the current beautiful girlfriend for several years: they had a mortgage. Recreational drugs were no longer his main business. He had property in the town and was negotiating positively with the IRS over certain discrepancies in years gone by.

Spence had almost broached his big problem, sitting in Frank's kitchen—a kitchen more spotless than ever, still occupied by the menagerie—a rat (though not Keefer), cockatiels swooping, cats underfoot, Betty the iguana, and Jade the parrot—same as ever. But Frank was not the same. He spoke of leaving all this, waving a hand to indicate not his pets but the raffish, heaving coastal conurbation. Angela was looking at early retirement. They were thinking of Scotland, on a grouse moor. Early retirement, my God.

Ah well, too bad. Spence was getting too old to have a guru.

... "It was a hot, still day, in the middle of the Atlantic Ocean. The sea and sky were so drunk with sunshine they could do nothing but lie there helpless. The pirates had brought a tank of baby eels to the heart of the Sargasso Sea, for as you know, eels are born in that strange, weedy patch of calm in the middle of the ocean. These particular baby eels were a pharming venture, whereby the pirates hoped to make their fortune. It is well known that hardly anybody eats eels by choice, people will even prefer the *andouillette*, but this was going to change when Shere Khan's transgenic eels hit the market, tasting of blueberry ice cream and crème de menthe liqueur. Rafe Rackstraw, from the crow's nest, yelled "Ship Ahoy!" And Fiona McLeod, the pirate with a rude tattoo of Sean Connery that she was always wanting to show you, yelled out "That's confirmed on the scanner, Ma'am." Shere Khan was not averse to the distraction, as NASDAQ figures on the recent performance of biotechs were poor. The ship was a strange one, a three-masted schooner, bare of sail, her sides crusted with barnacles. She was so old a ship, so old, that you would think to see her mainmast turn into a tree again, and blossom like the rose. Her name, as far as they could read it among the shellfish, seemed to be *The Pride of Whitby*. And her crew was a crew of dead men. . ."

The new adventure, which as anyone ought to know from that last line and a half, was Spence's homage to Bram Stoker and had to feature Gil Bates, dastardly cybervillian. (His editor had loved Gil Bates in *The Eighth Sea* and demanded more.) He fancied pinning the plot to something about shifting ocean currents, adult jokes go down so well...

If only Spence could be at the start of a new adventure, but he was trapped in dark December, no respite from the muddy, lowering skies—

In all his years of monogamy he'd never tried to amputate his sexual imagination. That Filipina maid, Josie, of Number 3 on the poolside terrace at Nasser, whose sexy smile and lovely round butt had brightened his days. . . When he'd seen Meret with Charles and realized, o-oh, the kid's unhappy at home and I am playing with fire, he'd still carried on undressing her, handling in his imagination the sugary little peeled-almond body: slightly hostile fantasies, lust mingled with resentment. It was an addiction. And yet alongside this she'd genuinely become a friend, a great collaborator: she was such a sweet kid. Meret's admiration and respect—completely unexpected, a gift from heaven—had jumped him out of the dire malaise he'd been suffering the summer Jake started school. She had made him realize that he loved the Shere Khan stories, that this was his dream niche, the work that was play. She had been more of a companion than Anna, fuck it, over the past two years. He couldn't *drop* her: even if it were professionally feasible.

So much testosterone in distress about these days, gangs of angry young men roaming the seafront; you had to pity them, but there were other male role-models, even more annoying. He was continually irritated by seeing *his own life* featured on lifestyle pages, what happened to being ahead of the game, what happened to being like nobody else? It made him want to commit a regression. It made him feel that his slow, timid, undercover lust was ridiculous. Who would cure him of Meret? Shit, why did he need to be cured? A little harmless flirtation, what the fuck is all this fuss about? Better get back to the pirates. Ah, the days that were caught in the pages of these picture books: the taste of rain on wild raspberries, the hot dust of the roadside, the times when thinking up more Shere Khan for a fretty brat had been as much fun as having someone reduce a compound fracture without anesthetic. . . Every moment so precious, washed and shining in memory. He just wished he could make up his mind. Anything would be better than this pointless. . .

He decided to send Mer an email. Something anyone could read.

➤ ➤

Christmas was horrible for Meret. Misery settled in on Christmas Eve, when they were dressing for Julie's party. Charles gave her, in his off-hand way, a jeweler's box.

"You might as well have them now," he said, "since we're going out."

He knew she'd have preferred to open her present on Christmas day. It was typical of Charles. He would ruin something for her, pretending he was being sensible: but she would see that sly smile in the back of his eyes, and *she knew he was doing it on purpose.* In the box was a pair of earrings, set with large diamonds and emeralds, ostentatious and dull, the kind of trophies his middle-aged friends' wives wore: nothing to do with Meret or who Meret was. What cut her to the heart was that *she* had made a big effort, as she always did, to get him things she knew he'd like (an expensive science book with beautiful photographs, a snakeskin belt, a heavy silk shirt in his best color). She threw the earrings across the room and shouted and sobbed. They had to go to the party anyway,

Meret with pink eyes, Charles in a sulk. Christmas has a terrible power: nobody dares to break the rules and stop pretending.

The disappointments continued the next day, as she sat with her mother and father and Charles and the children, and they opened their presents over Bucks Fizz and a breakfast of fresh muffins and scrambled eggs with slivers of truffles and organic smoked salmon. Dad didn't look at his presents, just grunted and sat there shoveling food into his face. Florrie and Tomkin started squabbling. Charlie wailed because nobody was paying him enough attention. Mum was the only one who was happy, having license to drink at breakfast time. Meret opened her presents with hope, though she knew this was fated, because nothing you hope for ever comes true, the only joys are unexpected. Not one of them was anything she liked. Charles had already left the table and settled in his armchair in front of the business results, as if neither his family nor Christmas existed: first switching off the Christmas tree lights so they didn't interfere with the picture on the screen. It was such a beautiful tree. There had been a moment—yesterday, some fleeting moment when she was hanging up her favorite crystal star and Charlie was sitting on the floor being sweet—when she had been truly happy... She stared at the oblivious top of her husband's head with hatred.

"I think we should subscribe to many-To-many. It's the best supplier; they have the radical quality channels and unbiased news coverage."

"It's too expensive. They don't get the advertising; what can you expect?"

"Spence and Anna have mTm."

Charles made a derisive noise.

In the darkening afternoon she wandered despondently around the house. Her brother Blondel and his wife were here with their children, and Mummy's sister Madeleine with her grown up sons. Meret had cooked herself to death while her mother and her aunt infested the kitchen, sniping at each other. She had laid the table beautifully, with ivy and Christmas roses and tinsel ribbons. What was the use? As soon as everyone sat down Charles started trying to force Tomkin to eat things he didn't like, which was STUPID and IMPOSSIBLE. Then Blondie started a fight with Dad over nothing, and the rest of them quickly pitched in to make things worse. Now the children were running up and down the stairs shrieking, and as far as Meret was concerned the pudding, for which she had carefully simmered the brandy sauce and saved a perfect holly sprig, could stay in the microwave until it was concrete.

Tomorrow must be divided between Charles's father, and his mother and stepfather, and Tony, the stepfather's divorced son—who'd come home to live and who hated Charles.

Oh, God.

Someone had left the door of her studio open. Kilmeny was crouched on the highest shelf of the bookcase, bug-eyed with terror, while her father's two fat Blue Persians stalked below like disgusting live fur-covered cushions. One of the bastards had been sick on Meret's desk, so copiously that not only was the work she'd been doing ruined, sick had run down the frame of the desk and was splattered over the books and papers and scarves and pens and paints that were lying on the floor. Weeping, she threw the brutes out and fetched a roll of babywipes. The filthy grey sick was still warm. She screwed up her drawing and threw it in the wastebin, and knelt there wiping art books and crying, under the big framed photograph of *Le Déjeuner en Fourrure*. The photograph was by someone famous, a friend of her father's. It had been there since she was a little girl, when this had been her bedroom. She'd never had the courage to tell Dad that she *hated* that fur-covered cup and saucer. She couldn't look at it without feeling the choking hair in her mouth, as if someone were pushing it down her throat. The horrible cats were yowling and scratching at her door. It opened and her father came wandering in, the gangsters gliding smugly ahead of him. He strolled to the windows and stood there swaying slightly, fists thrust in the pockets of his saggy trousers, gazing out into the grey Christmas night.

"*Diffugere nives...*" he rumbled. "Mmm, how does it go? *damna tamen celeres reparant caelestiae lunae...* But whatever the seasons mar the moons repair again, while we go down into the dust forever. Not any more, eh? We're the immortals now, and all creation else is doomed, emasculated, tortured into unnatural forms, on the way to extinction."

"Get those fucking monsters out of here," wailed Meret. "Or I'll *kill them!*"

Godfrey did a lumbering turn and fixed the delinquents with a stern eye and an admonishing finger: "Xerxes! Darius! Go to your baskets at once!" The Persians went on staring balefully up at Kilmeny, with heartless orange saucer eyes.

Meret laughed, through her tears of rage.

"Do other people have Christmases like this, Dad?"

"Of course they do, darling. We may not be perfect, but we're excruciatingly normal."

"Spence says. . . Spence and Anna think the way to be happy is to learn to do without *things*, luxuries and modern inventions. It's weird, isn't it. Considering what she does."

"Perhaps it's guilt. Or perhaps the puritans know something we don't, about the riches of the modern world, or something we prefer to ignore. Who knows. Your mother's drunk as a skunk. Madeleine told me to fetch you, to help get her to bed."

She helped to put her mother to bed, tried to persuade her grown-up cousins to help her clear up the kitchen, failed, and stayed at home with the children while everyone went to the pub. She had some peace then, cuddling Charlie in front of *A Muppets' Christmas Carol* until it was time to put the older ones to bed. She had planned a Christmas sleepover for them in the basement playroom, airbeds and sleeping bags as if they were pirates camping on a treasure island, and a grab-bag of Christmas goodies for a midnight feast. She tried to read to them, from *Shere Khan and the Canary Wharf Tower*, the first of the Shere Khan books and her favorite: with the beginning in the Southwark fog, the sewer rats and the archbishop, and the terrific fight up in the top of the glass pyramid. It didn't work; the little beasts wouldn't listen. Juniper and Maisie were bored; Tomkin kept making fart noises and carping comments.

"Why are they eating chips? It's stupid to have pirates eating chips."

"Because they're poor."

"It's stupid. Why are they poor?"

"When pirates have money, they spend it. Then they have none. They're feckless outlaws; they don't plan for the future. Can't you relate to that? Oh darling, leave Florrie alone, you're being horrible. *Florrie, don't bite him—*"

Her children were hell, simply hell. Why couldn't she have a child like Jake Senoz, who never had a tantrum in his life? *Just say no*, said Spence. *Tough it out.* It's easy if you have only one child, she'd told him. If you have three, you can't spend your whole time toughing it out. You have to give in to them or you'd have no life... Easy enough to have only one child, he had coolly pointed out. He was right, Meret had made a mess of everything. Why didn't she get Charles to hire a nanny? Because she loved these children unbearably—and because Charles was disgustingly stingy. He said, you're at home all day, what d'you need a nanny for...? Oh, but sometimes, deep in her heart, she longed to take Jake along to McDonald's, feed him a Big Mac and fries and a chocolate shake, and have him gobble up the dreadful food of the evil empire, just to *show* Spence.

She left the children to do what they liked, returned to her studio and coaxed Kilmeny down from her perch. Kilmeny was tortoiseshell and white, gentle and pretty and affectionate, everything the Persians were not. Meret set her on a cushion and knelt in front of her, giving her the admiration she craved: "Oh bonny Kilmeny, Ye're welcome here!" Since everyone was out, she could check her email. There might not be a message; he probably hadn't been able to get away. But oh, if there were...

She didn't ever phone him; or he her. Tones of voice could put you off; she wanted words she could think about. She wanted lines, so she could read between them. She wrapped herself in a shawl that had escaped the cat-vomit and sat at her computer. Yes, there was a message, a beautiful tingling message.

Oh dear, she thought, planning ahead, in spite of herself. He'll never leave Anna. But the thrill of having a romance...it was her only consolation.

➤ ➤

Another year had begun, in wind and storm. Anna lit a candle at bedtime, for the coziness of it, and cuddled up with Jake under his duvet. Ah, how time flies. She was reading him *The Lord of the Rings*, what happened to Spot and Pookie and *The Very Hungry Caterpillar*?

"Why is Saruman the head of the White Council?" asked the child. "I mean Gandalf's got the ring of fire, which is the top elven ring, and he's a main character. Saruman is so nasty and selfish, why did they have him?"

"Well, Gandalf was Galadriel's candidate. I expect that didn't help. The White Council is a humans' thing, even if it's made up of wizards. Tolkien never says so, but I would bet that's how it happened. The humans wanted someone who would push their point of view, which meant Saruman although everyone knew he was a jerk and probably on the take. Does that make sense?"

"Sort of. Not really."

"Yeah, well, that's office power struggles for you. Shall I go on?"

Snowstorms on January the twelfth: there was no need to come back to report that... There were shadows looking over the hedge into Anna's garden. Sometimes, in stolen moments of domestic art, she would raise her head from the treasured task (chopping vegetables, polishing furniture, sewing buttons on Jake's clothes) and find herself listening, with her heart in her mouth. For what ogre's footfall?

I will make it all right. Afterwards. First I have to take the ring to the fire.

◆ ◆

She tried hard, and mainly succeeded, not to think about the human implications of Transferred Y, and in this Nirmal was her perfect ally. Human sexual identity? Leave that for the psychologists. If you find out anything about human sexual identity from infertility genetics, it's that there is *no* straightforward match between variations in chromosomal sex and the behavior of the individual. Such a stupid thing to fight about. Wasn't there enough trouble in the world? If you followed the news, if you ever looked up from the unbelievable grind of work and caught a glimpse of the grim salvation that might be hurrying to the rescue of Clare's precious living world, you had to recoil in horror. Not that! There's got to be another way! Is there another way? Will anything break us out of this dreadful fall?

She did not want to think about the meaning of what she was doing, but she had recurrent nightmares of looking down into a dark mirror, as if into the reflecting lens of a telescope. In the dark something appeared and grew: beautiful and terrible, a devouring vortex. All human life ends in there.

And so it went on: Spence prevaricating, Meret like a child at a sweetshop window, Anna racing against time. For the first time in her life she knew what it was like to live like an ambitious scientist: scouring the journals, jumping at shadows, convinced that there were competitors leaping on her trail. Any moment, any day, some other team might snatch her victory... It was poisonous, but it was exhilarating.

She didn't talk to Spence about Transferred Y because the thing was *sub judice*. None of the team talked about it. There came a point when they knew they had information (the survey) that was dynamite, but they never discussed the outside-world implications. They were in the home stretch, nothing else mattered.

In January she found out that one of the Australians had privately warned Nirmal that Anna was going too far. How come this man had had access to the unpublished material? The time for secrecy was almost past, but even so! She came near to having a fight with the boss about it. This is my department, said Nirmal. The work we have done will appear with my name on it. But if you wish to continue, in spite of this advice, I will support you. Anna was oblivious. She put the incident down to stage fright. The paper had been accepted. How could they withdraw it? Why would they? Then the paper was published, and immediately the storm broke.

One day in early spring, Nirmal called her to his office. She went along unsuspecting. The tabloid journalism was a joke, and the actual scientists who had leapt to the attack were the usual suspects, nothing credible. She thought that Nirmal had called her in to discuss tactics. Instead he showed her a private email, from the team leader in Melbourne, casting doubt on the existence of the male XX effect, suggesting it was an experimental artifact. Anna laughed. She should not have laughed. The interview went into a destructive spiral, while Anna sat reading the printed email upside down and remembering too late that behind the Melbourne team lay their guru, a certain senior geneticist called Dr Pat McCreevy, Nirmal's lifelong rival. Oh, the pure realms of scientific endeavor are riddled with these enmities, and you're a fool if you don't take them seriously. Oh shit... To be called into question by Pat McCreevy was guaranteed to make Nirmal irrational.

She heard herself say all the wrong things. What does it matter? The so-called "male" human chromosome changes shape, so what? This is about something far more important! She did not accuse her boss of absurd sexual panic, but when he told her that there is nothing more important than human dignity, she did not agree. When he said he now believed their announcement had been premature and must be withdrawn, she objected furiously, and so—

It was the school half term. She came home in the middle of the day and was hurt to find the house empty. But Spence didn't know there was a problem. She'd told him long ago there would be controversy, how could he know anything worse had happened? She went round to the Rectory. Spence and Meret had left the children with Meret's mother and gone out together. They came back to find Anna waiting for them with a face like death and thunder. "Hi," she said to her husband—and dimly, dimly, it crossed her mind that it was strange they'd left the children behind. "Hello Meret," she added politely... "I've been fired."

➤ *iv* ➤

Once Ramone came down to the south coast conurbation for a gig and pulled out at the last moment, because she was sick of the game, these "lectures" that were really fucking *Tupperware parties* for the product. She walked around the streets that had been familiar long ago, saw a woman with a child, and followed them. It was dusk, the moon riding high in a clear abyss of blue. The trees in the park were leafless; it was winter. The woman was wearing a slim black coat to her ankles and a close-fitting cap. The child was in a dark red duffle coat with a brightly colored muffler. It trotted to keep up, holding tightly to Mummy's hand... Ramone seriously considered becoming a stalker. She would move to Bournemouth secretly and follow this contented young mother about, up and down the promenade, in and out of the funky shops, around the parks and gardens. She decided later that it couldn't have been Anna.

That night she went back to London, to her rooms high above the canyons of the City. Her living space still had the air of a student bedsit: a haphazard, temporary, and uncared for setting, in which only the heaps and piles of books possessed any validity. She spoke tenderly to the onlie begetter of her affections, Pele the blue rabbit. You are all I have and all I need, little one. The rest of them, those others with their families and friends and lovers, are deceiving themselves with pitiful illusion. I'm better off. You will never let me down. I call you *Pele* because that was what you were called when I was a baby. But don't worry my dearest, my sweetheart. I know your real name. Actually, it embarrassed her to look at Pele, or speak to him as if aloud. Like all true lovers, he was a creature for smelling and touching. When she slept, with her darling nuzzled in her arms, then she was truly happy.

She faithfully visited Lavinia in the nursing home. On the good days she found Lavvy bright-eyed and young looking, her hair brushed and styled to the taste of the nursing staff, and spent ten minutes or so chatting to a timid, affable elderly lady who knew Ramone well but hadn't a clue who she was. Ramone could relate to that. She frequently found herself in a similar situation: only when she had to talk to people who expected her to recognize them, she wasn't half so nice about it.

But Lavvy had no choice. On the bad days, Lavinia remembered enough to know what was happening, and that was terrible.

When she decided to move to Manhattan, she knew it wouldn't make any difference. Lavvy wouldn't notice if Ramone's visits were six months apart. Her clock had stopped; her watch on time had bust a spring. Maybe she knew something, because on the visit that Ramone intended to be her last, Lavvy (in affable old lady mode) suddenly asked if she could *have something to hold*. Always before, in response to Ramone's ritual question *Is there anything I can bring for you?* she had answered blankly, *no*. She did not want anything to read; she did not want flowers or pictures or smuggled forbidden drugs. She wanted for nothing. Ramone had struggled with herself, but won the victory and went back the next day with Pele. He was welcomed with puzzled approval. (Lavinia of course didn't remember that she had asked for something to cuddle, but the need was still there.)

Afterwards, when they asked her why she had left England, and why she was no longer available for raucous feminist comment, she gave them the kind of answer they expected. Professional feminists are snouts in the trough, arselickers to the male media, and their fans are a bunch of closet-genderist lesbians, bitter housewives, and fat people. Feminism stinks, I've said it before and I'll say it again. There's nothing anyone can do for women; they deserve all they get. This was entertaining copy, though not new. The truth had more to do with the fate of that blue toy rabbit, whose absence nothing could mend. In her heart, she was not living in Manhattan. She was not "involved" with the post-modern idiocy of Karel and Ri, or the least interested in the crappy "art" the three of them produced together. She was in phase transition, waiting for the day when her life would be restored to her.

Waiting to move on.

She found out about Lavvy's final illness from Roland. Lavvy's brother called her up to tell her his sister had contracted viral pneumonia, and the prognosis was not good. "She seems to have lost the will to live," he said, with false gravity. Ramone knew that this was code for euthanasia. Shocked energy raced through her limbs. She would return to England at once. With positive nursing Lavvy could come back from this. She was only, what was it, sixty-five? Not old! She could live long enough to be there when mind power could be restored to Alzheimer's sufferers, even the ones like Lavvy, with complications—

"I'm coming back. Tell her I'm on my way. Tell her, no matter if you think she doesn't know my name." Already she'd decided to phone the nursing home and get them to relay her voice to Lavvy's sickbed. It could easily be done, and she did not trust Roland.

There was a long pause at the other end of the connection.

"Umm. I was trying to break it to you gently, Ramone. I'm afraid she's gone."

"Fuck. YOU BASTARD! YOU KILLED HER! You HAD HER PUT DOWN!"

"The funeral is next Wednesday—"

"YOU TOLD THEM WHAT TO DO. YOU SAID LET HER DIE!"

"Actually," said the pained middle-class voice, intolerably pleased with itself. "Those were *my sister's* very words. Let me die. She had made a deposition to that effect, a living will. Didn't you know?"

When she went to the funeral, rage and hatred were still her principal emotions. She didn't want to admit that she had known this was coming when Lavvy, who was never queer for soft toys, had asked for Pele. . . It wasn't the first time she'd seen a friend cremated, so she wasn't much bothered by the ceremony. In the middle of it, she remembered with horror that her darling had not been recovered—

She rushed out of the chapel, or whatever they called it, and took a taxi fifteen miles to the nursing home. It was November: the straight, slim Dorset beeches in the grounds were laden with red gold. She had dressed in New York Bohemian chic, to annoy the family. The nursing home staff reacted with fear and revulsion to her makeup, her hat, and her shoes. They closed ranks. They said that Lavvy's effects had been removed by her relations. If Ramone wanted a memento, she should ask the Kents. When Ramone broke down in tears, they softened but insisted there was nothing they could do. Anything the family had left behind had gone to be incinerated days ago. She pushed them aside and ran, a mad woman dressed like a scary clown, past the tv lounge and the ranks of folded wheelchairs, to the room that she remembered. It was empty. It had never been other than empty. Lavinia had never lived here.

At the open window, polyester net curtains flapped. The fresh air didn't hide that grey disgusting nursing home miasma: piss and feces, stale food and disinfectant.

She walked out of the building sobbing without restraint. She had nothing to gain by keeping a straight face, so why not howl. . . At the bend in the drive, something halted her. It was like a voice, calling very softly. It was like the smell of damp leaf mould, in the dark undergrowth of the Embankment Gardens. Instead of going straight ahead to the gates, she turned to the left along a moist, rutted track between banks of rhododendrons. There it was: the rubbish corral, a big shoveled-out space cut into the shrubbery, stacked with bulging black bin bags. Oh my God, whispered Ramone, without the slightest doubt. A beautiful, grey-haired lady in a vivid pomegranate dress, walking away from Ramone, had turned and looked back. . . She fell on the first bag in the front row; then the next; scrabbling among all kinds of litter, soiled dressings, reeking incontinence pads, things that definitely shouldn't be left to fester like this. I'll get the place closed down, she thought vindictively. . .and saw the tip of a faded blue ear.

She had found Pele.

He stank. He would have to be washed. Otherwise he was fine.

Oh, miracle. Oh dear god who makes mistakes, thank you for this.

It had begun to rain, but she was too shaken to leave, and in any case she felt at home in this place. She spread one of the cleaner bags to sit on and used another—draped over two branches—to make a roof. Anyone who saw her now would know she was completely mad. Roland would be happy. Ramone didn't give a shit for their definitions. She had been saved by Lavvy, long ago, from the terrible trap of other people. She had been taught *to live*. No one could catch Ramone; she slipped through all their nets: not the feminists, not the intellectual bullshitters, not the spirituality groupies, not the sex-gang children of Bohemia. They were all the same, all conforming to some lying code they were afraid to defy. No one could tell her any different; she knew that she had hold of the important thing, here in her arms. In her own way, which was like no one else's way. Something to love.

The Entrainment

— *i* —

The journey must end. She must leave the toll system; she must drop into the familiar evasion pattern to deal with Bournemouth's aversion-therapy traffic control. Why did she feel such a sinking in her heart? She had never felt so bad about coming home before: not even when returning to Leeds, across the Pennines, meant returning from the haven of her work to the house that held only Lily Rose's death. Why feel so bad? The disaster had happened, the struggle was over, all she had to do was adapt. To be happy, with Spence and the child. How could she ask for more, remembering the icy sleets of March, than this—

It was Spence who spotted the paparazzi.

"Fuck!"

"Holy shit," breathed Anna.

The road beyond their house was blocked by cars. Dark figures were leaping out of them at Anna's approach, a premature camera flash sprang white above the glare of headlights. She braked hard and in a panic began to swing the wheel, flinging her head to see behind her. But they were being closely followed. No escape that way.

"You *both* said naughty words—" began Jake. But then he started to cry.

The newshounds were banging on the windows, pressing their lenses against the glass.

"Get out of the car," said Spence. "I'll park it. Be cool, smile. Get Jake indoors."

Anna and Jake scrambled out into the barrage. *Mrs Senoz, Ms Senoz! Dr Senoz! Have you anything, could you just, what do you, Hey, Hey, Anna! Look this way!* She put her arm around Jake and smiled, but then ran stooping as if through a storm of hail, up the steps, unlocked the house door, and slammed it behind them. The narrow hall felt cold as a cave. And it was here. The dread was here, indoors, not out there with the hellhounds. She stood, shocked and puzzled, trying to get the measure of this feeling, this cold waft of fear that had invaded her safe den. . .

"Can I tell you about my goal again," said Jake, wiping his eyes.

"Yeah, do."

"The one I got that was declared offside. . . I headed it in from the edge of the box, off a free kick from Matthew—"

"But it *was* offside, you know," said Anna, who'd been there. Once she'd found out that Charles never came to football, she had made it a priority to support the babes, last season. "You weren't offside, but Henry was. I saw him. It was rotten luck."

"It was still my goal, though. I hardly ever get a chance to score. But Andy says my tackling's very good. Did you know, Andy once trained with Alan Shearer, when he was my age?"

"Yeah, I did know. He won it in a competition in *Match*. He told me. Amazing luck."

She went into the ground floor study, where the piano lived, with their bicycles. *Is it here?* There were hounds scrambling over the front garden. They stared in at her, faces bloated with sexual rage. She wasn't making it up. There was nothing more blatant than the sex in bastards' furious hatred. She closed the curtains.

"Why are they so horrible?" asked Jake, who had followed her.

"Because they are sad bastards. I'm sorry, I said a naughty word. Can't help it."

"I don't mind."

"Let's get away from the street."

Spence found them handfast, sitting on the edge of Jake's bed, Werg the bear in close attendance; comforting each other with talk of the beautiful game. Jake was still wearing his mother's jacket. The ambush had not yet dispersed: Jake and Anna had heard its war cry start up again as Spence came through. MR SENOZ! they called him, but the ones who thought they were clever yelled, HEY, SPENCE.

"Sorry I was so long, couldn't find a parking place. Those *assholes*." He dumped Jake's rucksack. "I've left the rest of the bags downstairs,

I thought I'd better empty the car. D'you feel like making a cup of tea? Or d'you want something stronger?"

Anna shook her head. She never wanted to move or to let go of Jake's hand. "What's the *point* of it? That's what I don't understand."

"Simple. You refused to feed them; it makes them mad; there's nothing more in it. I must admit, I thought the fuss was over."

The rough love of public interest had reached them almost as soon as Anna's findings hit the press. *Is this the end of the line for the male chromosome???* Anna, partly from shock and partly because it seemed like common sense, had stonewalled: she'd tried denying these idiots the oxygen of attention. It hadn't worked. There'd been skulkers in the street, reporters on the doorstep. Neighbors had been interrogated; Jake had been followed on the way to school. When they found out she'd been fired, the frenzy had intensified. SEX SCIENTIST DENOUNCED; they'd loved that. Spence was right; she should have given the pack what they wanted straight away, when she was still to some extent in control. It was too late now. She knew she wasn't capable of handling an interview.

"They'll give up," she insisted. "They'll go away."

"Thank God they didn't track us down in Manchester."

There had been phone calls, which Anna's mother had calmly fielded: nothing worse. Maybe the media people had been restrained by legal considerations.

"Poor Jake!" said Spence. Anna heard the accusation: so did Jake, of course.

"*I'm* all right," said the child stoutly, hugging her. "Poor *Mummy*!"

Over his head, Anna and Spence exchanged challenge and truce. I know you think this is all my fault, signaled Anna, but please try not to act nasty to me, for his sake. They put Jake to bed together, with a show of parental solidarity: brush your teeth, no, it's too late to have a bath, wash your face and hands. No we can't go and fetch Fergie (his hamster) from the Rectory, we'll get her in the morning. Into your pajamas. Through the bathroom window Anna saw figures prowling in her garden. There was no access to their garden except through someone's house. How much was that worth? Which of our neighbors took the money? She closed the blinds.

They said prayers: Anna thought of Lavinia Kent. Never underestimate the power of ritual; never think yourself above the comfort it can give. How can it be false comfort if it palliates the suffering, for a little while? Beggars can't be choosers. God bless the bad reporters, said Jake firmly. And help them stop being bad soon. They lay together, Anna and Spence on either side, Jake in the middle, squeezed into precarious shelter. Anna held Jake close against her breast, and turned her face into Spence's shoulder. She'd never felt so much like a woman—the mythical nuclear-family, dependent, stone-age woman, huddling in the shelter of a male arm—in her entire life. Ironic, or what? She'd have liked them to spread sleeping bags on the floor and stay with Jake all night, but Spence wasn't in the mood to play shipwrecks. As soon as the child slept he withdrew his arm, as a matter of course, and they went to bed without speaking to each other.

She did not sleep. How soon would it be dawn? She would get up and do her yoga: paschimottanasana, where are you little fish? No wonder Spence was furious. It must seem to him she'd maliciously kept the destructive power of her paper a secret, until all hell broke loose. Did she deserve his anger? She'd known there would be trouble. Way back in Sungai, when her intuition had been strong that those bizarre results *would* stand up to verification, she had known what would happen. There would be an uproar, and it would be based on ideology, not science, so it would be truly vicious... So why had she done this to Spence? Why? Because like any scientist she couldn't leave a puzzle alone, and it was instinctive, innate, to deny the troublesome aspects. She had treated her husband badly; she shouldn't be surprised that he was bitter and distant.

She shouldn't have been surprised that Nirmal fired her, either. He'd warned her, but as always Anna Anaconda had tuned out the warning. From his point of view she had dragged his fledgling department into scandalous controversy. He'd taken vengeance for what he saw as a personal betrayal, exactly the same as long ago in Leeds. . .

She lay drowsing, mulling over the situation. She had been called a naive fraud, a man-hating hysteric, a deranged eco-terrorist. (What did they think? That she'd been tipping vials of fast-breeding TY viroid into the global weather systems?) Impossible to stop the tabloid machine, but the serious trouble was mostly her own fault, she could see that now. If she hadn't panicked... She felt better. She could see her blunders, her tactical errors: better to know you've been *stupid* than feel yourself in the grip of an incomprehensible nightmare. She must have slept, because she woke, and Spence was not beside her. A trapezoid of light lay across the landing outside their bedroom, coming from his work room next door. She put on her dressing gown and went to see what he was doing.

He was at his keyboard, wearing the worn blue cotton djellaba he used as nightclothes; it was a long time since they'd slept naked. He was checking his email. No, talking to someone online. She watched as he typed, paused to read a reply, typed again. Ah, the quirky old intimacy of chatroom-world. She felt envious and affectionate. Who was he talking to? How strangely alive he looked, so poised and so alert. . . From the past she had visited on the journey home there rose an image of Spence at the foot of the stairs to the chill-out loft in the Riverrun. He was tossing his head and teasing poor Wolfgang. Spence, at home among the tropical clubberati, drowning the air around him with the pheromones of a fine sexual animal, certain that he is desired—

"Hallo?" she whispered.

He logged off, so quickly that he must have left somebody puzzled.

"Who were you talking to?"

"Meret," he said, turning in his chair with a stern expression. He seemed to wait for her reaction, but Anna was too slow. "Got some Shere Khan problems we have to sort out."

"Oh."

They went back to bed, without another word.

But Anna knew. She knew because she'd known already, with a secret, normal-person part of her brain that she usually ignored. The world fell into a different shape, a new gestalt.

She slept. When she woke again Spence was by the bed, with a mug of tea and a newspaper. They hadn't taken a newsstand paper for years. They relied on mTm and the freesheets to keep them up with current affairs. "The hounds have gone," he said. "But here's something that explains their excitement last night. Some guys in Canada have supported your results." He laid the folded paper by her. Anna picked it up and looked at the headlines, feeling no interest. Of course her results were real.

She didn't know what to say to Spence. She put the paper aside.

"Not the right *kind* of support," said Spence, and sighed, with compressed lips. "Nothing satisfies you, does it? Jake's not going to school. We'll collect Fergie from the Crafts, bring her back, then I'm taking him to see a movie. Is there anything I can get you?"

"No thanks." She lay back listlessly, closing her eyes.

━━　━━

The hellhounds were under an injunction to approach nobody except Anna herself, and this morning they seemed to be respecting it. As long as she stayed indoors and never answered the phone, as long as she refused to give interviews, killed their email, they would have to give up in the end. Spence and Jake were in and out. Anna went through the house, tidying clothes into drawers and books onto shelves, setting cushions straight, tasting the horror and dread that filled the air. When her wanderings took her into Jake's room, Fergie the anarchist hamster was wide awake. She watched Anna with concern through the bars of her cage.

On the last of their camping summers, they had found a good spot above the Gorge du Tarn, to hole up and avoid the mayhem of *le quinze*. They were chilling around the yurt, after a hot and exciting walk, scrambling limestone crags, and Jake had implored his daddy to give *Charlie and the Chocolate Factory* another try. Anna had spread a blanket in a secluded corner of the *emplacement*, to do some yoga: Spence lay on an airbed in the evening sun, the book propped on his smooth, tanned chest while Jake walked up and down, tried to play with his diabolo, exhibited terrible adult signs of nervous distress. *Please*, thought Anna, between pity and laughter, please, Spence, stretch a point, be kind. Finally Spence sat up, shaking his head.

"I'm sorry kid," he said, holding out the book. "This still stinks pretty bad."

Jake walked over.

"Will you let me explain to you why? You see, this guy's take on poverty is just *vile*—"

"No!" yelled Jake. "No no no! Don't EXPLAIN!" And he ran, hugging the paperback, jumped over the low wall at the back of their site, disappeared into the scrub oaks.

"I'd better go after him," said Spence, sorrowful but unrepentant.

"You stay where you are, Rhadamanthus. You've done enough damage. For God's sake Spence, it's only a kiddie's book. And he loves it."

"Well, he shouldn't."

She found her little boy sitting on a ledge of warm stone, on the very edge of the gorge. Under his dangling feet a mass of treetops fell away. Far below the river snaked, a ribbon of sea-washed bottle glass, striated with tiny moving rods of bright color: those were kayaks. He turned his head away, a tear glistening on his cheek.

"Where's the book?"

"It's here. I was going to throw it away, but I didn't."

"I'm glad you didn't. It's not the poor paperback's fault."

She put her arm around his small, warm, naked shoulders. Almost at once he relaxed, and she rocked him, murmuring soothing words, don't worry, dearest Jake-boy, don't cry, I love you... "Maybe you ought to let him explain, so you'd understand. Jake, you can't *make* a person like something. Especially not your daddy. What's the use in forcing him to say what he doesn't mean? That's not what loving people do. You're going to have to accept that he's just not keen on Roald Dahl. Think of you and porridge." He was so in love with his father, so touching in his heartbreak: down there the river runs, up here the lizards blink on the hot rock. I hug my baby, I love them both so much:

Throw this jewel memory away; it is fouled.

One winter Monday morning. Anna discovered to her horror an unheard of thing. She had forgotten to make her sandwiches! "I hate Mondays!" howled Anna, running around looking for the hairbrush for Jake's hair. Every Sunday evening from time immemorial she had prepared five frugal lunches, packed in plastic bags and stowed in the freezer, five because though she was often at work on a Saturday (not to mention Sunday), there were days when her apparatchik duties turned up a free meal, and it averaged out. Spence, who in honor could *never* be asked to make these lunches, began to slice bread, the bread he baked himself, grinning very sweetly. "No!" she cried, "I've done that! I got that far, and then I couldn't find the butter! It was in the freezer, remember, because Jake had unpacked it there——" She unearthed from the crock five pairs of slices, but Spence took them out of her hands.

"Hey hey hey," she boasted. "Look at this, I'm getting my sandwiches made for me!"

"Under close supervision from the gaffer." He divided slices of organic salami into five modest portions. "How much mustard? One dyne, ten dyne, how many nanograms?" and then someone let rip a fart.

"Cor!" said Anna. "What a woofter. That was you, Spence."

"The one who smelt it dealt it," said Spence.

"Ha! The one who said the rhyme, done the crime. . ."

Jake had found the hairbrush and stood in the kitchen doorway giggling, gently smoothing his own curls, ready to dart away if attacked. His parents, if they could catch him, were far too thorough.

Sweetness, sweetness, in every living moment—

Throw it away

All the farting, nose-picking, bottom-scratching, snuffling intimacies of the nest, robbed of foundation, collapsing like the iridescent surface of a bubble when it bursts.

In the cold snap, before last Christmas, Spence and Anna lie in front of a coal fire in the piano room, bicycle stable, occasional winter parlor, sifting charity appeals. Anna meant to spread their contributions, but it always ended up being Christmas and Easter. Spence liked being coaxed. He liked having her take charge of this part of life, the mothering he missed in her professional daze. "Well gee whizz, *marmee,* I'm just waiting for the day when you send me and Jake out into the snow, to give our Christmas dinner to the poor..." And here, another jewel. A snowfall at dusk, Anna and four-year-old Jake are trotting along by the park gates, in the magic glimmering. They have been to see the dentist, and they both got a clean test. They are proudly wearing stickers to this effect on their coats, to take home and show to Daddy. Jake is telling his mummy about a new Shere Khan character Spence has invented, called Billy Blue.

"Billy Blue isn't a grown up, mummy. He's a little boy like me and you."

Throw it away, it's fouled.

➤ ➤

Anna had hoped that she wouldn't have to know the Crafts, but it had not worked out that way. Insidiously, helplessly, she'd had to endure it while the two families and the children became "friends." Birthday parties, barbecues on the beach, lunches at country pubs, treats for the kids: McDonalds, the ice-rink, the flumes, the laser-gaming. Anna didn't like it. This wasn't the way they'd reared Jake, this endless, greedy, placatory circus. How can you expect them to make sense of the world if you believe one thing and behave completely the opposite. And it didn't even work: Meret and Charles's kids were horrors… She knew she had no choice, and anyway, she didn't want to admit Charles Craft was a problem. She couldn't possibly tell Spence that old story now.

Secretly, irrationally what she'd hated *most* was being able to keep up with the Charles Crafts because of Spence's earnings. At least this aspect was a private humiliation: Spence was convinced that his Anna was indifferent to material reward, and the people they met at the Crafts expected Anna to have a "wife" job, something minor, a second-income thing.

One Saturday last summer it had been Anna's turn to cook for one of the gatherings that she didn't like. She'd been late home, the guests had been in situ, Spence hadn't done a thing about the food, which was a tiny bit bloody-minded of him, but fair. Anyway, she was happy to have an excuse not to join the party. My mother used to do this, she remembered, when annoying Senoz friends and relations turned up… When a woman disappears into her kitchen it's not a submission, it's a statement: a retreat in good order. She was peeling roasted peppers and aubergines for *pisto castellano*, a finicky job, and feeling irritated because Charles, along with a children's writer called Neal Hight, had elected to take roost in the kitchen, watching her while she worked. They were talking about Sheltered Housing in the Algarve. Neal's old Mum was installed. Charles was very interested in getting Meret's parents sorted out, but he had to convince Meret. She must see that her work was suffering, and it was so important to her—

"It's your wife's drawings that make those books," said Neal, "Spence is a lovely guy, don't get me wrong. But he has no idea how to write for children—"

Meret and Spence suddenly appeared and passed between the gossiping pair, crossed the kitchen and went out through the open door into the June garden. Neal mugged embarrassment at Charles, but Anna's eyes followed that visitation, the lucky Spence who didn't have to cook, out into the tiny paradise where three tiers of flowers beside the path were in bloom together: carnation, lily, lily, rose. A frog croaked, among the yellow flags by the pond where Jake's famous DRAGONFLY had lingered. Meret and Spence stood by the pool. Anna felt a prickling in her shoulders. She looked round and found that Charles was staring at her, a strange glare she couldn't read, except thank God it didn't look like sexual interest.

Truth doesn't go away. It stays, patiently waiting to be understood.

Of course everyone had known. The situation was so obvious! Anna's teammates on campus had probably talked about the affair whenever she left the room. Publishing folk had talked about it, in those after-work gatherings for cheap wine. Rosey McCarthy herself had issued a serious warning (and Anna had been embarrassed and disdainful, feeling that she was above women-talk, bitchy gossip).

She stood in the bathroom and stared at herself in the mirror above the basin.

Here I am, within another of those sanctuaries. I have become a woman. I can be a matriarch like Rosey, who though she loves Wol truly, never forgets to treat him with contempt. Throws him out when he fails to satisfy, allows him back on sufferance. It is what they expect, it is the way relations between the sexes have to be. You have to keep the whip hand, or else they will turn on you. He'll want a divorce, because Meret will want another white dress, another hired Rolls. I will have one of those complicated families: ex-husband, husband's new girlfriend, son, girlfriend's children, all around the same table. I will buy one of those huge gas-guzzling people-carrier tanks to carry them all around. Correction, I'll make Spence buy it. I will take his money and sit with my elbows on the kitchen table and gossip about what a shit my ex-husband is, men are all the same. Could she endure such a life? Of course. A woman can endure anything.

She could see the huge black jagged malign complacent shape of *female power*, the greedy rancor of it, reflected in the mirror, breaking through her skin. I was afraid of Transferred Y, and I pretended other reasons, but this is why. I didn't want to think of what it meant for real people because *that means me, that means Spence...*all the dirt about sexual relations, that I didn't ever want to handle.

A shadow moved in the depths of the mirror. A floorboard creaked. "Spence?"

Spence and Jake were out. She was so certain that she had glimpsed someone behind her that she went through the house from top to bottom. She looked in closets and behind every door, convinced that one of the hellhounds must have broken in. There was no intruder, only the dread and fear that had greeted her last night. Maybe the house has always been haunted, she thought. How would I know? My life has been lived elsewhere; that's why I'm in trouble.

━ ━

Another day began. Spence took Jake to school, then retired to his room. The Shere Khan industry must go on, the breadwinner must win bread. Before they left for Manchester, Anna had invented some post-employment therapy for herself: she would sort a career's accumulation of papers, in the loft. She went up there to think.

You get fired, then you realize your husband is having an affair. It often happens to people that way; it's not really a coincidence. Before you lost your job, there was a period of stress and anxiety, a situation that naturally affected your marriage, and you didn't have time to pay attention. Everything here is normal, perfectly normal. She sat on one of the old tin trunks that had traveled the world with them and stared into the gloom.

Why is it so hard for me to understand ordinary things?

Anna used to get goosebumps when she ran across descriptions of Asperger's Syndrome, the mild form of autism, the super-male trainspotter personality—especially reports from victims about how it felt, because they sounded so like herself. But *I'm not a man. I'm meticulous, obsessed, a little bit strange, but ain't I a woman?*

You can't be a woman. If you were, you would understand.

Maybe she'd known that Spence and Meret were having an affair. From the way he was behaving, she guessed Spence thought she knew. The day she'd had that awful interview with Nirmal and walked out of his office, fired, she'd gone round to the Rectory. Meret and Spence had been off somewhere together. And then Spence had...he'd been so cold, so unsympathetic, about her terrible disaster. He'd been cold and unsympathetic ever since, and now she could see why. To Spence, what had happened that fatal day had been...*my wife came home unexpectedly and caught me out.* Maybe Anna had known all along and cynically ignored the affair, because without Meret there'd be no Shere Khan, and she'd have had to to go back to being a prudent breadwinner. *It's as if I made a deal, in my sleep, traded my career for my marriage. I bet that's how Spence sees it...* This is the part of the Faustian bargain they don't tell you about. Oh, and by the way, while you are wrestling with God, your personal life will be a disaster, your home will be crawling with miserable secrets, carpets heaving with the dirt swept under them. But the Faustian bargain is supposed to be for men, anyway. Someone was walking around downstairs. It wasn't Spence. She would have heard him leaving his room, which was right below her. How strange if she had been living in a haunted house all these years and never known it. . .

Piles of shit in the corners.

She had tried so hard, she had made such sacrifices. Ah, Lily Rose. Little Jake, your deep eyes gazing at me over the curve of my breast, those nights when you were first born: but I did the right thing, I gave him to Spence, can't ask for equality and then refuse to give up your own privileges. She had been so sure that she and Spence could win the game together, with their new rules. But here she was in the filthy pit. The shit was where she lived, not tucked away in some children's literature conference hotel (as she had hoped): it was inside her life, her personal space. Anna's parents had brought her up to bolt the toilet door, had discouraged dirty talk about farts and poo. Anna and Spence had taught Jake differently. They were poor and aspirational too, but these things are relative. For them the killing squalor of real poverty was generations in the past; they didn't have the same ingrained fears. Nothing wrong with shit. The stuff is harmless, attractive even. From time to time bothered by constipation, a little struggling and heaving, sore anus after passing a knobbly great stool at last, but she was not *afraid*. In her childish fantasies, shitting had been her model for sex, not because sex was dirty but because Anna was ignorant, didn't know which bit of her anatomy down there was giving her pleasure. At Easter in third year, she and Ramone had spent a weekend with Martin Judge, another arts student, someone Ramone hated. She couldn't remember why, one of Ramone's strange freakish fits... He'd rented a cottage in the Lincolnshire Wolds. They had a picnic by a strong-flowing ditch of a river, in a field margin on a warm April afternoon. They ate sandwiches made of hardboiled egg and sliced onion that had been steeped in vinegar. Anna went apart, behind a bush, made a scrape in the ground and laid such a big fine turd, plump and brown and pointed at both ends like a rugby ball. Nice shit, good shit. Goodbye shit, I'm leaving now. If you can't walk away from it, that's not so good. Shit is anything in your life that you *don't want* and *can't use*, but there it is anyway. Her mouth was full of shit, she had finally found something Anna Anaconda could not swallow, she was choking.

At the end of the day Spence fetched Jake. "We have a stalker," he reported, in the stern, superior tone he'd been using ever since the day she lost her job. "Maroon jeep, parked outside number thirty-nine. The guy got out of the car and followed us half way to the school this morning; the jeep's still there now. But he didn't try anything, and the rest of them have gone. D'you think he's your police bodyguard?"

"I doubt if I have a police bodyguard."

He shrugged and turned away.

Anna went to hide in the kitchen, because her eyes were full of tears. She heard Jake say, "Why are you being mean to mummy?"

"I'm not being mean, kid. Mommy is very sad because she lost her job."

"I think you're making her sadder. *Please* don't get in an argument. I hate it when you two get in an argument. If we're in trouble, we should be sticking together."

Spence came into the kitchen and gave Anna a fake hug, which she returned in the same spirit. She thought: soon we'll start taking him to the ice-rink and stuffing him with sweets. He'll behave badly and I'll whimper *Oh, Jake, don't be horrid*! and let him get away with murder. The unhappiness of Meret's marriage, written over her children's lives as plain as print, now to be scribbled all over Anna's child. Spence cooked. They ate, Anna in disgrace. After the meal, she kissed Jake goodnight and went back to the loft.

It was late when she came down again. Spence was in the living room, sitting cross-legged on the rug, putting together a joint. Smoldering resin perfumed the air. The mellow light of their standard lamps fell over the beautiful wide spaces of this first floor room, with the balcony (skinny little balcony) from which you could glimpse the sea, where Anna grew pelargoniums and tomatoes and the little strawberry tree that was doing so well. They'd bought this house, when they came back to England and everything about the country had seemed drab, poky, and mean, because it had a balcony with a glimpse of the sea... But the folded futon couch was gone, it had been retired to Spence's study. A new sofa, big and soft and expensive, stood against the back wall. Anna and Spence always bought top of the range, when they emerged from Holy Poverty to make a consumer purchase: a compromise, as Spence would joke, between his taste and hers.

Spence works long hours; Anna works long hours. They come to the lovely room together and commiserate. Terrible day, nothing went right, totally exhausted. They work too hard, to distract themselves from the state their world is in, the private and the public spheres, but then at last the distraction fails.

"Hi," he said, noncommittally. "Want some?"

"No thanks." She knelt beside him. "God bless the drug," said Spence.

On the wall behind the new sofa there hung a Shere Khan original, several panels of gangling, raffish pirates doing piratical things and speaking Spence's words in cartoon speech-bubbles. She wished he had not said *God bless the drug*, because it made her think of all the other private things he would say to Meret, things that she would have to share with the other woman. She would have to get used to that. "We're gonna need a new supplier," said Spence. "Frank's really getting ready to move out of town. Sure you won't?"

"I'm sure."

He stubbed the joint out carefully. They would make a hefty one last for days. Anna put the pack of condoms, which she'd found exactly where she'd left them months ago, on the rug between them. "Tell me about you and Meret."

He drew himself up. "I didn't use them."

"I can see that you didn't use this pack. It would have been some trick, to fold them up again and stick it all back together—"

"I think. . .I think I wanted you to find them."

"Yeah," said Anna, suddenly rancorous. "I think so too. You wanted me to find them, you wanted me to find out what you were up to, without your having the trouble of telling me. Who the fuck do you think I am. Your mother?"

"Anna—"

"Actually, I think that's *exactly* who you think I am."

He closed his eyes, set his jaw, and turned his face away. "Will you let me explain?"

"Okay, explain. You admit there's something going on?"

He drew a sharp breath through his nostrils. "I find her attractive, and she's made it clear she feels the same way about me. We're close, we're friends. It's something that's built up gradually between us."

"So when we got back from Manchester and I was in hell and the street was full of paparazzi, naturally you dialed her up for a midnight chat—"

"It was a first. If you want to know, we were finally, for the first time, talking about meeting somewhere to have sex—"

"What, *last night!*" wailed Anna, not believing this unlikely story for a moment. "Kick me when I'm down, why don't you—"

"It wasn't last night; it was the night before. Anna you are not *down*. You make it sound like a prizefight. You lost your job; it's not the end of the world. This is not fair. Why the fuck are you getting at me? What about you and the Amoldovar kid?"

"I've never fucked Miguel. I'd never do a colleague, except possibly, though it has never happened, if I was stupid drunk. I have more sense. I know we're supposed to be free. If you'd had a fling *somewhere else,* that didn't ever come home, I wouldn't be too upset. Meret's not only your collaborator, not only someone you're close to, you've made her a friend of the family. She's here all the time, in my face, in my life. You don't do something like that to me and not even think it is wrong!"

"Oh, for God's sake. You're making too much. It isn't *serious*—"

"Not for you. For you it's fine. Now you have two wives. The boffin one for a trophy, and the not-too-clever sweet feminine younger one, who looks up to you and thinks you are such a wonderful *Daddy*—"

She saw that she'd stung him, and was glad.

"I've never been your intellectual equal, Anna. I know that."

"*Yes you are.* You are my equal. What you're not is my superior. That's what you can't stand, that's why you backed out, why you decided not to compete, why you gave up. The moment, the *moment* it became clear that I had a reasonable chance, an even chance of real success in my career, you decided you weren't going to play. If a woman can do it, achievement isn't worth anything, achievement is for sissies. I knew you resented me, and playing the househusband was your way of taking the shine off what I had done—"

"I don't know where this is coming from. Where the *hell* is this coming from? You want to play dirty, okay lets play dirty. You've never been here, Anna. You haven't shared my life, Meret has. We've been down among the mums and kids, while you've been up in the empyrean, exercising your genius. You've been a puritan patriarch in this house, keeping me and Jake in line with your perfectionist rules. Yes, I've been going behind your back to have some fun. What d'you expect? All you care about is your fucking work—"

Then all the pent up anger, the *enjoyment* of a fight, breaking out after such weeks of strain, suddenly drained from her, because she realized it was true. It was true, worse than her worst imagining. He was not her Spence anymore. She burst into violent sobs.

"Oh God, oh no. I thought it wouldn't happen if I didn't have another baby—"

"*What?* I don't know what you're talking about. What are you talking about?"

"Not my Spence, you're not my Spence—"

"Don't yell at me. If you cry like that, you're going to waken Jake."

He stormed out, she followed him. They had another round in the kitchen, she commanding: *don't you dare run away from me...* This went on for a while. In the end, as Anna ran through the house, howling like a banshee, she succeeded in frightening him. He left her crouched in a corner of their bedroom, keening and jabbering *please god, please god, don't let it, don't let it be real...* This Anna who never cried, or if she had to cry, managed it so quietly. He came back with a pill bottle and a glass of water.

"Anna, c'mon. Take this."

"What is it?"

"Temazepam."

"No!" Anna had a horror of leaning on prescription drugs. "What do you mean, *temazepam*, why do you have sleeping pills?"

"They're Mom's, from last time she was over here. Look, you haven't slept for weeks, you're in a state, you need to switch off. We'll talk in the morning." She looked at him as if she was staring from the nethermost pits of hell. "*Just swallow it,*" he said, in his stern, superior tone. He helped her to bed and pulled up the quilt.

◆ ◆

Spence went back to the living room. He took a cigarette from the joint-makings box and lit it. Long time since he'd smoked a whole one of these. The box must be returned to its hiding place. Jake would be horrified if he knew that his parents used tobacco. They should give up, should smoke only grass, but secretly they were hooked on the little nicotine hit. Maybe Spence would die of lung cancer: yeah, soon. That would be a result.

He thought of Meret: of something profoundly intractable and devouring in the heart of his little Japanese wood-cut, something that Charles Craft could deal with maybe, but not Spence. Of the resistance, almost revulsion, he had felt for all female desire until Anna had made desire innocent. He thought of the rough, soft and rapid sighs that would be drawn from her in extremis; she was never a noisy lover. He would have been out of his fucking mind to try to climb into bed with her, though often they'd had blazing fights that had ended in sex, fights fueled by pent-up lust. But it was what he'd wanted, when he saw her so vulnerable. He still had a tingling half-erection, right now. Explain that to Anna Anaconda.

Yet there was still Meret. Explain that.

You reach the stage when every thought in your head sounds like a line from Chekov (we long since passed through the Solzhenitsyn phase). When there is nothing ahead but pointless toil and waiting for the grave, what is the sense in virtue or restraint or even self-preservation? He went on smoking: thinking of Jake, on that mountain in Slovakia last winter, crying from tiredness, refusing to be carried, he wanted to do it himself. And Spence's heart had twisted inside him, because in that exhausted little face he knew that he was seeing the last, the very last of his baby son, gone forever, never to be seen again. Thinking of poor old Father Edmund at St Mary Magdalene's, where the family attended the occasional Mass. All he hears about is pedophile priests and the evil deeds of the Vatican; but what is the guy to do, he just keeps on trucking, though he knows it's all over. Soon this creed to which Spence was so irrationally attached would pass from the world in dishonor, just another soiled old religion...

I have fallen from grace.

He could have done better by Meret. He could have been a friend to her, she needed a friend, poor directionless kid. He hadn't been able to resist that reverent touch on his sleeve. The way she looked up, expecting *everything* from him. . . He thought of the beach at Pasir Pancang, Boolean Algebra, Anna's shining eyes. It seemed to him that he could hear, far off, the murmur of that tide, and see the ocean glimmering, calm and wide under a starless sky. But meaning changes, truth decays, and a sound knowledge of the Latin of the twenty-first century wasn't going to help him now.

━ ━

When Anna woke, the gulls on the rooftops were screaming, and rain was splattering against the bedroom windows. She was still dressed, her eyes were sticky, and her throat was sore. It was like some morning from the last weeks of the lab work, the terrible scraping out of final reserves of energy, eyelids that burned whenever she tried to close her eyes—all that effort; was it really over? Spence was there, looking at her.

"Where did you sleep?"

"On the couch next door." He was subdued. "Jake's in school. He doesn't know anything, he managed to sleep through the firefight. Here's your tea. Drink it; take a shower. Then I want you to come on a drive with me." He grimaced. "Yeah, I know. You hate cars because they kill the countryside, it hurts you to make an unnecessary trip. But I'm still an American, just about. I think better when I'm driving."

As they set out, he touched her hand. "What say? We put the hamster in the back, pick up Jake, and head for the ferry?"

She looked at him with incomprehension.

They drove up onto the New Forest freeway, where the ponies were standing heads-down into the rain; and somewhere back there, between the big road and the University of the Forest campus, Spence's sun terrace lay under the icy wind: but whatever thinking Spence did, it didn't come out in words. At length they came back down to the conurbation frontage, back to Bournemouth promenade. He found a parking space near to where Anna and Daz had once shared a room. They walked onto the pier. There was a thin crowd of visitors, old people, kids bunking off school. Young gulls, shrieking, skimmed the leaden waves.

"What do you want to do?" she asked.

"What do you mean? About what?"

"Please don't take Jake away from me."

"For God's sake!" He sighed hard. "Anna, you're over-reacting, outrageously. Can't you see that?"

"I know." She sniffed, and wiped her nose with her fingers. "I can't help it. It's because the way you feel for Meret can't be...can't be trivial. You wouldn't start fooling around with someone I have to meet every day, just on a whim. This isn't a fling, it's something long term. I may as well start facing that, face the whole problem. My new life."

"You always take things straight to extremes. You are still the woman I love, you and Jake are my family, and I don't want anything to change, ever."

"What about Meret? How does she feel? She made Charles marry her."

"Shit." Spence stared at the horizon. "Do you remember, a few months before this blew, you phoned me in the middle of the night, to tell me Jake was ill and you were going to take the day off, and stay home with him. So I didn't have to rush back—"

"Yes, you and Meret were up for some award or other."

He smiled. "It's called the Carnegie. Well, we didn't get it: probably never will now. A thing like Shere Khan gets one chance. I don't care. She's still the best thing I'll ever do. The captain, I mean, not Meret. Anyway, that night when you called, Meret was with me in my room. We were snogging, for the first time, when the phone rang."

"I must be psychic."

"Yeah."

"Well, I'm sorry. I didn't know I was being tactless. I thought I was being useful, telling you didn't have to rush back. It wasn't the middle of the night, it was ten o'clock, and I'd been trying your mobile all evening—"

"Whatever."

"That day when I came to the Rectory. Had something happened then?"

He didn't answer. Suddenly she knew that they had been here. The seafront was a place for Meret. You could take her on the funfair rides, you could win her an ugly oversized soft toy, you could buy her ridiculous food to eat. Meret would glow. She saw the two of them, standing at this rail. Meret looking up with that wistful smile. She would want to hold his hand, but Spence would withhold that privilege, considering it too risky.

She resolved to ask no more questions.

"When I went to fetch the hamster," he said, "Meret asked me, when I went offline so fast the night before, was that because you had come in? You see, you're not the only one who's psychic. I told her yes, and that there'd be no more late night chat sessions, because you needed me. She got the message, and I haven't spoken to her since. She's afraid of you, you know."

Psychic, thought Anna, staring at the sea. Yeah, or you could call it common sense... The banality of all this was so miserable, so unlike "Anna and Spence." "Afraid of me?"

"She respects you, but you frighten her. Anna, please believe me. *It's not serious.*"

"Then what is it?"

He looked away from her. "An addiction." The gulls cried, the crowd passed by. "Maybe I've reached the point where most guys start out," said Spence. "So low-down that I'd do anything for a free fuck and a momentary sense of achievement."

They walked back to the car. Anna thought: I give up, she might as well have him. This ordinary-looking marriage, the Spence-and-Anna relationship, had been too strange, deep in its secret heart: too strange and too fragile for this world. The pact they had entered into was broken, and it could not be mended.

➤ ➤

Spence fixed a secure hitching post on the wall outside their front door, something he'd been meaning to do for some time. The bikes moved outdoors. The bicycle stable, tidied out, became Anna's study, so that she would have a place of her own to match Spence's work room upstairs and would no longer have to mope in the loft. She spent her days in there, trying not to look at a large bouquet of lilies, roses, and carnations that stood on the table in the window bay: the expensive bouquet that said plainly *marriage on the rocks.*

She pined for her refuge of dust and gloom; she didn't like being down here, listening to imaginary noises. But she obediently stayed in her kennel, steeling herself for the years to come. Meret and Spence would get back together (if they'd ever broken up: she knew her husband was likely to be lying about everything; she'd picked up *that* much women's lore). Anna would live with the situation, asking no questions. She'd thought about it, and as long as Spence was prepared to carry on, she preferred the old-fashioned solution. She did her best to behave normally, they had sex and it wasn't so bad, it was okay. She told herself she would take the offensive, very soon. Defend her work, get her job back, be Anna again in this new world. She just needed to stay away from her husband's room, which was where she felt Meret's presence.

The reporters had gone, except for their faithful retainer in the maroon jeep. Spence said Anna was getting agoraphobic, so she went to fetch Jake from school. It was strange to be on the street, she felt otherworldly, as if she were convalescent after a long illness. The beggar-girl with the Golden Labrador and the two Lurcher puppies was in her regular pitch outside the corner supermarket, but the shop wasn't the Happy Shopper anymore; it was something else. The Broken Down Blue shop, which used to fascinate Jake because you could see right through it into the back garden, was selling cheap underwear and stationery. Surely there was a lot less plate glass on their local shopping street than there used to be... She went walking on, forgetting she ought to be at the school gates. When did Khan's the halal grocers go; when did the dry-cleaners close down? All these changes must have been going on behind her back or in plain view, but they didn't register; change doesn't register until it makes a difference (the Congregational chapel had become a pizza parlor), until suddenly one day some last insignificant item shifts and the whole street flips into a new state: suddenly this is not a local shopping street any more (the video hire shop was boarded up)... Anna began to tremble and tremble. It was like being struck down by malaria. She felt her forehead; it was cool. Agoraphobia, she thought. Oh fuck, oh damn, what a pathetic girlie complaint; is there no end to my shame?

She picked up Jake. "Sorry I'm late. I got distracted."

"Everything okay?" he asked kindly.

"Yeah, why do you ask?"

"You and Daddy made it up?"

"What makes you think we've been fighting?"

"Oh, dirty looks." He gave a distant, grown up shrug. "Shut doors. That sort of thing."

"We've made up. Everything's okay."

They held hands, walking home. In profile, his face had already lost some of its childish sweetness. She saw the beaky nose, the adult mouth, starting to take shape. It would be Spence's features that would emerge from the bloom. You killed my daughter, she thought, watching the boy child coldly. You murdered Lily Rose. Briefly, she wanted to kill him back. It didn't seem a terrible idea, just the kind of thing that flashes through your mind sometimes.

In the middle of that night she sat up, bolt upright, electrified out of sleep.

She suddenly understood what had happened to her, the whole thing.

Lily Rose was dead. Spence was no longer Spence. Jake was an arrogant little stranger. The whole world had changed, slyly, secretly: giving no sign, no warning. It had held itself together on the surface so that no one would know, while out of sight, shuffle shuffle tick tack click clack, it was moving the pieces around, changing into something different and malign. No one knew except Anna. She had found out: that was why the world was trying to kill her, why something was driving her mad. But the punishment was sheer revenge, because there was nothing Anna could do, no matter if she could get anyone to believe her. It was too late.

She was in the Biols coffee bar—a place she had thought she would never enter again after that hateful interview with Ilse. Everything had changed (the prices, the foodstuffs, the furniture, the makeshift posters on the walls), but everything was the same. She was having coffee with Jennie Nasrat, one of her two overseas doctoral students, the other being Ursula Masood. Ursula was always bunking off, unable to take the horrific hours you have to put in, serving the gods of molecular biology, no matter how fantastic the tech gets; Jennie was a trouper. They were gossiping. No, the words didn't come back, only the sweet slenderness of Jennie's wrist, encircled by the leather strap of her old-fashioned watch, the delicacy of her shoulders, her clear voice, her gentle bearing.

The loveliness of a young woman—

Oh no, oh no, not gone forever, please, don't tell me that, please no—

She went down to her new room and sat at her work table, afraid to look behind her in case those flowers were still there. The date on the phone pad was the twentieth of May, she had no idea if that was today's date. Her mind was wiped clean.

So, Dr Senoz, you finally understand what everyone was getting upset about?

Yes, I do understand. Meret Hazelwood has explained it to me. There will be no more beautiful young women, no more swaggering young men to court them. It's awful.

The psychological effects of this development, if it proves to be fact, must be immense. If our genes no longer talk the talk, how long will we go on walking the walk? Already the social boundaries of gender have become thoroughly uncertain, and we see the repercussions everywhere. So much of our philosophy, of our humanity itself, rests on this most vital opposition. I seriously wonder if we can be human without it—

She stared down at this text, on a newspaper page, head propped on her hands, rubbing her fingers along her hairline. Spence collected her clippings for her and left them on her desk. How cruel he could be, this new Spence. Meret's welcome to him... Anna Anaconda had plain resented all the philosophical fuss about TY. She could understand the grief about clinical problems, fertility problems. She just didn't get this kind of claptrap. *I seriously wonder if we can be human without it—* Get a life, pundits. It was only a deformed chromosome, make up another way to tell being from nothingness, for heaven's sake. Now Anna could feel the fear and such a sense of loss and betrayal. She had wasted her life. She needn't have bothered trying to fight fair; the game was over. This jagged flaw running through the human world, crisped all along its boundary with such complex variation, was closing up of its own accord. It would become a shallow ditch; it would fade and be gone... No need to dress down, modestly avoiding male attention. No need to make any of her sacrifices, evolution just evolves. But this was a circular argument, because of course it must have been the TY effect that had made Anna like that, given her the puzzle of being a woman and a scientist, decreed every detail of her behavior. *I didn't do it.* I didn't create the Transferred Y effect, I am the effect. It was as if she had said, I am God. The enormity of her situation, the abyss into which she had plunged the human future came rushing over her—

She went round to The Rectory to look for her team. They weren't at home and she badly needed them. Isobel Hazelwood greeted her at the door.

"Ah, Anna. I expect you were hoping to find your husband here."

"Is he here?"

"He is not. He and Meret have left me holding the babies, once again. I suppose they think they can trust me to be discreet, well they cannot."

"Can I take Jake home now?"

"I think the children are in the basement." She called them, "Tomkin! Florrie! Tell Jake, his mother is here!" and floated ahead of Anna: gliding first to the newell post of the rather grand staircase, propelling herself from thence to another handhold, a doorway further along the hall, and so by stages to the breakfast room. A bowl of dying flowers stood on a table among what looked like the debris of several days of casual meals. The pictures on the walls were of nude women and children. "My daughter tries to keep the place tidy," said Isobel. "Or so she tells me. I think the effort is chiefly mental. It never seems to reach the outer reality. We should hire someone. Would you like a sherry?" Isobel sat down and Anna sat down. It was strange that this lean, handsome woman, in her fantastical antique Japanese kimono in the middle of the day, was Meret's mother. She looked so old, her features blurred, all the life gone from her tired rusty hair.

"Your son is a lovely child. I'm surprised that you let him come here so much."

"What?"

"I can't be everywhere at once. And children, pretty children are so flirtatious."

"What?" repeated Anna, unease creeping up her spine.

"You must know about my husband, surely? Someone must have told you. He's an artist and a free spirit, and it's no real harm. People make such a fuss these days about things that were accepted, quietly:

things that have always gone on. I must admit I sent Blondel to school soon as he was seven: and I keep a close eye on Tomkin and little Charlie. But I think he knows not to foul the nest. We have no money. We're dependent on Charles's good graces."

"What about Meret?" whispered Anna.

"It's a pity Jake is so *friendly*. You shouldn't let him out of your sight, if that's the way you bring him up. Still, let's hope the old tom cat has lost his urge for conquest."

Tomkin and Florrie appeared at the door of the room. "Ah," said Isobel, "Where's Jake?"

The boy rolled his eyes and grinned. Florrie, her white tee-shirt slipping from a tiny, softly rounded white shoulder, pointed upwards. "He's upstairs with my granddad." The little girl's rosebud smile was full of lascivious knowledge—

"Anna? *Anna!*"

Spence was bending over her. She was lying on the floor.

"Come back to bed."

"I haven't been to bed. I went to the Rectory to look for you."

"Shit. Anna, I haven't been near her since... It's over, honey. I'm here for you now. I'm your Spence." He knelt beside her and stroked her hair. "Anna, don't yell at me, do you think you should see a doctor?"

She didn't want to see a doctor. The appalling vast crime she had committed was stuck in her throat, like a piece of poisoned apple, what could a doctor do? She would have to live with these dreams: like this dream where she walked into Meret's studio and found Spence and Meret with Jake, all three naked, the child being sodomized by his father while Meret held his head, his baby tongue lapping at the furry lip of this cup of flesh between white thighs. These images are part of the repertoire, human folklore is full of them: fuck the child, eat the child. They come to the surface when a society is disintegrating (Hansel and Gretel, oh Philomel with melody), and things like this will really happen; and equally they come to the surface when an individual mind is breaking up under pressure. The nightmares were so real she woke believing in them completely, convinced it had all happened, and then she'd been spirited back to her bed. It was all she could do not to TAKE THE CHILD AND RUN! But that was the last thing; that would be terrible... She must hang on, through these difficult few days, until she got used to her new life. But it was an unkind extra turn of the screw that this house, her own house, had to be haunted.

At first she saw nothing. She heard no more of those light, wandering footsteps that had puzzled her when they got back from Manchester. She was only aware, very much, of the ghost's presence: aware that someone unseen had left a room the moment before she walked into it, aware that someone had passed her on the stairs, had looked in through the bathroom door while she was brushing her teeth or running Jake's bath water. She said nothing to Spence or Jake. If Spence thought the house was haunted he'd have said something about it long ago, and she didn't want to give Jake scary ideas.

She tried to behave normally and believed she was succeeding, though she felt like a paper balloon in the shape of a woman, like a dry puffball that would fall into dust at a touch. The ghost did not seem hostile. It was a woman. Maybe she'd lived here when the house was young. Anna began to see, in her mind's eye, a woman in Edwardian dress, a sensible dark skirt, short enough so it would not become draggled when you were in the street on foot, stout boots, a neatly belted waist, a tailored jacket. The face was indistinct in feature, but it gave an impression of briskness, endeavor, hope. This figure was not an apparition, but an inner vision that felt like a real visitation, not something imagined.

She passes Anna on the stairs. Her skirts brush the dust left by Anna's poor housekeeping, but she doesn't condemn, she is in full sympathy. She shares the impatience of a talented woman, determined to escape from pettiness and drudgery and make her way in the world. She is often found sitting in the room called Anna's study, when Anna walks in there in the twilight. She is working at the desk: perhaps writing articles, or learning a foreign language. Finally, strengthened by Anna's repeated gaze, she is still there when Anna turns on the light. She is a benign spirit; she means no harm. She is refreshingly unsexual in her demeanor, though not at all mannish.

Anna decided the haunting was a good sign. She had lost her job, lost her lover, and possibly her whole society had lost its sexual identity, all in the same short space of time. She remembered, from the time after Lily Rose had died, that bereavement takes strange comforts. If everyone thought she ought to have the psychotropic drugs a doctor would prescribe, what was wrong with taking the medicine supplied by her own brain? My ghost will keep me sane, she thought; and told no one. But you couldn't get away from the fact that a ghost was a dead person, and it was frightening to have a dead person wandering around. Couldn't get away from that.

One day she was sitting in the kitchen alone, trying not to admit to herself that she was afraid to go into that room next door, the room that used to be a bicycle stable. If she let herself give way to being frightened, Spence would notice, and he thought she was getting on so well. The world was not behaving normally, or forgetting Anna's name, but never mind that. Eventually things would calm down. She saw herself slipping into dependency: the wife who doesn't drive, who doesn't like to leave the house on her own, who doesn't work. But it would be okay. The ghost would take over her need to strive. A dripping tap, sunlight. It was the middle of the morning. Spence was out; Jake was at school. She stood up, carefully. Into the narrow hall, hung with its quirky mementos from many lands. Open this other door. The lilies and roses and carnations had died and been thrown away, thank god, but the ghost was there. She was sitting on the piano stool, bold as brass. Her face was indistinct, but the rest of her was very clear.

"What are you doing in my room?" said Anna. "You are going to have to leave!"

The ghost didn't speak. She had no mouth only a blur of lips. She wasn't actually a person, she was more like the shell of a chrysalis. She was a state of hope, a woman trying to be free and equal, a woman at the beginning of the great project. She was determined to escape from bondage: to take her fair share of glory and hand over in return, to the man she loved, the great gift of equality. Never thinking *where will it all lead?* Anna wanted more than anything to crawl back inside that shell. It's better to travel hopefully than arrive, believe it, sister… The ghost just sat there, indistinctly smiling.

"You think you want to be me," said Anna. "You DON'T. You want to try your wings and prove your worth, and at the end of the story go back to being the angel of the hearth. That's what you want; I know that's what you want."

Some changes are irreversible, but Anna could not believe she was helpless. She waded in. She clasped the ghost to her breast and tried to spread her mouth over its face. It was there and yet not there. It was like a paper balloon in the shape of a woman. She could not swallow this thing. She would have to climb back inside, not through the mouth, which was closed, but through the vagina and anus, through the pores of the paper skin, around the rims of the eye sockets. Somehow, she would force her way... She struggled, but it wouldn't happen, it just wouldn't happen. She was lying on the floor by the piano stool, half undressed. Her arms and legs were moving of their own volition, she couldn't stop them, she heard herself grunting like an animal, and couldn't stop—

She managed to stop the flailing, and sat up, pulling her clothes together.

Oh no, no more of this. I'm not going to let Jake see this happening to his mummy.

She packed her carry-on bag, quickly and efficiently. No one saw her leave the house. Her faithful retainer had given up his vigil... She'd left her phone behind. She would not need it, she was going to vanish. One lucky thing. She could get away from here a lot further and faster than if she were living in the ghost's time.

— *ii* —

She took the train to Gatwick, didn't bother with a Women Only compartment, what a useless amenity; you can't lock them, and any real nutter makes straight for them. There was a terrorist thing going on. She left them to their doomsday scenario (couldn't work out whether it was an exercise or real) and set off for Heathrow. Passing through London she sat with a woman who was taking her nine-year-old son to see a specialist. The mother introduced herself through rail chaos, "How many hours did it take *you* to get from East Croydon?" But she was desperate to talk about the child. He had so many problems: asthma, allergies, chest infections, blurred vision, weakness, rashes, lassitude. Finally the doctor had insisted on them seeing a consultant, to discuss the genotype results. The mother's face was marked with mortal dread. Anna looked at the little boy: noting his rather long, narrow skull, the large eyes, the slightly androgynous cast of his features. She picked up his hand—which he allowed with the sad passivity of a kid too often handled by doctors—and tested the mobility of the wrist joint; examined his nails. "When he was a baby he was hypokalemic. . .he needed a potassium supplement?"

"Why, yes—"

"And he responded well to that?"

"Yes he did. Are you a doctor?"

"Don't worry. He's going to be fine. The little glitches will sort themselves out at puberty, when the extra testosterone kicks in." She grinned at the boy. "You'll do."

"But who are you?"

Anna retreated behind her magazine. She felt happy and perfectly well. She was free. She had left her grief, her desperation, her terrifying symptoms, behind her.

The price of the plane ticket meant nothing. She reached New York easily, without further incident, and checked into the hotel she'd booked from Heathrow. It was a place she'd used before, on 42nd Street, an anonymous hive for budget travelers. The corridors seemed spookier than before, more numerous and more dingy. In the morning she would start her new life. Meanwhile, she filled two trays from the salad bar in a grocery nearby and retired for the night. The second tray was for Jake. When she lay down he was there, curled up snugly with Werg in the other bed. The make believe seemed a sensible recourse: Lavinia Kent would have approved. Fill your world with spirits; keep out the dark by any means necessary. Shadows moved under the sill of the door; strange thumpings proceeded down the corridor. Once, which was very scary, a keycard was tried in the lock. *It's all right, Jake-boy*, whispered Anna. *The bears are prowling, but they can't get in...* She told him what they would do in New York: how he would walk between the paws of the great ones, the beautiful monsters, and look up and see their roaring heads high above him, almost closing off the sky. How they would ride the escalators in the Trump building, which was made of golden glass, and sit by the fountains under a bank of fern and moss so green and pure you'd think you were in Lorien. They would talk to the Vietnamese tourists who clustered round the shrine-windows of Tiffany's, buy candy corn from the Russian street vendors; they would feed the squirrels in Washington Square.

It seemed to her as she whispered that she fell asleep and woke, and she and Jake got up and went out and did all these things, and she was blissfully happy. They climbed on the boulders that lay around in Central Park like sleeping dinosaurs, the way Margaret Mary and Anna Teresa Senoz had climbed on boulders by Lake Windermere long ago. They visited the *Ghostbusters* lions and the White People in Greenwich Village, where she told him a very funny story (somewhat bowdlerized) about what Miguel did to those statues one day, years ago. They lived on salad bar food, coffee, Coke, and hotdogs; they found places, great expanses of old cobbles, that in dawn light or deep twilight made you feel time and space had slipped aside, and you were in Prague or Kraków before the great wars. She was giving him a dream, a dream of the beautiful city that would be to him what the loveliness of lake and mountains had been to her childhood. Never make the mistake your auntie Maggie made, she told him. Don't try to move into dreamland. Maggie wanted to live in the country; she ended up in a mock-Georgian housing estate, shitting on the beautiful thing she loved... I said a naughty word, I'm sorry. Live in the city, but like this. Be an exile and a stranger. Enjoy the tastes and smells; leave the owning to those other people.

In the middle of the night she woke, and *oh god* the second coverlet was flat and smooth. Anna sat up and stared, her heart pounding, *where is my baby?* She lay down again with fire spiders crawling through her nerves, in intolerable distress, too horrified for tears, remembering that she had left him behind. Her nightmares about what went on in the Rectory seemed entirely real. Shambling old Godfrey fucking his daughter, drunken Isobel ignoring it all, Spence fucking Jake. . . Oh, God. It could be true! Often, nowadays, the doomsday scenario is not an exercise. It dawned on her that, since she couldn't trust Spence and Meret was a little girl, she had entrusted her child's well-being to Charles Craft. Charles, you bastard, you're not such a bad bastard, if any of it is true you must know: for god's sake don't let me down.

She lay thinking about her new, outlaw life. She had the name of a gallery, geniTALia: nothing else, no address. When she'd showered and dressed she used the room's online services to track down geniTALia and didn't even check what she was being charged, which was unheard of for Anna, but it was okay. She was no longer in danger of losing touch with her poverty. She would run out of credit soon enough. Armed with the address she set off on foot, her carry-on bag on her back like a rucksack. If she knew anything, she knew that she had an invitation, an open door with no time limit. *If you ever change your mind, about leaving me behind. . .* If you ever realize that I was right all along, come and find me. Nobody, especially not Spence, understood the permanence of this relationship: that if either one of them made the first move, it would always be there. The great alternative; Anna's other life.

She walked through the shabby, bohemian streets of Lower Manhattan—and the people she passed were so colorful, so insouciantly pierced and scarred, boned and feathered, it was as if she'd already joined the pirates. And here's geniTALia. She walked in boldly. The gallery was about the size of an English corner shop supermarket, with a floor of blond polished wood and a flat screen in the center of each of the three walls; no other items. In the middle of the room a spiral staircase climbed up to another floor. Beside this feature a girl with cropped brown hair and many piercings, dressed in a dark red shift to her ankles, sat at a spidery desk.

"Hi, I'm beebee. That's b-e-e-b-e-e, all lower case. Can I help you?"

"I urgently need to get in touch with Ramone Holyrod."

"Well, I don't know if I can. . . May I take your card?"

"You see, I need somewhere to stay, and Ramone said if I was ever in New York—"

She shouldn't have checked out of the hotel. Suppose Ramone was out of town? She'd have to find another hotel, with a room that DIDN'T HAVE TWO BEDS, because she couldn't stand waking up and finding Jake not there, not again. And what about when the credit on her cards was used up? What then?

"I'm afraid Mizz Holyrod is out of town," said beebee, sunnily. "And I can't reach her."

"What about—um—Karel and Rio?"

"Ri. I'm afraid I can't reach them, either." beebee pulled a little face, beginning to tire of her brush-off routine. But she read Anna's card and gave a yelp.

"You're Dr Anna Senoz?" She stared into Anna's face. "Hey, you *are* her! You look just like your pictures. I'm so thrilled to meet you! I wish my boyfriend was here!"

"Your *boyfriend?*"

"Ye-uh. I'm het." She beamed. "I know, I don't look it. But it's the way I am. He's a major fan! You've had email from him, but of course you can't read everything, you must have tons of mail. Look, I'm not kidding, I really don't know where they are. That's the way they like to be, sometimes they just disappear and they are *gone.*" She frowned, sucking on the silver bead that jutted from her lower lip. "Listen, this is what I'll do. I'll give you the address of their place, I'll call you a taxi, and I'll get the super to let you in. I'm unconditionally sure they'll be back soon, but no matter what, you've just got to stay in their place while you're in New York; it's a trip. You'll love it. If you're not doing anything this evening, I could take you to dinner somewhere? I'll call you. I'd come with you now, only I'm not supposed to leave this dump. Mother of God, the sex destroyer lady, in my shop; my boyfriend will *kill me!*"

Anna didn't bother trying to understand, she had never found the strange cheepings of the media world to make any sense. She took the taxi, which stopped outside a solid nineteenth-century building, dark reddish brown in color, that looked like the scene of *Rosemary's Baby*. So here I am. A row of gingko trees lined the sidewalk. It was a street of basement restaurants and dog-walkers, strangely lived-in and normal for a trio of in-your-face art-monsters, but perhaps they were wise to property values. Artists are the ants, after all, getting in their stores and establishing status with the minimum of effort. Anna had been the grasshopper, singing and dancing and wearing herself out for no profit at all. More fool Anna. But she felt proud of her folly, after all these years of believing herself the sensible, boring one. She had butterflies in her stomach. Her name must be on a list of People It Is Okay To Let Into My Flat, but now she had doubts. She wished she could remember exactly what Simon had said about Ramone's kooky ménage.

The building supervisor must have been watching her arrive. The doors were open, he was standing in a pleasant, black and white tiled hallway, with mailboxes and large, healthy potted palms. "Miz Anna Senoz?" he asked, looking Anna over. He was a big man, dressed in black. There was a large handgun in a holster on his belt: he looked more like a very ruthless bouncer than a man who replaces lightbulbs. Here is where I get raped, killed, and eaten, thought Anna. Nothing occurred, except that he kept casting sly glances, as he traveled up with her in the repo Art Nouveau lift: like a man identifying a well-dressed woman as a whore, on the grounds that she is sitting in a hotel bar alone. . .

"So you're the new house-guest. You know these people?"

"I know Ramone Holyrod."

"I guess this means they're coming home soon."

They reached the fourth floor. He led her to the door of the apartment. "Okay, you're just going to set down your bags, I'm going to show you how to use the door key and where you'll be sleeping, and then you're going to come with me to meet the recognition programs. Got to get you ID'd on the hard drive, or you won't get into the building."

He handed Anna two slips of plastic on a loop of bead-chain, showed her which one to use and stood by the doorway. She walked into the studio apartment, *studio* not meaning a bedsit but a large and airy set of open plan rooms. She felt uncomfortable about the way the man was standing there.

"Jeezus. Good luck, is all I can say. I used to feel real sorry for that little Ramone, until I saw the way she would bring home the extra guests, just to give her own hide a rest. Watch out for the Korean woman, I think she's Korean. Did you ever see that video game of theirs? I guess you must have done, called *The Blocks of Wood*. One Two and Three. My fucking god. You know their 'model' for that game? She's in the nuthouse for life. Young Canadian woman. She was their houseguest too."

In the middle of the biggest room, which was the one you walked into, stood a surgical table. It looked as old as the building, nineteenth century, scoured wood with a row of metal cleats along each side. She looked at it and passed on.

"Yeah, it was a major scandal. But what happens? Nothing. The shocking story of what they did to a girl makes the so-called artwork more desirable. Can you figure that?"

In the room that must be Ramone's because here were her books, here was her characteristic spartan disarray, there was an array of hooks and straps and pulleys above a bunk-shelf that looked like a butcher's slab. The leather looked well-used; it was stained with both sweat and blood.

"Some of those *feminists* ought to take a good look at what happens in this apartment. What it says in the literature is there's a pair of female artists getting in touch with their suppressed erotic desires. What I *see* is a guy who likes beating up girls, and the more they let him do it the more twisted he gets."

"Sounds like Tex," murmured Anna. "Sounds like she found another Tex."

"If this is what women do when they're on top, I say you girls ought to be taken down from there for your own protection. So tell me you still want to move in?"

Oh, trust you Ramone. You always did walk too far on the wild side for me. Trust you to whip the blanket away, the moment I decide to jump. Those *straps* were too much. She walked past the grinning man without looking at him, headed for a door marked STAIRS, and pushed through it. "Hey lady," called the supervisor, showing no inclination to follow. "Hey, lady, you forgot your bag."

Anna went out into the street. Someone in the coffee shop opposite Ramone's building seemed to be staring at her. She walked quickly, wiping away tears. Everyone was staring. Was Ramone's flat really furnished like a torture chamber? It couldn't be. She was having a relapse, a return of her horrible symptoms. She had nowhere to go, no one to turn to, nowhere to hide.

"*Anna?*"

Someone was holding her by the shoulder. A large face peered into hers.

"It *is* Anna! Gee, what an amazing coincidence. Here I was sightseeing, I love this city don't you, and suddenly I see Anna passing by! I had no idea you were in New York."

Anna gasped. "Oh, hello, uh——" It was a name she had never been able to use easily, a name censored by defense mechanisms from before the dawn of time——

"LouLou," the big face prompted her. "Remember me? Your husband's Mom?"

"Oh. LouLou. Yes." Anna looked around for her bag, which she had left somewhere. "What a coincidence. Are you here on holiday. I'm, umh, I'm sorry but I'm in a hurry——"

"I think I'd better take you home. You don't look too good."

"What. . .to Illinois?"

"Well, no. I don't spend much time there now. Fact is, I'd have sold the house years ago if it wasn't for Spence. Looks like you found me out. My secret life. Home is, well, you'll see when you get there. There's some people will be very glad to meet you——"

"I *really must go.*" Anna panicked and made a lunge for freedom. The hand on her shoulder stuck fast.

"Okay, you don't have to meet anyone. Just come with me."

◆ ◆

The urge to treat mental dis-ease as physical illness, thought LouLou as she put her daughter-in-law to bed, is a very good one. She'd have liked to put Anna in a properly comforting sick room, airy and windowed, decorated in pale yellow, green, and white: because Spring is the time when we get better. The commune house being full to overflowing (they were negotiating the purchase of a neighboring property) she had to make do with an air-mattress in the former family room in the basement, which was also the home of Andreas's drum-kit, several mildewed boxes of black vinyl record albums, some broken furniture, and a few other odds and ends. Still, it's the thought that counts.

Anna had been given a hot bath with cypress oil and put into borrowed pjs that were clean and warm; the elflocks of her damp hair had been combed into order; she had been given a bowl of chicken soup (she hadn't eaten more than a spoonful). All the proper things.

"You lie down and sleep. If you need to pee, there's a little bathroom through that door by the cymbal stand. We'll talk in the morning. Here's the button for your bedside lamp. The connection is a wee bit flaky, but if you wiggle it around it works fine."

Anna was distressed because in the bathroom upstairs, when she had been dressed only in a towel, she had glimpsed in the mirror the hair in her armpits. She was very conscious of the fact that her mother-in-law had seen this hair, which Anna didn't shave often enough, but very little conscious of anything else. She struggled with her shame and transgression, until she remembered that she could switch off the light. The basement full of strange traps of steel and cable was plunged into utter, unrelieved blackness. No amount of wiggling would bring the light back. She lay still.

When she woke up, LouLou was sitting beside her.

"You want some herb tea?" She sounded exactly like her son.

Anna shook her head.

"How are you feeling?"

"A bit confused," whispered Anna. "Can you explain anything?"

LouLou nodded. "Oookay. . ." She paused on this long drawn out reassurance, her big face calm. She was wearing her jet black hair combed straight back and braided at the nape of her neck, Indian squaw style, the same as when Anna first met her. Still wearing the same sort of clothes, a long multicolored Mother Hubbard smock with a fringed yoke, and feathers. Her very Spence-like features looked like undersized currants trying to push their way through the olive glaze on a large, smooth bun.

"Where shall I start?"

"Did you really run into me accidentally, yesterday? Was it yesterday?"

"It was yesterday. Well, yes and no. I've been watching Ramone's place."

"Huh?"

"You've been missing for three weeks, Anna. We knew you'd come to New York, we found your name on a flight. We could have traced you here, by your credit cards. But that would have risked the media people getting to know you'd disappeared: we didn't want to get into that; we knew you wouldn't like it. My no-good son said you had to be looking for Ramone Holyrod. She's out of town, but the best clue I had was her address. So, I staked out the building," she explained, with pardonable pride.

"Does Spence know you found me?"

"No, he does not. I've told him I now know that you are okay, and that I am on the case. Won't do him any harm to sweat a little longer. I'm not going to tell him anything at all unless you want. D'you want to tell *me* where you've been? What you've been doing?"

"I don't know. . . I think I was staying in a hotel on 42nd street. I thought I had Jake with me. Oh! Oh, God, I left him behind, anything could have happened—"

"Jake is fine. I talked to him yesterday. He just knows you're away on a trip, he's missing you but he's okay." Anna, who had shot upright, eyes starting in terror, fell back on her air-mattress pillow. LouLou refrained, with a mighty effort, from the questions that were on the edge of her tongue.

"D'you want for me to fix it so you can speak to him, without Spence knowing?"

"No," said Anna softly.

She looked around. The rotting boxes, the smell of damp and cats, the odd assortment of paraphernalia, the windowless walls: she had woken into a scifi apocalypse, a bunker for survivors after the end of the world. How could she speak to Jake and not to Spence? She was astonished that LouLou had suggested such a thing. The ruthless *cosa nostra* of the female world could still shock her.

"Where am I?"

"Geographically? You're in upstate New York, in a house in the woods by the Hudson river. Emotionally speaking, you're among friends." LouLou hesitated. "You might as well know the worst. Among followers." She picked herself up. "My Goddess, I've been so proud of you, Anna. You would have been embarrassed to death, the amount of times I've boasted of our acquaintance. What we're trying to do here is to find a way to live in the world that you've discovered, the future of the human race. At the moment we're feeling real pleased with ourselves, because the big cover-up has collapsed, thanks to you. The conspiracy of silence is broken. But you can catch up on the world news later."

Anna blinked at her dazedly. "Are you still a witch? I mean, last time I heard—?"

"Oh sure, I'm still a Wiccan and still practicing magic. You should know, Anna. Transferred Y doesn't change anything important. We go on being the same people we were. I'll bring you some breakfast. When you've eaten, you'll feel stronger. Then, if you feel like it, you can come on upstairs and meet my other family."

"*Transferred Y?*"

"Sure. What else is in the news?"

Anna lay staring at the ceiling in complete bewilderment.

➤ ➤

She met the household. They were nine adults and three children, a boy of twelve and two youngsters of six and eight. The eight-year-old, whose name was Hilary, was the only true inter in this group, a child born with indeterminate sex organs. The others, of varied sexual orientation, confessed to being anatomically male or female, though Clarissa had been born ostensibly male. Those who could afford it had been typed, and one member knew that his sex-pair chromosomes bore no trace of the infection: but there was no stigma. They called themselves Transformationists.

They looked on Anna as a living saint.

"You are a prophet," explained a Catholic nun called Dorothy, who shared the parenting role with LouLou. "For twenty years at least, there has been a Transformationist community and culture in the USA, and we have links with other groups all around the world. People in all walks of life, all kinds of people, have felt that the sexual divide was no longer working. We knew what was happening, we were *living it*. But you've given us a voice, Anna. You've given us—" Her eyes glowed— "a *rationale*. A scientific explanation."

"But. . . You're still a nun?"

"I'm in dispute with my bishop," said Dorothy with dignity. "My Mother Superior understands. Didn't the good Lord say, *that they all may be one, father, as you and I are one?* Wasn't he born a man and lived the life of a woman, tending the sick, feeding the hungry, minding the children? I think the message is clear enough."

Anna didn't know whether to laugh or to cry.

I've founded a cargo cult.

She settled, in the end, for a smiling silence.

The Transformationists seemed content with this. They would tell her things: like, the rumor about group sex was a base libel, Transformationists were as moral as anyone, and it wasn't true about the hormones either. There were no rules about taking hormones or not, or about orientation, or having a job or not having a job, or following any particular religion or occult practice. The only rule was to live together lovingly: part of which required that if you were a man you wore a dress, at least sometimes. And that was only a "rule" because nobody had to remind women to wear pants from time to time. She did not catch up with the world news, though she was welcome to do that. The cultists used their connectivity only to chat with other Transformationists and to watch certain treasured movies. She took her place in the cooking rota, her share of the household chores. She went with LouLou, in her big battered old car, to buy provisions and was surprised to find there was a town outside the commune house: buildings still standing, people going about their business. When she looked into the store windows, she was surprised to find she had a reflection.

She let it all go by. She felt that she was living a half-life, persisting as a statistical anomaly, fading into nothingness. Days passed. She ate, she slept, she did domestic work, she didn't speak, and no one bothered her. One afternoon she was in the garden, picking bugs off the tomato plants with Clarissa. Clarissa suspected that Chelo, the unwed father of Hilary and hir little brother Paul, was still carrying on with the children's mother, and that his girlfriend in the commune house didn't know about it. . . It was a crying shame, because this girlfriend Ronan was a recovering alcoholic, a survivor of parental abuse and maybe incest. Clarissa was going to tell Dorothy: something had to be said—

"What do I do with the caterpillars?" asked Anna.

"Oh, get a rock and mash them. We don't use pesticides, but you can't leave 'em for the birds; these days there just aren't enough birds."

Anna had come to the same conclusion at home. Get a rock and mash them; it was the only way. But cabbage white caterpillars were her downfall, so charming in their subtle tweeds, the fabric soft as velvet. She remembered, one day, she had decided she couldn't bear to kill any more of them. She had Spence and Jake carry a jam jar full of remand prisoners through the house. Spence lined them up and pointed down the street. "Off you go, bugs. Go off and join the circus!" Jake, looking up at his daddy, wondering if this could be normal behavior, even for *his* nutty parents. . .

Spence and Jake—

Solidity fell on her. She let the caterpillars fall and looked around her.

"Are you okay? Hey, I'm real flattered you *spoke* to me—"

"I'm okay," she whispered, "Uh, I think I'll go and find LouLou."

LouLou was sorting laundry in the utility room.

"Hi," said Anna. "Can we talk?"

LouLou beamed. "Oh-hoh. She speaks!"

"I've been behaving strangely, I know."

"You have not! My no-good son was cheating on you; you found out and took off. There's nothing strange about that."

"It wasn't like that."

"Of course not. Everyone's trouble feels different to them. So what *was* it like?"

How often she had seen Spence come down from his work room, or arrive back from a hard day on the kiddy-book promotion trail, and just *sit*. Anna, in much greater fatigue, would zoom about picking lint from the rugs. Maybe when you have to spend your life running faster than the Red Queen, you became addicted to high-speed drudgery. She picked up a sock and found its mate. I can't do nothing; I can't be idle, not ever.

"I was upset because of all the fuss about Transferred Y. Really, I don't mind about him and Meret. I'm all right now. Thank you very much for looking after me. Who do these pants belong to?"

"Chelo. Nope, Marcie. You can talk, but you still don't want to talk about it, huh."

"There's nothing to say."

"You know, Anna, maybe you should stop guarding that private territory of yours so fiercely. Like that Ramone Holyrod says. Become *epimeletic*. Try to treat everyone like a brother and a sister, be intimate."

Anna thought of a bedroom bisected by string.

"Epimeletic? Is that Ramone's new word?"

"Ye-uh. Like the bees. You know, kind of like the grooming, cuddling, stroking that goes on inside the hive, which is the future, and more our natural behavior than the poke and run of conventional sex."

"I suppose so."

"I know it would do you good, but if you won't talk you won't. I can still tell you this much. You won't start forgiving until you stop making excuses. I know you, Anna. You didn't deserve what he did. You'd never cheat on anyone. So what do you plan to do?"

Anna shrugged, shook out a shirt, and settled it on a hanger. "I'm going to hope Meret doesn't insist he gets a divorce, and learn to live with it. Is that epimeletic enough?"

"Oh, really? That's strange, because from what I hear Spence does not have polygamy in mind. What makes you so sure you can't show the girlfriend the door?" LouLou gave her daughter-in-law a dry, sideways look. "You saw his mom off soon enough."

And I'd do it again, thought Anna, compressing her lips. It was you or me.

"Atta girl," said LouLou, when the renewed silence had lasted until the basket was empty. "You carry on your own sweet way. Heaven forbid Anna Senoz should cry on her mom-in-law's shoulder, like the common herd."

Before supper every night the group would come together to care and share. Everyone took turns to lead the meeting. Anna usually sat with them, out of politeness. Tonight the leader was her least favorite, Andreas the former Mormon, a thickset, pale-skinned young man with red lips in a black beard.

"I want us all to tell something that we admire about ourselves... I admire the way I finally got up the nerve to wear my dress to work," he went on. "I didn't want to do it, because I felt I'd just be doing this *macho* thing of challenging the norm."

"Who's Norm?" piped up Ritchie, a bright eyed little terrier of a dyke who often sported a jaunty fake moustache: the house's self-appointed comedian. "A friend of yours?"

"Sssh."

"But here I am in a dress and pantyhose and high heels, and I spent my whole time today explaining I'm just a normal guy in a dress. I want to say it has felt good."

"I want to say I think the sheer pantyhose and heels are unnecessary," announced Clarissa, "and I think you were right about yourself first time. You try too hard."

"This is my thing, Clarissa. I want to go the whole hog, spike heels and all."

"The whole macho hog. Right."

"I wear heels," put in Marcie. "I love pretty shoes. Since these things are fated to pass away, I think we can enjoy them while they last. Like national costume. Like Christmas and Hanukkah and the Eid."

"I admire that I learnt how to juggle," announced Hilary the inter. "I didn't think I could."

"I admire," said Anna.

A little stir went through the circle, a quiver of attention,

"I admire my ability to buckle down an accept a new situation. There have been several times in my life when everything has fallen apart, but I've picked myself up and started again. I'm glad I can do that."

"Hey hey!" whooped Ritchie. "You didn't tell us it was short for *Polly*anna—"

"Yeah," said LouLou darkly. "You certainly have that ability."

"I know you know about me and Transferred Y. I don't know if you all know—" Anna blushed, "—t-that for me, TY has been all confused with personal problems. But I believe I'm sorting them out. I believe I'll get back on my feet."

They nodded, and waited, but their prophet had nothing more to say.

"Thank you, Anna," said Dorothy at last.

The sharing moved on.

The next day, LouLou and Anna made another trip to the store. The town center—a few streets of white clapboard houses, two antique shops and a library—was quiet as usual. They filled the trunk with brown paper bags full of treats, staples, and beer.

"That was a nice thing you did, last night."

Anna nodded.

"I take it this means you're feeling better. You thought about talking to Spence?"

"Not yet."

"What a grocery packer you'd make. No slouch at cleaning up or ironing, either. The world gained a scientific genius and lost a great talent in part-time employment and housewifery. Are you going to adapt to needing people a little more from now on?"

"Perhaps."

"Attagirl. Gee, you'd better not get much better. I don't know if our little community could stand a fully armed and operational Anna Senoz around the house. I don't mean that. You know you're welcome, as long as ever you want."

This was a pre-emptive strike. They both knew she was leaving.

━ ━

While she was with them, she'd thought the Transformationists had nothing to teach her. On the train going back to New York she changed her mind. Anna would never do what they had done, drop everything and follow the new, not if an incarnation of the living God made the blind to see and the paralyzed to walk right in front of her. She was a fixed star, a rooted tree: but she could admire their courage. Even if she suspected most of them would have drifted off to the next snake-oil show in a few months' time.

It was a slow train. A woman got on, a middle-aged woman with grey streaked hair and a fine, dark, aquiline face. She sat opposite Anna. She was casually, stylishly dressed. She looked good; it was a pleasure to have her sitting there. Their eyes met. It was only a glance, but the secret warmth of it ran through Anna's veins. She realized, intrigued and astonished, that this might, if she chose, go further. She imagined herself leaving the train with this very attractive person, in silent accord: going with her to a bar, the two of them both ready to get sexual. It wasn't impossible; it was the way some people behaved.

Ah, she thought, turning to gaze out of the window. Ramone.

Anna's secret nest-egg, Anna's ace in the hole. This long affair, which Spence had always found so threatening; did it really make all the difference that it had never been physically consummated? It made some difference, but not all the difference. So where did Anna Senoz get off, flying into despair because Spence had ruined the purity of their contract? It was never as pure as all that.

She had bought toilet things, tee-shirts and underwear, and a bag to put them in; she was on her way home. But her stay in the commune had only restored her mind's mechanical strength. There was still a great blank in there, a whirling void of confused fragments. It felt like the time when she had first been pregnant with Lily Rose. Here was the street with the gingko trees, here was the dark building: a *very* unpleasant color, she noticed, like dry, stale blood. She tried her keycards. The doors to the lobby opened, no problem. Perhaps that obligatory session with the "recognition program" had been an invention: possibly it would have involved the lady visitor being obliged to remove her clothing, something like that. She tiptoed to the lifts.

Apartment seven was emptier than it had been before. None of the surgical looking stuff had moved, but there had been a vase of dead tulips on a carved block of Perspex: they were gone. Some art books were gone, from a lectern by the fireplace-slab. Other things that she didn't remember in particular, except as patches of color and form, had been shifted around. It looked as if the owners had been here and they'd gone again. Or someone else had been here, to collect the trio's possessions. However, Anna's cabin bag was lying just where she had left it.

"Well," she said aloud, "*Tell her I came, and no one answered. That I kept my word.*"

She sat on the floor, her back against a cold, white wall, keeping an eye on her two bags, now propped against each other for company, as if she were in an airport. She had been in such a state, the last time she saw this place, that she now felt as if she had climbed inside a picture of a bad dream, a dream of which she remembered nothing but this decor and an acute, sickening disquiet. Who is Ramone Holyrod? she asked herself. Someone I invented. My exterior soul. The person I wished I could have been; my repository for those parts of my self

I couldn't use or didn't want in my real life. Feelings that would have come between me and ordinary happiness. Ideas that would have made it impossible for me to pursue my life's work. Truths that would have made me an outlaw.

Or a crackpot.

But my ordinary happiness is gone, my life's work is gone, and those outlaw truths—

She had come to the end of the journey, which had begun in those hours of silent, passionate remembering on the road from Manchester. As the beat of a bass-line can raise the ghost of ecstasy, so that it walks through the mind as delicately as the spirits of John Keats's claret; as REM the memory drug, the regressor, taken in mild doses, can bring welling from deep springs an inexplicable bliss, she felt rising towards her, joining with her, becoming one, the *Anna out there*, the wild girl on the other side of the dark glass. Well, she thought, I have achieved something. I'm battered and broken, I'm tattered and torn, I've suffered cruel losses. But what else do you expect, at the end of such a great adventure? I should be satisfied: and I am. The room grew dim. Anna stayed where she was, thinking: afraid she hadn't been and couldn't ever be fair to LouLou, wondering if Anna Senoz was a horrible person, and should she try to change herself or should she turn determinist and give up in despair? Or should she just go on being Anna, trying to be the best Anna she could be—

The cardlock clicked, a loud noise in the silence. The door to the apartment was opened, slowly, by someone unseen. A face peered around it. It was Ramone. She was clutching a bunch of letters. She looked about and seemed gratified by the emptiness. She turned and hauled in her bags and shut the door carefully behind her.

She saw Anna. "Hallo! What are *you* doing here?"

"Looking for you. Where have you been?"

Ramone smiled—a warm and happy smile that reached her eyes, totally different from the manic glaze one had seen in publicity pictures of the *ménage à trois*. Evidently the rabid one had found herself again.

"Having a second honeymoon."

She came over and sat down by Anna, the smile turning into a more Ramone-like malign grin. "So, the famous Dr Senoz, I presume."

"Notorious. Briefly notorious. It's over already."

Ramone cocked her head and narrowed her eyes. "I don't think so! I flatter myself," she added with a glint of resentment, "that I'm going to be mentioned in biographies."

"Knock it off, Ramone. If you know about my claim to fame, then you must know that I've been trashed. Fired by my university; denounced as a nutcase. So much for that."

Ramone drew out a battered dayglo tobacco tin and a zippo from the pockets of a jacket too heavy for the season. "Shall I skin up? Why are you here?"

"Please. I've run away from home."

"Why would you do that?"

"Spence is having an affair with his illustrator."

"His illustrator? Huh? Oh, yeah, I know. The kiddy books. I've heard of them. The bastard," said Ramone, looking pleased. "What's her name? What's she like?"

"Her name's Meret, like the surrealist woman, Meret Oppenheim. Her father's called Godfrey Hazelwood, a well known painter in his day, but she's never gone in for what," Anna managed not to look at the surgical table, "is known as pure art. She's small, dainty, and very feminine. She has long red-gold hair, green eyes, and the sweetest smile."

"D'you want me to get rid of her for you? Shall I kidnap her and torture her in a deserted house?"

"No need for that." Anna took the joint, and drew on it gratefully. "She's married to Charles Craft."

"She *isn't*!" Ramone cackled. "Charles Craft! What a fate, hahaha. Small world!"

"Isn't it."

Anna felt she had to make some kind of declaration, after coming all this way, but she couldn't decide what form should it take. *Here I am. Do I stay or do I go*? "How are you, anyway? What have you been doing, since you gave up being a feminist?"

"Oh God," said Ramone, curling her chimpanzee lip. "The feminists!"

"Lesbians, bitter housewives, and fat people," recollected Anna, with a grin. "I don't think you're going to eat lunch in that town again."

"Hahaha, I'd rather starve." Ramone looked worried. "I did qualify the lesbians."

"Ye-uh. You made some bullshit disclaimer that you were trashing only an unaware, full-of-shit, sexist kind of lesbian. I don't believe the targeted group was fooled."

"Umm... Oh well, I don't care." Ramone flicked ash across one of the room's beautiful pale fur rugs. "I'm flattered you've been committing my press-releases to memory. I tried to read a paper of yours once...the bits in English." She laughed. "You know what, Anna? When we first met, and I ranted about the disgusting way post-liberation women behave? Freed slaves, no political perspective, nothing but groveling, simpering opportunism. I was right, but I was fucking wrong about them being helpless. They're everywhere. Especially over here. They've got no interest in leaving gender roles behind. They are out and proud shameless female supremacists, and I don't *like* them. I used to say, women ought to be the Goths and Vandals, sweeping in to rape and pillage. Now, that's exactly what they're doing: and the joke's on me."

"At least you haven't lost your sense of humor. I dunno, the rape and pillage has never worked for me. I'm as screwed as ever a woman scientist was."

"Well, maybe." Ramone gave Anna another curious look. "Since you're here, you can explain to me what the fuss is about. As far as I get it, in about fifty or a hundred years or something, all human beings will have two X chromosomes. But about fifty percent of these human beings will be physically male and fertile, and about the other fifty per cent female, likewise. So what is so exciting about that?"

"Umm..."

"It's bullshit, isn't it? Nothing's going to change."

"Well, hmm... How much can you follow, if I try to explain? I suppose you know that in male mammals, the X and the Y chromosome don't exchange genetic material much, because they don't match up well. Whereas all other chromosome pairs reshuffle their genetic traits?"

Ramone rolled her eyes. "Everyone knows that. They bloody do now, anyway. I bet mammalian sex genetics is a big topic in Ulan Bator this season."

"What the TY viroid did was to snip a specific piece out of the Y and paste it into a specific site on the X, in a human male. Once this has happened, and been inherited, the X and the Y start to reshuffle, and in a generation or two, the Y becomes indistinguishable from a second X, with male-determining genes. But there are male-specific genes on the normal X also, anyway... Well, there's a process called X-inactivation, to prevent a female animal—she has two Xs, remember—from getting a double dose of X gene expression, in loci where that would be damaging or lethal. The TY transformation interferes with this, in tiny but important ways. Sometimes the results will be lethal, so the pregnancy fails. Sometimes there'll be lesser effects. This is already happening, because TY has been around longer than I thought when I first found it: it was in the germ cells, in our generation. It's happening, and it will get worse before it gets better."

"So it makes getting pregnant and staying pregnant more difficult. Is this a bad thing?"

"Everyone's already got it. I don't know if it's a bad thing," said Anna softly, "but TY is going to cause a lot of heartbreak."

"But the media storm says it could be the end of the line for genetically-determined patriarchy! Men become women with dicks!"

"Or women become men with tits. You can make the words do anything you like."

"Holy shit," Ramone began, absentmindedly, to roll another joint. "But if this is so momentous, how come it was so difficult for other scientists to see it?"

"Because the original transfer involves a really tiny number of bases, in a non-coding sequence and because that's what molecular biology is like. It's spooky. Different people can make different things work, or can't make them work. You can get different batches of chemicals, different culture media, that make things appear and disappear. You have to use the right protocol and the right chemicals to make the original TY effect visible. As for what happened after that, I don't know. We did a survey, a confidential survey on samples from all over the world, and we found the TY viroid everywhere we looked. I don't know why this result is in doubt or why the evidence is apparently invisible except to me and the poor sods on my team—"

"It isn't invisible anymore."

"What?"

"You've been offline for a while, haven't you? Two weeks ago, one of the major US genetech companies confessed they already knew about your epidemic."

"Really!"

"It gets better," Ramone grinned ghoulishly. "They've been trying to correct the damage, which they took to be an IVF problem. They killed a few thousand proto-rich-kid cell-masses, before they gave up. Anyway, since then, other labs have broken ranks. The Oz team is dead in the water, and TY is out and proud." She went on rolling the joint, smirking at Anna's expression. "But now they're saying the death of the male chromosome isn't going to happen, because everything depends on this virus, and this virus is going to mutate and become harmless."

"No."

"The virus isn't going to mutate?"

"Viroid. That's not the way it works, that's the old way of looking at things. The TY viroid isn't a disease What's happening is a situation of the Aether."

"Excuse me?"

"This is where I get down from the fence. This is my idea, mine and Clare Gresley's. Listen. For the last many years geneticists have been discovering that life is one, that DNA is common to all living things and what's more, the same genes do the same things in widely divergent species. That's common knowledge: you can cut an "and" from the middle of a passage in a novel, paste it into a science text, and it will do the same job. What TY gives us is experimental proof of another idea, which has been growing but has been suppressed: that the language in the textbook and in the novel are in conversation with each other *right now*. That the things we call species aren't separate—they are part of a continuous fabric; that the phenomenon we call evolution is not a competition between organisms—it's a co-operative effort, orchestrated by tiny particles going about their own concerns. And they do not respect our artificial boundaries. Our Darwinism is as observably true and fundamentally dumb as saying the sun goes round the earth... That's what's the big deal. Okay, now the viroid... You know how a genetic "disease" doesn't have to be inherited? You can get, say, cystic fibrosis or a vulnerability to breast cancer from having any one of a number of happenstance glitches or unlucky combinations of glitches——?"

"Um, yeah——" said Ramone, as one does to Anna's explanations.

"The TY viroid is a little like that. It was an accident waiting to happen, nested in the aether, which is roughly analogous to the genome of 'Life on Earth.' It's not going to go away. It's not a disease; it's something that was bound to happen." Anna sighed... "It's a devastating change for life science. It means rewriting everything, from a completely different perspective. It's an awful prospect. And I'm the fool who rushed in, thinking people would be delighted to have their house torn down——"

Ramone shook her head. "Well okay. Web of life, all connected, cool. It'll never sell. The death of the male chromosome is so much sexier, hahaha." A thought struck her, or she pretended it had just struck her. "Hey, what about us? Are we affected?"

"I don't know about you. I am, first generation."

"What about Spence?"

"Yes. I told you. Nearly everyone is 'infected' by now."

"Have you told him?"

"Nah. It would only piss him off. You know how he hates to be like everybody else."

Ramone giggled.

"So there you go. It didn't stop him falling for the red-headed babe."

"I noticed," agreed Anna. "I take comfort in that. He may have humiliated me, but at least I know that genetic determinism is still a crock. Lovers will betray each other same as always, no matter how our chromosomes get bent out of shape." She was ashamed of having taken a sample without Spence's knowledge, but in those last months it had seemed as if all rules had been suspended.

"Hey, something funny. Charles Craft is a full XX. I nicked a sample from him, too."

"So, basically, I was right. Nothing's going to change," said Ramone, when she'd finished laughing. Anna gazed at the smoke that rose delicately towards the ceiling.

"Oh no," breathed Ramone. "Oh, don't tell me there's *more!*"

"I think," said Anna slowly, "that human sexuality will be changed. This thing is not a fashionable fad, affecting only a miniscule number of people rich enough to have their kids' genes messed about with: it's bound to change everything, some way or other. And I think it doesn't matter. That's how I felt a few weeks ago; that's how I feel again now. In the liberal world we already live as if people can choose at whim whether to take on a 'male' or 'female' lifestyle. In nature, before any of this started, many people were sexual mosaics, whether they knew it or not. In time, TY may create a situation where there are no genetic traits exclusive to 'men' or 'women': when sexual difference is in the individual, not a case of belonging to one half of the species or the other. Will that be a lot different from the way we are now? I don't know. Frankly, I'm more concerned about whether I can get back over the Atlantic without the plane falling out of the sky. Or whether the famine in Central Asia is going to get worse. And will the bad guys in Southeast Asia start using nuclear weapons? Do you realize our Daz, the World's Most Gorgeous Malaysian, is probably already dead?"

"She's supposed to be alive, in incommunicado detention."

"Yeah, sure."

"I know what you mean," said Ramone, chastened and low. "It's like the fall of the Roman Empire. This leftover we call the liberal world is irrelevant, the war zones are the shape of things to come, and the one thing you don't want to be in a war zone or an armed camp is any kind of woman. . . And I used to say that too." She reached into her jacket and brought out a worn, blue rabbit and hugged it, mugging at Anna owlishly over the toy's battered ears. "Maybe it's all part of the same thing. All part of the Transferred Y phase transition."

"Maybe it is. Hi, Pele. Nice to see you. I'm glad you're still around."

"Pele will always be around."

How empty the big room seemed, and the two of them like mice in a giant's kitchen. Ramone sighed. "Oh, well. Probably none of it will happen. Your sexual revolution viroid will fizzle out, and so-called civilization will go limping on. Anna, changing the subject because I'm getting bored, if I was to let you get away with it you would live here twenty years, wouldn't you, and never mention the equipment."

"It's your business," said Anna.

"Why can't you accept that I happen to like weird sex. It is what I enjoy."

"What about the Canadian girl, who ended up in the nuthouse? Is that true?"

Ramone scowled. "She'll be in and out of nuthouses all her life. We didn't do her any damage; I don't care if you believe me."

Anna looked, deliberately, from the surgical table and its tall theater lights, to the medieval torture contraption that hung from Ramone's bedroom wall. "What I see, I'm sorry, but what I see is complicated ways to express self-loathing."

"This is *my* way of dealing with *my* problem. And it works."

"Fine, it works. We agree to disagree. So what was wrong with Plan A?"

"Plan A?"

"Where I don't mention that your current relationship involves gross physical abuse."

"Consensual. So-called 'abuse' that heightens emotional and physical enjoyment."

"If you say so."

Ramone had started to rub one of Pele's threadbare ears between the finger and thumb of her right hand. Anna had seen this before: she believed the gesture was of great antiquity. "I've finished with them, actually. I only came back to collect my stuff. I wish I'd known you were coming, I'd have never let you in here. I'd have met you somewhere nice. Now you've seen this I know you're sitting there despising me. Whenever we meet it's at the wrong time, and I always end up looking like a jerk."

Anna didn't know what to say. She wanted to hug Ramone, the way Ramone was hugging that rabbit, but the declaration that she had come over here to make was impossible in the presence of the real person: not a symbol, not a metaphor, nobody's tall dark stranger.

"You're on your way back to Spence, aren't you. You ran away from him and came to find me, but you've changed your mind. I knew that the moment I walked in here and saw you. I've been considered as a poor substitute, and rejected again."

"You don't want me, Ramone," said Anna. "You never did."

"Yes I do... Maybe not for long," added the rabid one, hurriedly. "Maybe once would be fine. But I really do want you. Honest."

They went together into the second guest room, which was free of big apparatus. They took a couple of the fur rugs, because there were no covers on the bed and the air conditioning was chill, got naked and lay between them, and hugged and kissed and nuzzled and licked and enjoyed each other, just for once, until Pele felt quite left out.

➤ ➤

Now she will go back to being Most Favored Slave, thought Ramone, watching Anna's sleep. I can't stop her, and I don't want to. In the prison at Kota Baru, where part of Ramone stayed forever, would TY set anyone free? It would not. In the future, when there were as many sexes as there were people (if she'd understood Anna at all), there would be prisons, there would be horrors. But what will I do with myself? *Modern culture, like modern science, rejects reductionism, becomes a maze of irreducibly complex specificity...?* Nah, it sounds familiar; it must have been done. How happy Spence would be, to see her facing an empty future. Well, too bad. It's good to have these *Now Voyager* moments from time to time. *Something* will happen.

Something different—

She saw that lonesome road ahead, as dark and stony and hard to follow as ever. But the blackness above was riven with stars, and from now on, a fair share of those bright shining stars would have women's faces. And this woman-hating woman was surprised to realize how happy this made her.

Something new—

➤ *iii* ➤

Anna woke up wrapped in white fur and bathed in sunlight. She thought she was on an ice floe, gliding under the midnight sun. Ramone was lying beside her, wide awake. As soon as she saw Anna open her eyes, she quickly got out of bed (either to avoid renewed embraces or in case Anna did not want to renew them; we will never know). They bathed in separate bathrooms, Anna exclaiming in disbelief at the level of bizarre luxury she found in hers: staying in this apartment would indeed have been a trip. By the time she was dressed, Ramone was in the kitchen making coffee.

"By the way," she called. "Some of the snail mail is for you."

"For me? Did you say for me?"

"What's the matter, cloth ears? Some of the *letters* in my *mailbox* were *for Anna Senoz.* You must have been giving out this address as yours. I'm totally flattered."

"I didn't know your address until I got here. . . How mysterious."

There was only one letter. She understood the sharpness in Ramone's voice, because the handwriting on the large envelope was Spence's. She opened it with trepidation, there was nothing inside but another envelope, this time University of Poole stationery. She sat down on a swollen red satin couch—

> My dear Anna,
>
> I take the liberty of a personal letter as the first in-stallment of my most heartfelt apology. I am a touchy, irascible old fellow, and without my beloved wife to restrain me, too swift to avenge imaginary injuries. I believed that, careless of my department's future, you had used us, used *me,* ruthlessly, knowing that our reputation would be a casualty of your premature pub-lication, and this severely clouded my judgment on the day when we last met. Dear Anna, I will not attempt to excuse myself further. I hope and pray that envy of your achievement played no part in my hasty action. I have never known a better scientist or a more faithful

colleague. As we used to say, in the old country, you are

my father and my mother. Accept an old Hindu's. . .

She could read no more. The thin, spiky handwriting blurred and swam—

"What is it?"

"I've got my job back, I think."

"Tell them where they can stuff it," said Ramone trenchantly, dumping two French coffee bowls on the perspex table. "There's fuck-all to eat, so I hope you're not hungry. Hey, Anna? *Anna*?"

Anna Anaconda was crying like a baby, crying the way a baby cries when fear has passed, without restraint, rocking herself with her arms wrapped around her knees.

"I thought nobody loved me," she sobbed, "I thought nobody loved me!"

◄◆ ◆►

Hello?

Hi

Anna! Where are you?

I'm still in New York

How are you? Where've you been? Have you seen the news about TY?

I'm okay. I think I've about reached the point where Slothrop turns into a tree or dissipates into the zeitgeist or whatever he does.

Please don't turn into a tree, Anna.

As soon as she heard his voice, all the heavy things she'd thought she wanted to say to Spence, all the lines she had honed for her day in court, vanished into nothingness.

"I came looking for Ramone, but she wasn't here. Then I bumped into your mother and went to stay with her, up state. Did she tell you?"

"She didn't, she was very righteous about not telling me, but I guessed. Did you get Nirmal's letter? I didn't send anything else, but he was anxious for you to have it."

"Yeah, I got it. Ramone was here when I got back to the city."

"Oh, right. How's Ramone?"

"Same as ever. How's Meret?"

A short silence, and then they both laughed.

"We haven't seen much of the Crafts. They've been in Portugal, setting up Meret's parents in their new digs. They're putting The Rectory up for sale. Charles wants a bigger place, with some land. He's looking at Suffolk, or maybe further north."

Charles. My man!

And I'm sorry, red-headed babe. But it was you or me.

Anna leaned her cheek against the inside of the callpoint hood, thinking of Nirmal's letter. It was good to know, from the date on it, that his change of heart seemed to have predated the upswing in TY's fortunes. Not that this upswing was unqualified good news, because she knew what would happen. All the story would be about the sex; no one was going to pay attention to Anna's vector of entrainment. Even within her own community, she'd have to fight like crazy to get the basic science back into the picture, and she would probably fail... If there were any future in basic science, anyway, she thought gloomily, here on the brink of the Dark Ages. But that letter... She would value that letter as highly as she liked. Nirmal didn't have to give her back her honor, no matter how right she was. Plenty of precedents for him, if he'd refused. But he had done it of his own free will; he had led her back into the sanctuary—

"Anna, are you still there?"

"I'm at the airport. I'll call you again when I know my flight."

The car was packed, the sky was blue. Fergie the hamster had gone to stay with Henry, the Under Tens mid-fielder. The dead and golden month of August had come around again. Time to escape from the uncertainties, the shortages and failures, of modern urban life. Live in a tent, be elective refugees, and stop worrying.

Anna double-locked the front door and stood for a moment, as if listening.

This house...

Her reinstatement at the Genetics Department might prove meaningless, if the University's financial position was as catastrophic as rumor had it. Most likely it wouldn't turn out so bad. As Ramone said: civilization would go limping on for a while. But every time, when setting out like this, she had found herself wondering. . . Were she and Spence intuitively *practicing*, for an inevitable future that was getting very close? Maybe it really was Transferred Y that was carrying things over the brink, bringing a terrible salvation for the living world that had been under such threat from the awesome burden of human wealth and happiness.

Maybe, maybe not.

Think about it later.

Lock the door and drive away.

Life: An Explanation

I was born in North East Manchester, a landscape of narrow valleys, many streams, willows and poplars —overlaid with a thick crust of houses, mills and factories; most of the wheels already stilled before my time. In the house where I was born there was a window in the bedroom I shared with my younger sister, where I could hide behind the curtain and see a shadow girl on the other side of the glass, wild and free. I've written about my childhood, and how I think it relates to my writing, you can find the essay here: http://homepage.ntlworld.com/gwynethann/SFEYE.htm. When I was grown I went to a south coast University, where I did not have a brilliant career (I didn't do a stroke of work); but I dreamed my dreams and read some very interesting books. Later I lived in Singapore and became a passionate admirer of the culture of that whole region. The Jakarta Regime was subjugating East Timor, and I met Indonesians who tried to tell me how bad it was, but I was too ignorant to understand. That's when the battle of the sexes, in all its cruel consequences and seductive appeal, began to be an obsession. I've written about that, too: http://homepage.ntlworld.com/gwynethann/OSLO.htm.

Back in England, living in frugal content, combining motherhood and "career" (of sorts), exploring France and Italy on a shoestring every summer; for years I never had any private money in my pocket: I was making less than a science post-grad. But I couldn't give up tussling with the questions that seem to me so important. How can something as fragile and unstable as human sexual difference *as it really is*, be the cause of so much suffering: the foundation of so many books of merciless law? How can this problem ever be solved? What would the solution cost?

The story of Anna Senoz is not my life story (the scruffy and pugnacious Ramone, Anna's shadow-girl, is more like me, if I could imagine myself a feminist media-star). But in ways it's the story of my life as a writer: the experiences that shaped me, the changes that swept over my world, the ideas that made me write the novels I've written, the people who have inspired me; the future I imagine.

Praise for Jones's Writing

"Jones's prose is vivid, finely nuanced, sardonic and precise, and offers the most energetic combination of polemical and lyrical energies that science fiction has seen since the heyday of Joanna Russ"

The Washington Post Book World

"She is one of Britain's most brilliant SF writers, and one of the few authors of SF worldwide to understand the scale of the opportunities the genre offers for the imaginative reconfiguration of our categories of familiarity and strangeness, thought and feeling, gender and individuality."

Francis Spufford

"Intelligent, articulate speculative fiction, written with grace and insight."

The Library Journal

Reviews of Midnight Lamp

"...a writer of visionary skills, with a striking and poetic narrative style..."

The Independent

"One of the most seductive things about Jones's novels is that beneath the beautiful, natural lyricism of her words is a vicious brutality just waiting to rear its head...gritty and deft, ignoring old clichés of future-fiction in favour of a short, sharp shock to the readers' senses."

Dreamwatch